"WHAT ARE YOU DOING?" LILY ASKED.

"I'm undressing myself. Then I'm going to undress you. Then I'm going to make love to you, right here, under this beautiful old oak tree."

She stared at Knight. He was musing about the history of the oak forest even as he began to unbutton his shirt. He couldn't be serious. No, it was impossible. It was the middle of the day.

On the other hand, he had entered her bed-chamber, had ripped open her nightgown, had touched her and kissed her and made her scream with pleasure. Oh dear, she had to do something.

"No, damn you!" Lily picked up her skirt and bounded away from him.

"Not again," Knight sighed.

Avon Books are available at special quantity discounts for bulk purchases for sales promotions, premiums, fund raising or educational use. Special books, or book excerpts, can also be created to fit specific needs.

For details write or telephone the office of the Director of Special Markets, Avon Books, Inc., Dept. FP, 1350 Avenue of the Americas, New York, New York 10019, 1-800-238-0658.

CATHERINE COULTER

NIGHT SHADOW

AVON BOOKS ◆ NEW YORK

This is a work of fiction. Names, characters, places, and incidents either are the product of the author's imagination or are used fictitiously. Any resemblance to actual events, locales, organizations, or persons, living or dead, is entirely coincidental and beyond the intent of either the author or the publisher.

AVON BOOKS, INC.
1350 Avenue of the Americas
New York, New York 10019

Copyright © 1989 by Catherine Coulter
Inside cover author photograph by Karen Evans
Published by arrangement with the author
Visit our website at http://www.AvonBooks.com
Library of Congress Catalog Card Number: 88-92969
ISBN: 0-380-75621-8

First Avon Books Printing: August 1989

AVON TRADEMARK REG. U.S. PAT. OFF. AND IN OTHER COUNTRIES, MARCA REGISTRADA, HECHO EN U.S.A.

Printed in the U.S.A.

WCD 20 19 18

To Frances Perine

The most irreverent and wittiest of friends
a staunch supporter
an intelligent voice in the industry
an opinion for all seasons
that's usually right on

PROLOGUE

London, England
September 1814

Knight pulled back and came up onto his knees. He looked down at Daniella's body, pale as ice and beautifully mysterious, as only a woman's body could be in the dark of night with just moonlight spilling over her. He touched his fingers to her breast. "You're exquisite," he said.

Daniella opened her eyes and looked at the man whose mistress she'd been for nearly four months now. "Yes," she murmured, unaware of what she was saying. Her hands swept over his chest, feeling the crisp hair, the smooth musculature, and she sighed as her hands stroked down his belly, flat and warmly hard, and found him.

Knight moaned.

"You're also greedy," he said and laughed, a pained sound.

"Perhaps," she said, caressing him, "but you are also a randy man."

"You're right about that," Knight said and came into her in one powerful thrust. She gasped at the shock of him, but her body rose to meet his and he clasped her hips, bringing her even closer.

Her eyes shut and her mouth tightened. He

pulled out of her, watching her face and seeing the disappointment in her eyes.

"Beast," she whispered and jerked her hips upward. When he filled her again, she moaned and wrapped her legs about his flanks.

Her prisoner now, he thought as he swelled and probed deep within her. She was nearing her climax. He knew her body well—the slight quivers that clenched the muscles in her belly, the spasmodic tensing of her thighs and buttocks, the ragged moans that tore from her mouth, raw and ugly and real. But he kept his rhythm uneven, first fast and shallow, then slow and deep, deeper still. Until she cried out, her fists striking his shoulders.

"Knight!"

He smiled and said very softly, "All right." His hand was between their bodies, his knowing fingers caressing her, and she screamed, jerking upward, her eyes wild and unseeing on his face, her forehead shiny with perspiration.

He felt utterly alone at that moment and supremely powerful. Not since his nineteenth year, the year he'd learned how to pleasure a woman, had he allowed his partner to go unsatisfied. Indeed, he allowed no feigning, and he knew women too well for them to fool him. He saw that she was still and limp beneath him, her pleasure well spent, and he let himself go, let the searing release flood through him.

"Well," he said, more to himself than to her after some time had passed and his heart had slowed to normal, "I believe I've been properly exercised."

Daniella smiled, that sated woman's smile of hers that was like every other woman's smile he'd seen after sex; it made him feel again that absolute power. He smoothed back her hair, lightly kissed her mouth, then rose. He stretched, lit a lamp, and kneeling, built up the fire.

"It's chilly tonight," he said some minutes later as he began to bathe himself in the basin atop the commode.

Daniella watched him, his powerful body silhouetted by the flames leaping upward and the soft candlelight from the branch on the mantelpiece. He was a handsome man, she thought, with his thick, nearly black hair. It wasn't a blue-black like those Irish rogues she'd met, nor was it the shiny coal black like hers that reflected light and held deep reds. No, it was thick and it was nearly black, deep-looking, and it curled slightly against the back of his neck.

It was his eyes that held one's attention. They were brown with yellowish flecks, the eyes of a fox, intelligent eyes, shrewd and cynical. He was lean and firm, endowed with a beautiful male body. He was an athlete and a renowned sportsman, the foremost rider in the Four Horse Club, she'd heard it said; also to his credit, he was a favorite of Gentleman Jackson, that famous fighter who now instructed rich men in the art of boxing, whose remarks were that Viscount Castlerosse was possessed of remarkable science, enduring strength, and wily intelligence. She didn't know what remarkable science referred to, but it sounded again as if he were superior and thus she savored it because he was hers, at least for a time. Four months now. It seemed so short a span. When would he tire of her? She shook her head unconsciously, unwilling to raise that dreaded specter.

He was beyond any woman's reach, she thought, even a lady of quality, which she wasn't. How many times had he laughed and stated flatly that marriage wasn't for him, that he believed ardently in the particular philosophy expounded by his father that the wise and sane man married no earlier than the age of forty and that he picked a girl no more than eighteen who was healthy as a stoat, a good breeder, and malleable as a sheep. He begat an heir, then left the child alone to grow without learning the vagaries of his sire.

Knight Winthrop, Viscount Castlerosse, was many years yet from that fateful age of forty, having attained his twenty-seventh year some three months before. He was a renowned bachelor, sardonic in his cynicism but rarely cruel in his wit.

She looked at him as he washed his long, muscular legs. His motions were fluid and graceful. He made love in such a way, never hurried, always in control of her and of himself, and always with skill. But she sensed, she *knew*, that he remained somehow apart from her, alone and apart. Beyond her, she'd thought once when she'd watched his face as he reached his own pleasure.

"Even your feet are lovely."

His head jerked up and he laughed. "What did you say? My feet are *what?*"

Daniella shook her head. She hadn't realized she'd spoken aloud. She knew better than to say something so stupidly revealing and quickly retrenched. "No, no, my lord. I said your feet are dirty and need to be washed as much as the rest of you." He didn't want to know of feelings. He would dismiss her if he felt she wanted him for more than as a generous protector. He wouldn't be unkind or cruel, but he would leave. She rose slightly off the bed and stretched languidly, aware he was looking at her. Then, equally languidly, she lay down again.

"Put on something or it will be the worst for you," he said and his voice was rough. She made him randy again, her negligent pose on her side, her bountiful breasts pressed together, the smooth line of her hip made even more enticing by her position. Her hair was as black as only an Italian's could be and her flesh as white as—not snow, he decided. Even in his thoughts he didn't relish being common. Her flesh was pale, that was all. And those dark, almond-shaped eyes of hers showed all the passion of her Neapolitan heritage. He tossed her a peignoir, a frothy peach affair that he'd bought her some weeks before.

He watched her slip into it, her movements so practiced that they seemed as naturally seductive as a virgin's. "Tea, my lord?"

He nodded. His stomach suddenly growled. "Anything to eat?"

"Didn't you eat your fill at the wedding banquet?"

He grimaced. "I was too nervous. Lord, the bride and groom oozed over each other until I felt sick. It was unnerving. And the ladies—of all ages!—giggling and looking at me as if I were a grouse ready to be set upon by the hunters. I overheard one matron say to another that her daughter was *just* what Viscount Castlerosse needed. Imagine the impudence of that old bedlamite!"

Daniella laughed and left the bedchamber. Her maid, Marjorie, was long abed, and her cook and housekeeper didn't stay in the house at night. Fifteen minutes later she returned to the bedchamber carrying a tray of cold chicken, sliced bread, butter, and honey, and the pot of precious India tea.

Knight had just pulled on his dressing gown. He helped her spread the feast on the bed. He slapped her buttocks as she climbed over him, and she giggled. "Ah," she said, "Is it that you have *need* of me, my lord viscount?"

Knight picked up a chicken leg and tore off a goodly bite. "My needs," he said between bites, "are at present in my mouth, just as appropriate in this instance as in others."

He saw that she didn't understand and merely smiled, handing her a chicken wing.

They ate in companionable silence for some minutes until Daniella, replete, said, "Do tell me about the wedding and the reception. Weren't your special friends there?"

He knew she loved to hear about the ladies and gentlemen of his acquaintance—a sort of vicarious envy, he thought, but he willingly obliged her. "You mean Burke Drummond and his wife, Arielle?"

"He is the Earl of Ravensworth?"

"Yes. They were there, of course, since the bride is his former sister-in-law. He and Arielle were looking well and fervently happy."

"Do you disapprove of their marriage? The earl hasn't yet reached the age of forty."

"You still remember that, do you?"

"You have remarked upon that particular sentiment at least three times, as I recall."

Knight chuckled. "I trust I don't grow tedious, my dear. No, Burke isn't close to forty. In fact, he's my age. As for his wife, well . . ." Knight paused a moment, picturing Arielle in his mind when he'd first met her at Ravensworth Abbey. "She is well now, I think."

"Well? What illness did she have?"

"Rather a sickness of the spirit, I would say." He liberally spread butter and honey on a thick slice of bread. "She is a beautiful girl. She is also brave and loyal. I like her."

"Does this mean that you will change your mind about marriage, my lord?"

"Good God, no! She is perfect for Burke, not for me."

"Laura much enjoyed the earl when he was in London."

Knight had the grace to look a bit uncomfortable. "I'd forgotten that," he said. "He was in a bad way, wanting Arielle so much and yet not being able to have her. They weren't married then, you know. Laura is now with Lord Eaglemere, isn't she?"

Daniella nodded. "She doesn't like him. He is a pig and not natural in what he demands of her."

"Tell her to leave him," Knight said, shrugging.

Daniella merely looked at him, saying nothing. He could, at times, be as obtuse as a turnip. It wouldn't occur to him that Laura couldn't leave Lord Eaglemere. At least not until she had more money from his lordship. Daniella wanted to change the topic and asked, "Do you dislike children?"

"Not at all. I don't know children."

"You knew yourself, surely."

"There is no reason for me to involve myself with children. As you will recall—isn't it the fourth time now?—my father never busied himself with me. Left me to grow up with all my own perfections and none of his imperfections. He was fond of telling me, on the rare occasion when he saw me, that all my faults were of my own making and owed nothing to him. Perhaps Burke and Arielle will have children. Then I shall become a distant but doting uncle. Now, my dear Daniella, pour me another cup of tea, then remove that annoying peignoir. All this food and conversation have appealed to my baser hunger"

* * *

Near Brussels, Belgium
September 1814

Tristan Monroe Winthrop hummed as he
quickened his pace. He was a man pleased with
his own cunning and his success. He smiled as
he hummed, not at all surprised that he could do
both at the same time. He was convinced he could
do anything. He thought of Lily, waiting for him
with his children, and he nearly broke into a trot.
He'd been gone but three days, yet he missed
them all. Of course, missing his children wasn't
quite the same thing as missing Lily. Beautiful
Lily, who would soon be his wife. He'd used his
children as levers, shamelessly, he admitted to
himself now, and it had worked. His children and
the fact that she'd had no other choice, not really.
Not yet twenty and on her own in a foreign city,
her father's funeral to pay for, his effects to be
seen to. Her father, Baron Markham, that bluff
but incredibly unlucky gambler, had been his
friend. Tristan had saved him not once but several times from gaming hells that would have
taken his beautiful daughter as payment for his
debts—without his consent. Then he'd just keeled
over, clutching his chest, Lily standing there
watching him, at first not understanding, then
staring at him, tears streaming down her cheeks.
He'd lived another two days. Then he'd died and
left her with nothing save the clothes in her ar-
moire.

But Tris had been there to help her. She liked
him, loved his children and they her. He'd in-
vited her to live with him and the children and of
course she'd refused, until he'd changed his tune
and requested her services as their governess. It
wasn't until two months ago that she'd agreed to

marry him. By that time, he'd proved to her that
he had no disgusting habits, that he was possessed of a modicum of intelligence and wit; and
his children, bless them, had wrapped themselves firmly around her loyal and giving heart.

Lily Tremaine. A girl so beautiful it nearly took
your breath away just to look at her. And she was
sublimely unaware of her effect on men. Her incredible honey-blond hair was thick and wavy,
and she paid it little attention, tying it up with
ribbons or twisting it into braids atop her head.
That didn't matter. Nothing could dim her
beauty. Her eyes were a pale gray, calm and serene, but the calmness was a mask, a carefully
tended facade, he was certain of it. She was filled
with passion, and he would prove it to her and
to himself once she was his wife. He quickened
his step even more. God, he wanted her. She was
seventeen years his junior, but it didn't matter.
She'd been the adult to her father's child for many
a year now. Seventeen years was nothing. She
was too slender for his taste, but she would fill
out when she was pregnant with his child. It was
all the worry, he supposed, taking care of a vagrant, fatally charming father for five years, wondering whether she would have food for dinner
or, on the rare occasion, donning diamonds and
silks and attending a ball.

Loyal, brave Lily. He still held clear the mental
picture he had of her as she and the children had
waved good-bye to him. He would very much like
to tell her that he'd succeeded beyond his wildest
expectations, but he couldn't. Lily, he'd come to
realize, had this odd streak of honesty that was
occasionally disconcerting, particularly given the
fact that her father had been a grand scoundrel,
albeit an unlucky one. Of course, *he* had no intention of telling *his* children that their father was

a thief; not just any kind of common thief, of
course, but a master thief and a master strategist.
And ruthless, at least this time. According to his
calculations, Monk and Boy should be well en-
sconced in prison by now. In Paris. Far away from
him and his family. The bribes had been large
enough to make him pause, but it was worth it,
indeed it was. No more of those cold, conscience-
less bastards to haunt him.

A master stroke, that was what he'd managed
to execute. He was the winner and he'd taken all.
Never again would he have to worry about food
and lodgings for the children. He could give them
and Lily everything.

He was almost to the small two-story house on
Avenue LaRouche. It was a quiet street, poplar
trees lining each side, respectable in the extreme,
but to his newly sharpened tastes, much too poor
for his soon-to-be-higher status in life.

Nothing would be beyond him now. At the age
of thirty-seven he at last savored success, lasting
success. He hadn't killed anybody, hadn't even
hurt anybody. Monk and Boy didn't count. He
was now rich. So bloody rich that it boggled even
his wonderfully inventive mind.

When he heard the harsh words behind him,
''Ye filthy bloody bastid!'' he turned only frac-
tionally. When the knife struck him in the back,
deep and smooth in one single thrust, he had no
idea what had happened. He felt a sharp chill and
shivered, quickening his pace. Then, horribly, he
heard another voice and recognized it as Monk's,
low and mean and frightening as hell. ''Awright,
boyo, ye'll pay, but first, what 'ave ye done with
the sparklers?''

Tristan couldn't believe his ears. He turned
slowly to face his erstwhile partner, Monk Busch,
a man who had the look of an early-eighteenth-

century pirate, dark and ugly. "Monk," he said.

"Where, damn ye, Tris? Boy, get over 'ere! I got 'im but good now!"

Suddenly Tris stumbled and Monk saw the red stain spreading over his back. "Boy, ye damned fool! Ye've stabbed 'im in the back! Idiot! I told ye to be careful!"

"Eh! Arrêtez! Qu'est-ce qui se passe?"

Monk cursed. It was the damned Brussels watch. Tristan shouted at the top of his lungs, first in English, then in French. "Help! Help! Aidez-moi! Aidez-moi!"

A whistle blew sharp and loud.

Monk and Boy looked at each other, cursed in unison, and fled. Tristan stared after them, then slowly, very slowly, fell to his knees. He wished he could see his children and Lily just one last time. "Lily," he whispered as he collapsed to the ground. He realized suddenly that he had to tell her about his coup. He had to reassure her that there would always be enough money for her and the children if she could only bring herself to be less pristine in her notions. God, he wanted to see her one more time. But it wasn't to be. He couldn't tell her where to look . . . The last face he saw was that of the young watch bending over him.

Damson Farm, Yorkshire, England
October 1814

Lily sat with her feet tucked beneath her on the narrow bed, Theo, Sam, and Laura Beth grouped around her. They were in her small bedroom on the third floor of Damson House, one of the servant's rooms. She was no longer shaking with

fear from Arnold's assault; she was no longer
quivering with rage; she was at last calm and
coolly thinking about what she and the children
would do now. They couldn't remain here at
Tris's sister's home. Gertrude's husband, Arnold, had made that impossible. Gertrude toler-
ated the children, disliked Lily heartily, and was
spiteful enough to enjoy making Lily feel like an
upper servant. Gertrude would discover her husband's amorous activities soon enough, and it
wouldn't be Arnold who would be shown to the
door, it would be Lily, and the children wouldn't
be allowed to leave with her.

What a ridiculous coil! All because Arnold
couldn't control himself, had whimpered and
begged her to let him take her, then had turned
nasty, as only a petty little bully could. Theo, her
protector, her nine-year-old overly serious and
overly responsible little adult, had prevented Arnold from raping her on the stairs, against the
wall.

"I'll kill him, Lily," Sam said and thrust out
his chin. "Theo should have!"

"Shut your mouth, Sam," Theo said to his six-
year-old brother in his surprisingly stern adult
voice. "You won't do anything. I stopped him,
but I don't trust him, Lily. He isn't a wise man,
nor is he at all honorable."

Trust Theo to phrase things the way a vicar
would, Lily thought as she leaned over to pat his
arm. Actually, Arnold Damson was a fumbling,
vicious beast and bully. Theo had saved her,
clearing his throat loudly, his hands fisting at his
sides. Arnold had stepped back from Lily, realizing that he had no other choice at the moment.
He couldn't rape her in front of a boy, and his
nephew to boot.

Lily looked at each of the children in turn: Theo,

tall for his age and too thin, his eyes the pale blue like his father's, and bright with a formidable intelligence; Sam, compact and fierce, independent and restless, an imp who loved life and excitement and hadn't a thought for tomorrow; finally, little Laura Beth, only four now, quiet and so beautiful that it made Lily ache just to look at that small face, at that small mouth with a thumb now firmly stuck into it. Laura Beth looked like her mother, so Tristan had told Lily, and Lily knew that Elizabeth must have been beautiful, fragile, petite, and delicate, with silky black hair and eyes so dark a blue that they appeared black in certain lights.

She cleared her voice, encompassing all of them with her calm smile. "We'll leave, that's all."

Theo sighed. "I suppose we have no choice now. I can't be certain to be around all the time to protect you."

Lily wanted to fling her arms around too-grown-up Theo and hug him until his ribs creaked. "No, you can't," she said, her smile a bit wobbly.

"He's ugly," Laura Beth announced, taking her thumb out of her mouth. "So is Aunt Gertrude. And fat."

"That's true," Lily agreed. She took Laura Beth's small hand in hers, hoping to keep the thumb out of the child's mouth for a few minutes anyway. Laura Beth allowed it and gave Lily a look that made Lily know that she was allowing it.

"I want all of you to listen to me," Lily said. "You know that before your father died, indeed, several months ago in fact, he told me that if anything happened to him I was to bring you here, to his sister, Gertrude. You also know that we had no choice but to do so. There was no money.

Now that Ugly Arnold has shown his horrid true self, we will leave. Your father had a cousin. This cousin's name is Knight Winthrop, Viscount Castlerosse, and he lives in London most of the time. We were to go to him second if things didn't work out with Gertrude.''

"Is he ugly?" asked Laura Beth. She pulled her hand from Lily's, and her thumb settled back into her small mouth.

"I have no idea. I think your father left him as the last resort because he is a bachelor.''

"I don't like the sound of that," said Theo. "He just might try to hurt you, Lily, like Ugly Arnold did.''

"Arnold's a toad," said Sam. "Filthy blighter!''

Lily blinked. Where had Sam learned those words? They were, however, exceedingly accurate and descriptive. "Yes, that's true," she said easily. "Perhaps, Theo, but we have no choice. I have just enough money to get us to London. To this cousin. If he has any sense of duty at all, he will provide for the three of you, at least.''

"We won't leave you," said Theo and Sam, and Laura Beth nodded solemnly. He continued thoughtfully after a moment. "I don't think, though, that you should tell this new gentleman that you were Papa's betrothed, like you did with Aunt Gertrude and Ugly Arnold. They thought you were an impostor and not a lady.''

"You can't be a governess either," said Sam. "That would be worse. This cousin could make you leave us or he could hurt you.''

"Sam's right," Theo said in his judicious voice. "You've got to be something else.''

"You're my mama," said Laura Beth, the thumb coming out only long enough to deliver this startling statement.

Lily stared at the child, but Theo said, "I say,

that's just the thing! No, really, Lily, you can't be
Sam's mother or mine for that matter; you're by
far too young. But if you were married very early
to Papa, you could be Laura Beth's mama. That
way this cousin couldn't make you go away. He'd
have to take care of all of us. And since you're a
widow, he would have to treat you with respect.''

"Mama," said Laura Beth again and moved
over onto Lily's lap, snuggling against her breasts,
her thumb in her mouth and her other hand
clutching Czarina Catherine, her doll.

And that, Lily supposed, was that.

1

London, England
October 1814

It was eight o'clock on a rainy Thursday evening. Knight Winthrop, Viscount Castlerosse, was at home at Winthrop House on Portland Square, seated in his favorite leather chair in his high-ceilinged, thoroughly masculine library. Voltaire's *Candide* lay facedown on his thigh. He was looking into the flames that were sluggishly throwing off embers, a snifter of French brandy in his hand. The wainscoted room was dim and shadowed, the only splash of light from the branch of candles near his right arm. It was a cozy setting, and Knight felt appropriately coddled and relaxed and pleasantly tired.

He grinned at the memory of Sir Edward's face when Allegory, Knight's chestnut Barb, bred at Desborough Stud, had left him and his nag in the dust only halfway to the finish line marked by the Four Horse Club on Hounslow Heath. Knight had placed a healthy bet on Allegory's speed and indomitable spirit, and on his own skill, and had come away with a thousand pounds in his pocket, at Sir Edward Brassby's expense.

Allegory hated to lose even more than he did, he thought. The chestnut got that mean look in his eyes when he saw another horse drawing close. Knight wondered if the gelding had gotten his mean look from him or from his famous sire, Flying Davie.

He took another slow sip of brandy, then leaned his head back, closing his eyes. Life was well-nigh perfect. He had no complaints, no suggestions to the powers-that-be for improvement. He was content. He was healthy, his teeth were white and straight and strong, he was in no danger of losing his hair, he currently mounted a mistress who met his every sexual whim, and no one save an occasional new stallion ever disturbed his very fine existence. No, there was nothing more he could ask for.

He picked up his book and thumbed negligently through the pages.

"My lord."

Knight cocked open an eye at the sound of Duckett's soft voice. It could be quiet as a vicar's closet and still one wouldn't hear Duckett approach. Just five feet tall, round as his nearly bald head, Duckett was blessed with an abundance of perception, knew his master better than did even his master's valet, Stromsoe, and endeavored to smooth away any rough pebble that found its way onto his path.

"What is it, Duckett? Nothing dire, I trust."

"That I cannot say, my lord."

Knight opened both eyes at that and looked at his butler. "I beg your pardon?"

"There are a Young Person and three Very Young Persons here to see you, my lord. The Young Person wishes to see you first."

"The Young Person, as opposed to the *Very* Young Persons?" Another thing about Duckett,

Knight thought, he had no sense of humor. Not even an echo of one. "Well, tell this person I've left the country, tell her—him?"

"A she, my lord."

"—I've fallen into the North Sea, tell her—who the devil is she anyway?"

"She says she is your cousin's widow."

"*My cousin's what? Tris?*" Knight stared at Duckett blankly. Tristan dead? Knight paused a moment, trying to remember the last time he'd heard from him. Lord, it had been five years at least. He rose to his feet and straightened his clothes. "Bring her in, Duckett. As for the three Very Young Persons—I assume they are Tristan's children—give them over to Mrs. Allgood. She'll feed them, or whatever it is that very young persons require at eight in the evening."

"Yes, my lord."

Tristan dead! He felt a wrenching sadness, deep inside him, for the Tristan he'd known as a boy. Tris had been his senior by ten years, and on the rare occasions Knight had seen his uncle's son, he'd worshipped him ardently. Gay, devil-may-care Tris. A man who fascinated women, from what the fifteen-year-old Knight had observed when Tris had visited Castle Rosse and gathered every young girl about him with scarce any effort.

His widow was here with three very young persons who had to be Tris's children. Why? Knight turned to face the door. It was opened by Duckett, who stepped aside and said in hushed tones, "Mrs. Tristan Winthrop, my lord."

A female, covered from the top of her head to her booted feet in a serviceable brown wool cloak, came into the library.

"How do you do," Knight said politely.

"Hello," said Lily, and he heard the fatigue in her voice. "My Lord Castlerosse?"

"Yes. Please come in. Let me take that cloak. You can warm yourself at the fire. It is not a pleasant evening, is it?"

"No, I suppose it isn't. However, you are home, and that is a relief."

Knight assisted her out of the cloak and immediately wished he'd left her as covered as a package. He stared at her a moment, then forced himself to offer her a chair close to the fireplace. She looked pale and very weary; her hair was pulled back in a severe bun, her gown was wrinkled and not of the best quality, and she was so beautiful it made his toes ache just to look at her. He realized he was staring and said quickly, "Please, sit down and tell me how I may help you."

Lily sat down gratefully.

Perhaps it was the dim lighting, he thought. No woman could look like that, at least not in the harsh light of day. "I shall order up some tea. Are you hungry? Some sandwiches and cakes, perhaps?"

"I should like that. Thank you."

"I told Duckett to give the children over to Mrs. Allgood. She'll see to them."

But Mrs. Allgood hadn't been able to see to a thing. At that moment there was the sound of scurrying footsteps outside the library door, agitated voices too high and shrill to belong to an adult; then the door was flung open and three very young persons ran into the room. Lily was on her feet in an instant. "Good heavens!" was all she had time to say.

"Mama," Laura Beth bellowed and flung herself against Lily's legs. Theo and Sam took up protective positions on either side.

"Are you all right?" asked Theo, his eyes scanning her face.

Lily laughed; she couldn't help it. "I'm perfectly all right. Now what is the matter?" She saw an older woman standing in the doorway, consternation obvious on her face, and said quickly, "Mrs. Allgood? I'm sorry, but the children, well, they don't like to leave me alone with strangers— that is, with strange men, and—"

"That," Knight said, cutting off this rapidly deteriorating explanation, "is perhaps understandable." Did the very young persons believe him a ravening beast? He considered the looks of the Widow Winthrop and found himself in general agreement with their overprotectiveness. "You may leave us now for the moment," he said and Mrs. Allgood withdrew, Duckett just behind her.

Lily drew a breath, placed her hand lightly on Theo's arm, and said to Knight, "This is Theo, Tris's oldest child."

The thin boy was giving him the most assessing look imaginable. "Sir," he said, his young voice clipped, "forgive our impetuosity. We don't like to leave our mother alone with strangers."

"Theo," Knight said, "I don't blame you. I wouldn't either."

Lily quickly said, "And this is Sam. Sam, this is Viscount Castlerosse, your cousin."

"Sir," Sam said, his voice not at all balanced toward the civil end of the scale. It was as aggressive and pugnacious as his small chin, which was stuck forward. The compact little body was tensed, ready for a fight.

"Hello, Sam," said Knight easily. He looked down at the little girl, who was sucking her thumb and clutching a doll to her chest. She was pressed tightly against one of her mother's legs.

"And this is Laura Beth. She's just a bit clingy

now. It has been a long trip and we weren't certain just how you would, well, that is, we weren't altogether sure that your temper would . . ." Lily's voice dropped off. She couldn't seem to phrase a proper sentiment or make a logical explanation.

"Believe me," Knight said, "I do understand. Hello, Laura Beth."

Laura Beth turned to face the tall man. "You're not very old," she said, staring at him with unblinking eyes.

"Laura Beth," Theo said sharply. "Mind your manners."

"Theo, that, I believe, should be taken as a compliment." Knight saw Sam shoot a quick glance at his brother. Neither of them looked like Tris. But side by side, their features together . . . the resemblance to his cousin was striking.

"Together, standing there, they remind me so much of their father," he said.

Lily turned to Theo. Laura Beth kept her hold, and as a result, pulled Lily's dress tightly against her thigh and hip. Knight swallowed. This was absurd, for God's sake. Here he was, experiencing old-fashioned lust for a woman who was the mother of three children! No, he thought, that was impossible. She was much too young. He shook his head, listening to her voice. With the children, it was soft and filled with sweetness.

". . . so, Theo, if you and Sam will help Laura Beth into bed. Are you still hungry? No? Well, then, let me call the nice Mrs. Allgood and—"

Sam said in a loud whisper, "We don't want to leave you alone with him, Mama. Laura Beth's right. He's not old at all, not even close to Ugly Arnold and look what he did—"

"Tried to do," Lily said firmly, wanting to strangle her two overly vocal protectors. "That is quite enough." She couldn't recall the last time she'd been so embarrassed. She opened her mouth to apologize, to say something—anything—but the viscount interrupted her smoothly.

"I swear upon my honor as a gentleman and your cousin that I shan't behave inappropriately with your mother. Please go with Mrs. Allgood. Your mother will follow you shortly." He paused, then gave Lily a faint smile. "I would let her be with you now, but, you see, I haven't the faintest idea what's going on. It's not that I believe any of you are dangerous footpads or villains bent upon robbing me, but you certainly can understand my caution."

"So," Lily continued, "it is only fair that I explain things to the viscount. Theo, please. Laura Beth, let me go now. Sam, you would like a biscuit, wouldn't you?"

"He's right," Theo said. "We could be villains for all our cousin knows. We'll go with the woman—"

"But," Sam interrupted, his small fists on his hips, "we will look at the clock. Mama mustn't be too long."

"I shall keep her no longer than I must to ensure that she isn't one of Napoleon's remainder spies."

"All right," said Sam, a trace of approval showing through in his tone.

Mrs. Allgood was duly fetched. Laura Beth was pried loose and was convinced to accompany her. Laura Beth put her hand into the older woman's and smiled up at her. "Sam and I would like a biscuit."

"Cuthbert makes an excellent raspberry biscuit," Mrs. Allgood said.

Lily stood silently for a moment, looking at the closed library door. She heard the viscount say from behind her, "She'll take good care of them. Don't worry. And don't worry further that I will try to ravish you. It really isn't my style, you know. Come and sit down again. I will ask Duckett to bring tea, raspberry biscuits, and other edibles."

Lily did as she was bidden. She was so weary, most of it from sheer nerves at their possible reception by Tristan's cousin, that she slid into the plumply cushioned chair with a sigh of deep pleasure.

When Knight returned from giving Duckett orders, he saw that she was almost asleep. He approached quietly and said in a soft voice, "If you should like to take to your bed now, we can speak in the morning."

"Oh, no! That is, you are too kind, but you must realize why we are here and wonder at it and—"

"Perhaps, but we are certain to straighten everything out sooner or later. Ah, Duckett, here you are. I suppose you had everything ready and waiting. Certainly you did. Just wheel the tray in front of Mrs. Winthrop. Yes, that will be all."

Duckett, loath to leave, fiddled a moment with a tray lid, then, at the low snort from the viscount, finally sidled out of the library.

"I'm not certain whether or not I've been approved," said Lily, looking after him.

"The consequences of having servants who knew you in short coats, I fear. Don't worry about Duckett. Now, Mrs. Winthrop—that sounds odd, you know, since I also am a Winthrop. I'm Knight Winthrop." He gave her a bow.

Lily blinked and rose, giving him a curtsy. "I am Lily Winthrop, Tris's widow, my lord. I am sorry to tell you, but he died last month in Brussels."

"I'm very sorry. How did he die? Was it a long illness?"

Lily looked away, but not before Knight saw the pain in her fine eyes. "No, he was killed, murdered. By footpads, so the watch told me. They weren't caught, at least not before the children and I left Brussels."

"Where have you been? It is nearing the end of October now. I'm sorry, please sit down, Mrs. Winthrop."

Lily gave him an utterly charming crooked smile, then cut it off as quickly and effectively as if shutting off a spigot of water. "To Tris's sister in Yorkshire."

"Good grief! I'd forgotten all about the Damsons. That is their name, is it not?"

She nodded, saying nothing.

Knight paused, gazing down at her. Firelight made her hair look like soft honey. He swallowed. Dammit, he didn't even like honey. "I gather we are speaking of Ugly Arnold?"

"Yes, he is Gertrude's husband. Theirs is not a happy household. We left four days ago." Lily hadn't been certain if Gertrude would feel it her duty to demand custody of the children, so they had sneaked out at dawn.

"That is a long trip. You came by stage, didn't you?"

"Of course."

"You can't be Sam or Theo's mother. You're too young. In fact, even Laura Beth—"

"Laura Beth is my child. She's four years old. Theo and Sam are my stepsons. Tris's first wife died some six years ago." Even that was a lie. She had died birthing Laura Beth four years before.

Knight said thoughtfully, more to himself than to her, "You even seem too young to be the mother of a four-year-old child."

Lily drew herself up. She had to be certain he was convinced now. "I am twenty-three," she said, and the look in her eyes made him back down.

He pulled a chair across from hers and seated himself. "Please, drink some tea. Cuthbert's sandwiches aren't to be despised either. Why did you leave the Damsons?"

He knew the answer, of course; just looking at her, a man could completely lose his head, his perspective, his honor, and any other positive virtue he ever possessed. He wasn't certain why he was asking.

"We weren't happy there, nor were we particularly welcome. And yes, there was Ugly Arnold, as the children called him. You see, Tris had told me months ago that if anything ever happened to him we were to go to the Damsons, and if they didn't suit us, well, then to you, his cousin." She looked him straight in the eye. "We're here because we have no place else to go. I can take care of myself, don't mistake my request, my lord. But I can't take care of the children. They are wonderful and deserve far more than I could ever provide them."

"Tristan left you penniless?" It was straight speaking, but he knew now that it was what the Widow Winthrop wanted.

"Yes, very nearly. After I saw to his funeral arrangements and sold off what I could, we were left with only forty pounds." She paused a moment and he saw her fingers nervously pleating the wool of her gown. Knight looked at the teapot. He said easily, "Will you pour?"

"Of course," said Lily, delighted to have something constructive to do.

He watched her, admiring her gracefulness, and knew she was a lady, a lady bred bone-deep, a lady regardless of her lack of funds and alternatives at this point in time.

"I like only a spot of milk."

Her hands were shaking slightly and he felt a spurt of guilt. She was doubtless very tired, worried, frightened even that he would turn her and the children out into the street.

He said quickly, his voice deep and calm, "I will see to everything. Please don't concern yourself further. You should eat; then Mrs. Allgood will show you to your bedchamber. You and the children are perfectly safe with me. I'm not an Ugly Arnold, I swear it. I will take care of you." The instant the words were out of his mouth, he was appalled. What the devil had he promised?

Lily looked at him and said faintly, "Thank you, my lord."

He handed her a plate of cucumber sandwiches. "Here, Cuthbert does quite well with these. You're welcome. Tristan was my favorite cousin, even though we hadn't seen each other in over five years. I am sorry he died."

There came a knock on the door. "Yes?" Knight called.

Mrs. Allgood, looking on the edge of consternation, poked her head into the room. She was obviously laboring under considerable distress. "Forgive me for disturbing you, my lord, and you, Mrs. Winthrop, but your little girl is crying for you. She's afraid. It is a strange and new house for her."

Lily was on her feet in an instant. "Excuse me, my lord."

She walked quickly toward the door, seemed to remember herself, and turned. "Thank you. I think I shall see to the children, then go to bed. Tomorrow, my lord."

Knight had no time to rise before she was gone,

Mrs. Allgood hurrying behind her. The door
closed. He turned to look into the fireplace. The
flames were sluggish now. He hoped she'd gotten warm enough. It was a chilly night, and the
damp penetrated to one's very bones. He saw his
copy of *Candide* on the seat of his leather chair.
He frowned at it. What was it he'd been thinking?
Oh, yes, that his life was perfect, that he was content, that he wouldn't change a thing.

Now, though, there were three children in his
house and one very beautiful, very young widow.

He shook his head. Even if she'd been dowdy,
he wouldn't have hesitated to assist her. Lily. It
was a lovely name. Her eyes were a pale gray, he
thought, but wasn't certain. Perhaps blue, rather.
He would have to check in the morning.

Three children.

Now that was something else. He knew nothing about children. He did know, however, that
one didn't separate a mother from her offspring.
He was struck again by the resemblance of the
two boys' combined features to their father. Oh,
damnation, Tris, he thought. Why, damn you?
Why couldn't you have been more careful?

What if he hadn't been home when she and the
children arrived? Surely Duckett would have admitted them. Then Knight remembered the several times he'd jested about children, Duckett
within hearing.

Upstairs in a lovely guest bedchamber Lily was
met by a sobbing Laura Beth, Theo and Sam hovering over their sister, looking about helplessly.

Mrs. Allgood made clucking noises. Lily said
sincerely, "Thank you, Mrs. Allgood. I will see to
them now. They will sleep in here with me. It's
no trouble at all."

Mrs. Allgood didn't know what to do. Once
Winthrop House had boasted a nursery on the

third floor, but it had long ago been transformed into servants' quarters. There hadn't been children here in more years than she could count. Where to put the boys?

Lily knew her problem. "Perhaps there are two adjoining bedchambers? Tomorrow, if his lordship agrees, we can move into those. But for tonight, the boys can bundle up on the floor."

Mrs. Allgood was routed. She hurried off to have blankets fetched.

The moment the door had closed behind her, Laura Beth stopped crying. She gave Lily a self-satisfied grin.

"I thought something wasn't quite right with your overly dramatic squalling," Lily said, hands on hips. "Now . . ."

"It was an act," Theo said. "We wanted to make certain you were all right. Our cousin seemed to be a gentleman, but we couldn't be certain. You were alone with him, after all, and you know what happens when you're alone with men—"

Sam piped in, "He could have locked the door and thrown the key into the fireplace, then he—"

Lily held up her hand. "No, he was a perfect gentleman. Come along, all of you. Let's snuggle on the bed until Mrs. Allgood returns with the bedding."

"It was playacting," Laura Beth said, taking her place curled against Lily's breast. Theo and Sam sat with their legs crossed at the end of the bed.

"Well, you quite impressed me. Poor Mrs. Allgood, I believe she thought she'd damaged your sensibilities! It's a beautiful room," Lily continued, looking about for the first time at the soft blending of pale blues and creams. The bed was on a dais and covered with a wool counterpane of darker blue. The Aubusson carpet was cream-colored, the draperies a light blue.

"It's a girl's room," said Sam with a snort of disgust. "Soft and blurry."

Lily was too tired to do anything but smile. Where did they get their energy? She felt Laura Beth's hand fall and the small body go limp against her. One down, she thought, smothering a yawn.

"At least her thumb is out of her mouth," said Theo. "Sam's right, this is a girl's room."

"Yeck," said Sam.

"You're certain he will be honorable, Mama?" said Theo.

Lily took his hand and squeezed it. He and Sam had made a great game of calling her Mama at every opportunity upon their abrupt departure from Damson Farm. Now it seemed utterly natural. "Yes, I believe so. He was surprised, needless to say, for we did appear suddenly upon his doorstep. But he behaved with perfect propriety and courtesy. Ah, here is the bedding for you two."

As gently as she could, Lily lifted Laura Beth from her lap and covered her with a blanket. She thanked Mrs. Allgood, dismissal implicit in her tone. She and the boys spread the bedding upon the sinfully thick carpet. "You can undress after I douse the candles," she said and gave each of them a hug and a kiss. Not a clinging hug, but the lightest of pecks. They were boys, after all.

Within thirty minutes, Lily and her family were soundly asleep. Knight, still downstairs in the library, was staring at Mrs. Allgood. "What did you say?"

"I said, my lord, that all of them are in the same bedchamber. I took up more bedding for the boys."

"That is absurd! Have them moved immediately. The young woman is exhausted and needs her rest. Four people in one room, well—"

"It is what the lady wanted, my lord," said Mrs. Allgood firmly. She remembered the viscount from the age of three. His tone was nearing the same pitch. "We can straighten things out in the morning. Good night, my lord. If there is nothing else . . ."

"No, no, go to bed, Mrs. Allgood."

"I gather the lady and children will be remaining for a while?"

"I suppose so," Knight said. "Do you know anything about children, Mrs. Allgood?"

"Certainly, my lord. It's been a long time since my Gladys was a child, but she has two babies now and I see them every week."

Knight had no idea that Mrs. Allgood was a grandmother. He felt suddenly oddly disconnected. She'd been with him forever. He'd never before realized that she was a person outside his household as well as inside. "I see," was all he said.

"In the morning, Mr. Duckett and I will move them into adjoining bedchambers. There is nothing to concern yourself over."

She was letting him know, in the kindest way possible, that he should mind his own business. He was forced to smile. "All right. Tell Duckett he can have the food removed. Mrs. Winthrop didn't have much of a chance to eat."

"I shall. Good night, my lord."

2

Where the devil was she? It was ten o'clock in the morning and Knight was pacing in his library. He finally gave in and rang for Duckett.

"My lord?"

"Good God, do you have to slither about like a bloody ghost? You nearly scared the fingernails off my hand."

"My apologies, my lord. You wished something?"

"Yes. Where is Mrs. Winthrop? Half the morning is gone, and surely even she would be up and about by now and ready for her breakfast."

"I inquired earlier as to her whereabouts, my lord. Breakfast was sent up to her bedchamber. She wished—as a mother would, I'm sure—to stay with her children."

That certainly made sense, although it wasn't unduly flattering to him—her host, her savior, her protector in a cold, very hard world. "Send word that I wish to speak to her in the library."

"Yes, my lord."

"At her convenience, of course."

"Certainly you would have no wish to sound peremptory, my lord."

"Damn you, Duckett, you can keep your opinions to yourself."

"As you wish, my lord."

"You will be murdered in your bed, Duckett."

"I, my lord?" Dark eyebrows soared toward his bald pate.

"Yes, I shall have Stromsoe do it."

"Your valet, if I may venture to be so bold, my lord, hasn't the stomach for violence of any kind. Indeed, I saw him pale at the sight of a squashed bug."

"Oh, go away!"

"The bug had just bitten him. Very curious."

"Out!"

The viscount's message was delivered to Lily some three minutes later by Betty, an upstairs maid who kept bobbing curtsies as she repeated carefully and slowly, "Mr. Duckett says it's at your convenience, ma'am. His lordship ain't—aren't—really in no big 'urry, you know, it's just that he wishes to see you before too much more time passes into the future."

"Thank you, Betty. I shall come down immediately."

"What does he want to see you for?" Theo demanded. "That maid was most curious," he added without skipping a beat. "Her speech made no real sense."

"And alone?" asked Sam, instantly contentious. "Why didn't he ask for all of us? I'll plant him a facer, I will."

"He's not old," Laura Beth announced, taking her thumb out of her mouth.

"You are the most suspicious lot," Lily said, much amused. "Doubtless he wishes to know what our plans are, or rather, what our plans are for him. I want you all to settle into your new bedchamber. Theo, please watch Laura Beth.

Sam, please don't do anything horrible. All right?''

"Like what?" asked Sam with great interest.

Theo gave him one of his patented adult looks. "Like hanging knotted towels out the window with a message on the end saying you're being held a prisoner in the house, you loony."

"Oh, that kind of horrible."

"If that's the yardstick," Lily said, "I fear I am in some trouble. Just don't do anything to embarrass us and make his lordship want to boot us out of his house. I'll be back soon."

Lily made a quick visit to the ornate dressing-table mirror, patted an errant strand of hair into place, sighed at her pale cheeks and shadowed eyes, knew there was nothing to be done about it, and left the bedchamber.

She hadn't noticed that her large eyes were grayer than usual and darker with worry, but Knight did. He wanted to howl and curse, for he'd prayed devoutly that the incredibly beautiful creature of the night before would dissolve into an ordinary mother this morning. But it wasn't to be. She wasn't wearing anything fancy or alluring. Her gown was of pale gray muslin, with very few ruffles and no flounces at all, high-necked and high-waisted and long-sleeved, yet it still managed to announce the fullness of her breasts and the slender line of her torso. Her hair was pulled modestly back from her face, the result being that this style emphasized her high cheekbones, the slightly exotic slant of her brows, her delicate ears, and her narrow Roman nose.

She was the most delicious female he'd ever seen in his life and she was his cousin's widow, responsible for three children. He decided then and there that he would move her to Castle Rosse, along with the children, in the near future; that way his life could resume its placid and quite acceptable course. There was no doubt that she was an unwelcome storm in his shoals.

"My lord," Lily said, sweeping him a modest curtsy.

"Please call me Knight. We are related, you know."

"Then you must call me Lily."

"That's an unusual name."

"My father, Francis Tremaine—he was Baron Markham, you know—well, he had few claims to virtue, but one of them was being knowledgeable about all kinds of plants and flowers. I was christened Lily Ophelia long before I was born."

"A reference to Shakespeare is preferable, I should say, to Lily Hydrangea or Lily Buttercup."

"I added Lily Gorse Bush to the list long ago!"

"And if you'd been a boy?"

"That is enough to make one pause, isn't it?"

"As in Ugly Arnold Yew Bush?"

"I like that," she said, chuckling. "My brother, had there been one, would have been christened Birch Hawthorne Tremaine. What can one say to that?" And she chuckled again, at her sire's vagaries, Knight supposed. Hearing her voice, seeing her smile, he felt as if the sun had burst through on a dreary cloudy day and shone over him and through him, warming him. Then he realized who her father was. Tremaine—seventh Baron Markham! Good God, he thought, the man had flown England some years before, head over arse in debt, leaving his ancestral home in Dorset, if Knight remembered aright, leaving everything, in fact. So he had gone to Brussels.

With Lily?

"And your mother?"

"She died when I was fourteen years old. She

wasn't a flower, but rather a plain, very straight-forward Jane."

"If she looked like you, there was nothing plain about her."

If he could have, Knight would have cut out his damned and blasted loose tongue. Lily withdrew, not physically, but he could feel it. She was wary of him, understandably so. He was a man and she was at his mercy, if the truth be told, and all this following on the heels of the disagreeable machinations of Ugly Arnold. Knight was a gentleman, for God's sake, not some randy rakehell whose only interest lay in getting between a woman's legs. He started to apologize, then stopped. No, he would simply retreat. That should do the trick.

Then she said easily enough, and if her smile was forced, only he was aware of it, "No, my mother was a beautiful woman." She paused a moment, looking toward the bow windows that gave onto the park across the street. She added in a very careful voice, "I could tell from your expression that you'd heard of my father. He wasn't a particularly wise man, but he loved me, truly, and he took good care of me."

Knight imagined that it was she who took care of him, but he said nothing.

He was being polite, Lily thought. She said abruptly, "You wished to see me, my lord? About something in particular?"

"Knight," he corrected absently.

"Yes, well, Knight."

"I understand that you and the children all slept in one bedchamber last night."

"It does sound a bit overcrowded, doesn't it? I assure you that we weren't packed together like a gentleman's cravats. You must realize that the children—"

"No, I perfectly comprehend your motives. And will you be moving this morning?"

"If it is all right with you. I believe Duckett is arranging matters even now."

"Doubtless he is." Knight waved a negligent hand toward a chair. "I forget my manners. Pray be seated." He turned and sat himself down in the very large and comfortable leather chair behind his equally imposing mahogany desk.

"Did Tris leave a will?"

"No, not that I know of. He never spoke of one at any rate, and I didn't find one in his papers."

"Then no one has been named as the children's guardian."

"*I* am their guardian." She sat straighter in her chair. "Surely that can't be a surprise to anyone."

"I would have thought that Tris would have named a gentleman to be responsible for them."

"Why?"

He regarded her with tolerance and patience. "You are very young. The boys will need masculine guidance. They will need someone to look out for them. You are a woman, and although you are attached to them, it is not the same thing."

She wanted to demand, *Not the same thing as what?* but she said only, "Perhaps."

"Further, you have no means of support. So it is to their advantage to have a male relative as their guardian, financially speaking, of course."

"No!"

"That male relative could be Ugly Arnold or it could be me. The choice is yours. But I fancy you wish to have things arranged legally so there will be no possibility of you later losing the children."

She fell silent at that dreadful possibility, and

he added gently, "It's obvious that you haven't had time to give this matter any thought."

"No," she said, "I haven't. I have been trying to find us a home. It's left little room for else."

"I understand, but now you must see that things are handled properly and legally."

"No one could take the children from me, could they?"

"I doubt it, but I'll have my solicitor, Tilney Jones, drop by this afternoon. He will know what is to be done."

"You're very kind."

No, he was in truth a cynical bastard, but one who didn't cause much harm to his fellow creatures when all was said and done. He merely waved aside her comment. "You do realize, do you not, that if I am to be their legal guardian, I will have ultimate power over them until the boys reach eighteen and Laura Beth becomes twenty-one. Or until she marries."

Lily said nothing. The thought of four-year-old Laura Beth being married brought to mind the image of a young woman standing beside a supposed groom, the young woman's thumb in her mouth. She grinned at the image, then harked back to his other words. Her fingers began to fret with the pleats of her muslin skirt.

Knight eyed her. Obviously she found the entire proposition distasteful, but she was holding her tongue because he could, if he wished, boot her into the street. He felt guilty, and a bit angry at the situation, and said abruptly, "You must be thinking that you wished you had enough money never to have come here in the first place."

"That's true enough," she said with unrelenting candor, her chin going up. Just like Sam's, he thought. She rose suddenly and her pale cheeks were flushed. With anger, he noted. Good. That meant she'd forgotten her wretched situation, at least for the moment. "I don't know you, my lord, except that you were Tris's cousin. You could be a saint or the devil himself, you could be Napoleon or Wellington, the Prince Regent or—or—"

"Difficult to find the other side to that coin, isn't it?"

"It doesn't matter! I will not give you control over my children. I won't."

"Do compose yourself, Mrs. Winthrop. You're a very young lady with little concept of this world—"

That smug bit of masculine pretension sent her over the edge. "Ha! If you have heard of my father, then you know that he was cursed with a gambling fever. It didn't leave him. On his deathbed he wagered the doctor that he would live another twenty-four hours, and that fool of a doctor told him it wasn't possible. My father wagered the doctor's fees, and do you know what? He lived twenty-five more hours! No, my lord, I wasn't sheltered and protected like your little English misses. I took care of my father, saved him from more scrapes and dishonest cutthroats than you have probably seen in all your advanced years—"

"I'm only four years your senior," he said mildly.

"You're certainly older than twenty-three!" The instant the words erupted from her mouth, Lily gasped and took a step backward. She hit the arm of a chair, hard; the chair slid back, leaving her to flail the air with her arms to regain her balance. That didn't work and she went down on her bottom with a thud.

"Lily! Good God, are you all right?" Knight quickly skirted the desk.

Her "Yes" was clipped. He stood over her a moment, seeing her chagrin, her fury, her tumbled skirts and beautiful ankles, and despite his better intentions, he laughed. "Here, let me help you up." He offered her his hand, which she finally accepted, and pulled her to her feet. He jerked a bit too hard and she stumbled against him. For a brief moment, he felt the length of her. A surge of lust went through him that was so powerful, so all-controlling, he almost couldn't recognize it for what it was. He couldn't believe—he refused to believe—that any woman could send him skittering into sexual oblivion. Still, he wanted to touch her—

"What are you doing to Mama?"

Knight quickly turned, his lust dead as ashes in a summer grate. He saw Sam and slowly released Lily, noting the small boy's hands were fisted, his sturdy little body ready for an attack. Knight sighed.

"You walk as quietly as Duckett. I'm not doing anything to your mother, Sam. She fell and I helped her up. What do you want?"

Lily pulled back and smoothed down her gown. She was embarrassed to the tips of her toes, needed an outlet, lost control, and yelled at Sam in a fishwife's voice, "Really, Sam, this is too much! Go back to your room and knot the blasted sheets! Where is Theo? Laura Beth?"

"We drew straws," he admitted, studiously regarding the toe of his shoe. "I won."

"Now that you've seen, you may take yourself off. I'm still speaking to your mother."

Sam stood stiff as a rod, his expression mule-stubborn.

Lily clamped down on her embarrassment, realizing her loss of control was not the child's fault. She said, more mildly now, "Yes, my darling, do

take yourself away. His lordship and I are trying
to make decisions."

He still didn't move and gave her a confused
look. Lily's voice became more cajoling. "Please,
Sam."

"Out!" Knight ordered after a few more moments of stiff silence from the boy.

Sam finally gave in. "All right, but we have
more straws."

Lily and Knight watched him leave the library,
his step lagging. Finally he was gone. Knight
strode to the door, pulled it closed, and locked it.
This was the first time in his life that he'd locked
a door. He stood there, shaking his head. What
had happened to the pleasant, altogether predictable march of events? Life had become noticeably
otherwise during the past twelve hours. It was
disconcerting. He turned to face Lily.

She looked guilty enough to don a hair shirt.
"I yelled at him," she said blankly. "I actually
yelled at him."

"I warrant he'll survive it. Now, if you're all
right and have no bruises from your fall, let's get
back to business. You will also wish me to educate the children," he said. "The boys at least."

"Oh, no, not yet! I will educate them, they are
still very young and—"

"How old is Theo?"

"He turned nine in August, but he—"

"He should be at school. At Eton."

"I will not allow it. I know enough to begin
their education. I've taught them for nearly a year
now—"

"Only a year? I thought you'd been married to
Tris for four years at least. That is Laura Beth's
age, isn't it?"

The wages of sin, the consequences of lying, Lily
thought. "Tris taught them," she said, and he

knew it was a lie, not a complete and utter lie, but enough of a lie to make his lips thin.

"I see," he said and turned away from her. "I will send for you when Tilney Jones arrives. I trust that will suit you, ma'am."

He'd turned colder than a frozen winter pipe and she knew that he knew that she'd lied to him. She sighed. This interview hadn't gone well at all. She'd fallen like a clumsy sweep, heard him laugh at her, then hold her, she'd yelled at poor Sam and disagreed with her host at every point . . .

"Thank you, my lord," she said in an emotionless voice. "Until later, my lord."

He turned to see her walking swiftly to the door, her head bowed. He called after her, "Lily, will you join me for luncheon?"

She paused, saying nothing.

"And the children, naturally," Knight added, then cursed himself silently for that addition. He couldn't imagine dining with children, for God's sake. How could one have an intelligent conversation? How could one discuss, for example, the farming policies of Lord Liverpool with children there?

He grinned at himself. He hadn't discussed anything remotely concerning politics for the past three months.

"All right," Lily said and withdrew.

I'm a perverse idiot, he told himself, staring at the closed door. Why did I invite her to dine with me? It had just slipped out. He didn't like it, not at all.

Knight took his leave ten minutes later. He met Raymond Cosgrove, Lord Alvanley, and Julien St. Clair, the Earl of March, and the three of them visited Gentleman Jackson's Boxing Salon. Knight was sweating, breathing hard, a bruise burning over his third left rib when he realized suddenly that it was long past luncheon. He wondered in a brief moment of honesty if he'd purposefully forgotten the luncheon because he'd felt constrained to be there in the first place.

"I have to get home," he said. "I forgot about luncheon."

"What the devil are you blathering about, Knight?" asked Julien. "You just flattened Canney over there and now you're talking about missing your lunch?"

"I've got visitors," Knight said, toweling the sweat off his face.

"Who?" asked Lord Alvanley.

"My cousin's widow and her children."

"Children?" Both Julien and Raymond looked at him blankly.

Sir Charles Ponsonby strolled over. "I couldn't have heard aright. Knight speaking of children? Did you run over some of them, my lord? Give them to Cuthbert to fry or broil or bake? This is altogether fascinating. What children?"

Knight looked about at his friends. "I just said that they're my cousin's children," he said evenly. "They and their mother are staying at Winthrop House."

"And you were going to have luncheon with them?" This was from Raymond. He managed it in a fairly calm voice, but then the laughter burst forth. "Oh, no," he gasped, the laughter coming in loud hiccups now. "Children, at your bachelor's quarters? Children at Winthrop House?"

"I see it now," said Sir Charles, shaking his finger at Knight. "It's the children's mother, isn't it, Knight? She's a beauty, I'll wager. Does she want to hang onto your sleeve, old fellow?"

"She's not at all a beauty," Knight said, lying without compunction. "For God's sake, gentlemen, she's destitute and she wants the best for her offspring. I had no choice in the matter. Now, if you laughing grouse will excuse me . . ."

"How many children, Knight?" asked Julien St. Clair.

"Three."

"Ah, I have it. One of the children is a beautiful girl, all of eighteen, right?"

"No, Raymond, they're all under the age of ten."

"And they're staying at Winthrop House?"

"That's right. Now, if you'll excuse me—"

"By Gawd," said Sir Charles. "I don't believe this. Maybe he meant they were staying *under* Winthrop House. Or perhaps beneath the oak tree in the backyard?"

Julien said slowly, staring after his friend, "I don't believe it either."

At Winthrop House, Lily waited as long as she could before allowing Mrs. Allgood to have their luncheon served. His lordship still hadn't returned. The children were hungry, bored, and testy. They'd moved their belongings into their new bedchambers two hours earlier, and time had hung heavily on everyone's hands since then.

Lily finally gave it up, praying their host wouldn't mind. In fact, she considered him abominably rude, but she wouldn't have admitted it to anyone. "Come," she said, "we'll have luncheon, then go for a walk. I'm just as bored as all of you, so cease your complaining."

"We weren't—"

"Yes, you were, Sam. Be quiet and sit down."

"I left Czarina Catherine upstairs."

"Laura Beth, she's not hungry, I swear it. Sit down now."

She did, and her chin came even with the table

edge. Duckett smiled. "I'll see to it, ma'am," he said, and a few minutes later, Laura Beth was seated regally on four stacked tomes.

"Sam, stop taking everyone's silverware! Sit still!"

"I'm just examining the design, Mama. It looks like cabbages with W's wound in and out."

"This soup is *green*, Mama."

"It's split pea soup, Laura Beth, and it's supposed to be green."

"I don't like ham," announced Sam, scientifically observing the thin slice of ham that was quivering on his fork.

Lily looked at the three children and wanted to strangle each of them. "If you do not eat this minute, you will go back upstairs and I won't take you out. Sam, stop trying to pull the books out from under Laura Beth!"

"But this one looks interesting. It's—"

"It's Francis Bacon," Theo said, then squealed, "Careful, Sam! Oh, no!"

Laura Beth went tumbling to the floor, yelling all the way.

Knight walked into the small breakfast parlor at that precise moment.

Lily bounded to her feet and Sam slipped under the table, hoping to escape retribution.

Duckett said calmly, "Good afternoon, my lord. Would you care for your luncheon now?"

Knight closed his eyes for a moment. When he opened them, he met Lily's gaze. She'd dropped to her knees on the floor, trying to calm a sobbing Laura Beth. Her face was perfectly white and he knew that she was afraid. He was overwhelmed by the chaos, but not angry. He said quite mildly, "I shall eat later, Duckett. Lily, are you and Laura Beth all right? Would you like me to thrash Sam?"

Sam poked his head out from under the table.

Theo, a moment before his brother's executioner, was now his staunch defender. "It was my fault, sir," he said, standing bravely in front of Knight. "Sam didn't realize what he was doing. It was the Francis Bacon, you see. His *Sylva Sylvarum*. That means—"

"I know what it means, Theo." Knight looked about the small room one more time, turned on his heel, his greatcoat swirling around his ankles, and took himself off.

"Oh, dear," said Lily.

"Don't worry yourself about his lordship, ma'am," said Duckett. "I daresay he'll come about."

"That's what I'm afraid of," said Lily.

"I'll plant him a facer," said Sam, crawling out from under the table.

3

Arnold Damson, brother-in-law of the late Tristan Winthrop, stood on the corner of Portland Square and felt his self-confidence ebb just a bit. The houses bespoke wealth, power, and ancient privilege.

He forced himself to square his shoulders. It didn't matter. After all, he had right on his side. And right dictated that he could have Lily Tremaine. And he wanted Lily Tremaine. He wanted her more than he dreaded the impending interview with Lord Castlerosse. He kept telling himself that the viscount wouldn't want to be saddled with Tristan's three brats. Of course, Lily was another matter. He wondered if the viscount had already lured her to his bed.

He shook his head at that. She hadn't been here long enough. Only one day, two at the most, by his reckoning. He was in time to save her from the nobleman's lascivious intentions.

She would have succumbed to him, Arnold, if not for that damnable brat, Theo, interrupting him on the stairway. Oh, yes, he'd get them all back and then remove the little monsters from Lily's influence, and her from theirs.

It had taken him two hours of examination, subtle and smooth as could be, of course, to get

Gertrude to remember the viscount's existence. He, a man of the world, of course, had known that the viscount would live in London. Locating him upon his arrival had been ridiculously simple. He wondered what Lily would say when she saw him.

Arnold Damson knew he wasn't a superb specimen of manhood. He wasn't one of the vaunted arrogant Corinthians or a superb horseman or a renowned athlete. But he was the children's uncle. He controlled the purse strings. He held power over their futures.

And that made up for all his shortcomings.

He marched up to the impressive dark oak doors and rapped smartly with the highly polished brass handles.

The door opened and he found himself staring at a rather plump man who was very short and very bald. Who would hire a paltry fool like this?

"Yes?"

"You will take me to Lord Castlerosse, my man."

Duckett smiled. A country squire, full of his own importance, slightly cowed by his surroundings, and contemptuous of a man of shorter stature than he. He was neither old nor young, Duckett saw. He was too thin and too sallow and his clothes were poorly cut, but he did have a beautiful full head of light brown hair. He also looked as if he pouted a lot—a discontented man who in all likelihood made those around him thoroughly miserable.

Duckett's perusal required only a split second. He said gently, "Who did you say you were? One of his lordship's bootmakers?" Duckett decided to enjoy himself. This pathetic specimen would have no knowledge of the incomparable bootmaker, Hoby. "Or perhaps you wish to sell his lordship a new brand of hair pomade? I regret to tell you that his lordship doesn't use such things, but you might like to speak to his valet. I can see if he has time for you. He is a rather flighty fellow, but he might be able to find a moment for you.''

Arnold was flustered. ''No,'' he managed after a moment. ''I don't want to see the damned valet. I am the children's uncle! I demand to see Knight Winthrop.''

''Your name, sir?''

''Damson. Arnold Damson.'' Arnold wished desperately at that moment that he had a ''sir'' in front of his name. It was too late to make up one now.

He gave Arnold a wide smile. ''Do come in, Mr. Damson. I will see if his lordship wishes to receive you.''

Duckett left a properly chastened Arnold in the entryway and took himself off with a slow and stately stride to the library, slower and statelier than usual. The viscount was dictating correspondence to his secretary, Trump Dickie.

After Duckett informed the viscount of his visitor, he waited. Knight looked startled, then began to smile. He rubbed his hands together and his smile bordered on the evil. Duckett was fascinated. ''Ah, send him in, Duckett. Trump, do take yourself off for, say, half an hour.''

When Duckett showed Mr. Arnold Damson into the library, Knight was on his feet, a wide smile on his face.

''How do you do,'' he said politely. ''It is a pleasure to meet Tris's brother-in-law.''

Left with no choice but to return the civility, Arnold dutifully responded with what manners he could muster, but he didn't like it. He'd known the viscount was a young man. Gertrude, the stupid cow, had remembered that he was Tristan's junior by many years. But the man wasn't the soft, pampered, flabby specimen he'd pictured in his mind. He was tall—the top of Arnold's head came to his chin—and damnably well formed: wide shoulders, narrow waist—no paunch for this fellow—and long legs thick with muscle. He was, in short, a sportsman. His face would interest women, Arnold thought, bringing all his critical faculties into the fray. He was forced to admit that the viscount was, at the very least, a moderately acceptable-looking man. It was assuredly a revolting development.

Knight kept himself from laughing aloud at Ugly Arnold's intense scrutiny. He wished he could ask him what his final conclusion was. He said instead, ''You are newly arrived from Yorkshire, I see.''

Arnold didn't know how his lordship could see anything of the sort, but he said quickly, ''Yes, my lord. Damson Farm is near Harrowgate. A fine holding.''

''Yes, I remember Tris telling me about it some years ago. He mentioned that it belonged to his sister, Gertrude. That was, of course, before she married you. How odd that you should change its name. As I recall, it was called Oberlon Grange. After a Winthrop of long ago.''

Arnold didn't like this at all. The viscount—arrogant bastard—was making him feel like a cheap interloper. ''I prefer my name to another man's,'' he said and managed to raise his chin a bit.

A weak chin, Knight thought, not changing expression. Perhaps he should recommend a beard. It would help.

He showed Arnold a chair and seated himself opposite, crossing his legs at the ankles. He looked to be filled with the milk of male camaraderie. "Now, would you like to tell me what I can do for you, sir?"

Arnold blurted out, "I am here to fetch my niece and nephews and their mother."

"I see. How very interesting." Knight flicked a piece of lint from his coat sleeve before looking up to add, "Whyever should you wish to do that?"

"I am their closest relative. Lily had no excuse to leave Damson Farm in such a hurly-burly way, and all because of a silly misunderstanding. The children, and their mother, of course, are my responsibility, after all."

"I see," Knight said again, and indeed he did see. He couldn't really blame Ugly Arnold for his infatuation with the lovely Lily, but to come all the way to London to saddle himself with three children, merely in the hope of getting her into his bed . . . the fellow had gone to a good deal of difficulty, and he'd done it very quickly. He deserved some hope. "This sounds extremely logical. If it is convenient with your plans, Mr. Damson, I should like for you to come to dinner."

Arnold didn't quite know what to make of that. He'd expected the viscount to be toplofty, perhaps treat him with condescension, but he'd found him entirely affable, much more so than that bald butler of his. And he seemed in agreement with Arnold's claim. Now an invitation to dinner!

"Will Li—the children's mother be present?"

"Should you like her to be?"

"Since she would probably insist that she accompany the children back to Damson Farm, it is entirely appropriate."

"I do agree," said Knight, his face entirely straight. "Now, my dear sir, I suppose that you have much to occupy your time. Tonight, say around eight o'clock?"

Arnold found himself on the doorstep a minute later, not really understanding how he'd got there so quickly. And so politely.

Betty was giving Lily another message upstairs. When Lily knocked on the library door, she heard a very mellow "Come in, Mrs. Winthrop."

She quietly opened the door, wondering what awaited her. Perhaps he would send her about her business now. The debacle at lunch still made her head ache. Sam had deserved to have his ears boxed. She just hadn't been able to bring herself to do it. He had given her his unrivaled orphan look and, as usual, she'd succumbed. Little heathen.

"Hello," she said and took only two steps into the library.

"Shut the door, Lily."

She did as he bade her.

"Now, I have some excessively interesting news for you."

"News?" She looked at him blankly. "You . . . you're not angry? About the children? Luncheon? Sam and Francis Bacon?"

"No. Just a bit numb. Actually, I'm feeling quite entertained. I was able to put off vastly boring correspondence with Trump—my secretary—in favor of a visitor who wasn't completely unexpected, but rather, here more quickly than I'd anticipated. He'd come such a long way and was so bent on getting what he wanted. In short, Lily, you and I are going to have the pleasure of dining with the one and only Ugly Arnold tonight."

"Oh, no!" Her hand went to her throat, and she knew she'd paled to the color of his cravat. All the implications burrowed through her brain. Arnold would tell him that she wasn't really Tris's widow, that Laura Beth wasn't her child, that she had only the claim of being Tris's betrothed. She stared at Knight, feeling hopelessness flow over her. They had been here but twenty-four hours. And now it was all for naught. She saw that Knight was smiling. Perhaps he'd made this up to punish her?

"No," she said, "Arnold can't be here. I didn't tell him anything about you, not a thing. You're making this up, aren't you, because of luncheon? Oh, please say it is merely a jest!"

Knight sighed dramatically. "I do wish you could show as much forbearance for me as you do for the children. I imagine that Ugly Arnold got the information about my existence from Gertrude. He certainly has moved quickly to find you. In any case, I felt such an excess of infatuation and nauseating devotion deserved some hope. Also, after Tilney Jones has left, in about two hours from now, we will be well on the way to legalizing my guardianship of the children. I assume you will have no more, er, problems with my proposal?"

"Ugly Arnold here," Lily said, more to herself than to him. Indeed he'd moved quickly! "He wants the children?"

"No, he wants you. He's willing to take the children in order to have you."

"He said that?"

"Don't be ridiculous. Well, he did, but not in those words. Let's just say that what he wanted was made quite clear. I fancy our Arnold isn't above blackmailing you to get you into his bed. That is, you may stay with the children if you succumb to his, ah, blandishments."

He saw her flinch but didn't soften. She said in a pitifully hopeful voice, "Perhaps he isn't quite that bad. He is their uncle, after all."

"He would tolerate the children. But what he wants to be is your protector. Now, what would you like to do about this? Do you find me more acceptable as a guardian? I do promise you, Mrs. Winthrop, that I won't try to blackmail you into my bed."

"Why should you want to? You don't even like me."

Goodness, he thought, staring at her, an arrested expression in his eyes. How had she come to that wonderful conclusion? "I like you well enough, ma'am. Now, what is your decision?"

She had no choice but to relinquish the reins. She rather thought that the viscount, even with all the legal power over the children, would not be much of an attentive guardian. "We shall do as you deem best."

"What the devil does that mean?"

"Will you be their legal guardian?"

"Yes. If it's possible, Tilney will know how to bring it off." Knight consulted his pocket watch. "Would you like to be present? He should arrive shortly."

Lily's hand flew to her hair. "I should change, perhaps. I have been sermonizing . . . Sam is such an angel, such a sweet little boy, he really—"

She broke off at the look of absolute incredulity on the viscount's face.

"He is! Perhaps he's a bit mischievous!"

"He's the devil's own spawn," said Knight. "I fancy the dons at Eton will cure him of his more unacceptable pranks."

"No, he's much too young. He's only six and—"

"Mrs. Winthrop, please shut up. You will do as I say, or you could perhaps find yourself with Ugly Arnold again."

"Blackmail," she said. "You are too above that sort of thing? You are not a—"

"A prince among men? A toad among princes? A prince in wolf's clothing?"

She laughed, she couldn't help herself. It was her cross to bear. Even when she was at her most furious, she could see another's point of view. Her father had taught her that; rather, he'd crossed the line so many times that she'd come to accept rage along with laughter.

It was a beautiful sound. Lilting, flowing over him like the sweetest honey or jasmine. Knight shook his head. He was fast becoming a blithering ass. The woman had laughed, that was all. At least she had a sense of humor.

"You don't need to change your gown or comb your hair. You look like a mother should look—slightly harried, harassed, and otherwise flustered. Ah, Duckett. I fancy Tilney Jones has arrived?"

"Yes, my lord. Mr. Jones, my lord."

Tilney Jones was a very pleasant-looking man in his middle thirties. Blessed with intelligent brown eyes, broad shoulders, and a graceful form, he was also endowed with an excellent sense of humor and a talent for telling tales that brought his audience to its knees with laughter. He was one of the viscount's best friends. He stepped forward and shook his hand. "Now, what is all this about children, Knight? I surely must have misunderstood! You and *children*—it doesn't merit serious thought. Wasn't Trump having a jest at my expense?"

"Actually, Tilney, if you will but pay attention to your surroundings, you will have the sublime pleasure of making the acquaintance of the children's mother. Mrs. Winthrop, Tilney Jones, my solicitor, and a fellow who sometimes doesn't look before he leaps with his tongue.''

Tilney turned on his heel, beheld Lily standing silently behind him, and became mute. He'd expected a mother, for heaven's sake, a woman who looked like his own mother, not this very young woman who was so exquisite. ''You can't be a mother!''

''She is, old fellow,'' said Knight. ''Of only one little girl, however.''

My God, he was thinking, observing his friend's instant bemusement, I swear I will never look at a woman—any woman—and fall so obviously and metaphorically at her feet. It was humiliating and degrading.

Knight said very gently, ''Now, dear fellow, say, 'A pleasure, ma'am. Forgive my impertinence. I am certain your children are wonderful specimens.' You may speak now, Tilney.''

Lily had had enough experience in her young life with reactions like Mr. Tilney Jones's. She simply ignored it. It meant nothing to her, nothing at all. She smiled and gave him her hand. ''Pay him no heed, Mr. Jones. I am delighted to meet you and I trust you will see to the solution of our problem.''

''Yes, ma'am,'' said Tilney, unable to take his eyes off her.

''Tilney, do get yourself together. You're embarrassing Mrs. Winthrop, and me, of course.''

Lily pulled her hand from Mr. Jones's grasp.

''Shall we proceed?'' asked Knight at his most sardonic.

* * *

Near Harrowgate, England
October 1814

"Aye," said Monk Busch, "we're 'ot on 'er
trail now, Boy. 'Er and the brats. We'll get 'em."

"I'm thirsty," said Boy, running his dry tongue
over his bushy whiskers. "And 'ungry."

"Ye always are. Skinny as a gallows tree, ye
are, and eat like a bloody fat whore. Jest shut yer
trap. We'll go to this Damson Farm, make sure
Tris's little lovebird is there, then 'ang back a bit."

Boy took up his familiar refrain. "We don't
know she's got anything to do with it, Monk. Old
Tris could have 'id 'em anywhere. Jeez, back in
Brussels, for all we know."

Monk gave his partner a look of acute dislike.
"We tore up 'is damned house, looked everywhere, even in the mouse hole. Nothing. And 'is
little tart takes off with the brats awful soon after
'e's shoveled underground. No, she's got the
goods, aye, she does."

"Then why she'd come 'ere? To a relative's?
Why doesn't she set 'erself up, what with all the
stuff?"

That bothered Monk as well. "Don't know,"
he admitted. "Don't matter anyways. She's a
smart piece, that one. Tris was head over arse in
love with her, let it slip once, 'e did, when 'e was
deep in 'is cups."

"She's a looker," said Boy. "I wonder if poor
Tris got in 'er before 'e croaked."

"*Poor* Tris? You're a booby! 'E double-crossed
us, Boy, bribed that damned magistrate, and left
us to rot in a stinking Frenchie prison! 'E deserved the skewer in 'is back! As for 'is little piece,
she was living with 'im, wasn't she? For Gawd's
sake, she was living and sleeping in 'is house . . .

looking after 'im and 'is brats. Tris weren't no monk—''

''No, not like you!'' exclaimed Boy, pleased with his witty effort.

''Shut yer trap, Boy. I don't find ye at all amusing. Ye're a bloody dolt. Now, maybe this little piece will want to do for us. Ye know—we let 'er keep a bit of the goods in return for a tumble or two in the 'ay.''

''She's a looker,'' said Boy again. ''I wouldn't mind plowing my rod in 'er, I tell you.''

''Ye don't have enough between yer legs to make it worth 'er while, not like me. But why not? Another thing, Boy. I wouldn't be surprised if she told Tris to do us in. A looker like 'er. Sees 'er chance and takes it.''

Monk was rather pleased with this analysis and continued after a moment. ''Yep, she took in poor Tris. I'll bet ye it were all 'er idea to buy off them coves and 'ave us in-car-cer-ated in that damned prison.''

''She ain't as smart as we are,'' said Boy. ''Come right to England, she did; didn't even try to cover 'er tracks. Gawd, every man from Brussels to York remembers 'er, and it ain't just because of the three brats cutting up their peace. No, remember what that coachman said? Just rolled 'is eyes, 'e did, and licked 'is chops.''

''She thinks we're in prison. She ain't worried, not at all. Old Tris was jiggered by footpads, that's wot the watch believes, that's wot she believes. Nobody will ever be the wiser.''

''How do we get 'er off this Damson Farm place?''

Monk shrugged and his eyes narrowed. He looked mean and cruel and determined. Boy shivered, just a bit; he couldn't help himself. Monk was a serious cove, bent on getting what he

wanted. Boy thought of himself as being filled
with the gin of human kindness, or whatever the
saying was. He wasn't like Monk. No, sir. He
would be very polite to everyone once he was
rich.

"I'll get 'er," Monk said, and Boy didn't doubt
his word for a minute.

Winthrop House, London
October 1814

"That's it, then," Theo said, his shoulders
hunching. "I can't imagine what his lordship will
do now."

Lily had told the children of their uncle's presence.

"I'll blast his liver," said Sam, but he didn't
sound like he really meant it.

"He's not a nice man," Laura Beth added.

Lily sighed. "What's done is done. I tried to
have everything tied up as completely as I could
with the viscount's solicitor, Mr. Jones. If Arnold
vents his spleen tonight, well, perhaps the viscount will feel compelled to keep you three."

"No!"

"I'll plant him a facer!"

"He's young."

Lily tried for a very reasonable, child-convincing
voice. "But, my dears, the fact is I've lied to him.
Evidently it hasn't occurred to Arnold that I
would change my status. If the viscount says
something, if Arnold gets distracted, it's over.
There will be absolutely nothing I can do about
it."

"If he finds out and he gets really mad, then
we'll all leave, that's all."

Dear Theo, he didn't know what the real world was like. How cold and difficult and mean it could be. But he and Sam were her protectors, so she tried for a smile and gave each of them a hug.

She donned her best gown two hours later. She kissed the children good-night, promising that she would come and tell them about the dinner. The boys were in a very large bedchamber that adjoined hers and Laura Beth's. She walked downstairs, managed a travesty of a smile for Duckett, and allowed him to open the drawing room doors.

"Lily!"

She paused a moment on the threshold. Standing directly behind Arnold was Knight, and he looked calm, utterly relaxed, though there was a glint of amusement in his eyes, she was certain of it. He hadn't guessed a thing. Arnold hadn't said a word against what he thought to be true about her. Realizing this had the effect of eradicating every ounce of fear she'd felt for Ugly Arnold—for all of one minute. During that precious minute she saw him as a rather pitiful man, with ignoble aims and an unfortunate predilection for her.

"Hello, Mr. Damson," she said pleasantly, nodding at him. "I trust you had a pleasant journey here to London? I hope Gertrude is well."

"Gertrude is fine. She is always fine, though she complains of her bile humors, as you know."

"It is kind of you to come and see that we are settled in and comfortable."

"No, it isn't! That isn't it at all!"

"You don't wish us to be comfortable? I assure you that Lord Castlerosse is a very polite host. He would never be—"

"That isn't what I meant!" Arnold wished the damned viscount would take himself off. He tried to calm himself. Right was on his side. But just looking at Lily made nearly all logical thought fly out of his head. She was tastier-looking than even he remembered. He recognized the pale peach silk gown. It was modest and perhaps a bit out of date, but on her it looked wonderful enough for a bloody queen. Her hair was piled on top of her head in a thick braid. Loose tendrils floated down her neck and over her ears. She looked calm, composed, that *serene* expression of hers he remembered so well firmly fixed on her face.

"I see. What do you mean, sir?"

"I mean that you and the children—"

"Dinner is served, my lord."

Arnold cursed, luridly, but only Knight heard him. He swallowed the bark of laughter. "Thank you, Duckett. Mr. Damson, would you please give Mrs. Winthrop your arm?"

Lily didn't want Ugly Arnold within six feet of her, but she merely smiled and waited for him to take her arm. He was trembling and she wondered why. It was she who was the fraud, after all, not he.

When they reached the dining room, Duckett was holding her chair for her. She moved toward him, but Arnold didn't release her arm. She tugged, but still he did not let her go.

"Mr. Damson, please."

"Oh," said Arnold and dropped her arm.

Knight looked at Arnold, a brow flaring up in utter astonishment at his unaccountable behavior.

Arnold flushed, Lily prayed he wouldn't say anything, and Knight decided to let the farce continue. Once they were all seated, he said to Duckett, "You may serve now."

"Very well, my lord."

It didn't take long for Arnold to drop the first shoe. Over a serving of braised mutton he said,

"I wish to leave on the morrow, Lily. You will have the children ready."

It was now or never, she thought, her fork poised halfway between her plate and her mouth. "No, Arnold. We aren't going anywhere with you. We're staying here."

Arnold then dropped the other shoe.

4

Damson Farm
Harrowgate, England

"Yes'm. We're friends of Lily Tremaine, yer brother's little gal. We're awful sorry that old Tris got jiggered, but we'd be mighty glad to see his little gal, yep we would."

Gertrude Damson managed to glean the essence of this unworldly speech, although it didn't much reduce her fear of these two villainous-looking creatures. The large man who had spoken looked mean enough, with his beefy face and flat dark eyes, to steal from the vicar's poor box and then throttle the vicar. As for his weaselly little partner, he looked as if he'd hold down the vicar while his friend was doing him in. She got hold of herself. So they wanted to speak to Lily, did they? They were Lily's friends? Not likely, but Gertrude didn't mind, not one bit. She looked about for that fool, Beem. He was nowhere to be seen. Why had he let these creatures in to see her?

Actually, Beem was five pounds richer, but worried nonetheless. He hovered outside the drawing room, praying that the man wouldn't strangle the mistress.

Gertrude knew deep down that she would have yelled her head off had the men asked to see anyone on Damson Farm except Lily Tremaine, the little slut. She still smarted from Arnold's miserable infatuation for the trollop. So he wanted the children back, did he? A man who had paid little heed to his own offspring now wanted to be the "father" to poor Tris's? Gertrude would have spit in his face if he hadn't been so pitifully obvious. But Lily had packed up the children and simply disappeared. Gertrude had more than a sneaking suspicion of what had caused that flight, but she would never admit it to herself, to the vicar, or to any powers higher than she herself.

Gertrude smiled at the two villains who stood with their grimy hats in their hands in the middle of her pristine drawing room. She said brightly, "Lily Tremaine is in London. I believe she's now living with Viscount Castlerosse. He was my brother's cousin, you know. I don't recall his address."

Monk wasn't prepared for such easy capitulation. He frowned at the blousy, big-bosomed woman and wondered if she was lying to him. "Are ye certain?" he demanded, at his most menacing.

Gertrude blinked. "Of course I'm sure. My husband left to fetch her and the children back here."

"Oh, ah," said Boy and tugged on Monk's sleeve. "Let's scuttle, Monk, let's go."

"All right," said Monk, still floored at the ease of his success. No need for threats; no need for the delicate little stiletto, his most valued possession and a long-ago gift from his sainted mother;

no need to curse. It was disheartening. It wasn't what he was used to.

After Beem had shown out the two villains, he immediately presented himself to the mistress and told her of their threats to his person if he didn't allow them entrance. Gertrude just looked at him and held out her hand. "Give it to me, Beem, all of it."

Beem fluttered, denied, tried his best to look both affronted and innocent, and ended up placing the five-pound note in his mistress's outstretched hand. It wasn't fair.

"They wanted Miss Tremaine," she said as Beem watched her stuff the note down her massive bosom.

Beem was instantly alert. "Oh, dear," he said. "I hope you don't know where she went, ma'am."

"Of course I know, and I told them, you old fool! Unlike the rest of you absurd men, I don't think they'll melt at the sight of her *beaux yeux*. Now get out of here before I have you kicked off Damson Farm!"

Winthrop House
London, England

"Tell us everything, Lily. Everything."

Lily shook the sleep from her eyes and mind. She looked at the clock on the mantel and saw that it was just six o'clock in the morning, and here were the three children, bouncing up and down on her bed. They'd been fast asleep when she'd checked on them last night and so had not awakened them to relate the events of the evening.

"All right. Just give me a minute. All of you get under the covers. It's cold and I don't want any of you to become ill."

Laura Beth, Czarina Catherine stuffed under her arm, slithered down next to Lily and snuggled close. Theo and Sam got under the covers at the end of the bed, propping themselves up with bolsters.

"Will we have to leave, Mama?" asked Laura Beth.

"I don't . . . no, we won't." Lily prayed she was telling the truth. She simply didn't know and was afraid to become an optimist. That was what her father had been all his life.

"Tell us," said Theo, and his voice was frightened. "We can take it." Lily wanted to hug him close and vow that she would never let harm come to him, never. Instead she gave him a warm smile, what she hoped was a reassuring smile.

"Well, Ugly Arnold was himself. Early into the evening meal I thought it was all over for us." She looked toward the portrait of an ugly woman swathed in a stiff farthingale the color of a bilious green. A long-ago Winthrop? With bad taste?

"Mama," said Sam, impatient, and she brought herself back.

"I'll tell you all of it." Not quite all, she amended silently to herself. Not the cursing, the nastiness barely coated with false civility.

"Lily, you and the children will come back with me," Arnold had said. "I am the children's uncle by marriage. If you refuse, I will take them away from you and no court in the country would gainsay me."

"On the contrary, sir," the viscount had smoothly disagreed. "Lily and the children will remain here. Won't you have some of the curried sweetbreads? Cuthbert is very fond of them and makes them very nearly edible.''

''No!''

''Surely you wouldn't like to just try them, sir?''

''No, I mean, Lily will come with me!''

Knight didn't look at her. He'd already seen her pallor, the stark fear in her fine eyes. He'd known her and the children for all of twenty-four hours. It was bizarre. They had turned his well-measured life upside down. And he was enjoying himself immensely. He didn't allow himself to dwell on the awesome fact that he would be the legal guardian of three—three!—children whose existence hadn't troubled his life until just yesterday. ''Mr. Damson, I should prefer to eat my dinner in relative calm and peace. We could discuss this, ah, slight disagreement later.''

''No,'' said Arnold, ''I want to settle things now.''

''Very well,'' said Knight on a long-suffering sigh. ''Duckett, you and the footmen please take yourselves off. We will serve ourselves. How, I don't know, but I assume we will be able to manage.''

''Very good, my lord.'' Duckett led Charlie and Ben away, much to their respective disappointment.

''Now, Mr. Damson,'' Knight continued, ''if you won't try the sweetbreads, perhaps the haricot mutton strikes your fancy?''

''There isn't any!''

''Ah, I see that you are quite right. Well, then, some fowl à la béchamel?''

''My lord,'' said Arnold, growing desperate now at this excess of affability, ''I came to dinner simply because I wanted to see Lily and tell her my plans. You are not a close relative; you can have no say in the matter."

"Not as close as Gertrude, that's correct. However, Mr. Damson, it really doesn't matter. The children and Lily remain with me. Very shortly I shall be their legal guardian."

"You can't! I won't allow it! I will get a solicitor—"

"Please do, sir. Perhaps my own solicitor could recommend an able fellow for you. But you know, such a case as this could drag on and on. You, sir, simply haven't a chance in the long run. No, even though your motives are doubtless elevated to the heavens themselves, you must relinquish all thought of the children. They are mine now, and that's an end to it."

"I shan't allow it, my lord. Never."

Knight said very gently, "Mr. Damson, did I neglect to tell you that I am excessively wealthy? I did, didn't I? Forgive me. I am, you know. You haven't a prayer. Now, can we finish our dinner? Lily, do finish your fricasseed chicken."

Lily very nearly choked. She couldn't believe her ears. The viscount was adamant. She had prayed he wouldn't toss her and the children willy-nilly into Arnold's panting arms, but to be her champion? It was beyond what she'd expected.

"You just want to bed her! You just want her to be your damned mistress!"

Lily gasped and flushed to her eyebrows, not in embarrassment, but in fury. "You horrible—"

Knight merely raised a hand to shut her off, then gave Arnold a look that shriveled his toes. He felt such a surge of rage at the man's rudeness, it was all he could do to stop himself from stuffing the sweetbreads down Arnold's skinny throat.

Arnold, seeing he'd wrought stunned silence, plowed onward, despite his gut fear of the viscount. "Lily, you can't stay here with him. He'll ruin you—you'll have no reputation left at all. You must come home with me. I . . . Gertrude wants you very much, truly."

Knight moved back his chair and rose to his feet. He said quietly, "Do stand up, Mr. Damson. I don't want to break your nose whilst you're seated."

Arnold knew he'd gone too far. But it was galling, the cheek of this damned man. Just because he was rich as Croesus and a damned peer of the realm, he believed he could do as he pleased.

"No, I won't rise! You won't break my nose— if you do I'll see you in Newgate!"

Knight couldn't help himself. Ugly Arnold had turned into a completely unexpected melodramatic comedy. He threw back his head and laughed deeply. "All right," he said, all neat amiability after he had caught his breath. "I won't break your nose. It is already of an undeniable ugliness. And, Lord knows, I shouldn't like to be in Newgate. Lily, would you please go into the drawing room now? I should like to finish the business with Ug—with Mr. Damson now. Please, that's right. Don't worry."

It was a half an hour later when the viscount joined her in the drawing room. He stood for a moment, just looking at her. She was by the fireplace, the flames crackling behind her, and she was so beautiful he wanted to . . .

"He's gone," Knight said as he strode into the room. "When Ugly Arnold realized there was no hope for it, he folded his proverbial tent. He didn't want to, mind you, but he did, cursing me, cursing fate, cursing, of all people, his poor wife, Gertrude."

"He . . . he didn't say anything? About me?"

Knight walked to the sideboard and poured himself a brandy. He held up the decanter, but Lily shook her head.

He sipped the wonderfully warm, wonderfully French, brandy. "About you? Well, I did offer him the children, but that treat he refused, which, of course, came as no surprise. Said it wasn't fair to remove children from their mother. It affected him profoundly—such a consideration." Knight saw the look of relief sweep over her features. Immense relief. He'd already told her that Arnold was gone. Why this show of relief now? He smiled thinly at her, then attacked.

"This afternoon when we were enjoying our verbal fisticuffs, I recall that I referred to the fact that I was but four years older than you. You corrected me, saying that I was older than twenty-three. Now, why don't you tell me the truth, all of it."

Lily had prayed devoutly that that horrid bit of information had slipped by him in the heat of ver- bal battle. It hadn't. She was a fool to have lost her head so easily.

"Lily?" His voice was very, very gentle.

She cleared her throat and said, "I will be twenty on the second of December, just a bit over a month from now."

"I see." He felt instant and utter rage toward Tristan. None at all toward Lily, the poor girl. Dear God, Tris had taken her to wife when she'd been all of fifteen! A child! And he'd gotten a child on her immediately. "You were a child bride," he said, and his anger would have been evident to the meanest of perceptions. "Your fa- ther indeed sounds like the honorable sort."

Lily looked at him blankly. The guillotine blade hadn't dropped. Then she understood. He'd drawn the most awesomely wrong conclusion. She sent a silent thank-you heavenward. "I suppose you could say that I was somewhat young."

"Somewhat! You were a bloody babe! I didn't realize Tris was such a . . ." His bile dried up. Tris was dead. Besides, if Lily had been as beautiful at fifteen as she was now, which was undoubtedly the case, poor Tris hadn't had a chance.

He forced an elaborate shrug. "We will finalize my guardianship soon. Why don't you go to bed?"

Lily walked backward to the door, thanking him with every step, until he threw up his hand to cut her off. "Do stow it, Lily! I'm not such a villain to give you over to Ugly Arnold. You *or* the children."

She nodded now at the children, just as she'd nodded the previous evening at the viscount when she'd ducked out of the drawing room.

"And that was really all there was to it," Lily finished and smiled at each of the children. "So I think we will perhaps be all right."

She heard Theo's very adult sigh of relief. She stretched forward and patted his arm. "That part about me being very young when I married your father, try to remember and not give it away."

"We're safe," Theo said, and Lily knew he felt as if the weight of the world had been lifted from his shoulders.

"I think that we will go shopping today. Each of you may have whatever you wish. How does that sound?"

"Anything?" asked Sam.

"Don't be a greedy looby," Theo scolded in an adultlike voice.

"Well, you know how much money we have," said Lily. "Just keep that in mind."

"Lily?"

"Yes, Theo."

"I'm sorry, I forgot. It's 'Mama.' Do you think Cousin Knight would let me borrow a book or two from his library?"

Lily hadn't the foggiest idea of the viscount's reaction to such a request. It seemed quite reasonable to her. "Why don't you ask him, Theo? He appears to have your well-being at heart."

"I want to ride his cattle," said Sam.

"That, my love," Lily said firmly, "is another matter entirely. I've heard it said that gentlemen are very particular about their horses and little boys. We'll see."

"There's one more thing," Lily said hesitantly, dreading what she had to tell them. "Your cousin Knight will become your legal guardian."

"Why? He isn't our mother," Theo said reasonably. "What difference does it make?"

"He'll just give us a bedchamber and food," said Sam. "And maybe a horse to ride every so often."

"He's pretty," announced Laura Beth, and that comment drew all eyes.

"You stupid little girl! Men aren't pretty!"

"Don't scoff, Sam," Theo said. He added patiently to his little sister, "Why do you say that, Laura Beth?"

But Laura Beth just shrugged and the thumb went back into her mouth.

Lily felt the lump in her throat. It was threatening. She had to get it out before she was a mute fool. "Your cousin Knight believes you boys should go to Eton. As to exactly when, I'm not certain yet. It's just that he will have the authority to see that you do what he wishes."

Theo whistled. "We've landed ourselves in the soup this time, haven't we, Lily—Mama?"

Trust Theo to see through to the consequences with great rapidity.

"I don't know yet," she said truthfully. "I just don't know. I do know that all of us need to stay out of his way. Now, we must concern ourselves about your ignorance, which is more vast than it should be. After we shop, we'll have lessons, all right?"

Sam was vociferous in the negative. Theo's eyes glowed and Lily felt guilt that he wasn't with a tutor, a real tutor who knew all sorts of things, so many more things than she did. She would have to speak to the viscount.

Since there wasn't a nursery, Lily asked Mrs. Allgood to have their breakfasts brought to her bedchamber. They were dressed and ready to leave Winthrop House by nine o'clock. Sam, thankfully, hadn't done anything dreadful during the thirty minutes when Lily had to leave him to bathe and dress herself.

They met the viscount at the bottom of the stairs. He was on his way out.

"He *is* pretty," Laura Beth said, her eyes on his pale biscuit-colored greatcoat.

Theo groaned and Sam scoffed.

Lily said easily, "Good morning, my lord. As you see, we are going out ourselves. I am taking the children shopping—each of them deserves a present."

Knight had turned at the sound of Laura Beth's voice. Pretty, am I? he thought, and grinned, unable to prevent it. But it was a shock to see a woman and three children trooping down *his* staircase to come to a halt in *his* entrance hall. The boys looked scrubbed and well turned out. Theo seemed faintly worried, and Knight realized the boy was reacting as would an adult uncertain of his reception. Sam looked like he owned the world and even if he didn't, he'd still do as he wished. All of them were bundled up warmly. Lily was particularly ravishing in a thick, white-ermine-lined cloak of pale blue velvet, an expensive garment of the highest quality. Her muff matched and was of the softest ermine, though neither cloak nor muff looked particularly new. He wondered when Tris had given them to her. The cloak was also a bit short. Of course, Tris had married her before she was even fully grown, for God's sake. Knight shook his head at his errant thoughts.

He smiled. "Good morning to all of you. May I give you a lift somewhere, Lily?"

"Oh, no, I don't wish to impose," she said quickly. "I spoke to Duckett and he told us where to go."

"And that is?"

"To the Pantheon Bazaar."

Knight winced. He saw no hope for it. He didn't entirely trust Ugly Arnold to slither away in defeat. It was possible that he was watching the house, hoping to get Lily and the children alone. Would he abduct them? Knight cursed very softly, then raised his head and forced a smile. He would have Duckett send Raymond a message that he wouldn't be coming to his house for the Four Horse Club meeting.

Manfully, he said, "I should very much like to escort you. After all, we haven't really become acquainted as well as we should be yet."

"But surely you have other plans, sir!"

"Not at all," he said smoothly, and Lily held her peace even though she knew he was lying. "Consider my poor self at your disposal."

Two hours later, Knight considered his poor self had been disposed of at least a dozen times. He was testy and quite fatigued from Sam's exuberance and limitless excitement whenever he saw something that struck his fancy, and a fancy-striking something was at nearly every shop and booth. As for Theo, he tried to calm down his brother, but that seemed only to have the opposite effect. Laura Beth, equally tired, whined when her thumb wasn't in her mouth and wanted to relieve herself at every odd moment.

The Pantheon Bazaar was filled to overflowing with shoppers. It was a place Knight had visited many years before, at about Theo's age, if he remembered aright. It was a place he never wished to see again. Theo dawdled at every bookstall, much to Sam's contempt. Lily knew that the viscount was becoming less charitably minded by the minute. She didn't blame him. She herself would have liked to grab Sam's earlobe at least a dozen times and shake him. The viscount wasn't used to children, and today was the first day they'd been let loose, so to speak, in nearly a week.

She was on the point of telling them that they would purchase Laura Beth's present and leave, when Laura Beth pulled her thumb from her mouth and started waving Czarina Catherine wildly in the air. "There he is!" she shouted at the top of her lungs. "There he is—Ugly Arnold!"

Lily's blood turned cold. Knight looked in the direction of the waving doll, and sure enough, there was Arnold Damson, lurking behind a booth of multicolored ribbons. There was a cretinous specimen with him.

"Oh, no," Lily said and pulled Laura Beth against her. "Sam! Theo! Come here, both of you."

Theo immediately turned, but Sam, in the throes of a new toy that was a hay wagon with real wheels and straw, paid her no heed.

"Sam," Knight said in his most menacing voice, "get your butt over here now!"

Sam looked up, saw his cousin Knight standing there like the imperial emperor, and didn't hesitate. He dashed to him.

"What's wrong?" Sam demanded.

"We have company," said Knight. "None of you leave your mother. Sam, do you understand me?"

"Yes, certainly. I'm not a dumb looby!"

"That, my boy, is a matter of conjecture."

"Ugly Arnold," said Laura Beth. "He's old."

"Yes, love, he is," Lily said. "He isn't a very nice man either. But don't worry, your cousin Knight will take proper care of him."

I will, will I? Knight thought. She'd said it with such calm conviction. "Come along," he said abruptly. "Let's say hello to Ugly Arnold."

Lily shot him an uncertain look but didn't question his decision.

Arnold saw them approaching and panicked. They weren't supposed to come toward him, for God's sake. They weren't supposed to have seen him! And they weren't supposed to have been with that bloody sot of a viscount. Damnable fellow—he'd found out very late the previous evening, after ingratiating himself with a group of downy fellows, that Viscount Castlerosse was a bachelor who defined the word itself. Him with *children*? Ludicrous! Ridiculous! Yet here he was, guarding them as if he were their bloody parent. It wasn't to be borne. He said to Boggs, the villain with him, "Let's go, dammit! We'll get them later when he's not about."

Boggs, not at all a shy sort and wanting his five pounds, dug in his heels. "It's just one gentleman, a dandy by the looks of him. I'll clean up the ground with him."

Arnold was undecided. Boggs was a brawny specimen, but the fellows of the night before had also said that the viscount was an athlete, a horseman, a man who took anybody in the ring and beat the wadding out of him. "No, later, perhaps. I want no fighting here. It's too dangerous."

Boggs had to be satisfied with that. He had to obey the bloke what had the quid.

"He's a coward, Cousin Knight!" Sam shrieked, pointing and jumping up and down. "He's running away!"

"Shut your trap, Sam," Theo said quickly. "We don't want people staring. It's not good manners."

"Indeed," Knight said. "Restrain yourself, Sam. If Ugly Arnold tries anything, I'll put you on him. All right?"

"I'll smack him good," said Sam.

Knight looked faintly approving at this well-meaning threat.

With the excitement over, the children finally realized their own fatigue. Sam was hungry. Theo was tense and exhausted. Laura Beth was fretting, her voice a high whine.

Lily turned to Knight. "I'll see to them now. Please, I know you're not used to children. I'll take them home."

Knight, who would have given just about anything to be freed from the pestilence of the three little beggars, said perversely, "Not at all. We still have a present to purchase for Laura Beth. We'll do that, then I'll escort you to Gunthers." He turned to Theo. "Would you like an ice?"

The yelling approval was enough to smack through his eardrums.

What have I done? he asked himself. Just as he'd tried to insist that he pay for Theo's book— a thesis on the feasibility of the steam engine—

and for Sam's ten-gun schooner, he again tried to insist on paying for Laura Beth's sleepily chosen small white leather gloves.

Lily said no.

Knight, infuriated, said yes and drew out a pound note.

"My lord," Lily said, her teeth gritted, "we have already been through this twice. The children are my responsibility. I am not a pauper. I have the funds. I will buy their presents. They are from *me*, after all, not from you."

Knight ostentatiously folded his pound note and gave her an exaggerated shrug. He was, quite frankly, too tired to think of a sharp retort.

Gunthers wasn't as horrendous an experience as he'd expected. Once Sam had a large bowl of ice cream in front of him, his mouth drained of all words, complaints or otherwise. Laura Beth was snuggled against Lily, accepting an occasional spoonful. She insisted on wearing her white gloves. Theo, looking wary and tried, ate his ice in silence, throwing an occasional uncertain look at Knight.

"My God! I don't believe this!"

Knight looked up to see Julien St. Clair, the Earl of March, staring at him and his small herd. Beside him stood his countess, Katherine St. Clair. She poked her husband in the ribs and stepped forward, a smile on her lovely face.

Introductions were got through. The children were subdued, but the earl and the countess weren't to know why, Knight thought sardonically. They were polite and civil and diffident. As for Lily, she was what he would have expected: a lady with appropriate social graces and a kindness of spirit that made her new acquaintances want to continue in her company. Knight also noticed that Julien wasn't bowled over by Lily's beauty. His smile was social, not infatuated or lustful. That was a relief. Knight was beginning to believe that he would have to watch every male closely when one swam into Lily's waters.

Julien St. Clair couldn't come to grips with *this* Knight Winthrop. What had happened to his cynical, clever, completely irreverent friend? This man who was sitting at a circular table with a beautiful woman and three—three!—children. It boggled the mind. It left one stunned.

He heard Knight say to the older boy, "Theo, why don't you show your new book to his lordship? I understand he's fascinated with the subject of steam engines."

Julien shot Knight a look that promised retribution, but the smile he gave Theo was warm and interested.

"She's lovely," Katherine St. Clair said to Lily. Laura Beth, shy and sleepy, said a blurry "Thank you" and buried her face against Lily's shoulder.

"She's also getting heavy. I trust she outgrows her desire to use me for a bed in the near future."

"I declare, are those new gloves? How very smart they are!"

Laura Beth opened both eyes at this comment and thanked the lady again. "Mama bought them for me. Cousin Knight wanted to, but she wouldn't let him. I think she wanted to smack him, but she didn't. Mama said that—"

"You close that mouth of yours, my dear child. Here, have some more ice cream." Lily looked up to see the countess regarding her intently. "She's a very sweet little girl."

"I would agree," the countess said, nodding pleasantly.

Several other acquaintances stopped by briefly within the next fifteen minutes, and their reactions all fitted the incredulous mold of "By Jove, old man, *children?*"

"Good God, Knight, you in the infantry?"

"Bloody bedlam," muttered the dazed Marquess of Bourne, shaking his grizzled head. "We might as well surrender to old Boney."

Lily's attention, for the most part, was on the children, primarily Sam. But even he minded his manners. Lily saw that Knight made certain he was given another bowl of ice cream the moment he finished his first one. In short, he had no time to turn his schooner's cannon on any of their incredulous visitors.

"It's ten-gun and wonderful," Lily heard him say to Julien St. Clair. "I could kill every Frenchie if only I was just a few years older."

"No doubt," said Julien, smiling faintly.

"He's rather bloodthirsty," Knight said, and to his surprise, he ruffled Sam's soft brown hair.

Julien stared. My God, it was simply more than a mere mortal could comprehend. When he and his countess took their leave, he remained silent and in a state of advanced confusion for the better part of two hours.

The carriage ride back to Winthrop House passed in similar peace.

"So that's the trick, huh?" Knight remarked to Lily. "Glut the little heathen and peace is restored."

"That about covers it," Lily said, grinning widely.

The children were dispatched upstairs with Mrs. Allgood, Laura Beth and Sam to nap, Theo to pore over his new book.

"I think I'll take a nap, too," Knight said, stretching.

Lily gave him a crooked smile that made him instantly randy. "Parents say that children keep

them young; however, I tend to think they age
you.''

Knight gave her an answering smile, unable not
to. He'd been too aware of her today, all day, and
it bothered him tremendously. He decided then
and there to take himself off to Daniella. She
would ease him; she would restore his perspective. Further, visiting her would save him from
the inevitable roasting from his friends. He didn't
doubt that his exquisitely aberrant behavior would
be the talk of the ton by evening. He wondered if
it would be attributed to the beautiful Widow
Winthrop. ''I'm going out,'' he said abruptly to
Lily. ''I shan't be back for dinner.''

He left her standing in the entranceway, asking
herself if she'd said something to offend him.

By ten o'clock that evening she was trembling
with trepidation. There was something that would
surely offend him now. She wouldn't be surprised if Knight booted them out into the waiting
arms of Ugly Arnold.

5

Knight was pleasantly relaxed. He leaned his head back against the hackney squabs and closed his eyes. Unfortunately, that made him remember and he shuddered. It had been too close there for a while. But things had worked out, thank all the powers that had taken pity on him. He didn't want to dwell on it, but he couldn't help himself. It had never before happened to him, never in all his male adult life.

Despite his randiness, he couldn't seem to make things happen. Daniella was as she always was—beautiful, alluring, marvelously adaptive—and in the end, it was her skilled mouth that had brought him up to snuff, so to speak.

All because of a damned woman he'd known for such a short time it was objectively absurd.

And he'd thrown his head back and shouted her name at the moment of his sexual release.

It wasn't to be borne. He would send her and the children to Castle Rosse. Soon.

He had to get his life back on its wonderfully predictable course before his mistress stabbed him for stupidity and his friends had him committed to an asylum. He could just hear Julien St. Clair telling all their mutual friends of his very odd encounter at Gunthers with Knight and his gaggle.

81

Why, he was eating an ice, surrounded by children eating ices! And by toys! They were his family. Knight, with a family! Ah, but the mother, an angel of beauty, yes, our Knight . . .

He moaned, cutting off his imaginary monologue as he realized he could not send the brood away until he was officially and legally the children's guardian. He couldn't take the chance of sending them to Castle Rosse in case Ugly Arnold was still lurking about with evil intent in his heart.

He would speak to Tilney Jones on the morrow, hurry the fellow up, instruct him to grease every upturned palm. He didn't care what it would cost.

Twenty minutes later, Knight let himself into his home with his latchkey. To his surprise, he saw a light coming from the drawing room. It was late, after midnight. He frowned and strode into the room.

He came to a stunned halt. "Lily! What are you doing up? Is something wrong?"

She looked pale and nervous and breathtakingly beautiful. Damned woman!

Lily tried to avoid mendacity. "Nothing is really wrong, if you mean that someone is ill," she began.

"Excellent. We make progress."

He was at his most sardonic—his voice smooth and bland, his left eyebrow arched upward, his look one of ironic hauteur. He walked past her to the sideboard and she smelled the subtle attar of roses perfume. He'd been with a woman, his mistress, no doubt. She swallowed.

She watched him pour himself a brandy. She was about to speak when he said abruptly, his voice meditative, "I am twenty-seven years old. Not all that far removed from childhood. But I'd forgotten that children have such separate and distinct personalities. Theo—good Lord, the lad's so intense, so grown up. Was he ever a little boy?''

''A bit more before his father died.''

''Ah.'' Knight looked down into his brandy snifter. ''That's another thing. The children haven't spoken at all of their father. Isn't that somewhat odd? Shouldn't they say something? Shouldn't they grieve?''

They *had* grieved, Lily thought, each of them in his or her own way, in private, which wasn't all that good, especially for the children.

''Since his father was killed, Theo has tried to become the head of the family. He always was a serious little boy, but now—'' She shrugged. ''Perhaps you're right about Eton. Perhaps in the company of other boys his age he'll become younger, more carefree. I should like him to get into just one Sam-like scrape. But he's a scholar, you know, and I don't see anything changing that.''

''Well, now our scholar will become an expert on steam engines. And Sam?''

''Sam is just the opposite. Since Tris's death, he's become a handful. He's always been an imp, but now it's as if, well, he *has* to misbehave. Please realize that since Tris's death, the children have known no security. We made the long trip from Brussels to Yorkshire not knowing if the Damsons would take us in. They did, but Gertrude didn't like any of us, and then there was the debacle with Arnold. I had to uproot them yet again, very quickly, to bring them here. Once more we weren't certain of our reception. The children are frightened, though they'd rather die than admit it.

''Sam's very aggressive, always wanting to plant someone a facer. It's his way, I think, of handling his fear. As for dear Theo, I believe he thinks that the more mature, the more adult, he acts, the more at bay he keeps his fears."

"Laura Beth seems to have escaped."

"Not at all. Since her father's death, she won't let Czarina Catherine out of her sight, or her arms, and she won't take her thumb out of her mouth. As you've noticed, she's also clingy with me. As for a show of grief, I have heard Sam crying late at night and gone to him. He's had his fist shoved into his mouth so Theo wouldn't hear him. I wasn't able to bring myself to intrude on his grief. It would unman him, I think."

"He's a little boy!"

"Yes, a very proud little boy."

"I see," Knight said slowly. "You appear to have figured all this out in vast detail."

"I love them. I care about them. The changes are obvious to me, as are the reasons for the changes. Cause and effect, I suppose you'd say."

Knight set down his snifter. "Why are you still up?"

"Sam," she said, expelling a deep breath.

"Sam? Ah, I see. He's been indulging in an impish little-boy prank?"

"Yes."

After a few more moments of silence, Knight said on a deep sigh, "I'm waiting, Lily."

"I suppose I should tell you, particularly since I waited up to do so, but—"

"I won't eat you or Sam."

"He stole Cuthbert's rising bread dough from the kitchen and wrapped it around the stairs leading to the servants' quarters on the third floor. That staircase isn't well lighted. In fact, it's quite dim."

Knight simply stared at her. "My God! How incredibly inventive. Did anyone scream? Die of fright? Go catapulting down the stairs into oblivion?"

"Betty shrieked the house down. She thought she'd put her hand 'inside a dead body,' as she so aptly put it. 'Sticky and puffy and oozy.' I don't know about the oozy part. It would seem to me that Cuthbert wouldn't make oozy bread dough, but then again—" She stopped to stare at her host, who looked not at all angry but rather bemused and somewhat admiring.

Actually, Knight was trying to remember twenty years before. Had he ever executed such a clever prank? He couldn't remember.

"You . . . you're not furious?"

"As in will I kick the lot of you out of my house?"

"Yes, that's exactly what I mean."

"No, but I will have Sam clean off the bread dough."

"I'm not that doting a mama! I made him do that immediately. It was quite a prolonged task." She drew a deep breath. "There's something else."

"I begin to think I should bring a priest into the house, for confessions, you know. It appears there'll be a steady stream of work for him. Is there more to expiate tonight?"

"It's Cuthbert. He bellowed to the entire neighborhood that he was going to leave."

Knight's look and voice were weary and cynical. "Don't let Cuthbert's threats dismay you. I pay the fool much too much for him ever to consider leaving my employ."

"But he was quite voluble in his threat that if we didn't leave, he would."

"Fine. Let him. I don't care."

It was Lily's turn to stare at Knight. "You're not angry? Truly not?"

"No, but I am tired. Let's retire now, Lily."

The instant those words were out of his mouth—
double-edged only to him—he felt lust flood
through him.

He turned quickly away from her, only to halt
at the door as he remembered his valet's snide
comment to him just before he'd left to visit Daniella. "Have you had any difficulty with my valet,
Stromsoe?"

She had, but she didn't want to get that man
into trouble. She shook her head.

She couldn't lie well, he thought, but he let it
go. He said a clipped good-night and took himself
off to bed.

As for Lily, she followed more slowly upstairs.
Stromsoe hadn't really troubled her, not really.
He'd been rude, true enough, but he was just being protective of his master. She'd handled him
quite well; at least she thought so. He'd stopped
her in the upper hallway earlier in the evening. . . .

"May I ask where you are going, ma'am?" he'd
demanded in his prissiest voice. He was actually
barring her way.

Lily looked at the pompous, pomade-haired,
very rosy-cheeked man and grinned. "No."

"No what?"

"No, Stromsoe."

"Madam, if you please!"

"Very well, Stromsoe, you may not ask. It is
none of your business."

That had taken him aback. "Then may I assist
you with something, ma'am?"

"If you will fetch me a glass of warm milk. It is
for one of the children."

His rosy cheeks became fiery. "Why, that isn't
my job!"

"Then why did you ask if you could assist me?
You aren't making any sense, Stromsoe."

And that had routed him thoroughly. She wondered what the prissy little man had said to the viscount to make him mention it to her. He'd probably referred to her as an encroaching female with a passel of indigent brats and stuck a disdainful nose in the air. But it was all true.

Lily was tired, and if the truth be told, she was every bit as frightened as the children. Because she was a grown woman, she was able to hide her fears more successfully than the children, but they were there nonetheless.

She shook her head as she quietly undressed. She could hear Laura Beth's soft breath from the bed and knew that the little girl would be sprawled in the middle, her arms and legs flung wide, Czarina Catherine nestled close.

Before she fell asleep, Lily realized that she wanted peace. She wanted security. She wasn't able to think beyond that.

Knight had wondered why they hadn't shown grief. She should have told him that there simply hadn't been time.

The next day Knight, deep in thought, walked into his library to fetch several papers Tilney Jones had requested. He came to an abrupt and very surprised halt.

On her knees in his chair was Laura Beth.

She was studiously poring over a large piece of foolscap on top of *his* desk, *his* quill bearing down until he was certain it must split.

Some rather important papers surrounded her, moved by her, he saw, in piles that were precariously positioned very near the hand-carved onyx inkwell. He cleared his throat, saying softly so as not to frighten her, ''Laura Beth.''

The child jerked up and stared at him, her dark blue eyes large and wary. He was struck again about how different she looked, not at all like Lily, or Tris, for that matter.

"Oh," said Laura Beth. "Hello."

"May I ask what you're doing here?"

Laura Beth stood on his chair, leaning her hands on his desktop. "I'm drawing," she said. "Would you like to see?"

"In a moment," he said quickly, one eye on that damned inkwell. "Why are you drawing here? This is my room and my desk."

"Oh," said Laura Beth again, not looking one whit abashed.

"Where is your mother?"

"Mama's in bed. She's sick."

Knight took a quick step forward. "Of what? Why did no one tell me?"

"She's not really sick, just her tummy."

"Her tummy? Did she eat something that didn't agree with her?" Cuthbert, he thought. Had the damned fellow blamed her for the bread-dough fiasco and fed her something bad? No, that was absurd.

"I'll go see her."

"She said she wanted to sleep for a while, then she'd be all right."

It was Knight's turn to say, "Oh," which he did. "Did your mother tell you to come here to my study?"

Laura Beth had the grace to look down. "No," she said barely above a whisper. "She thinks I'm in her room. But I didn't like the charcoal, it's messy." She bounded up suddenly in the chair to show him the charcoal streaks on her pale pink muslin gown. He saw her shove at the desk and send the chair spinning backward on its casters. The inkwell flew up, toppled, and spewed thick black ink on every important paper that had held a place of prominence on his desk.

She shrieked and Knight dashed forward to catch her before she was flung from the wildly spinning chair. He felt the ink end of the quill brush his cheek. He felt Laura Beth's skinny arms go around his neck and squeeze as hard as she could. The chair bumped against his knee and for an instant he lost his balance. He landed against the edge of the desk and felt black ink seep through his immaculate buckskin trousers.

Knight closed his eyes. Laura Beth squeezed tighter. Duckett opened the door and gaped.

"My lord!"

Laura Beth whimpered and buried her face snug against Knight's neck.

"It's all right, Duckett," Knight said. "We've had a minor accident. I'd tell you to take Laura Beth to her mother, but Mrs. Winthrop isn't feeling well." Knight ground to a halt. What was he to do with the child? He was saved by Theo, who had heard the commotion.

"Oh, dear," Theo said, stopping beside Duckett. "Oh, sir, what has she done?" Theo saw the answer to his question. Black ink was everywhere, on the viscount's trousers, on his pristine white cravat, even on his cheek. Theo closed his eyes to blot out the horror.

Knight, who was ready to toss Laura Beth out the study window, saw Theo turn as white as his collar. He saw the flash of fear in the boy's eyes. He smiled. "It's all right, Theo. No harm done. Laura Beth and I just had a minor accident. Is your mother awake, by any chance?"

"No," Theo managed, trying not to moan at the awful black-ink mess. "She's not well. I'll take Laura Beth, sir."

"Very manly of you, Theo, but I fear that both Laura Beth and I have been tarred, so to speak, with the same brush. I'll take her upstairs and bathe both of us." He saw the boy swallow convulsively and he felt a wave of compassion so strong it made him blink. "Should you like to do me a favor, Theo?"

"Oh, yes, sir. Anything!"

"Go to the drawing room and tell Mr. Jones that he is to be denied my presence this afternoon. Tell him I'm occupied with a very strong-armed little monkey and I'll get the papers he needs to him on the morrow."

Theo nodded quickly, and Knight knew in that moment that the boy would bow and scrape and indulge in all sorts of unnecessary apologies to Tilney.

"Theo," he said easily, "just deliver my message. You're a Winthrop and this is your home. You belong here. Don't ever forget that, all right?"

Theo swallowed. "Yes, sir."

"Good boy. Now, Duckett, if you would be so efficient as to remedy the destruction in here."

"Certainly, my lord. Er, would you also wish me to take Miss Laura Beth?"

"No, she comes with me." Knight grinned at his butler. "Besides, I don't think anyone could pry her off my neck."

If anyone had told Knight that he would be bathing a four-year-old girl in *his* roomy copper tub in *his* bedchamber, stripped down to his trousers, he would have laughed his head off.

As it was, he had to face Stromsoe, who looked as though the world as he knew it had finally exploded. Knight supposed that it had. "Fetch a tub of hot water and lots of towels, Stromsoe. Laura Beth and I are going to have a nice scrubbing."

"My lord!"

"Good God, man, obey me! Go!"

When the now speechless Stromsoe backed out

of the viscount's room, Knight said to his rider, "Now, sweetheart, down with you. We're both a mess." He managed to unpeel her arms from about his neck, and in the process his pristine white shirt, which hadn't known a day's soiling in its existence, was covered with small handprints amazingly detailed in black ink.

He stripped Laura Beth and wrapped her in a towel. "Sit on that chair and don't move." His tone held just enough menace to ensure the child's obedience. He wondered for a moment if it was proper for a gentleman to strip off some of his clothes in front of a little girl. There were doubtless rules governing such a situation, but he didn't know them. It really didn't occur to him to wonder if there were also rules governing the bathing of little girls. He shrugged and stripped down to his trousers. Laura Beth giggled when he applied himself to his boots.

"You find that funny, do you, you little hellion?"

"I'll help," said Laura Beth, all eagerness and black ink.

"No, you won't. You'll sit quietly until the hot water comes. Sit!"

She obeyed. They had some minutes before the water arrived. Knight stretched and scratched his chest. Laura Beth said, "You're pretty. Can I touch?"

Knight dropped his arms. "You already did. You nearly choked me."

That brought forth another giggle.

"You have hair all over you."

"Well, you can't touch and I don't have hair *all* over."

Laura Beth subsided at that, and Knight watched her try to untangle several tresses of hair that were ink-coated. He said thoughtfully, more to himself than to his guest, ''I guess what we need is a nursery. You know, a place where you can destroy things without it mattering. I'll have to think about that.''

Stromsoe returned, directing two footmen with buckets of hot water. Knight, knowing his dignity was in serious question and not wishing witnesses, dismissed all of them, stripped off Laura Beth's towel, and placed her in the water.

She shrieked and splashed. He winced at her enthusiasm, believing his eardrums shattered, and got as wet as she. He ended up washing her hair as well as the rest of her. He was pouring his cupped hands of water over her hair to get out the soap when he heard a gasp from the doorway. He looked up and saw Lily.

''Hello,'' he said, grinning. He gave her a small salute with one wet hand and finished his task.

''Mama!'' Laura Beth yelled, her legs pumping in the water. ''Cousin Knight is washing me! Look at my hair! He's not as good as you, but he's fun!''

''You insult me, you ungrateful little witch?''

She gave him a beatific smile. A very small hand touched the hair on his chest. Two fingers tightened and tugged.

Knight yowled, more for effect than from pain. Laura Beth laughed and laughed.

Lily couldn't think of a thing to say, nor could she look away from the viscount. She'd seen her father and the boys, of course, in a similar state of undress, but never a man of Knight's age and physical endowments. Laura Beth was right, he was pretty. More than that, he was beautiful. She stared at the long, smooth line of his back, the deep, firm muscles of his shoulders and arms, the sworls of dark hair on his chest. She swallowed, wondering at her reaction. Then he turned, suddenly, and met her eyes. She flushed to her eyebrows, quickly looking away. Oh, God, here she was, gawking at him like an idiot half-wit! Stromsoe had knocked on her door, pulling her from sleep. He'd told her that the *child* was in his lordship's bedchamber, that the *child* was in his lordship's tub. He was mortally offended, and Lily, terrified of what the *child* was doing, rushed down the corridor.

"Laura Beth, hold still!" Knight lifted the wriggling little body from the tub and wrapped her in the huge towel.

It was another game, and Laura Beth shook with laughter when he pulled the towel from her face.

"My turn! My turn!"

"Your turn for what?" Knight asked as he dried her hair.

"I'll wash you now."

"Oh, Laura Beth," Lily said, having finally discovered her tongue. "Knight, I'm so sorry, I didn't mean for her . . . what did she do? Oh, dear, you're covered with black. What is it?"

"Ink," said Laura Beth, peeking out from the towel.

"Ink," Lily repeated blankly.

"From Cousin Knight's desk."

Lily went blank. Knight had seen the surprised awareness in her eyes when she'd first rushed in, and he realized she hadn't seen him as a man until that moment. She'd liked what she'd seen, he knew enough about women to sense that quickly enough. It pleased him inordinately. But now he saw the same fear in her eyes as he'd seen in Theo's. It made him feel like some sort of monster. He said sharply, "For God's sake, Lily, stop it! I'm not going to kick you out of my home, never. Will you please contrive to believe me?

Now, I understand you're ill. Go back to bed. You look like hell.''

Actually, she looked exquisite.

"I'll take Laura Beth.''

"No, you're sick. I'll call Mrs. Allgood to dress her.''

"No, I'm not really sick. It's just that . . .'' Her voice dropped off like a stone from a cliff.

"Your tummy hurts—at least that's what Laura Beth told me.''

Lily turned mute with embarrassment.

"Mama said it was just her *woman's* tummy,'' Laura Beth said in a confiding voice to Knight.

Lily closed her eyes. She was beyond embarrassment. If she had Laura Beth's throat between her hands, she would have wrung it.

Knight said not a word to that startling explanation. "Lily,'' he said, all business, "go back to your bedchamber. Now. Go.''

Lily fled.

"As for you, you remarkable child, I'm giving you over to Mrs. Allgood. No, you're not going to wash me. You behave yourself, do you understand?''

Laura Beth, her face as guileless as an angel's, nodded, and Knight, having seen that look before, groaned.

6

Knight stretched his legs out to the fire, cupped his brandy snifter between his hands, and leaned back in his exquisitely comfortable chair. He remained that way for perhaps a minute. But it wasn't the same. Not at all the way it had been before Lily's arrival, hers and the children's. He sighed, hoping she felt better, knowing, of course, that she felt just fine again, since her malady wasn't in truth a malady.

He'd seen Lily only in passing for the past three days now. She was obviously avoiding him, and he supposed he couldn't blame her. She'd seen him half naked in his bedchamber, and Laura Beth had embarrassed her to the roots of her glorious hair.

To spare her, he'd eaten dinner at his club for the past three evenings, then spent the majority of the nights out. He hadn't visited Daniella, which was excessively odd of him, he thought in stray moments, but he had won five hundred pounds from Davey Cochrane at whist in the card room at White's. Just as he'd expected, several of his friends had tortured him mercilessly about his newly acquired family. He'd found himself merely smiling, the memory of Laura Beth's wriggling little body clear in his mind. He'd played peekaboo

with a damned little girl! It made him smile even
now to think about it. As for all the ink-covered
papers on his desk, well, poor old Trump hadn't
been completely delighted to recopy them, but
he'd set himself to it sharply. The papers Tilney
had needed had been duly delivered to his office.
Now it was just a matter of time and proper palm-
greasing before the children were Knight's legal
wards.

He started to rise. It was early afternoon and
he must be on his way to Tattersall's. Old Baron
Setherly was selling up, and there was a magnif-
icent black Barb amongst his cattle that Knight
wanted to look over. He heard the library door
open quietly. Lily? He eased back down in his
chair. His body tensed and he felt something in-
sidiously warm and wonderful spread from his
toes to his ears.

He said not a word. He didn't move. Slowly,
he looked around the side wing of his leather
chair. There was Theo walking—no, creeping, on
his tiptoes—across the expanse of Aubusson carpet to the long wall of floor-to-ceiling book-
shelves. He watched the boy. He realized that
Theo was thinner than a nine-year-old should be,
and he was pale. As Knight looked at him, he
found himself seeing more and more of Tris in
him—the tilt of his head, the fine, aquiline nose,
the stubborn chin. Why the devil was the boy
skulking about?

Theo was terrified. He didn't know if the viscount was home or not. He hadn't been for the
longest time, but the house was Cousin Knight's
and he could be anywhere. Lily had told them all
so earnestly to keep out of the viscount's way and
he'd known she was worried, particularly after
Laura Beth had dumped ink all over his desk and
papers and himself. Theo looked furtively about,

then climbed the ladder to fetch the book he wanted from the second-to-top shelf. It was a black leather volume on the remarkable properties of the ancient *omaya* root, written by an obscure monk from northern Italy sometime during the sixteenth century. It was old and delicate, and Theo held it as carefully as he would Lily's favorite broach, a heart-shaped amethyst that had belonged to her mother.

"Theo."

The quiet voice from behind him made him gasp with alarm. His grip on the valuable old book loosened and he watched in horror as it dropped to the floor. The ancient binding split apart and several sections flopped out. Theo closed his eyes and swayed. He wanted to die.

"Sir," he managed to say finally. "Oh, dear, I'm sorry—oh, no!" Theo twisted about on the ladder, saw the carnage, knew he'd see it until the day he died, and lost his hold.

Knight, startled to his boots, was nonetheless swift of reflex and managed to catch him in midflight. The boy's momentum sent them both to the floor, but Knight held him firmly, cushioning his fall with his own body.

Theo struggled to be free, his voice catching on sobs.

Knight immediately came up on his knees over the boy and quickly examined his arms and legs. He could find no broken bones, but that didn't mean Theo wasn't hurt internally. He grasped his shoulders, shook him slightly so that he would look at him, and pulled him to his knees. "Are you all right, Theo? You're not hurting anywhere?"

Theo dashed away the damnable tears and shook his head, afraid to speak.

"You're certain?"

"Yes, sir," Theo said in the thinnest voice Knight had ever heard.

"Good," Knight said briskly, felt his heart stop its terrified pounding, and rose, offering his hand to Theo.

Theo wanted to sink quickly and quietly through the floor and land squarely in hell.

"Come along, my boy."

The viscount took Theo's hand and gently jerked him to his feet. "You look none the worse for your adventure. I escaped as well. I'm sorry I scared you."

Theo stared up at him. The *viscount* was apologizing? It was too much. He shook his head stubbornly and knew the truth must come out. "Sir, I destroyed your book!" There, he had admitted it. Now he waited for the viscount to see the destruction and turn on him, which was nothing more than he deserved.

Knight frowned down at the bent head. What book? He saw the old volume lying on the floor and said, "What the hell is that? I don't even recognize it."

"It's a first edition."

"It is, huh? Well, it must be deadly dull, for I've never read it."

"Oh, no, sir! It's all about this strange root that can cure all sorts of wicked diseases and—"

Knight grinned, relieved at the renewed animation. "In that case, let's put it back together—there's a bookbinder I know on Court Street. He can fix anything, even ancient tomes on miraculous roots. Should you like to come with me, Theo?"

"Oh, yes, sir, and I . . . I'll pay for it, sir."

"All right," Knight said easily. "Tell you what, why don't we ride there?"

The change in the boy was remarkable. Before

Knight's fascinated gaze, Theo lost all claim to stooped shoulders, his eyes—not at all like Tris's—glittered with excitement, and he looked ready to burst the seams on his coat with excitement. Then, just as suddenly, the light left his eyes, and he looked ready to cry again.

"What's the matter? Don't you ride?"

"I did something very bad," Theo said. "You can't reward me. You should punish me. I truly deserve it, sir."

"You dropped a damned book because I startled you. It is nothing. Less than nothing. Now, cease your recriminations—I do find them excessively tedious, Theo—and go get on your riding clothes. All right?"

Theo gave him the hopeful look of a child who knew he hadn't heard aright. He was waiting for the correction and the proverbial blows to strike.

"Theo, I'm becoming very impatient with you. You have fifteen minutes, not an instant more. Do ask your mother's permission, all right?"

"Oh, yes, sir!"

There was a thoughtful look on Knight's face as he watched the boy dash from the library. He leaned down and gathered up the book. "Dreadful-looking thing," he said to himself, stuffing the separate hunks of pages back into the broken binding. "The only reason it's a first edition is because no one wanted a second, except perhaps for the monk's mother."

As he waited for Theo, Knight decided he'd first take the boy with him to Tattersall's; then they'd go to Mr. Milligan's shop on Court Street. He wondered if the boy had any money to pay for the repair of the book. He doubted that he did. Now he had set himself a problem. Talk about proud—he could imagine Theo's reaction if he, Knight, paid for the repairs. What to do?

And then he knew. Knight smiled and strode out of the library, whistling and quite properly proud of himself. He strode right into Lily.

"My God, are you all right?" He grabbed her arms, dropping the book and further demolishing the binding.

"Yes, certainly."

He released her, shaking his head in some amusement. "I seem to be bringing everyone low today."

She merely smiled at him, and it was enough to make him want to instantly throw her down on the entrance-hall floor, very gently, that is, and have his way with her.

"Where's Theo?" he asked, unable to look away from her. She was still smiling, though it wobbled a bit from the strange look on his face.

"He—he's changing his clothes. I wanted to thank you, Knight. I haven't seen him so excited about anything since . . . well, since before his father's death. You're very kind."

Now he frowned down at her. She was as pale as Theo. Had they all remained indoors since they'd arrived here? He said abruptly, "Go upstairs and change. You do ride, don't you? Of course you do. You'll come with me and Theo."

He saw a leap of excitement in her fine eyes at the proffered treat, then it was gone. "That is a wonderful offer, but I must stay with the children. You know Sam—if he isn't watched, he could do the most dreadful thing. Oh, I forgot to tell you. He apologized to Betty about the bread-dough railing. She called him an 'awful little tadpole' but did forgive him finally."

"Excellent," Knight said, but he wasn't really paying attention. He was thinking. He realized he shouldn't dilute Theo's outing with him by bringing along the other children. He didn't want to say it, but he forced himself to. "You're right. You must remain with the children—to protect my house and all its denizens. As for Theo, don't worry about him. We'll be gone for several hours. Does he ride well?"

"Yes, his father taught him ages ago. He has light hands. Of course, he hasn't ridden in the past couple of months—"

"It isn't a problem. I've a hack in the stable that will suit him nicely. Oh, Lily?"

"Yes?"

"Will you be dining with me this evening?"

His voice was gentle and Lily felt something skitter over every covered and uncovered patch of flesh on her body. "If you wish," she said, and saw him at that moment naked to the waist, wrestling with Laura Beth in the tub. She heard his laughter, saw him lift Laura Beth high in his arms and wrap her in the huge towel.

"I do wish. Don't worry about Theo. I'll take good care of him."

"I know you will."

"Did he, ah, say anything to you about what happened?" This he asked in a carefully neutral voice.

"Yes, he did. Theo is painfully honest. He asked me if I thought it was all right for him to have so much fun when he'd been so wicked."

"Wicked! For God's sake, he dropped a stupid book!" Knight pointed to the dilapidated specimen at his feet. "This is the book he's so distraught about—I doubt it's worth the paper it was written on." He leaned down and picked up the book.

"Theo takes things seriously, including any lack he sees in himself. He did damage something that belonged to you. But I told him that keeping you company would be his good deed for the day."

"You *what?*" Knight gave a shout of laughter. "What a master stroke, Lily. Well done. Now, I don't imagine that the boy has any money, and—"

"I gave him five shillings."

Knight cursed and Lily stared.

"Forgive me, but I wish you hadn't done so. I wanted to lend him the money and then let him work it off. He needs his own money, even if it's only a few shillings a week."

Lily couldn't believe this. He hadn't wanted to box Sam's ears for the bread-dough debacle, he'd laughed over Laura Beth's ink devastation and even bathed the child himself, and now he was thinking about what to do for dear Theo.

To her utter horror, and for the first time since the night of Tris's death, Lily burst into tears.

Knight was appalled. Tears because he'd said Theo needed a few shillings a week? It would be the most natural thing in the world to pull her into his arms and press her face against his shoulder. It would be even more natural to whisper soothing absurdities to her and lightly stroke his hands over her back. And it was the most pleasant feeling to breathe in her subtle scent. Was it jasmine or perhaps lavender? Or maybe just Lily herself. . . .

"You—you unwoman me," she whispered against his shoulder, and her fingers clutched at his jacket lapels.

"Unwoman? Now that is a new word and concept for me. I think I like the sound of it." He was pleased that he could speak so lightly and that his voice actually sounded teasing.

She gave a somewhat watery laugh.

"What are you *doing*, sir?"

"Oh, dear," Knight said and gently pushed Lily away from him. "Your protector, my dear,

his fists at the ready." He grinned up at the
ferocious-looking Sam who was standing on the
bottom stair, his sturdy legs planted wide apart,
his fists on his hips.

"Well, sir?"

"Well, nothing, Sam. Put your fists back into
your pockets and stop calling me sir. I'm your
cousin Knight. Now, your mother was crying because she didn't have any bread for her breakfast."

"But I did, Cousin Knight."

"You had very *old* bread. My cook, Cuthbert,
you know, well, he's leery about making more,
because a little boy who lives here doesn't know
that bread goes into the belly and not on a stair
railing."

Sam fell against the railing, he was giggling so
hard, and Lily laughed, a clear sweet sound that
made Knight so randy he wanted to howl.

"You're the most complete hand, sir," Sam said
between giggles.

"Don't you forget it, my boy. Ah, here's Theo.
Looking smart, my lad. And Laura Beth not far
behind. How are you, snippet?"

"I want another bath," said Laura Beth past
the thumb in her mouth. "And we'll play towel
again."

"Laura Beth!" Theo exclaimed, horrified.

"It's peekaboo," said Sam with disgust.

"Perhaps in a few days," Knight said easily. "I
must first recover from our initial bout. You very
nearly drowned me."

Laura Beth giggled, and Knight felt the urge to
swing her up into his arms and kiss her pink
cheeks. Instead he grinned over at the hopeful-
looking Sam and said gently, "No, Sam, you can't
go with us today. Pick up your lower lip and don't

sulk. Boys don't sulk. We'll all go on a picnic to Richmond next week, all right?"

"What's Richmond?" asked Laura Beth.

"Silly gudgeon, it's a place that's pretty and has spots for picnics."

"Excellent description, Theo," Lily said.

"Now, Theo, we're off. Your mother told you, I hear, that it is your duty to keep me company this afternoon. Sam, Laura Beth, mind your mother and don't destroy the house—"

"Or its danzans," Laura Beth added.

"Denizens," Theo corrected.

"Exactly," Knight finished. "Lily, I'll see you for dinner."

"If you wish it."

"I most assuredly do."

Lily nodded to Charlie, the first footman, and he deftly refilled her wineglass with the sweet bordeaux.

"This is the best wine I've ever tasted," she said, smiling at her host. He looked exceedingly handsome in his black evening garb. Ever since she'd seen him in his bedchamber, in only his breeches and absolutely nothing else, she couldn't seem not to see him as a man now, a very handsome man at that.

"My father was quite the spirits connoisseur," Knight explained. "He passed on a bit of his knowledge to me. I'm delighted you like tonight's choice. Incidentally, you look lovely this evening."

"Thank you."

Her voice was light, disbelieving. It wasn't an act. It struck him again that she didn't know how instantly delicious she was to the male eye. She thought he was merely indulging in masculine flattery. It was disconcerting. Actually, he'd had his usual reaction when she'd come into the drawing room earlier. Her gown was modest by London standards, but the color of soft peach made her skin glow, her hair seem more lustrous; in short, just looking at her made his muscles go into spasm.

He said abruptly, "You haven't worn mourning for Tris."

She paled but answered in her composed voice. "No. There wasn't time, and I didn't want to spend our money on unnecessary things." Her chin went into the air—a small act of defiance.

"I'm sorry," he said quickly. "It's none of my affair. Now, back to our Theo. He's a bruising rider. He needs a more spirited horse than poor old Bruno. Wicket would be just the horse for him, I think."

"Knight, please, you mustn't let him ride one of your best horses. Really—"

"Be quiet, Lily, and try a bit of the crimped cod and oyster sauce. I shall do exactly as I please, contrive to remember that. Now, after we left Tattersall's—oh, yes, Theo is quite a good judge of horseflesh—we went to the bookbinder's. I was all for throwing that dashed old tome into the Thames, but Theo, well, he was still indulging in a complete attack of conscience."

"Did he have enough money?"

Knight briefly considered lying to her. But he couldn't. Theo didn't lie, so she would find out. "No," Knight said easily. "It was a most interesting situation there for a while." He fell silent, remembering the look on the boy's face. There had been chagrin, but most of all fear, and that had smitten Knight as nothing else ever had in his benighted years.

The boy had drawn a deep breath and said to the benign Mr. Mulligan, "Sir, I have but five shillings. Could I perhaps pay the remainder off next week?''

If Mr. Mulligan wondered at the boy's apparent lack of funds, and that boy in the company of a very wealthy peer of the realm, he didn't let on.

''My mother doesn't have much, you see, and—''

''Theo.'' Knight's low, firm voice brought Theo to instant and complete silence. ''I have a proposition for you. We'll leave the book with Mr. Mulligan, then ride to Hyde Park to discuss it. My proposition will not make you rich, but it will make you more affluent, shall we say.''

''Oh, sir, I'll do anything!'' . . .

Knight forked down a substantial bite of roast partridge with bread sauce, one of his favorite dishes. He grinned over at Lily. ''Theo will pay me back the other five shillings by next week, don't doubt it. He, my dear Lily, is now my librarian and cataloger. My library is in a rare mess, and Theo has already prepared to gird his loins and take it on. Trump will aid him when it is necessary. Theo will work no longer than two hours a day, five days a week.''

''But—''

Knight held up an imperious hand. ''It is between Theo and me, Lily. I am not a mill owner, nor do I believe in sweathouse conditions for nine-year-old children. So hush. You are only his mother. You have no say in the matter. Now, do try a bite of that crimped cod. It is one of Cuthbert's better efforts.''

Lily ate.

Knight watched her eat. He watched her throat muscles as she swallowed her food; he watched the drops of wine on her lips as she drank from the fine crystal wineglass.

After a moment, he asked abruptly, "Why did you cry?"

Her eyes flew to his face.

"Why?" he repeated.

Lily tried to look rueful, but she doubted she achieved it. She probably looked like a pathetic fool. "You have been wonderful. I couldn't bear it."

"Now that's interesting. Shall I be cruel to you and the children? Shall I threaten to beat Sam? Cut off Laura Beth's hair? Would that make you laugh instead of cry?"

She was forced to laugh. "No, you're being absurd. I didn't mean it like that precisely. You have just been so very unexpected. It is more than I— we deserve."

"And it just came crashing down on your head, is that it?"

"Yes. I'm sorry I got your cravat all wet."

"You're forgiven. And there is something else. The boys need a tutor. I've decided that they shouldn't be enrolled at Eton until next term. The tutor I have in mind is the third son of a vicar who holds his living from me. Actually, he's the younger brother of Tilney Jones, my solicitor. He's just finished at Oxford and is free for the next few months. He will also provide the boys with the proper exercise. Theo, I noticed today, is far too pale, and when he is not with me, then—"

"*You* decided?"

Knight brought his flowing monologue to an abrupt end and stared at the beautiful Lily. She was also pale; not from lack of exercise, but from anger at his high-handedness. He continued mildly, with the ease of a man born to privilege and the occasional brain flashes of a diplomat. "Actually, if you approve of him, he can come here on Monday next. If you don't like him, then we will forget it. Also, we need to redo the second floor so the children will have their own nursery. Only don't say that denigrating word in front of the boys. But they need their own rooms, their own area. You and I will meet with the architect and—"

"Why are you doing all this? I don't understand!"

He saw her confusion and understood it. As a matter of fact, his own confusion at his behavior was much greater. He said very quietly, "I'm not Ugly Arnold, Lily. I have no intention of trying to seduce you on the stairs. I have no intention of trying to gain your favors in my bed by being nice to Tris's children."

"But why?"

"You know something? I haven't the foggiest idea, if the truth be told. Now, should you like some dessert? Perhaps some damson pudding?"

Lily slowly shook her head.

"Then shall we adjourn to the drawing room? I should like you to play for me, if you would. You do play, do you not?"

"I'm out of practice."

"I can't imagine you stumbling over your fingers to the extent that I would cry hold."

"You are an optimist, sir!"

"Now, about that architect, he can be here tomorrow, if that is acceptable to you."

Lily leaned forward, and he saw that her right hand was fisted on the table beside her plate. "I don't want you to . . . disrupt your life for us, at least more than you have already. I don't want you to feel compelled to tear down walls and build new ones. I'm trying to keep the children quiet and out of your way. I don't want you to feel that you must—"

"That is quite a lot of things you don't want me to do, Lily. There was once a nursery on the third floor of this house. It is now servants' quarters. I don't wish to displace them. So that leaves the second floor and several unused bedchambers. We will make do. I daresay it will add value to the house if sometime in the future one of my misbegotten heirs decides to sell. Incidentally, I don't feel that I must do anything. I am simply doing what I wish to. Now, are you quite through?"

Lily just looked at him. "You don't wish any damson pudding, my lord?"

"Knight, if you please, and no. I wish to hear you trip lovingly over Beethoven."

Lily was out of practice, but she played well enough to make Knight exceedingly relaxed. He didn't turn the pages for her. He sat opposite the pianoforte, watching her face as she played. He wished she were a hag. He wished she had the temperament of a fishwife. He wished the children were obnoxious brats.

He wasn't forty yet. Thirteen years to go. And here was Lily. He frowned at that. She'd been Tris's wife and was now a widow of only one month or so. She was grieving for her dead husband. What the hell was he doing thinking like this, for God's sake?

He rose abruptly when she came to the end of the third movement of the Sonata in C major. "I'm going out, Lily. Thank you. I will see you tomorrow." *In the daylight. In candlelight I want to ravish you.*

She rose quickly but not quickly enough. He was gone.

Lily frowned. Had she said something untoward? Had her playing been so error-riddled? She left the drawing room and walked upstairs. It was

only nine o'clock. There was time yet to play with
Theo and Sam. Laura Beth was long asleep,
sprawled, Lily knew, in the middle of the bed.

Two days later, Knight Winthrop, eighth Viscount Castlerosse, was named legal guardian of
his cousin's three children.

7

Boy had never been in London. He felt instantly at home. Everyone spoke English, after all. It was a treat after France and Brussels with all those Frogs making their prissy foreign sounds.

Monk, a man from London, took him to see all his former haunts down on the wharf, and together they enjoyed the odors of the squalid alleyways and found the suffocating fumes of the slatternly taverns ambrosia.

"We 'ave time, Boy," Monk said as he swilled down a long draft of warm ale. "We'll find 'is bloody lordship soon enough and with 'im Tris's fancy little piece, don't ye doubt it. We'll treat this as a bit of a congé, as them damned Frenchies say. Yes, sir, I'll show ye all about my city."

"Aye," said Boy, trying to ape his friend's actions and ending up coughing up his toes. "I love Lunnon."

"A long time since I've been 'ere," Monk said and gave a lecherous wink to a frowsy barmaid. "A long time."

"Wunnerful city, Lunnon."

"Oh, aye. Way back in '02, I think it was, it was even nicer. I was just a little button and a bloody watch caught me with my paw in a merchant's pocket. I escaped, o'course. Ma was dead by then and it was jest me. I found ye in '04 in Liverpool, don't ye remember? Then it was off to France wot with them quid we stole off that Lady Whatsername in Dover.''

Reminiscences followed, more ale was ordered and swilled, and soon Monk and Boy were snoring in drunken splendor, oblivious of their surroundings.

Boy wanted to see all the sights, particularly the Tower of London, and Monk, feeling well in control of their destiny and filled with gracious bonhomie, took his friend to see the spot where the lovely Lady Jane Grey lost her pretty head. They assiduously avoided Bow Street.

Julien St. Clair, the Earl of March, seated himself next to Knight in the reading room at White's. He said without preamble, ''There is talk, Knight. Lots of it. Probably because we were so busily twitting you, we didn't spare a thought to those possible fools who overheard us. A lucky few were even blessed to see all of you at the Pantheon Bazaar.''

Knight had slowly lowered the *Gazette*, and regarded his friend with somber eyes. ''I see. Please go on, Julien.''

''I hate it, you know that, but your Lily is naturally your light o' love, and little Laura Beth is obviously your child. It's unfortunate that her hair is nearly as black as yours.''

''I hadn't noticed, but I do believe you're right,'' said Knight, a bemused smile on his face. ''Her eyes are a very dark blue, though, unlike mine.''

''I suppose the gossips draw the line at claiming all of them your offspring. After all, the older boy is nine years old, isn't he? You would have had to have gained sufficient potency by seventeen to have fathered him.''

And Lily would have had to have been all of ten years old, Knight thought. He didn't say it aloud. He didn't want Julien to know that his cousin had married a fifteen-year-old girl and immediately gotten a baby on her. He tried to listen to his friend. Certainly he'd heard bits and pieces, had vague acquaintances give him thoroughly cold looks, but he'd ignored all that. It was absurd, no one had done anything wrong, and he couldn't be bothered with such nonsense. However, if Julien was concerned enough to run him down and tell him, it was bad. It was more than bad. It would shortly be intolerable. He cursed softly.

''I agree,'' said Julien. ''I have spread the truth, as have all our friends, but you know the gossips.'' He shrugged. ''It's like a wheel gathering speed down a hill. Unfortunately, there's not a more titillating scandal just at present, thus yours must do until another one comes along.'' Julien grinned. ''I have never seen my wife more incensed. I feared she would screech a very unladylike curse at Lady Gregorson the other evening at the Ranleaghs' musicale—a dreadful experience, by the way. You were fortunate to miss it. Some yelling soprano from Milan.''

''I guess I shall just have to send Lily and the children to Castle Rosse. I was made their legal guardian, so Ugly Arnold must now forget any nefarious plans he has for her.''

''I saw the announcement in the *Gazette*. It only caused more furor, as you can well imagine.'' The earl, who was privy to Ugly Arnold's attempt the day at the Pantheon Bazaar, asked with a slight frown on his forehead, ''I trust the fellow can read?''

''Julien, I'll have you know that dear Arnold is a squire of the first order. His wife is my cousin, more's the pity. Well, thank you for telling me, but—''

''Of course,'' Julien interrupted smoothly, ''you already knew about the wagging tongues.''

''Yes, but it's worse than I'd expected. I haven't taken Lily to any balls, routs, or even musicales simply because she's in mourning for her dead husband, and she doesn't like to leave the children alone.'' Knight grinned. ''She's afraid Sam might plug up all the chimneys and send us scrambling and coughing out of doors in the dark of night in our nightshirts.''

''You don't wear a nightshirt.''

''That could prove most embarrassing, to be sure.''

''Lily is a beautiful woman. Were she plain, the gossips would probably never have taken a plow to this particular field.''

''I know.'' Knight paused for a moment, steepling his fingers and tapping the tips together. ''It's the strangest thing. She doesn't realize her own beauty. It's disconcerting, particularly for a man who's spent so many years on the social scene here in London. I think I've been treated to every ploy, every machination, that the fertile brains of matchmaking mamas could devise. Of course, you were in the same kettle until you met Kate.''

''True, but not to the present point. Must you really send them to Castle Rosse?''

''What the hell else can I do?''

Julien studied a well-buffed fingernail. ''I suppose you could marry Lily.''

Now that was a stunner, Knight thought as his jaw dropped. He stared at the Earl of March as if he'd lost his powers of reasoning as well as his ears and his teeth. "I am not forty," Knight said slowly, precisely. "I am twenty-seven. I have thirteen more years of freedom before I—do—that—thing."

"It's called marriage, Knight," the earl said easily. "Just a suggestion, old fellow. No need to speak so slowly, as if to a half-wit."

"I've hired a tutor for the boys." Knight paused again, then added a bit ruefully, "Actually, John Jones—yes, that's really the fellow's name—will come to be interviewed by Lily on Monday."

"He would escort them to Castle Rosse, then?"

"I suppose so."

But Julien knew that this as-yet-unhired tutor would never be in charge of Lily or the children, not if Knight had anything to say about it, which of course he did and would. This would be a wholly unpredictable and quite amusing situation were it not for the gossips. Julien couldn't imagine, after having met Lily, that Knight would emerge from it whole-hide. Every time he mentioned the situation to his wife, Kate, she always ended up howling with laughter, choking as she managed to say over and over, "Poor Knight! I shall write a play about him. The clever man who vowed and swore endlessly and with great wit and verve that a wise man never married until he was forty years old, and then only to beget an heir. Oh, no, nothing so foolish for Knight Winthrop! And now he is twenty-seven and the steppapa to three children. Oh, it is too wonderful. *The Fitting End to the Man Who Protesteth Too Much*—that will be the title of my play."

"Your new tutor—he'll probably fall head over arse in love with her, Knight."

Knight looked exceedingly grim. Then he sighed. "Yes, I know he will, even if he's half

blind and an idiot, which he won't be." He sighed
again. "Have you ever heard of a female tutor?"

Julien laughed. "Then you would be in the
suds, old fellow. She'd fall in love with you."

"Oh, go to the devil, St. Clair." Julien rose easily and Knight stopped him, saying. "Thank you
for telling me. I will do something. I must protect
Lily and the children."

Julien just looked at him, his head cocked to
one side.

It was, oddly enough, the picnic to Richmond
on the following morning, Saturday, that decided
Knight that Lily and the children must go to Castle Rosse. The sooner the better. For everyone.

For late October the weather was uncommonly
warm, the sun bright overhead, and only a faint
breeze stirred the hair. The children were in tearing spirits. After much discussion, Knight decided to allow all of them to ride, Lily insisting
that she would carry Laura Beth and Czarina
Catherine in front of her. Charlie, the footman,
and Lucy, Cuthbert's assistant, would come behind in the carriage with the picnic supplies.

Knight hired a pony for Sam and bought a spirited bay mare for Lily. He didn't tell her he'd
bought it for her, simply shrugged when she saw
the mare in his stables on Saturday morning. If
she wished to conclude that the mare was hired
as Sam's pony was, it was none of his concern.

"Oh, she is lovely! Her name is Violet? Beautiful, aren't you, my girl? No, no, I haven't a car-
rot, but I shall fetch you one presently." She
turned to Knight, nearly dancing in her excitement. "What are you doing with such a fine lady
in your stable, my lord?"

So she hadn't concluded that the mare was
hired. He said nothing. He wasn't so stupid as to

open his mouth and put his foot in it. He looked at her, his look unknowingly hungry. Her riding habit had seen several years of wear, but it was well cut and of good quality material. It was royal blue, emphasizing her high full breasts and slender waist, and severe in design, all save the pert little riding hat perched atop her head with its ostrich plume sweeping along the side of her face. Slung over one arm was the beautiful ermine-lined cloak he'd seen her wear once before.

As for Sam, he approved of his pony, though Wicket, Theo's grown-up mount, made him want to protest heartily that he wasn't a little boy, after all. Laura Beth simply smiled at everyone, her thumb in her mouth. When it finally came time to mount up, Laura Beth held up her arms to Knight.

He stared down at her, nonplussed.

"I want to go with you," Laura Beth said in an endearingly innocent voice that brooked no argument to the discerning ear.

Lily laughed a bit uncertainly. She didn't look at Knight. "You, my darling little pest, are to ride with me. Are you afraid that I'll drop you, Laura Beth?"

"No, Mama, but Knight is my special man, my special cousin."

"I am your *only* cousin."

That fact didn't bother Laura Beth or her logic even a little bit. She sucked happily on her thumb.

Lily choked. "Nonetheless, we can't bother Cousin Knight, my love. It is very kind of him to take us on this picnic, you see. We don't want him to feel that he's here to serve us. You will ride with me. Come along now."

Knight heard himself say, "I don't mind. Hand her up to me, Lily."

Lily stared at him. He looked startled that he'd

offered. She remained silent for a moment, waiting for him to retract the offered treat. But he didn't.

"Are you sure, my lord?"

"My name is Knight, Lily, and yes. Give me the little snippet."

"What's a snippet?" Laura Beth wanted to know.

Knight leaned down, tweaked her nose, then lifted her in his arms. "A snippet is a small little fragment of something, usually something of . . . great account."

"Girls," Sam snorted as Charlie gave him a leg up onto his pony, a fat little chestnut named Darby.

Theo smiled benignly upon the cavalcade, saying to Knight, "If you tire of her, sir, I shall take her. She's just a little girl, after all."

"I shall survive, Theo." He mounted easily, Laura Beth tucked under one arm. Then he settled her in front of him. "Onward, troops."

It was just as they turned the corner onto Oxford Street that Knight pulled to a halt to allow a barouche to pass. It held the glacially correct Countess of Bormaine and Mrs. Frazier, a sharp-tongued termagent who had managed to insinuate herself into the highest echelons of the ton, probably by blackmail of some sort, Knight had always thought.

"Oh, do look, my lady," he heard Mrs. Frazier's shrill, penetrating voice call out. "I vow and declare it is his lordship with his darling *family*. Hello, Lord Castlerosse!"

Knight had no alternative but to pull up his horse, careful that the boys and Lily did the same. His arm tightened about Laura Beth and she grunted. "Shush, little one," he whispered to her and unwittingly dropped a kiss on her head.

"How sweet," said Mrs. Frazier. "And look—I vow it is the charming *widow*. She is *living* with you, is she not, my lord? Without any sort of older woman in residence, I understand."

"Mrs. Frazier, Lady Bormaine, may I present Mrs. Winthrop, my cousin's widow, and her three children."

The two ladies looked from him to Lily, avidly taking in her beauty, the richness of her ermine-lined cloak—doubtless a present from the viscount to his mistress—the quite expensive mare she was riding.

"This goes beyond the line of what is tolerable," Mrs. Frazier said loudly behind a gloved hand.

"It's a disgrace," the countess said in an equally loud whisper. "His doxy togged out like a lady!"

The coachman, after a commiserating glance toward Knight, pulled the barouche away. Knight felt as though his jaw was locked together, he was so furious.

"You're hurting me!"

"I'm sorry, Laura Beth," he said automatically and loosened his hold on the child.

"I think," said Theo, looking at the departing barouche, "that they were being quite rude. What's a doxy? I don't understand, Cousin Knight."

"Forget them, Theo. Stupid, vicious people, that's what they are and they're nothing to us."

Knight turned to look at Lily. She was as pale as the white ermine lining her beautiful cloak. She was also furious; he could see the pulse beating in her throat, her hands fisted on the reins.

"I'm sorry," he said simply.

"Ow!" cried Laura Beth.

"Be quiet, snippet. You said I was your special man. You must put up with my vagaries."

"What's varities?"

"My peculiarities, my limitless stupidity in this case. Now, let's continue to Richmond."

They did. Lily said not a word. Laura Beth bounced and giggled, and Knight had his hands full to keep the little girl atop the horse, himself as well.

Luckily, Knight told himself as they gained the main road to Richmond, Sam was so excited he hadn't heard a word. Thank God. He could just imagine Sam threatening to poke his fives in each lady's face.

Not that the two old bitches didn't royally deserve it.

The day became warmer, the sun brilliant overhead. Knight saw Lily slip off her cloak and fold it over her saddle. He made haste to remove the outer layer of Laura Beth's clothes. She wiggled and hooted with laughter at his clumsy efforts.

"Hush, Laura Beth, and help Cousin Knight!"

"It's all right, Theo," Knight said as he finally pulled the little girl's arm from the sleeve. "I'm bigger, so logic dictates that I should prevail, eventually."

"You don't know Laura Beth," Sam said, giving her a darkling look. "She's a silly little girl and a nuisance."

Theo said in a priggish voice, "At least she doesn't scare Betty to death with yucky bread dough in the dark."

Sam looked ready to say something completely out of line to his brother when Knight quickly raised his hand. "Quiet, all of you. Now, look at the scenery. To our left is the Thames. It's muddy, but it's English, therefore ours, and is to be appreciated. Sam, watch your pony."

Lily tried to become unfrozen. She truly did. She watched Knight handle the children and knew it was an exhausting job. But he was doing it and with unexpected skill. She just couldn't bring herself to say anything. Those two awful ladies had thought—no, truly believed, since they'd called her a doxy—that she was Knight's mistress. His paramour, his whore. She shivered with anger. But why would they? For God's sake, there were three children. Did the ladies believe the children to be Knight's? Impossible; he was far too young. Hers? That was truly ludicrous.

It was beyond ludicrous. It was dreadful. She felt fury, not only for the insult to herself but even more for Knight. He hadn't asked for it. He was so completely innocent of anything remotely objectionable that she wanted to scream invectives to the heavens.

"Mama, what's wrong?"

Lily finally managed a fake smile for Laura Beth. "Nothing, my love. Stop wriggling about or Knight will drop you. He might be your special man, but he said nothing about you being his special little girl. He just might roll you into the Thames."

Laura Beth looked up at Knight, removed her thumb from her mouth, and asked, "Would you roll me into the Tims?"

"In an instant, if you disobey me."

"Oh." After that brief remark, Laura Beth put her thumb back into her mouth, hugged Czarina Catherine close to her chest, and looked with great interest toward the river.

They arrived at a lovely small park near the river thirty minutes later. The boys dashed away to skip rocks across the water, Laura Beth demanded bread for the loudly squawking ducks, and Lily said not a single word. Her movements were stiff, wooden, angry.

Soon the carriage arrived. She helped Charlie and Lucy, somewhat to their consternation, spread the beautiful white linen tablecloth on the fall grass.

"Go play with Laura Beth," Knight said. "She needs to be watched."

Lily obeyed instantly.

Knight stared after her, wondering what the devil he should say to her. He himself was still furious. God, he'd been a fool not to have taken the appropriate measures to protect her.

The luncheon itself was demolished; that was the way Knight thought of it as he stared down at the continuing and growing devastation. The boys ate as though it was either their last meal or their first in years. As for Laura Beth, she *tasted* everything, leaving bits and pieces piled on and around her plate. Lily scolded, threatened, cajoled. Finally, to everyone's utter surprise, she jumped to her feet, placed her hands on her hips, and said in the shrillest voice he'd ever imagined from her, "All of you, stop it this instant! Do you hear me? STOP IT!"

Three sets of hands instantly stilled; three pairs of startled eyes flew to her face. She was pale, her hands shaking slightly.

Knight, who was frankly enjoying the children's antics, much to his own surprise, added his own look at Lily. She was truly upset. He watched her splay her hands in front of her.

"Theo, Sam, I am ashamed of you. Knight is giving us a marvelous treat and you're acting like . . . convict children! He surely must believe you have next to no breeding, certainly no manners! Please, just behave!" She looked as if she would say more, but didn't. She turned on her heel and fled.

"Oh, goodness!" Lucy cried.

"Mama!"

Knight said in his sternest voice, "You do somewhat resemble convict children, though I've never personally observed any. Mind your manners and stay here. I will see to your mother. Lucy, Charlie, watch them!"

Knight caught up to her very quickly, for her direction was erratic and soon completely halted by the riverbank.

He made no move to touch her. She was sobbing, her shoulders hunched, her arms wrapped about herself. He hated her pain, brought on by those damnable harridans.

Finally he said quietly, "Lily."

She hiccuped and he saw her straighten her shoulders, knew she was trying to pull herself together.

She said in a dismal voice, filled with self-loathing, "I yelled at the children and they were just having fun."

"Well, yes. So what? I venture to guarantee that they will survive. You can't always be Miss Perfection, Lily."

"It's Mrs.," Lily said.

He smiled. "That's much better. Here, take my handkerchief." He handed it around so that she didn't have to turn and face him as yet.

"Thank you."

"You're welcome. Now, why don't we take a short stroll and talk about this?"

"There's nothing at all to say! You saw them, you heard them! I'm your doxy, your whore! It's done and I'm responsible! I'm going to leave, I must. Now that you're the children's legal guardian, they're safe. I'll go in the morning and everyone will be nice to you again.''

"How old did you say you were?"

She turned to face him at that, her expression a study of confusion. "I am nearly twenty."

"For one who has reached such an advanced age, you're showing remarkable signs of stupidity."

"I am not! Listen, Knight, the children are now safe. They don't really need me, not really, and I can go away. Maybe soon you could send me Laura Beth."

"I've always thought martyrs the biggest bores alive."

"That's why they normally get burned at the stake or some other awful thing. That's why they're martyrs."

"A good point. You make me forget my logic. In any case, you're being a bore, Lily. You will not leave the children." *You will not leave me.* "This nastiness you witnessed was unfortunate. It was entirely my fault, not at all yours. I knew what was happening. You hadn't a clue. Now, this is what I propose."

"I don't want to hear you propose anything!" The ambiguity suddenly struck her, and her face flamed with color. She whirled about and ran away from him, sticking close to the riverbank.

Knight watched her for a moment, then strode after her. He hoped Sam wasn't observing this sterling performance, else the little boy might be thinking that Knight was attacking his mother.

He called out, "Lily, you're tiring me out and I'm not enjoying it. Stop your damned nonsense! Stop your damned running! Stop, period!"

She did, beside a willow tree.

"That's better."

Lily looked at him, then blurted out, "I can't

stay here and watch your reputation be torn to shreds, all because of me and the children. Don't you understand? I simply can't allow it."

"You can't, huh? All right, then. Here's what we'll do. You, my dear, and the children will go to Castle Rosse. It's my country seat in Dorset, not even a full day's journey from London. After your interview with John Jones, everything will be set. All right?"

"No."

Knight hadn't ever had a woman gainsay his wishes, not since his mother had departed to more heavenly climes many years before. He merely stared at her, nonplussed. "What?"

"No, I won't do it. You won't sacrifice yourself."

"Remarkable," Knight said, more to himself than to her. "I hadn't thought you so stubborn, Lily. I had indeed believed you to be quite malleable, yielding. I would have thought that since Tris married you when you were scarce even a young girl, he would have molded you into a more submissive creature."

"Tris didn't believe in molds," Lily said, thrusting her chin up. That, she supposed, was the truth. He'd wanted her to marry him so badly that he'd never shown her any dominant sort of male traits. She'd always assumed all men wanted to rule whatever size kingdom they could manage to obtain, be it only a wife. Her father certainly had ruled with an iron fist, until they'd had to leave England. Odd how she'd become the power then. She hadn't thought of it in those particular terms before now. "He wanted me to be happy, that's all," she added, aware that Knight was simply staring at her.

"And were you? Happy, that is?"

Lily couldn't bring the glib answer out. She

couldn't even make herself nod. She just stood there, her fingers tearing at the bark on the oak tree, feeling stupid and helpless and altogether useless.

Knight sighed. "All right, Lily, that was impertinent of me. Come back to the picnic before Sam attacks me for assaulting his mother. We'll speak of this later."

"I shan't change my mind, Knight."

"You will do as I tell you."

Lily just shrugged. Let him rave and rant and carry on. It didn't matter. He would learn that she was just as stubborn as he. She wouldn't let him ruin his reputation, his family name, lose all his friends, just because of her.

"I'm hungry," she said and strode back toward the picnic.

"Good, that must mean you're returning to a more equitable state of mind."

It occurred to Lily sometime after midnight as she lay awake in her bed that perhaps she'd overreacted to the meeting with those two old ladies. Perhaps they were just two out of many. She would have to think about it.

The following morning, however, riding in Hyde Park with Sam and Theo and Laura Beth, she discovered that she hadn't begun to learn the extent of the damage to the viscount's reputation and good name.

8

Like the previous day, Sunday morning continued beautifully mild, the sun shining as if it had never known a moment of dark clouds. It was so unlike the end of October that one would be a fool to remain indoors. At least that was what the servants were saying, and Lily agreed with them.

She sent word to the stables that she and the children would ride. Knight, it appeared, had already gone out. She wondered if he'd gone riding. She wondered, too, where he had gone off to the previous evening. When they'd returned from Richmond, he'd bidden her a polite good-evening and left.

This morning she felt buoyant, more optimistic, ready to take on anyone and anything. She had indeed overreacted the previous day. She'd made everyone miserable just because two very rude ladies had had nothing more important to do than shred someone's character.

She was humming as she dressed Laura Beth. She listened intently to Theo tell her about the wondrous properties of something called the *omaya* root. Even Sam's carping at Theo for his bossiness drew nothing more than a mild reproof from her.

Sam, incensed, declared, "I'm six years old! I don't need Theo to tell me to fold my shirts. Why, Papa would have told him to go prose to an ant, Mama!"

That, Lily thought, was probably the truth. Tris had had the gift to tease Theo out of his over-adultness. However, Sam's shirts did look a mess. She just shrugged, such was her excellent mood.

She gave both Sam and Theo firm instructions when they reached the gate to the park. "You will remain with me or else we will return home immediately. Do you promise?"

They promised, but Lily knew Sam forgot things like promises very quickly.

There were few riders in Hyde Park this morning and they were all gentlemen. They touched the tips of their hats as they passed. One man drew his horse to a halt, stared at Lily for the longest time, then sighed dramatically, his hand over his heart.

"Bloody ass!"

"Sam! Where did you hear that?"

To her surprise, Theo filled the uncomfortable silence. "Well, Mama, he's right, and it's not his fault. Cousin Knight's stable lads all talk like that. But the point, Mama, is that the man was stupid." Theo paused, his head cocked to one side, the way Tris used to do. "But you're the problem, Mama."

"I?"

"Yes," said Sam, looking at her critically. "You're too pretty. Men can't help but stare at you and act like ass—fools."

"Bloody ass," Laura Beth said clearly.

Lily simply stared at them, then laughed. "You are the greatest pair—what a corker! Laura Beth, don't repeat that again. It isn't nice. Enough now; let's canter a bit."

They were enjoying themselves immensely until Lily turned to see a lively chestnut mare draw up beside her. Atop the mare sat a young lady, quite beautiful, with the exotic dark coloring that made Lily think she was either French or Italian. Just behind her rode a gentleman on a startling pure white gelding. His expression was bland, his manner seemingly detached. He was older, perhaps forty, handsome, she supposed, were it not for the coldness of his eyes, a winter gray. She recognized the signs of dissipation; she'd lived with them long enough with her own father. He was dressed entirely in white. He didn't smile, he simply looked from the lady he was with to Lily and waited silently.

"You are Mrs. Winthrop, are you not?" the young woman asked, neither smiling nor frowning at Lily.

"Yes, I am. These are my children," Lily added, sweeping her hand to include Theo and Sam.

To Lily's surprise, the lady didn't introduce herself. Nor did the gentleman. Her dark eyes narrowed, and Lily braced herself. For what, she wasn't certain, but it wasn't long in coming, and it was awful. The lady said very calmly, "You are Knight Winthrop's whore, and I for one am appalled that you would remain here—in his very house, with your farrow of little bastards—whilst he is ostracized. Talk grows, and soon every moral gentleman and lady of London will cut him dead. You are despicable, madam. Take your brood and leave London."

Lily saw red. "How dare you! None of that is true, none of it!"

"I will not stand by and watch you destroy a man everyone admires! You miserable harlot!" The lady sent a contemptuous glance that encompassed all the children, dug her heels into her mare's flanks, and was off. Belatedly, Lily saw that the gentleman had not as yet galloped after her. He studied Lily's furious flushed face and said after a long moment, "Should you like to leave Lord Castlerosse, my dear, I would be delighted to take you in. I'm a generous man and I'll see to it that your bastards are well fed, if you please me."

Lily stared at him, dumbstruck. Just as he rode away, torrents of words streamed from her mouth, but it was too late. She shut up, aware of Sam and Theo sitting quietly on their mounts, both boys as rigid as statues.

Laura Beth removed her thumb from her mouth and announced, "I think I'll roll that lady into the Tims."

"Mama, she's nothing but a stupid bitch!" Sam looked ready to spit nails. "How dare she say those things about us!"

"What about that miserable man?" Theo all but snarled, making Lily blink with his unusual display of anger. "What did he mean by calling us bastards? We're not bastards!"

"What's bastard?" Laura Beth inquired mildly.

"Oh, stick your spoon in it, Laura Beth!"

"Now, Theo, he's gone. He and the la—female were both horrid, but we shan't see them again." Odd how calm she sounded. Lily supposed she had really been waiting for the other shoe to drop, so to speak. It had—and a hundred boots with it.

"He was the bastard," Sam said, shaking his fist toward the retreating pair. "Not us."

"Mama," Theo said, his voice suddenly as gentle as a spring shower, "let's go home now. I want you to forget what they said. All of it was silly. Come on."

Lily nodded. Dear Theo, recognizing that she

was nearly blank-brained with shock. She heard him say something to Sam but couldn't make it out. A moment later, Sam cleared his throat loudly and said, "I'm sorry for saying that word, Mama. I shan't do it again."

"Which word, love?"

"Bitch, Mama."

"Oh. Thank you, Sam. But you want to know something? I should like to ride after the both of them and tell them exactly what I think of them."

"Throw her into the Tims!"

Lily laughed, and Theo felt himself relaxing. He prayed that Cousin Knight was home. He was worried. Very worried. Lily was pale as wax and he knew that she was holding herself together by a thread. Horrid, horrid people. Why couldn't things be fair?

Knight was home, but Lily forestalled Theo and his good intentions. They were still in the stables, ready to go into the house, when she said quietly and very firmly, "Theo, Sam, neither of you is to say a single word about this to his lordship. Do you promise me?"

Theo looked troubled.

"Promise me!"

"All right. I promise."

"Sam?"

Sam nodded.

"Good," Lily said, hugged each of them, and strode off toward the house, clutching Laura Beth's hand in hers. Only Sam noticed that two of the stable lads stood very still, admiring Lily. Stupid oafs. She was his mother, for mercy's sake.

Knight was coming down the stairs when Lily and the children entered the house. He paused, his eyes covering every inch of her in a brief instant. Something was wrong.

"Where have you been?" He'd meant to sound mildly curious but heard the underlying worry in his voice.

Sam started to say something until Lily sent him a look that could fry him. "We've just been riding in the park," she said. "I think all of us will now breakfast, then dress for church."

"Oh, Mama!"

"No whining, Sam. You will not grow up to be a heathen. May we borrow the carriage, my lord?"

"Certainly," Knight said. It was on the tip of his tongue to offer to accompany them to St. Paul's, but he did have an appointment that couldn't be missed. "I will see you for dinner, Lily?"

"Perhaps," she said and forced a smile.

"I should appreciate it. There is much, I believe, that we have to discuss."

Lily was deep in thought the remainder of the day. The homily given at the service was sufficiently erudite to allow her mind to wander freely. Luckily, Laura Beth held her peace. By the benediction Lily had made up her mind. She would leave—Knight, his beautiful, safe house, and the children. But then she realized she couldn't do it. She couldn't leave Sam and Theo and Laura Beth.

What to do?

Actually, something very silly changed her mind that evening. Laura Beth wanted Betty to tuck her in for bed. Lily felt a stab of pain, then just after it a sense of relief. She could be separated from the child for a little while. Laura Beth wouldn't miss her; she had Betty, and Betty was a good-hearted girl.

Lily wrote a letter to Sam and Theo. She sent

word to the viscount that she had the headache
and wouldn't be joining him for dinner. She purposefully stressed that she wanted to see him in
the morning to discuss all the matters at hand.
The note she wrote him was much shorter. She
realized that she didn't know where to put it. She
stood blankly in her bedchamber, the envelope in
her hand, staring at nothing. In the end, she tore
it up. He would learn about her departure from
Sam and Theo.

She packed one valise. At precisely eight-thirty
that evening, she slipped down the servants'
stairs and out the back entrance. She heard Cuthbert, the cook, in a Gaelic tirade directed at the
scullery maid, but saw no one. She hurried to the
street corner and hailed a hackney that had just
left off a passenger. She told the driver to take
her to the Tottingham posting house, where she
and the children had arrived the week before.
Only a week! It seemed impossible. It felt like
years, as if she were leaving everything she loved
and held dear.

A coach for Brighton was scheduled to leave at
ten-thirty. Lily settled herself in the waiting room,
oblivious of the men's stares. Her expression was
so forbidding that she was left alone. She accepted a cup of tea from the innkeeper's spouse
and removed herself to a small table in the corner
of the dining room.

It required only thirty more minutes for her to
fully grasp the extent of her folly. "Oh, God, have
I lost my wits?"

An older woman, her single black valise
clutched to her enormous bosom, started at her
words. " 'Ere now, dearie, ye got a worry?"

Lily automatically shook her head. She'd been
completely and utterly stupid, thoughtless. . . .
She grabbed her valise and rushed out the door

of the inn. The yard was well lit but she could see
no hackneys near. She ran out of the inn yard
toward the corner. And right into Ugly Arnold.

Knight frowned down at his nearly full dinner
plate. He wasn't hungry. He wanted to see Lily.
He wondered if she was truly ill or just avoiding
him. He cursed softly at the green beans.

"My lord?"

"Oh, nothing, Duckett."

"My lord, Mrs. Allgood informed me that Betty
informed her that Mrs. Winthrop was behaving
oddly. Obviously her headache was pulling at her
and—"

Knight shoved his plate aside and waved Duckett to silence. "It doesn't matter, damn you. Mrs.
Winthrop will do just as she pleases. As to my
lack of appetite, tell Cuthbert I'm in mourning or
something." He tossed down his napkin and
rose. "I'll be in the library."

Damn Duckett and his impertinence, Knight
was thinking as he strode across the white Italian
marble entrance hall. He heard what sounded like
a squeak and looked up to see Betty clutching at
the railing as she careened down the stairs, her
cap askew.

"What the devil!"

"My lord! Oh, dear, oh, dear!"

He drew on his patience. "What's the matter,
Betty?"

"It's Laura Beth, my lord! She's very upset!"

"Why?"

"Mrs. Winthrop, my lord, she's gone!"

Knight froze. "Where?" he heard himself inquire and marveled at how calm he sounded.

"I don't know!" Betty wailed at the top of her
lungs. "She's just gone!"

"Very well," he said. "I'll see to the child."

It made no sense, he told himself over and over. Betty was mistaken. Lily was probably tucking in Sam and Theo. She was probably reading them a story. She was . . . no, she was ill. He hurried down the corridor to her bedchamber and pushed open the door.

A branch of candles was lit. Laura Beth was sitting up in the middle of the bed, Czarina Catherine clutched to her chest, her hair in two skinny braids over her shoulders, her small face blotched from crying.

"Cousin Knight!" She hiccuped loudly as she came up onto her knees.

"What is this all about, snippet?"

Czarina Catherine fell to the counterpane unnoticed. Laura Beth held out her thin little arms and Knight, without thought, gathered the child to him. Her arms went around his neck, her legs around his waist, and he felt her wet cheek press against his. "It's all right, snippet. I swear it's all right. No more crying; it smites me right down to my knees."

She giggled and ended up with a hiccup. Knight carried her to the chair in front of the lazily burning embers in the fireplace. He sat down, holding her close, and rocked her, not really realizing what he was doing, acting purely by instinct. "Now, what is this about your mama not being here?" He must sound calm; he mustn't alarm the child.

"She's gone," Laura Beth wailed and pressed herself even tighter against him.

"I'll find her," Knight said confidently, and he was confident. Lily would appear at any moment in the doorway. She would be embarrassed that he was here in her bedchamber, holding her daughter, but she—

"It was because of that awful lady," Laura Beth said.

"What? What did you say, snippet?"

"Mama took us riding in the park this morning. It was nice until this awful lady and a man on a big white horse stopped us. I wanted to toss her in the Tims. She was horrid and rude and called us names, and Mama was awful upset."

"What names? What did the lady say to your mama?"

His heart was pounding. He was afraid to hear what was bound to come out of the child's mouth. He knew, he knew what it would be.

"She called Mama a hore and a har-let and me and Sam and Theo bastards and she said that you were a good man but people would orsta—orchestra—"

"Ostracize?"

Laura Beth nodded and her thumb found its way back home to her mouth.

He wanted to curse the house down but he couldn't, not with a four-year-old baby in his arms. So Lily, in a spate of martyrdom, had fled the scene, a bloody stupid thing to have done. Curse her for being so damnably sensitive! Didn't she realize he could bloody well take care of himself *and* her *and* the children?

"Laura Beth, you and I are going to see Theo and Sam. I'll just wager that your mama left them a letter."

"Why not me?"

"You can't read, that's why. Come along now."

She was like a clinging monkey, but Knight didn't notice. He told her to keep as quiet as she could and together they tiptoed into Theo and Sam's room. Sure enough, Knight spotted an en-

velope propped up against the wash basin atop
the commode.

He carried the child downstairs to his library.
He held her even while he tore open the envelope
and read Lily's letter to her boys. It was what
he'd expected. It tore at him and at the same time
made him want to wring her neck.

My dearest boys,
Your cousin Knight is now your legal guardian.
You are fond of him, I know, and he is fond of
you. Try to behave and don't make him angry
with you. I'm leaving for a while so that the
dreadful gossip will stop. Please try to understand. It isn't fair for me to stay when your
cousin is being treated so horribly by all his
friends. Please forgive me and try to understand. I love you and I want you to be happy
and safe. Take care of Laura Beth. I will write
to you soon. All my love,

Mama.

Knight's fist crumpled the single sheet. Laura
Beth was asleep, sprawled over him like a blanket. He kissed her lightly on her temple, then
strode back upstairs and put her to bed. His
movements were decisive and calm, although he
was terrified that something dreadful would happen to Lily. She was a beautiful woman and she
was alone. In London. Damned stupid woman!

He wanted to beat her senseless.

At least the boys wouldn't have to read this
now. He wondered where her letter to him was.
He knew she'd written to him, doubtless more
absurd pap, just couched in different terms.

He was on the point of calling Duckett to dispatch the footmen to the various posting houses
in London. He stopped, his fingers inches from

the bell cord. Oh, no, he knew where Lily had gone. Undoubtedly she'd taken flight to the only posting house she knew of. He realized he was taking something of a chance with this assumption, but he was certain enough to continue.

Knight drew on his cloak and gloves and said to Duckett, "Mrs. Winthrop is an idiot. I am going to fetch her. Don't say anything to anyone."

"Certainly not, my lord."

"Arnold! Whatever are you doing here?" Lily wasn't afraid, but she was startled and dismayed to see him.

"Hello, Lily."

"Yes, hello, Arnold. I repeat, what are you doing here? Are you preparing to return home?" She turned to wave toward the posting house, and in doing so, she pulled away from him, very matter-of-factly, and straightened her cloak.

"You look beautiful," Arnold blurted out.

Lily became very still. She said quietly, calmly, "How is Gertrude, Arnold?"

He said nothing, merely stared at her, like a hungry Bedouin at a lone sheep.

"Haven't you written to Gertrude? How long ago did you leave Yorkshire?"

"I followed you, Lily. I want you. Please, I'll give you whatever you want, but you must come with me. We'll go to France, to Italy, wherever you wish, Lily, only—"

"Stop, Arnold. Just be quiet." She had to think. Lord, this was a ridiculous situation.

"You are rid of the children, thank the powers. You did it for us, didn't you, Lily? You made the viscount their legal guardian so we could be together?"

"Arnold," she said, riled now, "your oars are not in the water. The viscount very properly became their guardian for two reasons. First of all, it was his duty; second, he saw to it that you couldn't coerce us—me—into coming back to Yorkshire to endure Gertrude's contempt and your pawing!''

''Lily, no! I won't paw you, truly I won't. I love you!''

She saw his pallor, the widened pupils, heard the quavering in his voice. Oh, dear, what had happened to Ugly Arnold? ''Listen to me,'' she said, lightly placing her fingers on his coat sleeve. ''Let's go inside and have a cup of tea. You would like that, wouldn't you, Arnold? You are not looking at all well.'' He wasn't—he looked like a man with a fanatical mission. Was she his mission? Lily shuddered, unable to help herself.

''You want me to touch you, don't you, Lily? I saw you quivering for my fingers to touch you, my mouth. Oh, God, Lily, let's leave right now. We can be to Dover before morning and—''

''No! That's quite enough!'' Lily jerked away from him and turned on her heel to stride back to the inn. In the next instant Arnold grabbed her arm and jerked her backward, against him. She felt his hot breath sting her cheek. She felt his hand cup over her mouth, felt his other arm go around her waist.

This was insane!

Where were all the people? It was dark, clouds obscuring the quarter moon. She could hear men and women laughing, talking, from the posting house, not more than thirty feet away. Then she felt a frisson of fear. Don't be absurd, she told herself. It's Arnold. Only Ugly Arnold. She could handle him, surely. The way she'd handled him back at Damson Farm?

He was dragging her away from the inn. She sent her elbow into his stomach. He grunted but

held on tightly. Lily began to fight him with all
her strength and she knew her blows struck well,
causing him pain. Yet he held on as a mongrel
would to a bone. She tried to bite his hand, but
her teeth only scraped against his smooth palm.

This was ridiculous!

He dragged her behind the stables, into a mal-
odorous alleyway. "Not much further," she
heard him pant near her ear. "I have a room for
us nearby. We'll be alone, Lily, finally alone, and
you'll see, you'll want me."

Lily closed her eyes for an instant, then knew
she had to calm herself. She had to think, to out-
smart Ugly Arnold. Surely that wasn't beyond
her; surely she wasn't that bereft of sense. Then
she heard another man's voice and her heart sank.

"Ye got 'er, eh, Mr. Smith?"

"Aye, I've got her, Boggs. No more need for
you now, my lad. Wait a moment and I'll pay you
the two quid I promised."

"Gawd, what a purty piece she be!" Boggs
marveled. "Lookee at that hair, soft as a kitten's
fur, it is, and that smooth white face, Lordy, purtier than when we saw her at the Pantheon Bazaar, and I want—"

Those were the last words Mr. Boggs spoke.
Lily stared dumbfounded as the huge man fell in
a soundless heap three feet away from them.

Knight! He was standing there in the shadows
gently rubbing the gloved knuckles of his right
hand.

"I suggest, Mr. Damson, that you release her
immediately."

He sounded amused. Really, Lily thought,
didn't he realize that this was at least a little bit
serious, that Ugly Arnold was kidnapping her?

"No!" Arnold screeched. "She's mine, damn
you! Mine and I'll have her, do you hear me?"

"You are yelling loud enough to bring Bow Street down on yourself. Surely I can hear you. However, you may not have her. Let her go now."

Arnold yanked her back harder as he took a step away from Knight. Lily gave him another elbow, this time lower, in his belly. He howled but still held onto her as if she were the only raft in the middle of an ocean.

"You bore me, Arnold," Knight said, "and you are obviously annoying the lady." In the next instant Lily was free, falling to her hands and knees on the filthy ground. She jerked about to see Knight lifting Arnold off the ground by his shirt collar. He shook him like a rat, speaking slowly and forcefully as he did so. "You will go home, Arnold, or I will put a bullet through your arm. Do you understand me?"

"No! I want—"

Knight slammed him against the side of a building. "Listen to me, you miserable little slug. I won't have her bothered again, ever. You come around again, you let me see your ugly face just one more time, and I won't put a bullet through your puny arm, I'll put it through your little black heart. Go home to your wife!" Knight released Arnold and he slid down the wall to the ground. He didn't move. Arnold wasn't stupid when things were properly explained to him.

Knight turned. "Lily, are you all right?"

Lily was still on her hands and knees, looking up at him. "How did you find me?"

He merely shrugged. "You aren't the most creative runaway. I had a feeling that you would return to the posting house you arrived at. And you did. Here, let me help you up." He offered her his hand and she grasped it. She staggered a bit when on her feet, but Knight made no move to assist her. When she was firmly standing again, he took her arm and drew her away from the alleyway. "I would just as soon say what I have to say to you without fear of interruption from either of those two scum."

She didn't utter another word until they reached the hackney that waited on the other side of the inn. "My valise," she said.

Knight didn't pause. He gave her the coldest look. "Forget it." He opened the door and gave her a hand up. He stepped back and said to the driver, "I want you to drive around. I will tell you when to stop."

"Aye, governor," said the driver and clicked his nag into motion. Knight sat himself opposite Lily. Suddenly, without warning, the hackney hit a deep rut and Lily was tossed into his lap. It was as if the dam had broken. His hands were on her upper arms and he was shaking her.

"You damned stupid woman! How could you pull such a ridiculous stunt!"

"I don't know," Lily said, aware that her legs were tangled with his, her breasts pressed against his chest, and that he was holding her up.

Knight cursed luridly, lifted her onto his thighs, clasped her tightly against him, and kissed her, hard.

9

Knight was a wild man. His tongue was probing for entrance—he wanted to taste her now—and to his besotted joy, she parted her lips to him. He felt the moment she responded to him, and her response—uninhibited, incredibly passionate—sent him over the edge. His tongue was in her mouth, delving, learning her textures, reveling in her sweet taste; then, finally, he managed to gain a semblance of control. He drew back a bit, his lips, his tongue, slowing, gentling. But he couldn't gentle his hands and arms. He was clutching her, pushing her back against his arm, and his right hand was at her breast, kneading, *learning* her, and he felt her shudder and arch her back upward, giving herself to him utterly.

He heard a small moan and that sweet siren's sound brought him abruptly to his beleaguered senses. His hands dropped from her so quickly that she nearly fell. He grabbed her about her waist and put her on the opposite seat.

Then he looked at her. The light was dim but it didn't matter, he could still see her, and it shook him to his toes. She was staring fixedly at his mouth. Her incredible eyes had darkened in color with her passion, her hunger for him still there for him to see.

143

It hurt him to breathe. "Lily, don't look at me like that."

She didn't know what he was talking about. She wanted to tell him that she felt the oddest sort of heat deep in her belly, and an ache so insistent and wonderful that it made her press her thighs tightly together. She heard her heartbeat pounding loudly, drowning out everything. She tasted him on her lips with her tongue; her breasts swelled and ached. She felt alive, wildly alive, for the first time in her life. She stared at him, not understanding, but wanting to tell him, to have him make her feel all those things again.

"Stop doing that, dammit!"

It required all his resolution not to pounce on her again. His hands were fisted at his sides. He told them to stay there. Still she sat there just staring at him as if she didn't comprehend what had happened, as if she hadn't wanted him to stop kissing her, to stop touching her, caressing her. . . . "Stop it!"

"I heard you," she said, and her breath expelled on a soft sigh. "I'm not doing anything at all."

He said brutally, to save himself, "You are looking at me like you want me to ravish you, to take you right here in this damned filthy hackney! Is that what you want, Lily? You want me to toss up your skirts and ram myself into you, right here, right now?"

Her wildly beating heart slowed quite suddenly to a painfully diminished pace. The coursing waves of heat receded. She tried to put his angry words together, to make meaning of them.

"The devil take you, woman! Your virgin act is ludicrous! Tris had you since you were fifteen damned years old! What is it? You miss a man? Is that it? You're as randy for me as I am for you?

Why didn't you stay with Ugly Arnold in Yorkshire? He would have been more than willing to
plow your belly whenever you wished it. Lord
knows, it would have saved my sanity!''

He thrust his fist against the ceiling. In a moment, the hackney came to a stop. ''Go home and
go to bed. After all, you do have the headache,
don't you?''

He wrenched open the door and jumped down,
then slammed it. Lily heard him give the driver
directions. She said nothing, merely sat on the
cracked leather seat, her hands tightly clasped in
her lap. It started to rain. She listened to the rat-
tat-tat on the roof of the hackney. Foolishly she
hoped Knight wouldn't be caught in it. She didn't
want him to take a chill.

Fool.

Duckett was waiting for her. He took one look
at her disheveled, dirty clothing, her tangled hair,
her pale face, her shocked eyes, and quickly called
for Mrs. Allgood.

Mrs. Allgood immediately took charge. She
gathered Lily to her side. ''You just come with
me, lovey. I'll tuck you in. No, now don't you
worry about the children. Laura Beth is sound
asleep. His lordship saw to that before he left to
fetch you. No, no need to say anything. I understand, truly I do.''

Lily wondered how she could understand. How
could anyone understand? She didn't herself.

''Oh, dear, I fear your gown is quite ruined.
But your beautiful cloak is all right. The ermine
isn't damaged.''

Within fifteen minutes, Lily was in her long
flannel nightgown, in her bed, Laura Beth clasped
against her side, deeply asleep.

Plow her belly. She supposed that referred to the
act of possession by men. Her fingertips lightly

touched her stomach, then moved slowly lower to where that wonderful throbbing ache had centered. She wasn't stupid. Although she'd never seen a man's body, she knew it was very different from hers, that it had a rod that stuck out from the groin when the man felt desire. One time when Tris had held her closely after her father's death, his sex had pressed hard against her belly. She'd felt nothing except vague distaste then, but later, when she thought about it, she knew he'd wanted to come inside her body.

She'd never really dwelt on the subject of sex after that one time, and on the surface of things the entire business seemed odd in the extreme to her and horribly embarrassing for the man. But it hadn't seemed at all distasteful while Knight had been kissing her and fondling her breast with his wild fingers, molding her against him. She'd wanted more and more and she hadn't realized that he'd stopped wanting her until he'd pushed her away.

Lily shuddered. He'd accused her of driving him mad. Well, she could go to Bedlam with him, for what he had done to her in the hackney had certainly made her become another person, a woman who had no control over herself. She shuddered again, wondering how it would feel to have his long fingers raise her flannel nightgown and stroke her naked flesh. Stop it, you half-wit. She didn't, though, until sleep finally claimed her.

Knight had himself firmly in hand. He realized that he'd placed himself behind his desk to give himself distance, to put her in the position of the supplicant. He didn't care. He needed every advantage with her that he could devise.

Ten minutes later, a light rap sounded on the

library door. "Come," he called, pleased that his voice sounded as indifferent as he planned to act.

Lily slithered into the room. There was no other way to put it, he thought, watching her and feeling himself swell with instant desire. Damn her, why? This morning she was wearing a simple gray muslin gown, cut high under her breasts, sleeves long and fitted, the collar so high it nearly touched her chin. Her luxuriant hair was drawn severely back. He should tell her that such nunlike efforts only made her appear more alluring. It was true that she was incredibly lovely, but he'd known lovely women before, made love to them, enjoyed them, and left them eventually without regrets. What he needed to do was make love to her; then all this ridiculous aberrant behavior would disappear. But he couldn't. She was a lady, the widow of his dead cousin, and she was so passionate that it made him tremble just to remember. He stiffened ramrod-straight in the chair.

"Do come in and sit down, Lily." He himself didn't rise. It was rude, but he didn't care.

She didn't once look at him.

That helped.

"How is your headache this morning?"

That brought her head up and she stared at him blankly.

"Ah, of a certainty that was a lie, wasn't it?"

"Yes," she said as she eased down into a chair. She sighed. "I fear that it was. I should have been more thoughtful before I spoke."

He frowned just a moment, then forced his features into no expression at all.

"Are the children all right?"

"Yes."

"John Jones will be here in three hours for you

to interview him. I trust you plan to remain here for that length of time?''

"I won't leave again unless you toss me out.''

"Oh, I shan't do that. It would doubtless make the children impossible to handle. Also, how could I make them understand that their mother is obviously a very foolish, very stupid woman, who willy-nilly leaves her offspring because of some kind of inexplicable martyrish streak?''

"You probably couldn't. Make them understand, that is. Sam would probably hit you first, particularly if he thought you were insulting me.''

He paused. At least she was speaking to him now. Good. "All right, enough sniping. It brings me no pleasure, especially since all you do is act like a whipped dog.'' He saw her cheeks gain color and knew he was getting her goat. She deserved it. He raised his hand to stop her. "I know why you left yesterday evening. I know about the lady and gentleman who accosted you in the park yesterday.''

That brought her to the edge of her chair. "But Sam and Theo promised, they—''

"Laura Beth didn't promise. She was the one who told me. She told me she wanted to toss the lady into the Tims. She said the lady called you a harlot and a whore and accused you of causing me—a fine, upstanding man of high moral character—to be ostracized by society. My question is, why didn't you bother to enlighten me, Lily? It is a vague possibility that I could have provided some alternative other than flight for you.''

Lily studied the globe that stood beside Knight's huge desk on a brass stand. She said finally, ignoring his question, "It's true. I didn't want you to be upset. I suppose I wanted to protect you, for you don't deserve any of the horrid talk.''

"My God, woman, I pray your form of protection is never in the hands of my enemies!"

"Also, I didn't want you to blame the children or look at all of us and curse the day we arrived."

"I've already done that, innumerable times."

Her eyes flew to his face and he saw pain there and blank surprise.

His hand slashed through the air. "Who was the lady? And the gentleman?"

"She didn't introduce herself. She evidently knew us, though. The gentleman didn't say anything either until after she rode away, and then—" She stopped abruptly and began a concentrated study of the globe.

Knight's gut tightened with cramp. "What did the gentleman say to you?"

"Nothing."

He stood up, flattening his palms on the desktop. "Lily, I swear I'll thrash you—"

"He simply wanted me to be his mistress instead of yours! Isn't that what everyone thinks I am?"

"Ah," he said. "I thought as much."

"If you thought as much, why did you make me say it?"

"Describe them," he said, his voice sharp.

"The young lady was beautiful, dark-haired, foreign-looking, I thought, very exotic. As for the gentleman, he was older, a rake, I believe the term is, and he was riding a pure white stallion and was dressed entirely in white as well."

"Good God!"

"You know who they are?"

"Yes, indeed." Then he began to laugh. He wrapped his arms around himself, his laughter deepening. Lily just watched him, completely at sea. Finally Knight got himself under control. "That lady," he said, "wasn't a lady at all. Her name is Daniella and she is—*was*—my mistress. You're right about her foreignness. She's very much Italian. As for the gentleman, he's her latest protector, Lord Daw by name, and he certainly isn't a nice man. You were right about that, too."

"Oh."

"You see, my dear Lily, I am such an upstanding, moral gentleman that I dismissed my mistress all of two days ago. Actually, she'd begun to bore me excessively." That wasn't precisely the truth, but Lily couldn't know that. "In any case, I'd already heard that Lord Daw had been sniffing about her, and I've never been one to share. I suppose that Daniella wanted some revenge. On you, it appears. It seems I made the immense mistake of yelling out your name when I took my pleasure with her."

Knight stopped. God, what was happening to him? Speaking like this to a lady, to his cousin's widow? He watched her face. Her eyes were open to him. He saw confusion uppermost, saw her tilt her head to the side in question. He wanted to shake her for her absurd act. He wanted to kiss her until she made that siren's sound again, until she fell on him and tore off his clothes.

"Lily," he said, and he sounded as if he were in pain. "Forgive me for my loose tongue. It was a most improper thing to say and—"

"You should hear Sam if you wish to learn about improper."

He smiled at that, but the smile didn't reach his eyes. "What you did was more than stupid. I shan't tell the boys, you may be certain of that, but Laura Beth knows you were gone. She yelled her head off and Betty came for me."

"I thought she was sound asleep."

"Well, she was until something woke her and you weren't there, nor were you to be found."

"Mrs. Allgood said you took care of her."

"What do you expect? That I would leave her bellowing to the rafters? Of course I took care of her. Indeed, she resembled a little clinging monkey and I her mobile tree, carrying her about."

It was Lily's turn to raise her hand to quiet him. "The problem still remains. Do you truly believe people will stop talking about you if the children and I are gone from London?"

"Naturally. Out of sight, out of the gossip mills, the saying goes. If you approve of John, then all of you will leave for Castle Rosse in the next couple of days."

"I don't believe you."

"That people will cease their talk?" Knight shrugged. "You don't know society the way I do. This is my particular jungle, Lily. I know the rules—Lord, I helped form some of them!—and I know how their minds work. You aren't here to be ogled and you no longer exist."

Lily rose from her chair. "All right," she said and looked yet again at the globe.

"Do you wonder where Ceylon is? Or are you trying to locate a small island to flee to?"

"No, it's just that I'm embarrassed . . . about last night. I didn't thank you, Knight, for saving me from Ugly Arnold and his awful friend."

"You're quite welcome."

"I'm also embarrassed about what happened later, in the hackney. I'm sorry I upset you."

Upset me! He was stunned into silence. He'd attacked her, for mercy's sake!

After a moment she continued, sounding genuinely confused. "I'm sorry I behaved so oddly. I don't understand how I could have done such things. If I offended you I am truly sorry. I hope you will forget it."

"You may be certain that I shan't."

She looked at him helplessly, her expression strained.

He spoke very softly. "Do you have any idea what it is like for a man to have a woman offer herself so completely, so freely, to him? To trust him with all of herself? No, of course you don't. Dammit, go away now or I'll say more stupid things. You could at least demand an apology from me, Mrs. Winthrop. I wasn't particularly a gracious gentleman last night. Good God, I not only attacked you, I insulted you." He sighed. "Oh, Lily, please leave now, and if you wish, take the globe with you. It is better, I think, than looking at the idiot male who stands before you."

She moistened her lips. "I'm sorry, truly I—"

"Be quiet! Do you think me an idiot? I know it wasn't me in particular you were responding to. God, how insanely happy Tris must have been for the past five years. To have your passion, your trust; to possess you."

Even as he spoke, she turned on her heel, picked up her skirts, and ran toward the door. He watched her tug fruitlessly on the knob until finally it gave. He thought he heard her sob but couldn't be certain. He was a bastard. He'd hurt her again. He hadn't meant to; he'd just meant to put her in her place.

Whatever that was.

John Jones, Tilney's younger brother, was a likable young man of slight build, wide forehead, and intelligent brown eyes. Better yet, he had a sense of humor, and more importantly, Lily didn't appear to send him into instant tongue-tied infatuation. Knight didn't leave her alone with him. He simply couldn't bring himself to do so. If the fellow succumbed, he wanted to be there to personally boot him out.

After John, as he'd insisted Lily call him, had gone, Knight said, "So you approve, Lily?"

"Oh, yes. He is a very nice young man. The boys will get along quite well with him, I'm sure."

"Better yet, he didn't fall instantly in love with you."

She merely smiled, as if he were speaking childish nonsense. "I wish the boys could have met him."

"They'll meet him on Wednesday. Sam and Theo trust your judgment."

"And yours, of course."

"That's right. Oh, by the way, Theo begins his stint in my library in an hour or so. Trump will assist him to get things started. When he arrives at Castle Rosse, he will continue his work in the library there. It is smaller but, as I recall, in much worse shape."

"Thank you."

He waved that away with a show of impatience. "Should you like to go out for a while? It's warm enough, at least the sun is out, and you can bundle up."

She actually shrank back into her chair. "Oh, no!"

He eyed her. "Coward."

"You're right about that if it means I want to avoid more awful insults."

Knight said nothing, merely took a turn around the room. Lily stayed put and watched him. She couldn't seem to help herself. She sighed, remembering the feel of him, the sensation of his hands on her, how his mouth . . .

"Lily! Stop it!"

Knight swallowed. He'd turned to say something and there she was, staring at him as if he were naked, or soon would be, by her hands, her eyes hungry for him. God, it was wonderful and intolerable.

"I'm going out, Lily. I shan't be here for dinner this evening." He headed for the door, then stopped abruptly. "You will be here when I return, will you not? You don't intend to bolt again?"

She shook her head, saying nothing.

"I bid you good day." And he was gone.

And Lily thought, I keep driving him from his home, but I don't know how or why. She rose slowly and left the library just as Theo and Trump came in, Knight's secretary laughing at something Theo had said. Lily heard Theo exclaim over the very excellent collection his lordship possessed on horse breeding.

"Hi, Mama," Theo said, smiling brightly at her. "This is just wonderful, isn't it?"

Lily patted his arm, then smiled at Trump. "Thank you for your assistance."

She was halfway up the stairs when there came a knock on the front door. She paused, hearing Duckett walk to the door in his magisterial way and open it.

His greeting to the visitors was glacial. Tradesmen? she wondered. Then she heard her own name—Lily Tremaine. Oh, God!

Duckett regarded the two suspicious specimens that stood on the front steps. One of them looked fit enough to kill his own mother, with his low forehead and mean eyes; the other one had bloodshot eyes, a weak chin, and an altogether disagreeable countenance. And here they were asking for Mrs. Winthrop, save they had her name wrong. He said in a voice cold enough to freeze honey, "She isn't here. There is no Lily Tremaine in residence here."

Monk eyed the short and dark and impressive

butler. What a scabbler, this puffed-up little cock. "Lookee 'ere, we knows she's 'ere. Fetch 'er, else ye'll be sorry. We're friends of 'ers, we are, and—"

Not at all likely, Duckett thought, and very efficiently slammed the door in their faces. It was done so quickly that Monk had no time to react. Boy automatically took a step back at the black rage on Monk's face and nearly fell down the remaining five stone steps.

"Ye bastid!" Monk yelled at the closed door. He raised his fist to pound, then thought better of it.

Duckett turned, his face troubled. He saw Lily and quickly went over to her.

She looked more puzzled than scared, he thought, but she was clutching the railing. "Who were they, Duckett?"

"A couple of scoundrels, ma'am. They're gone now. Odd, they asked for you by your father's name. It was Tremaine, wasn't it?"

She nodded, relief flooding her. She felt the full weight of her lie in that moment but resolutely shrugged it off. She'd gotten a brief glimpse of the big man, the one who'd spoken to Duckett. He was a villainous-looking creature and she wouldn't trust him as far as Sam could spit, a phrase of the child's that she found particularly apt at this moment. They had known Tris, obviously. They had known of her, just as clearly. What could they possibly want with her? It was a question that couldn't be answered, she realized.

"They probably made a mistake," she said finally to Duckett, and that stately individual just looked at her.

She went upstairs to the guest chamber that overlooked the front of the house. She saw the two of them standing in the park opposite. One was speaking, the other gesticulating toward the house. Lily quickly pulled away, twitching the curtain back into place.

She was afraid. Something was very wrong.

"Mama?"

Lily turned to see Laura Beth standing in the doorway, Czarina Catherine under her left arm. "Yes, love?"

"Czarina wants to play now. With a grown-up, she told me."

"All right," Lily said, her voice distracted. She had to get hold of herself. She and the children would be leaving London in a couple of days. She had to stay in the house until then. She said with smiling calm, "Let me see what Sam's doing first, Laura Beth."

She was just in time. Sam was standing on a chair in front of a very old oil painting of some Elizabethan Winthrop complete with a wide white ruff, silk doublet, and stuffed trunks.

There was a quill in his outstretched hand and he was poised on the brink of artistdom.

"Sam! Don't you dare!"

He whirled about and tumbled from the chair, landing on his bottom.

After seeing that he wasn't hurt, Lily allowed herself full rein. "What were you going to do?"

Sam twitched and hemmed and hawed and admitted finally, "I was going to give the fellow a mustache. He needs it, Mama. He's got no upper lip. It makes him look shifty."

"Oh, Sam, how could you? I admit that the fellow isn't such a wonderful specimen to look at, but you can't do things like that. The painting doesn't belong to you. I should draw a mustache on you!"

"That is a sight I should much enjoy."

Both Lily and Sam stiffened in appalled silence.

Knight came down the corridor to them. "That, my dear boy, is a great-great-great-someone whose noble appellation, fortunately, I am unable to recall. He was, I was informed by my tutor, quite a villain." Knight moved closer to the painting and stood there studying it, stroking his chin. "I think you're right, Sam. He has no upper lip. I should, however, appreciate it if you would refrain from including a mustache at this time. Perhaps he'll improve given another century or so."

With that monologue completed, Knight saluted Lily and left them, striding down to his bedchamber at the end of the corridor.

Stromsoe suddenly appeared. He harrumphed as he passed, giving Sam a look that could curdle milk. "Evil boy!" he was heard to mutter under his breath.

"Clodpole prig!" Sam called after him.

Stromsoe paused and Lily held her breath. She grabbed Sam's hand, squeezing it hard. The valet didn't turn in the end, thankfully, but continued after his master.

"Oh, dear," Lily said on a sigh. She rose to her feet and pulled the chair to its rightful place.

"Give me the quill, Sam."

"Ah, Mama—oh, all right."

Sam expected a good tongue-lashing, but it didn't come. He saw that Lily was frowning, a worried frown, and he felt guilty about the silly portrait and the prig valet, though not that sorry. Stromsoe also had little upper lip and a weak chin to boot.

"I'll play with Laura Beth, Mama," was his handsome offer.

"Thank you, love. Be gentle with Czarina Catherine, you hear?"

"Yes, ma'am."

* * *

Mrs. Allgood cleared her throat. Lily looked up from the puzzle she and the boys were putting together.

"His lordship requests your presence for dinner, Mrs. Winthrop."

Theo, who was studiously examining a likely piece to fit into the corner of Brighton's Royal Pavilion, looked up. "Oh, do, Mama. And tell Cousin Knight how much I accomplished in the library today!"

"Do," Sam seconded. "Tell him I shan't draw any mustaches on anyone, including the pictures of the ladies."

"He'll be very relieved, I'm sure," Lily said, and perforce, nodded.

"I'll go, too," Laura Beth announced.

Mrs. Allgood smiled. "His lordship did request that you bring the children down so he could enjoy them, Mrs. Winthrop."

Lily agreed. There was nothing else to do. Sam and Theo were excited and Laura Beth was dancing a little jig, far too close to the partially assembled puzzle.

She didn't trust Knight. She imagined that Duckett had informed him of their visitors. And of the name by which they'd requested her.

"Oh, dear," she said. She looked at the boys. "Never," she said, "never tell a lie. It turns into a monster maze with more twists and turns than you can imagine. It doesn't end. Don't do it."

Theo gave her an odd look, but Sam, who couldn't wait to see his lordship, was already at the door.

"Let's go, Mama," said Laura Beth and lifted her arms.

10

Knight stood in isolated splendor in the middle of the drawing room, waiting. He was dressed in evening garb, stark black and white, a most impressive display, so Stromsoe had assured him earlier.

"You've the form, my lord," Stromsoe had said in an unheralded emotional outburst, "the form so, er, well formed to make gentlemen gnash their teeth in envy."

Knight had regarded his usually morose valet with some amazement. Then Stromsoe had ruined his promising beginning by quickly moving from compliments of his master to a whining diatribe about Sam's naughtiness—if indeed it was *only* naughtiness—to the inappropriateness of children in general in a gentleman's town house, to ladies who were widows who behaved most improperly in his, Stromsoe's, view.

Knight had halted his monologue, harking back to Sam. "That painting would not have been hung even by the artist's doting mother. My ancestor was very likely blind, or possessed of execrable taste. It would only have helped had Sam added the mustache. In fact, I may yet let him do it. Now, Stromsoe, you will cease your complaints. Mrs. Winthrop and the children will be leaving Wednesday for Castle Rosse.''

Stromsoe had looked as if he'd burst into happy tears at the news, or at least shout a few halleluxjahs, and Knight wondered suddenly if he and all his servants had become so used to their placid, predictable existence that threatened change upxset them inordinately.

Knight now looked toward the double doors, wondering what was keeping Lily and the chilxdren. He'd backed her against the wall, he knew, smiling at his strategy. With the invitation to the children, she would be forced to come. And that, he'd already admitted to himself, was why he'd returned home. He had truly intended to stay away until midnight at the earliest. He'd planned to visit the opera and take Janine, a lovely and large-breasted courtesan, to bed with him, but it hadn't happened. He'd been walking along, tryxing to enjoy the late afternoon, but had found his thoughts going to Lily. Always Lily. It was damxnably porous of his brain to do this to him.

She was the only woman in his entire adult life who had made him lose control, who'd brought him to his knees. He'd behaved abominably. Had he continued his assault the previous night in the hackney, he wouldn't have given her pleasure, he would have hurt her. He'd been a savage, a barbarian, and he was appalled at himself. He didn't like it, not at all.

Damnation, he was a gentleman. He'd menxtioned that fact to his brain on and off since the previous night, but it hadn't slowed the furious desire he felt for her, the instant and overpowerxing effect even her name had on him.

He'd known her for such a short time in the infinite scheme of things. His reaction to her was absurd.

He heard her soft voice just outside the drawing room doors and felt his body respond. He cursed, swallowed, and willed himself to indifference. All in all, a very tall order.

Sam bounded through the door and came to a panting halt six inches from Knight. "Sir, I'm sorry, truly, it wasn't Mama's fault, she stopped me and scolded me but good, and I swear I won't do it again!"

Knight looked down at the worried little face that wasn't anything like Tris's face but nevertheless was becoming dear to him, and thought, I never wanted to protect my mother as much as he does. And she's his stepmother, not his real mother. "I never assumed it was your mother's fault," Knight said mildly. "It has all the earmarks of a Sam operation, not a Lily operation."

Sam laughed, as Knight had intended.

"He won't do it again, sir," Theo said, coming up to stand beside his brother.

"Don't ever make assurances you have no way of keeping, my dear Theo. Given Sam's record, I shouldn't venture even one very small assurance."

"Oh, sir!" Sam said. "I'm not that bad."

"You're probably a good deal worse," Knight said and then grinned, ruffling Sam's hair.

Knight looked up to see Lily, a wriggling Laura Beth in her arms. She wasn't dressed for the evening—he hadn't given her the time. But she looked so exquisite in her plain muslin gown that his heart ached. He wanted her, desperately.

"Good evening, Lily."

When she raised her eyes to his face, he had the overwhelming urge to grab her, throw her over his shoulder, and ride away into the night with her. Good God, he thought, appalled, if his sire could see him now he'd howl with uncontrollable laughter. And call him a fool, among other things, to confuse old-fashioned manly lust with something else, a something else that didn't exist except in the minds of weak females and between the pages of lurid romances.

"Hello, my lord."

He cocked an eyebrow at that formality but had no time to respond. Laura Beth was at his feet, tugging at his trouser leg. "Good evening, snippet." He hoisted her up and felt her thin arms go about his neck. She gave him a very wet kiss on his cheek.

"Yeck," Sam said in rampant disgust. "Don't, Laura Beth. That's slimy."

"She's just a little girl and doesn't know better," Theo explained and earned a sotto voce "Prig" from his brother.

"I brought them to see you," Lily said quite unnecessarily.

"Yes, I appreciate it. Now, all of you come over by the fire and tell me what you did today."

Lily hung back, watching the viscount with the three children, smiling at how each of them clamored for his attention. Laura Beth sat in marked splendor, quite like a little princess, on Knight's lap, while the boys took up positions on either side, both of them talking at once. She heard Knight laugh and slow them down.

She seated herself in a stiff-backed chair away from the group. I could have stayed gone, she thought, staring at the intimate family tableau. They wouldn't have missed me. They have him, they—

"Mama," Sam called over to her, "what did you say the name of that thing was?"

Lily shook off the altogether silly thought. The fact of the matter was that she couldn't do without them.

"What thing, love?"

"Come here, Mama," Theo said, moving away from Knight. He patted the chair to the right of the viscount.

Lily walked over to them. She met Knight's eyes, and the look in them nearly undid her. Fierce and tender, all at once, and hunger—wild and gentle—again, both at once. She shivered, wondering how he could evoke such opposites together to such a devastating effect on her.

"Come closer to the fire, Lily."

She wanted to shout at him that he was the one making her quiver and shake and shudder, not the temperature of the bloody room. Instead she smiled.

"Now, my dear Sam, what *thing* are you talking about?"

"The thing I found behind that ugly chair in that awful green bedchamber."

Lily swallowed, her eyes avoiding Knight's. "I don't remember anything about that," she said very firmly. "Now what—"

" 'Course you do, Mama. It was long and skinny and very old, you said, like something out of the sixteenth century. Cousin Knight wants to know all about it."

Cousin Knight realized at that point that this *thing* of Sam's was likely something forbidden and that Lily was covered with fear that he'd pounce on the lot of them for disturbing a precious family heirloom of yore. He said easily, "Tell you what, Sam, why don't you bring me this infamous *thing* tomorrow morning. We'll examine it together, just the two of us."

"Yes, sir!"

There, Knight wanted to tell Lily, does that convince you that I'm not a monster?

Thirty minutes later, after the children, complaining and carping, were finally induced to go with Betty to their beds, Knight and Lily were seated in the formal dining room, she at his right. There was silence save for the sound of clattering forks and knives. Duckett was flanked by only one footman—Charlie.

"More rump steak pie, ma'am?" Duckett inquired.

"No, thank you, Duckett. I'm quite stuffed."

"On what?" Knight asked, eyeing her plate askance.

"I could say the same of you. You haven't given a thought to your roast suckling pig."

She was right, he knew, but all appetite had fled when she'd first come into the drawing room. Only an insatiable appetite for her filled his mind. He drank his wine, then dismissed Duckett and Charlie. When the door closed quietly behind them, he said abruptly, "Duckett told me about your visitors."

Lily froze, her fork suspended over a cold mound of mashed potatoes, and automatically began shaking her head.

"I see. So you wouldn't have mentioned it to me, would you? Just like the lady and gentleman in the park—you would have been protecting me? Or is it something else? You have a stained past, Lily?"

"No, how absurd!"

"Duckett told me they had all the earmarks of thieves, smugglers, or even murderers." Knight paused for a moment, looked at her full in the face, and added in quite a grave voice, "He also said they asked to see Lily Tremaine."

Lily quickly looked away from him. She stared hard at those mashed potatoes. They didn't move.

She forced an indifferent shrug. "It is odd, isn't

it? I have no idea who they were. Duckett got rid of them. He's completely unflappable.''

Knight rose and fetched the brandy decanter from the sideboard. She was telling him the truth. It was strange, but after so little time he knew her, really *knew* her. ''I'll pour each of us some. I fancy you need it.''

She didn't demur. She sipped at the fine brandy, feeling its warmth down to her knees. It was wonderful. She'd never tasted brandy before. She said as much.

Knight chuckled. ''It has a way of soothing all the world's ills. That is why, I think, gentlemen drink it after their meals. It helps digest their food and fortifies them for the female company waiting in the drawing room.''

''How very cynical you are.''

''I used to be, in any case,'' Knight said and frowned.

''What's the matter now?''

''Those two men. You're positive that you've never seen them before?''

''I don't think so. No, I'm sure. I haven't the faintest idea who they are.''

''But you've thought about it, haven't you? Obviously they knew of you from Brussels. Could it be that they were cohorts of your father's? Of Tris's?''

''It seems likely,'' she said truthfully. ''After Duckett slammed the door, I went upstairs and saw them across the street in the park. They're truly horrid-looking men, candidates for Newgate, as my father would have said. What could they have had to do with my father? Or Tris, for that matter? I assure you, neither my father nor Tris hired assassins.''

''Why did they call you Lily Tremaine?''

She didn't move a single unnecessary muscle. "I haven't the remotest idea."

"It does give rise to speculation, does it not?"

"If one is a speculator, I suppose."

He laughed, then asked quickly, "What did Tris do to support all of you?"

Lily blurted out, "I don't know, he never told me, but—" She broke off, her eyes flying to his face, knowing that he'd baited her into unwise speech and she'd almost given too much away.

"Continue, Lily."

She shook her head, mute.

"What could you possibly not want to tell me? What does it matter? Tris is dead, well beyond our mortal coils. I must confess that you confuse me, Lily."

"Very well," she said. "If you are so interested, I can tell you that with Tris things seemed to be either feast or famine." *Careful, Lily. You didn't live with them until six months ago!* But she remembered the previous two years when Tris would visit her father. "More feast than otherwise," she added. "My father was just the opposite."

"More famine than feast?"

"Exactly." Lord, that was certainly true. If it hadn't been for Tris, she and her father would have been booted out of their small house in Brussels innumerable times.

"Feast or famine," Knight repeated, looking into his brandy. "That must have been difficult for you, as his wife, during the famine times. And as a daughter during your father's lean times."

"Perhaps."

"You have no idea how Tris made his money?"

"No, I truly don't know, except . . . no, that's ridiculous, just a feeling I had, but—"

"What feeling? Come, tell me."

"I understand that ladies consider such things as money quite beneath their notice, as do gentlemen."

"I don't. You might as well spit it out. What were you going to say?"

Lily frowned. "I said that my father or Tris wouldn't ever have needed assassins. Well, that's true, I'm sure. But occasionally Tris would be gone for up to two weeks at a time, without explanation, really, and he invariably came home with money, lots of it. He'd just laugh if I or anyone asked him what he'd done while away, and give the children the most outrageously expensive presents."

"You're thinking perhaps that Tris was involved in some shady dealings?"

Lily shrugged. "I don't know. You wanted me to tell you and I did. That's all there is to it."

"Did you ever see him with other men? The criminal-looking sort?"

He saw the look of surprise on her face as she nodded. "Yes, once I did. Not those men who came today, but two others who were equally repulsive. When I asked Tris about them, he just laughed again in that dismissive way of his and told me my imagination was far too active."

"Possibly it was." She'd given him a lot to think about. He said after a moment, "Drink your brandy, Lily. Then perhaps you'd care to play piquet with me?"

Lily hedged. She wasn't a complete fool. To spend more time alone with him would lead to her complete undoing, she knew it. "I'm really not very good," she said at last, giving one final look at the mashed potatoes.

Knight chuckled. "Lily, don't lie to me. Tris was a gambler; more than that, he loved any card game. I will not believe that he didn't teach you every single game of chance in existence during your five years together."

Lily rose and tossed her napkin onto her plate. "Very well, my lord. I shall trounce you. I was merely trying to save face for you."

Knight, an excellent card player, said mildly, "I appreciate your consideration, Lily, I surely do."

Knight was still awake when the clock at the end of the corridor struck twelve. Lily hadn't quite trounced him, but she had won two out of three rubbers with a more than respectable difference in their scores.

"What a Captain Sharp you are," he'd remarked after she'd caught him holding a spade guard, and been delighted at her light, carefree laughter. He wanted more lightheartedness from her. He wanted to rid her life of worries and fear and insecurity.

"I fancy," she'd said quite honestly, "that you also have been called that in your lifetime. You aren't an opponent to be despised, my lord."

"What an accolade," he'd said. "Should you care to wager on the outcome of our match?"

She'd cocked her head to one side in question, but her eyes were sparkling with excitement, with challenge. "You know I will win, Knight, so why do you wish to lose a wager to me?"

"Ho, madam, you grow cocky. 'Tis just one rubber we've played. And you did hold the better cards. Now about that wager."

"I don't know. I haven't much money and I'm not such a fool as to believe myself invincible. There is such a thing as bad cards, you know."

"Your skill isn't great enough to overcome bad cards?"

"I'm something of a gambler, I'll admit that,

but I'm not an idiot, nor will I play fast and loose with my few guineas.''

''I wasn't thinking of wagering money, Lily.''

''What, then?''

He sat back in his chair and looked thoughtful. He tapped his fingertips together and knew that Lily was watching him closely. What was she thinking? Perhaps she wanted him again? Knight shook himself. Talk about fools and idiots. . . .

The wager was set, though his had made her suck in her breath in surprise and look at him with ill-disguised excitement.

'' 'Tis too much, Knight, far too much!'' But he knew she wanted him to insist; he saw it on her face.

Ah, but that leap of pleasure in her eyes—he set himself to convince her and she let him.

As for what he would gain if she lost to him, she just shook her head and told him he was being quite silly, inappropriate, and most importantly, he wouldn't win in any case.

He shrugged. ''Then what matter?''

Their play became more serious, their concentration greater. Her mind was agile, her decisions made quickly with no regrets, her game sharp and decisive. Even her voice changed, from soft and serene to crisp and cool. A different Lily. He enjoyed himself thoroughly.

They played three rubbers and he lost. He would have liked to continue, but he knew that she was tired, knew that Laura Beth would more than likely be hopping up and down on the bed at the break of dawn, wanting her mother's attention.

''I lost,'' he said and grinned at her. The candle at his left elbow was nearly gutted.

''You sound pleased about it. That is not natural in my experience.''

"Still, you now own your own mare, Lily. You two are perfect for each other. Violet's bloodlines are impeccable, you know."

"Thank you, Knight. She is wonderful."

Knight wasn't about to tell her, ever, that he'd already bought Violet for her. Well, perhaps someday. His brain stopped cold. He wasn't thinking clearly. *Someday?* He wondered what Lily would have done had she lost to him. Would she have accepted a new wardrobe from him? With him in attendance to help her with the shopping? He grinned again, wickedly.

"What is it?"

"Had I won the wager, I was wondering if you would have paid up, so to speak."

"Justice was done in my opinion," Lily said, trying to sound forbidding and failing woefully. The humor came across quite clearly to Knight's ears. "You are impossible! Further, the only reason I agreed to your very improper wager was because I knew I would win. You really shouldn't make wagers that will make your pockets to let no matter what the outcome. Now, I am going to bed, my lord. Good night, and thank you for Violet."

He rose and stood there for a moment. He didn't say anything, merely towered over her. He raised his hand and lightly stroked his fingertips across her smooth cheek. "Good night, Lily," he said, leaned down, and lightly kissed her mouth.

He turned away quickly, leaving her to stare at his rigid back. . . .

Now the damned clock was moving quickly toward three-thirty in the morning. Next time he would wager the same thing and next time he would beat her. He smiled at the thought and finally fell into a deep sleep.

* * *

John Jones said in a humorous voice to Lily, "My youngest brother is just like Sam, ma'am. My mother used to tear her hair and call him her towheaded nemesis. His name is Robert. He's all of eighteen now and terrorizes the dons at Oxford."

Lily groaned at that. "Does it never end, then?"

"Who knows? I have to say, though, that one is never bored in Robert's company."

"At least you have experience, John."

"I love my brother a good deal, ma'am. I found that if he had direction and activities that ran him ragged, he tended to fall into fewer scrapes. Now, may I meet the boys?"

Lily made the introductions, then stood back to watch. Sam did a thorough, very nearly rude examination. Theo smiled shyly at the new tutor but was noticeably wary. John remarked to Theo, "His lordship tells me you've undertaken the cataloging of his library. Lord, what a task. Perhaps you'll be able to tell me about it."

Score one for John Jones, Lily thought, smiling to herself.

"I shall be an artist," Sam announced, interrupting Theo after a good four minutes had passed. Lily was pleased at his un-Sam-like show of patience. Four minutes was an eternity for Sam.

"An artist?" John said, turning.

"Yes, Cousin Knight said I should begin with one of the Winthrop ancestors up in the eastern corridor. The fellow in the portrait needs a mustache. He has no upper lip."

John didn't crack a smile. "Perhaps it would behoove you to practice drawing mustaches a bit before you attrempt the real and lasting one. Once drawn, you know, it's there for all succeeding generations to observe. You wouldn't want your great-grandson to say, 'That's my great-grand-father's handiwork. He had talent, obviously, but he didn't practice enough.' ''

Sam appeared much struck by this display of logic until he remembered his duty. He shot a look at Lily, then said, "Sir, Theo and I must ask you your intentions toward our mother."

"That's right, sir," Theo added, unconsciously moving closer to Lily.

Lily laughed at John's aghast expression. "I—I don't understand, boys," he began. She could see the red flush creeping up his neck above his collar.

"We must be careful of our mother," Sam said. "Men act stupid around her and we have to protect her."

"Sam! Do stop it!"

"I swear to you," John said, getting hold of himself and the situation, "that I shan't ever have one single stupid thought of your mother." He placed his hand over his heart.

"Or act?" Sam pressed.

"That's enough," Lily said, stepping toward John. "You've quite embarrassed him, you know, and probably insulted him as well."

"No, no, ma'am," John said. "Really, Theo, Sam, I shall be the model of rectitude around your mother."

"All right," said Sam. "But we'll be watching, sir!"

"Are you certain you still wish their company, Mr. Jones?" Lily asked.

"Yes, ma'am. I think we shall all suit wonderfully."

"Very well. I shall leave you now. Boys, do as Mr. Jones tells you. I'll be with Laura Beth."

Well, Sam thought, kicking a pebble from his path, he'd practiced a good fifteen minutes. Indeed he had. He'd even shown John the portrait, pointed out that just a few brush strokes would cure the ancestor's problem, but John had insisted he practice more. Sam had filled up the drawing paper with mustaches, so many he knew he'd dream about them, not a pleasant dream either. He'd slipped out of the room, bored, tired of listening to Theo prose on about those steam engines of his. And it appeared that their new tutor was equally enthralled.

It was enough to drive a fellow out of doors, which was exactly where Sam had been driven. Duckett hadn't been at his usual post, and no one observed him leave. The afternoon was overcast and cold. The wind cut right through Sam's jacket. But he didn't want to go back. It wasn't fair that Theo held all John's attention. He was nearly as bad as Laura Beth.

Sam walked a good four feet off the path to kick another pebble. At least tomorrow they'd go to Castle Rosse. He wondered if there were other children, if they'd be able to play outside, if there'd be a stable and lots of horses. He felt a moment of guilt at disobeying Lily. But who cared? He would just be outside for another ten minutes, then he'd go back into Cousin Knight's house and no one would be the wiser.

He started whistling.

"My Gawd! Ain't that one of Tris's nippers?"

Sam's head came up at the sound of his father's name. He saw two vastly ugly men, both bundled up against the shrill north wind. They were staring at him. One of them was gesticulating wildly at him.

"Aye, his littlest nipper, I think. No, there's a little girl, too."

Monk shot Boy an annoyed look at his ridiculous accuracy. "Right into our 'ands, eh, Boy? 'Ey, you! Little nipper!"

Sam stopped, but he was poised for flight. He watched the larger of the men stride toward him. His boots were dirty, the bottom third of his greatcoat covered with mud. He was not a pleasure to behold. However, he didn't need a mustache. His upper lip was quite thick and prominent.

"I'm a friend of yer pa's. Yeah, Tris Winthrop. Me and Boy 'ere was 'is pals."

That seemed more than unlikely to Sam. "You're a lying brute," Sam shouted.

"Bloody mouthy little nipper! Ye come 'ere!"

Sam, no fool, turned on his heel and ran as fast as his legs would pump. Suddenly he felt a huge arm close around his middle and lift him straight off the ground. He could see the Winthrop town house in the distance. Oh, dear, he thought, and sent his elbow backward.

"Ouch!" The arm tightened and Sam couldn't breathe.

" 'E don't look like Tris, Monk. Ye sure 'e's one of 'is nippers?"

"Aye, I'm sure. What's yer name, ye foul little brat?"

Sam shook his head. "I don't know any Tris. I live just over there. You don't let me go and every Runner in London will be after you. They'll hang you and put your heads on pikes and cut out your guts and make you eat them."

Monk laughed. "Wunnerful creative powers the nipper's got, eh, Boy? Ye don't look like yer pa, brat. Ye sure yer mother didn't play ole Tris false?"

"Let me go," Sam yelled, trying again with the elbow in the big man's belly. Again the arm tightened and choked him and he gasped for breath.

"Tell ye what, little fellow. Me and Boy 'ere think you're a gift, just for us. Ye'll come with us, and then your ma—your pa's whore, I mean to say—will give us wot's ours."

Sam heard only the insult to Lily. These terrible men would hurt her.

What was he going to do?

Even at the age of six, Sam wasn't much of a believer in divine providence. Thus, when he saw a man in a stylish beaver hat and swirling great-coat come into view, he was able at first just to stare at him dumbly. Then he yelled at the top of his lungs.

"Help me! Kidnappers! Kidnappers!"

"Ye damned little brat, I'll cook yer hash!"

11

The gentleman paused, frowned, then shouted, "Drop the boy! Now, or it'll be the worse for you!" He suited action to words. Quick as a flash the top came off his cane and out came a glittering sword stick. He brandished it in the air and began to run toward them.

Monk was furious. "Ye damned little brat! Oh, damnation and blast!"

Boy picked up a rock from the side of the path and threw it at the charging gentleman.

"Ye blinking ass! Oh, damn, let's scuttle the pike!"

Monk dropped Sam like a stone and scurried off in the opposite direction.

"You bloody cowards!" Sam yelled, waving his fist toward the running men. "You'll pay, I'll see to it! My cousin Knight will slice your ears off!"

The gentleman stopped, carefully resheathed his sword, then offered Sam a hand.

"Hello, Sam," Julien St. Clair said. "How nice to see you again. Who were your friends?"

"Oh, sir! I don't know, but they knew who I was. They were up to no good, that's certain."

"Doubtless you're right. Do you remember me? I'm Julien St. Clair, a friend of your cousin Knight's."

"Yes, sir, I remember you. I met you at Gunthers. Your wife is nearly as beautiful as my mother."

"Thank you. I'm certain my wife would appreciate hearing how you, well . . . never mind that. What are you doing out here alone, Sam, if I may ask?"

Sam flushed and Julien raised a brow.

"Of course you have your mother's permission?"

Sam wondered briefly if he could get away with a lie but quickly decided he dared not try it. Julien St. Clair knew Cousin Knight. He'd be found out. The deck, as his father used to say, was stacked against him. "No, sir, my mama doesn't know. She was playing with Laura Beth, and our new tutor was listening to Theo prose on and on about his stupid steam engines."

"I see," Julien said thoughtfully, studying the boy. "Why don't we return to Winthrop House? You can share a cup of tea with me, perhaps." Actually, Julien had his mind set on a brandy.

"You wouldn't mind, sir?"

What adult could be immune to that plea? Julien wondered. He knew exactly what the boy was asking and it amused him. "I'd make a wonderful alibi, no doubt," he said. "But, Sam, it won't work. Knight must be told about those men. It wouldn't be right to keep such a thing from him."

Sam looked as if it were the rightest thing in the world, but he managed, wisely, to hold his tongue.

Knight, who had arrived home just five minutes earlier, was rather surprised when Julien, with Sam in tow, appeared in the library doorway.

"Good day, Knight. Behold a savior delivering your cousin to you from the maw of kidnappers."

"What the devil are you talking about, St. Clair?" Knight paused at the look on Julien's face and quickly added, "Sam, go ask Duckett for some tea and cakes. Go!"

"Now, what happened? Oh, yes, come sit down, Julien."

"My thanks. Yes, well, I came along—quite minding my own business—to see Sam being held under the arm of the most contentious-looking creature imaginable. His cohort looked little better. Sam was yelling at the top of his lungs, bless his presence of mind. I had my sword stick, thankfully, drew it, and dashed forward like a regular St. George. The fellow dropped Sam and the two of them fled in the opposite direction. I didn't go after them, needless to say. After all, there were two of them, and I had no wish to have my gullet carved out, not even to impress Sam with my heroism."

"I see," Knight said slowly.

"You know who those men are, perhaps?"

"I have an excellent idea. Did Sam tell you what they wanted of him?"

"No, we didn't speak of that. Hopefully they said something of value to him."

Knight was silent. He paced the library and continued silent. He turned abruptly. "Don't say any of this to Lil—Mrs. Winthrop. I don't want her unduly worried. She and the boys will be leaving for Castle Rosse tomorrow morning. They will be well out of the way of any more villains."

"Doesn't she have the right to know?"

"No. I will decide what she should and shouldn't know."

"Quite the autocrat you've become, old man."

"Brandy, Julien?"

"Yes, thank you."

Knight was in the process of pouring when he

heard Lily's and Sam's voices outside the library door. He closed his eyes a moment, vowing Sam to silence. But it wasn't to be.

There came a knock on the door. As it opened, Knight heard Sam say with great descriptive relish, "They were ugly and awful, Mama!"

"Sam loves his mother," Julien observed. "You truly didn't expect him to keep mum, did you?"

Knight cursed softly, downed his brandy in one long drink, and stared balefully toward the half-open door. "Come," he called.

Lily's face was pale, but she appeared otherwise composed. "Good afternoon, my lord," she greeted Julien. "I trust your wife is well?"

"Yes, certainly, Mrs. Winthrop. Please, ma'am, you needn't pursue social vanities with me, not when you're bursting with questions."

"Thank you, my lord. Come here, Sam. You will tell me and Knight exactly what happened." To Julien, she added, "If you will interpolate when necessary, my lord."

Sam knew he was in for a scold at the very least. From the thundercloud expression on his cousin Knight's face, he suspected it just might be a hiding. He drew a deep breath and plunged forward.

". . . and then the huge man said real loud, 'Isn't that one of Tris's nippers?' Then they called each other by their names—Monk and Boy—I'm sure, even though they sound odd."

"Just a moment, Sam. Describe these men."

Sam described Monk and Boy with some inaccuracy due to the perspective of a young child well under five feet of height. Julien ably assisted to right the matter. When all was said and straightened out, Knight spoke in a voice that he'd scarce ever used in his adult life. "Go to your room now, Sam. You will stay there until tomorrow morning. You will have your dinner, but by yourself, in your room. What you did was stupid and ill-advised. Apologize to your mother, then off with you.''

''I'm sorry, Mama.''

Lily scarce heard Sam's abject words. She was staring at Knight in growing fury and surprise. How dared he discipline Sam! Still, she knew the value of adults sticking together when it came to punishment. She herself, upon hearing of Sam's escapade, had wanted to strangle him, spank him until he couldn't sit, and hug him tight since he was safe again. She and Tris had formed a partnership in that regard. He never gainsaid her orders, nor she his. She held her tongue now, but it was difficult. This man wasn't the children's father.

But he *was* their legal guardian. She realized quite suddenly that he had more to say about their behavior, and about the consequences of their behavior, than did she.

Sam, his lower lip nearly pouched down to the floor, left the library, his step as slow as a snail's. Lily still held her peace. Knight said, his voice laced with amusement, ''Lily, don't let Julien's presence stop your flow of outrage. Come, spit it out before you choke on your bile.''

Her chin went up. Julien sat back on the settee, an interested spectator. Knight was regarding her with open amusement. He was, she realized, goading her.

''I would have thrashed him soundly,'' she said. ''I would have locked him in the attic and given him only bread and water for . . . three days.''

That took him aback, Lily saw, and was more than pleased with her outrageous lie. ''Sending him to his room—which he shares with Theo—

isn't at all a punishment. He will enjoy himself immensely, and because Theo loves him, he won't leave him to any isolation. He will consider it his duty to amuse him.''

''Your logic is shattering. I shall send him to spend the evening with Laura Beth.''

Lily laughed at that, unable to help herself. ''Now, that would be a punishment. Sam would probably poke out Czarina Catherine's painted eyes were he banished to spend even an hour alone with Laura Beth.'' To Julien, she added with a faint smile, ''Czarina Catherine is her doll—''

''An extension of her arm, more's to the point,'' Knight said.

''Yes, her constant companion. Now, Knight, you may as well say it. Those two men are the same two who came here yesterday.''

Julien got to his feet. He smiled gently at Knight, then at Lily. ''You are doubtless wishing me to Jericho at the moment. Not that I'm not fascinated with all of this, but you need to work it out between you. Also, I don't account myself a sterling referee. Actually, before all the excitement, I was just coming to see you, Knight, to inquire if you wished to attend a mill with me. Near Backlesfield, tomorrow afternoon.''

Knight's eyes gleamed, but he said with commendable fortitude, ''No, I think not, Julien.''

''Why not?'' Lily asked. ''We knew you wouldn't be accompanying us to Castle Rosse,'' she continued, disappointment lying heavy on her tongue but, thankfully, not sounding through in her voice. '' 'Twould be a great waste of your time.''

Knight was torn. He was worried that the men would see them leave and follow. On the other hand, he knew if he accompanied them, he would have the very devil of a time keeping his hands off Lily. He needed space from her, and time. He needed very much to regain his perspective on life and he needed to take Janine to bed, at least a dozen times. He needed to get his rudder back on an even keel. If he could ensure that she and the children would be safe . . . "Very well, Julien. Fetch me at two o'clock."

"Excellent. Mrs. Winthrop, a pleasure, ma'am."

Once they were alone, Knight said quickly, "I will send two Runners with you to Dorset, to Castle Rosse. You will have ample protection."

Lily was both regretful and relieved that Knight wouldn't be coming with them. She would miss him. Dreadfully. "I'm sure we'll have no problems. The men can't be observing the house all the time, and we can make certain they're not around when we leave tomorrow morning."

Knight waved her observation away. "The question is why, Lily? What is it they want? They called him Tris's nipper. Obviously they were cohorts of Tris's, or associates, or something, for God's sake. They were quite willing to take Sam. As a lever? Quite possibly. Think. What could they want?"

Lily moved away from him, toward the bowed windows that looked onto the park opposite.

"Lily, you must have something of value they want."

"I don't know!" She whirled about to face him as she spoke. "I'm telling you the truth. I have no idea what they want."

"Tris was murdered just before he arrived home. Is that true?"

"Yes."

"Murdered, perhaps, before he could tell you what it was he had of value."

"There was nothing of value in his house or in

his personal things. Nothing. This is a great deal of speculation, Knight."

"Have you another suggestion, ma'am?"

"You needn't get in a snit!"

"Have a cup of tea, Lily."

"Duckett hasn't brought it yet."

Knight, frustrated, strode to the door, yanked it open, and bellowed, "Duckett! The tea, man!"

"My lord."

Knight jumped a good foot. Duckett was at his elbow, silent as a shadow, the tea tray in his arms.

"Damn you," Knight said under his breath.

"I trust you will retract that, my lord, when you have found your good nature again."

"I'm fast running out of good nature."

"I devoutly pray that isn't true, my lord."

"Serve the tea, damn you."

Duckett served the tea in the tense silence. "The children, my lord?" he asked, once done.

"Yes, take them tea, if you please," Knight said. "Sam also. He must have a mighty thirst after his excitement."

"Not much of a punishment for his disobedience of me," Lily said, her eyes narrowing.

"So I'm not used to being a parent! I did what I thought he deserved. You want me to flog him? Well, I won't do it."

Lily chuckled. Her smile was crooked, endearing, and made him so instantly randy that he gulped down his tea and scalded his mouth. He gulped again and groaned.

Duckett said not a word. Prudently, he left the library, after nodding to Lily.

"I'm sorry," Lily said after a moment.

"What? I'm burned and you're sorry?"

"Not about that, that was your own fault. I'm sorry for baiting you about Sam's punishment. I couldn't physically harm him either. I do want sometimes to wring his neck, but in reality, I would just as soon wring my own. I will leave you now. Do forgive us for cutting up your peace.''

''Are you going to rescue Sam?''

She shook her head. ''Of course not. If adults don't stand together, there would be chaos. And believe me, you don't truly comprehend chaos until you've seen children in control.''

She turned and he heard himself say, ''Lily.''

''Yes?'' She faced him again, and for several moments, all he could do was just stare at her.

''You're . . .'' *So exquisite all I want to do is kiss you, every inch of you.* ''I will see you at dinner.''

''I don't think so, Knight. I have a lot of packing to do.''

''As you wish,'' he said, trying his damnedest to sound indifferent.

It was only seven o'clock in the morning. The sky was overcast, the fog thick, so thick Lily couldn't see more than two feet in front of her. It was cold, too, a damp, roiling cold that cut through any amount of cloaks and scarves and vests to one's very bones.

Knight would have shivered as well, but he was too busy checking with the two Runners to ensure that Monk and Boy were nowhere in the vicinity.

''I've told the Runners to keep a close watch,'' he said to Lily. ''They have complete descriptions of this Monk and Boy. You're not to worry. You will arrive at Castle Rosse this evening. They're expecting you.''

''Thank you, Knight.''

''Cousin Knight!'' Theo's head poked out the carriage window.

''Yes?''

"I'll finish the library when we return to London."

"I know, Theo."

Sam's head appeared, then Laura Beth's. Knight stepped to the window and lightly touched his fingers to each child's face. He said in a low voice, "You will take good care of your mother. Don't drive her to the brink of insanity, all right? And keep an eye out for Sam's villains."

"Yes, sir!"

"And mind Tucker, you hear me?"

"Yes, sir!"

Knight assisted Lily into the carriage, then quickly closed the door. "A safe journey," he said and stepped back.

He nodded to Tucker Dilly, the coachman, and the carriage rolled forward. Three children, John, and Lily were in one carriage. Knight felt a good deal of pity for the two adults. The Runners, two men of unprepossessing mien and decades of experience, gave Knight a confident salute, then spurred their horses after the carriage.

Knight stood quietly on the lowest step until the carriage had disappeared into the fog. Back in the house, he made his way upstairs to his bedchamber. He paused for a moment in the corridor, hearing Stromsoe say in a pleased voice, "Ah, the quiet! Finally, quiet! A gentleman's house shouldn't be filled with children. Ah, finally."

Knight grinned. It *was* quiet.

Janine, an ingenue of sorts who played a milkmaid in a current production on Drury Lane, had a limpid sort of beauty, little conversation, and thick, very long blond hair. She was as skilled as Daniella, and Knight had sex with her three times before stumbling home at three o'clock in the morning

At least he hadn't shouted out Lily's name when he'd come to his release with Janine.

The next morning, he lay in bed a while, looking up at the fancy molding on the ceiling. He grinned at himself, remembering his vagrant thoughts the previous afternoon at the prizefight in Becklesfield. He'd kept wondering what Theo and Sam would have had to say about the two fighters. He feared he hadn't been the most entertaining of companions to Julien. As it was, though, he'd won four hundred pounds in wagers on the champion.

"You going to buy a new hunter with your ill-gotten gains?" Lord Alvanley had asked.

Knight just shook his head. He thought he'd buy Sam and Laura Beth ponies and have them taken to Castle Rosse.

Sir Charles Ponsonby strolled over to Julien's phaeton. "Where are your children, Knight?" He made a big show of looking all about the phaeton.

"They're at Castle Rosse."

"And their glorious mother?" asked Sir August Krinke, a fellow with more money than good sense and an odiously leering eye.

Knight paused, looked directly at Sir August, and said with a deep drawl, "With her children, naturally."

Sir August took a step back at that look. Knight Winthrop was known as a very urbane gentleman, but the look in his eyes was enough to make a civilized man pause.

More acquaintances stopped by, and Knight, once into conversation, was pleased that Lily didn't cross his beleaguered mind more than three or four times during that hour. There was drinking at the Mordant Tooth Inn just outside

Becklesfield, the six or so gentlemen in the party
filled with high spirits and ribald comments, none
of them, fortunately, directed at Lily or Knight's
children.

Then he'd gone to Drury Lane and suffered
through the awesomely bad comedy and taken
Janine, the milkmaid, to bed.

At least now, he thought, he was well rested.
He stretched as Stromsoe came into his bedchamber. ''Ah, my lord, you're awake. I've brought
your coffee.''

And so the day begins, Knight thought, pulling
himself up on two very fluffy pillows.

The day seemed empty and yet, at the same
time, frenetically busy. Odd, but it was so.

The house was so bloody quiet.

Knight could even hear Duckett walk into a
room now.

''May I inquire if you will be dining at home
this evening?'' the butler inquired.

Knight shook his head. ''No, and I shan't be
home until very late.''

Duckett knew that ''home very late'' meant a
female to ease his lordship. He withdrew as silently as he'd entered. Goodness, but the house
was quiet!

Castle Rosse
Dorset, England

Lily was exhausted. Finally, alone in her own
bed, without three pairs of hands demanding this
and that and three mouths all speaking at the
same time. She fancied John was just as relieved
to find himself alone as was she.

The butler at Castle Rosse, Thrombin, had

greeted them with pleasure—much to Lily's relief—as had the housekeeper, Mrs. Crumpe. The Runners were duly taken care of, assuring Lily before they left for their return to London that there hadn't been a sight or a sniff or a sound of the two men. No, ma'am, not a single thing to worry about now.

Lily had burrowed more deeply under the pile of wonderfully warm covers when she heard her bedchamber door open. She froze, jerking upright in her bed.

"Mama?"

Laura Beth. "Come here, lovey," she said quickly, not fighting the inevitable.

Twenty minutes later, Lily, Laura Beth snuggled against her, fell into a deep sleep. Even with her small bed partner, Lily was well rested the next day. She met John downstairs in the morning parlor, eating breakfast with the boys. He was saying easily to a rapt Theo and a bored Sam, "Castle Rosse is a country seat of antiquity and history. It was built by Sir Peter Winthrop, then Baron Rosse, in 1568, during the reign of Elizabeth the First."

"That's why it's so drafty in our room," Sam said, not stopping in his chewing of bacon. "It's bloody ancient."

"It's historic," Theo said with a frown at his brother. "And mind your tongue, Sam. You know Mama doesn't like it."

John managed to keep a straight face. "It is something of a rabbit warren, but we will enjoy exploring, I doubt not. I was even told that there are priest holes. Perhaps we can find one."

Lily said a quiet good-morning and took her place, listening to John and the boys.

". . . and in the early eighteenth century, it is

said that the then Princess Anne stayed here but a fortnight before she became queen."

"Mama showed us a picture," Theo said. "She was a very fat lady."

"I also pointed out, if I recall correctly, that she was ill and that was the cause of her being fat."

"Yes, well, then Castle Rosse was also a meeting place for some of the high-ranking ministers of George the Second."

Sam yawned over his toast and Lily shot him a look. He began, very quietly, to torment Laura Beth.

Lily realized after some minutes that she kept looking toward the door, waiting for Knight to enter. It was absurd. She found she had no more appetite.

Castle Rosse *was* a rabbit warren, but an immensely beautiful one, Lily discovered during the next several days in the company of Mrs. Crumpe. Floors dipped and rose, several feet at a time; stairs ended abruptly; small rooms of no use whatsoever gave onto smaller passages that led nowhere in particular. And it was cold, dreadfully so. The children's nursery was on the third floor in the West Wing, and it took a good ten minutes to reach it from the drawing room on the second floor in the North Wing, if one didn't lose one's way, that is.

"This is ridiculous," Lily announced the second morning. "John, I'm going to have all of us moved together in the East Wing. There are so many vacant rooms, and many of them adjoin, two and three at a time." John heaved a sigh of relief. He was getting chilblains.

And so the Winthrop party occupied the second floor in the East Wing of Castle Rosse. The servants were most appreciative of this collective grouping. "I vowed I would stop breathing,"

Mrs. Crumpe said, beaming at Lily. "It is very kind of you, ma'am, to stay all together like this."

The only bedchamber that wasn't taken over was the master suite, located at the very end of the corridor.

"I remember your husband, Mrs. Winthrop," Thrombin said unexpectedly one afternoon as he straightened the tea tray on the low marquetry table in the drawing room. "A very fine gentleman. I am sorry that he is gone."

"Thank you," Lily said. "We all miss him."

She looked up to see Sam standing in the doorway, unabashedly listening.

"Come in, Sam. Perhaps Mr. Thrombin will tell you about your father."

To her pleasure, Thrombin did. He hadn't seen Tris in over ten years, but he remembered the handsome, brash young gentleman and his impact on his cousin, Knight Winthrop. "A dasher, your father was, Master Sam, always ready for any trick, any dare. Your cousin Knight, our master, you know, well, he worshipped your papa. Followed him everywhere, and your papa, he was the real gentleman, he was, and nice as could be to his younger cousin."

But it was from Mrs. Crumpe, one day later, that Lily discovered Knight's precepts of life.

12

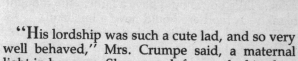

"His lordship was such a cute lad, and so very well behaved," Mrs. Crumpe said, a maternal light in her eyes. She paused, frowned a bit, then added, "Well, most of the time he was well behaved. Like all gentlemen, he was occasionally a wild young stallion. But not malicious, no, never petty or mean was our little lordship."

Lily smiled at that, just imagining the kinds of scrapes young Knight had got himself into. He most certainly had been more like Sam than like Theo. She and Mrs. Crumpe were touring the long, narrow portrait gallery in the West Wing. Lily couldn't take her eyes off the nearly life-size portrait before her. It showed a fifteen-year-old Knight standing beside a bay gelding. He was tall, straight, and there was humor in his eyes, mocking, fun humor. He was a winsome boy who gave promise of becoming a handsome man, which he had.

"His mama died when he was ten, you know. He'd never seen much of his father, as his lordship believed firmly that a child shouldn't be cursed with the faults of his sire but left to develop a set entirely his own."

That bit of information startled Lily into exclaiming, "What? That is absurd! You mean that the former Viscount Castlerosse simply ignored his own son?''

''Why, yes, but on purpose, you understand,'' Mrs. Crumpe said, now dusting the portrait. ''He was an older gentleman when our lordship was born. He didn't wed until he was forty, and his viscountess was a girl not yet twenty. But he got her with child almost immediately and then took himself back to London and his life there.''

Lily was appalled to the tips of her toes. Goodness, a little boy should have a father, she thought blankly. A mother should have a husband.

''I'm sure all this is nothing new to you, Mrs. Winthrop, knowing the viscount the way you must,'' Mrs. Crumpe continued in her comfortably certain voice. ''He holds the very same philosophy as his father. He won't marry until he's forty. I will tell you, Mrs. Winthrop, Mr. Thrombin and I were surprised—yes, we'll admit it—that you and the children actually *stayed* with his lordship in his London house for such a long time. His lordship, like his sire, feels that children should be left strictly to their nannies and tutors.'' She marveled out loud again, shaking her head in wonder. ''Almost two weeks. I fancy he was near insane with all the children's noise and shenanigans.''

No, Lily thought, he'd been wonderful. Not to be married until he was forty? He was only twenty-seven!

Something deep inside her protested in a dull, thudding way.

''And this was his mother, Lady Elysse. Lovely, isn't she? His lordship has her eyes—fox's eyes, everyone called them. It's that gold mixed in with the brown, you see. Very unusual.''

''Did the former viscount love his young wife?''

Mrs. Crumpe allowed a bit of reproof to show

through. "Indeed not, Mrs. Winthrop. He thought such emotions pure sham and absurd. Love, he would say in that contemptuous way he had, was for weak heads and for those who hadn't the wit to see six inches in front of their faces. Love wasn't for a strong-headed gentleman like himself, oh, no, indeed. I fancy 'tis but another of the beliefs his lordship holds dear."

Lily trailed dutifully after Mrs. Crumpe, taking in everything she was saying. Somehow she couldn't seem to picture Knight as a mirror of his father's beliefs.

For some unexplained reason, the beautiful house and immaculate grounds, first beheld as a sanctuary and a home, now seemed a prison. There was no love here, she thought, no caring . . . no shouting, no arguments, no *life.*

Near Winthrop House
London

Knight was whistling. His body felt marvelously drained, quite sated; all in all, very pleased with itself. Everything was set into motion now. It was just a matter of waiting. And keeping alert. Whistling always helped.

The only thing was, he thought, frowning as he recalled yet again his session with Janine, Lily's hair was a richer, more variegated blond than Janine's and it was softer. At least he thought so. He had touched Lily's hair the evening he'd saved her from Ugly Arnold, then attacked her in the carriage. Whistle louder, he told himself, and think about other things.

Mr. Wheat, one of the Runners who had escorted Lily and the children to Castle Rosse, had dutifully reported to him. No sign of the men. All was well. Monk and Boy were nowhere near Castle Rosse. They had to be here in London.

That was a relief. He wondered when Monk and Boy would make their next move. They perforce had to make one. It was just a matter of time and opportunity, and for the past two days and nights, Knight had been giving them more than ample opportunity. Now he was walking alone, a perfect target.

He grinned. It obviously hadn't occurred to Lily that he would have to be their target, since she'd left the scene. Otherwise he hadn't a single doubt that she would have insisted upon somehow protecting him.

He saw a cloaked man turn out of a side street, pause for a moment beneath a light on the eastern corner of Portland Square, then nod politely toward Knight and continue on his way. Knight wanted to laugh aloud. That certainly wasn't Monk or Boy. This gentleman was the epitome of civilization.

Knight began whistling again.

When the attack came, it was quick and quiet. Knight *felt* their presence rather than saw them, and was able to free his sword stick.

"Ah, 'tis the fancy governor, all right," Monk said with great relish. Knight finally made him out in the shadows, crouched over and feinting back and forth as he tossed the gleaming silver stiletto from his right hand to his left and back again. "Circle 'im, Boy, but stay out of the way of 'is sticker."

"Gentlemen," Knight said loudly, all amiability, "finally you show yourselves. Why don't you question me rather than try to cut out my innards?"

Knight saw Boy's figure from the corner of his

eye. He wasn't a stealthful mover, thank the powers for small favors.

"Awright, ye fancy cove, ye tells us where the sparklers are and we'll let yer innards stay in yer gut."

"What sparklers are you referring to?"

"Tris's fancy piece knows, oh, ah, she does! Ye tells us or she does, and we'll find 'er, don't ye doubt that."

Tris's fancy piece? Knight shook his head. "I repeat," he continued, taking a quick step away from Boy's outstretched arm. "What sparklers?"

"Billy's Baubles, 'tis wot Tris called 'em," Monk explained. "It was this cove named Billy who 'ad these sparklers made in Paris for 'is little lady friend, a female sort named Charlotte. Then this Charlotte breaks off their betrothal and Billy sends back the sparklers, only we get 'em and snab off afore anyone's the wiser."

"Tris 'id 'em, no doubt about that," Boy put in. "Then 'e shoots us the trove, 'as us snabbled and tossed on our ears in jail, 'e does, and takes the sparklers. Now, ye tells us and we'll let ye go. Surely Tris's little whore told ye. Ain't ye taking care of 'er now?"

Jewels, in other words, Knight thought as he mentally translated their cant. So Tris was a jewel thief, was he? And he double-crossed these two. Not too wise a move. What the hell had happened to his devil-may-care cousin? A damnable criminal? He tried to close his mind to their other words. *Tris's little whore . . .*

"Sorry, fellows," Knight said as calm as could be, "but you've got the wrong cove. I don't know a thing about Billy's Baubles, not a damned thing."

This announcement didn't endear him to either Monk or Boy.

Knight carefully positioned himself. Monk and Boy weren't strategic fighters. They were dirty fighters, sewer rats, but Knight was dirty enough himself and he knew he could best them. "I regret to tell you, gentlemen, but I think my best course of action is to dispatch the both of you to hell. You do most certainly deserve it. I assume you murdered Tris?"

"'O, the proud cove's got quite a big dose of arrogance, eh, Boy? Old Tris turned traitor on us, I done told ye that, so there wasn't no choice now, were there?"

Those were the last words Monk spoke. Knight lunged forward, his form perfect, his sword finely balanced and deadly. He caught Monk off guard and felt the tip of the sword sink into the man's shoulder, fluid and easy and sickeningly liquid-feeling.

Monk yelled and dropped his stiletto, jerking back against the building wall as Knight pulled the sword out of his shoulder. "Damned bastid! Kill 'im, Boy, we don't need 'im! We'll go after Tris's little whore!"

Knight whirled on the quickly advancing Boy. Damnation, the fellow had a pistol. His own pistol was tucked inside an inner pocket. No time to pull it out. He darted to the left as Boy fired. He felt the bullet graze the side of his head. He heard Monk yelling at Boy as he felt himself slowly, slowly, sink to his knees.

"Damn and blast, there's another cove coming. Let's get the blue blazes outa 'ere!"

The last thing Knight saw was Boy, clasping Monk under his arm, half dragging him away, cursing and wheezing with every step.

"Good God! You're hurt!"

Knight managed to cock his right eye open. Julien was bending over him. "I was stupid," he said. "That damnable Boy had a pistol, and like a bloody fool, I left mine in my coat pocket."

"I was coming, old fellow. Now, let's get you home. Your face is covered with blood."

When Julien St. Clair, the Earl of March, strode through the front door of Winthrop House carrying an unconscious, blood-covered Viscount Castlerosse over his shoulder, Duckett actually moaned.

"Oh, my God! Sir, he isn't—"

"No, he's not dead," Julien said quickly. "Have his physician fetched immediately, Duckett."

Duckett screeched for a footman and gave him disjointed instructions. God, all that blood! What if his lordship was fatally wounded . . . what if . . . oh, God, no! But he couldn't ignore his duty.

The Winthrop physician, Dr. Tuckman, as old and fragile as a venerable first edition, soon arrived.

Dr. Tuckman had seen everything in his nearly sixty years, but the young viscount, his face streaming with blood, was still an unwelcome surprise.

"Let's see what we have here," he said, moving Julien aside.

After Knight's face was bathed, Dr. Tuckman said in a voice of mild reproof, "Why, 'tis barely a scratch. Look here. The bullet grazed along just above his left temple. Messy, but not at all deep or dangerous."

"Then why is he unconscious?" Julien asked.

Stromsoe had kept his distance, much to Duckett's disgust, even though he knew the valet's distress at the sight of blood.

"Shock, most likely," Dr. Tuckman said. "He'll have a mite of a headache on the morrow, but nothing more serious than that. Footpads shot him?''

Julien decided on believable fiction. He nodded.

''Disgraceful, utterly disgraceful that such things still happen in a city as modern as London.''

At that moment, Knight groaned.

''Thank the Lord,'' Julien said.

''Nothing divine about his recovery, nothing at all,'' Dr. Tuckman said in his sour old voice and began packing his black bag.

Duckett didn't know what to do now. He'd tried to do what was best, truly he had. He hoped Charlie had followed his instructions. Who was to guess or know that things would have turned out this way?

He heard horses come to a halt in front of the house and groaned again. Oh, dear, oh, dear.

The door flew open and Lily, her riding hat askew, her riding costume, once a rich deep blue, now bedraggled and filthy, came rushing toward Duckett.

''Is his lordship all right, Duckett? Please tell me he's not dead!''

''Mrs. Winthrop,'' the butler began, then stopped to lick his very dry lips. ''You are here very, er, speedily.'' He was starting to sweat; he could feel it on the top of his bald head. ''You didn't take a carriage.''

Lily waved away what she considered nonsense. ''Of course not, we rode. His lordship, Duckett, how—''

''What the devil are you doing here?''

Lily spun about on her heel to see Knight standing at his ease in the doorway of the library, his arms crossed over his chest. There was a white bandage around his head, but he was fully dressed, his color healthy; all in all, quite the picture of blooming health.

She was flooded with relief. All her frantic prayers had been answered. "You're not dead," she yelled and ran full tilt toward him.

With all the presence of mind he could muster, Knight caught her hands, holding her away from him. "Lily, what are you doing here?" he repeated.

Lily blinked, then moved back from him, aware suddenly of her precipitous and utterly unwelcome dash to him. He dropped her gloved hands. "Charlie came for me at Castle Rosse. He said you were shot and possibly gravely wounded. I came immediately, of course."

Knight looked over her head at Duckett, who was standing as straight as his five feet would allow, trying to look more self-righteous than a judge.

"You were covered with blood, my lord. Quite covered and horribly, well, dead-looking."

"That's the truth," Charlie added.

"Mrs. Allgood had two maids scrubbing the blood off the entrance hall this morning," Duckett said, deciding to go in the direction of gruesome detail.

"Quite a lot of blood," Charlie added.

"You weren't even here," Knight said in an acid voice. He was aware that he was starring at the moment in something of a spectacle. "Mrs. Winthrop, please come into the library. Duckett, send in some tea and refreshments."

The library door closed.

Lily stood, her back to the door, staring at Viscount Castlerosse. He was different. The look in his eyes when he regarded her was different. She didn't understand. "Who shot you?"

"Actually our two villains, Monk and Boy."

She gasped. "No! But . . . I knew it, I just knew it!"

"I see you're quick to grasp the implications. Yes, Lily, I knew they would come for me with you gone. I'm not quite the fool you must believe me to be."

"I've never believed you a fool! You are far too noble, if you would know the truth."

"Noble? How nice of you to say so. I'm pleased, I assure you. I was hoping they would come to me. I gave them more than enough opportunity. They took their chance last night. My only claim to stupidity is that Boy had a pistol and shot me with it. I hadn't expected that, and my own pistol was in my coat. Knives in the dark seemed to me to be their style. On the other hand, I'm certain that Monk hadn't planned on having my sword slice into his shoulder. I would say that he is sorely wounded and on his back now and for the next week. Julien, of course, was part of my plan. He brought me back here. My head wound made me bleed like a stuck stoat, but it wasn't at all serious."

"I see," Lily said finally. She drew a deep breath. "I've been terrified for you."

"Thank you," he said in the driest tone she'd ever heard from him.

What was wrong with him?

Duckett arrived with the tea tray and plates of scones, cakes, and biscuits.

Lily suddenly realized that she was starving. She seated herself, then said as she smoothed her riding skirts, "Oh, dear, I'm filthy—"

"Eat first; then you can go straighten yourself up."

"Thank you. I'm quite famished."

Knight watched her sink her teeth into a slice

of Cuthbert's lemon cake. He waited until her mouth was full before he said, ''I discovered what the fellows want. They want sparklers. Jewels, in other words.''

She nearly choked. He quickly slapped her back, then handed her a cup of tea. ''Oh, forgive me. Yes, I'm all right now. I know of no jewels! Goodness, why—''

''They were Tris's cohorts. They murdered him, unfortunately before they found out what he'd done with the jewels they'd stolen. He evidently double-crossed them, an act, I think, that wasn't very well thought out. Tris called the jewels Billy's Baubles, after a fellow named Billy who had them commissioned for his fiancée, Charlotte. Charlotte appears to have broken the engagement, and the jewels were on their way back home—wherever that is. Tris and his fellows stole them.''

Lily could but stare at him. Slowly, very slowly, she said, ''I don't believe that. Tris wasn't a criminal. He was a fine man, a wonderful father—''

''And an exceedingly loving husband as well?''

Lily couldn't bring the words out for several moments. She stuck her chin upward and said firmly, ''Yes, of course he was. He wasn't a thief. He wouldn't have asociated with the likes of those men.''

''Lily, it's true. Stop railing against the facts. The only question I have—well—actually, there are two questions. First, where are the sparklers? Second, from whom were they stolen? Who is this Billy fellow?''

''I tell you there aren't any jewels! Don't you think I would have found them after Tris's death?''

''Monk and Boy firmly believe that you know. They also firmly believe that Tris hid them. It is up to us to find them and give them back to their rightful owner. It seems logical to me that Monk and Boy would then have no more reason to do away with us.''

Lily drank down the remainder of the tea. It couldn't be possible, no . . . She squeezed her eyes closed, fighting the tears. Oh, Tris, no, no.

''You shouldn't have come here.''

She heard his words, the flat tone of his voice. It took her a few more minutes to gain control. ''I had to,'' she said, opening her eyes to see him regarding her with no expression whatsoever on his face.

''Why? You and I are no relation, Lily. None at all,'' he added, his voice deliberately cold.

He was different. Very different. He was acting as if he hated her.

He continued softly, not waiting for her to reply. ''Perhaps . . . perhaps you are playing a very deep game. I am now the children's legal guardian. I am now responsible for them. And you, ma'am, well, you could now leave the children in my care and remove yourself to wherever you wished to go, a fortune of jewels with you.''

''Wh—what did you say?''

''You heard me.''

She jumped to her feet, nearly upsetting the tea tray. ''Why are you acting so strangely? So cruelly?''

''Did you come back with Charlie to spend my last hours with me? Perhaps you thought I would be so grateful for your concern that I would marry you on my deathbed. I would make you a very wealthy woman, you know. Probably far more wealthy than the stolen jewels would.''

She was pale now and very, very cold inside. But composed. Her chin went up. She was bedraggled, dirty, her hair a ratty nest, and she looked beautiful.

Knight held firm. He had to.

"Or, *Mrs.* Winthrop, you figured that even if I survived my bullet wound, your presence here in my home—without a chaperon—would do the deed for you. I would feel compelled to marry you. Certainly you know how much I want to bed you, I've been unfortunately very obvious about that. But marriage, ma'am? I am not that great a fool. You will leave Wintrhop House whenever it pleases you. I care not if your reputation is in shreds. I wouldn't marry you, won't ever marry you."

Lily said quietly, "The two men—they told you, didn't they? They told you I wasn't married to Tris?"

Knight laughed, a harsh, low, ugly sound. "If you mean they referred to you as Tris's *fancy piece* and Tris's *whore*, yes, they told me you weren't married to him."

Lily didn't make a sound. She just stood there, looking incredibly composed, incredibly . . . wounded.

He had to hold steady. He would no longer be taken in by her beauty, her remarkable acting ability. "You act the doting mother to perfection, ma'am. Everyone who's observed you must agree with me. Loving, kind, all the things one expects from a mother. So your father gave—rather, sold—you to Tris when you were all of fifteen years old? He recognized a harlot even if she was his own daughter. Or perhaps Laura Beth isn't even your child. Perhaps that is just another ploy to gain sympathy for the poor, grieving widow. Spare me the truth of that question. It doesn't matter. Not to me. Finish your tea, ma'am. Do eat more of the cakes. You are rather thin at the moment, and you need to gain flesh to assure that your next protector is a man of wealth and position.''

She felt frozen, a wasteland of pain, more than she'd believed possible.

''What, no comment to that, *Mrs*. Winthrop? Well, no matter. I do recall how such a very short time ago you did escape on your own. What a pity that Ugly Arnold must needs ruin all your carefully laid plans. And I, of course, just like a fool of a St. George, came galloping to your assistance. You didn't even want my assistance, did you?''

She just stared at him, mute. Slowly, she nodded.

Knight didn't notice. He was pacing now, not looking at her, the words flowing from his mouth. ''Very wise of you not to run from me after I'd dispatched Arnold and his miserable hireling. And then I had the utter misjudgment to attack you in the carriage. And you loved it, didn't you, Lily? You, my dear, have all the theoretical attributes of a very skilled whore. Unfortunately, you are honestly passionate, I think. Take my advice. A truly successful whore is as cold as a corpse.''

Knight, finally exhausted of words, gave her a mocking salute, then turned on his heel and strode from the library. He didn't slam the door behind him but closed it very slowly and very quietly.

Lily eased down onto the settee. She stared straight ahead, seeing nothing, wishing, quite simply, that she were dead.

If she'd had the energy, she would have left at that moment. But she was simply too exhausted, both physically and mentally. She went upstairs to her bedchamber. Betty brought her bath. Mrs. Allgood brought her dinner on a tray.

"Is his lordship at dinner?" Lily asked.

"No, he's dining at his club this evening. Why, I don't know." Mrs. Allgood frowned. "I would have thought that since you came all the way from Castle Rosse—" She shrugged. "Well, 'tis none of my affair, is it? What do you think of Mrs. Crumpe?"

"She is most kind. To all of us."

"She should be. She's my cousin. Emily's her name. I wrote her, of course, that you and the children were coming and told her how nice all of you were. I'll bid you good night, Mrs. Winthrop."

A small world, Lily thought. She was asleep by eight o'clock, her dreams dark but undefined.

At one o'clock in the morning, Knight gently squeezed down on the handle. The door swung open without a sound. It was dark as pitch. He strained to see Lily but couldn't even make out her outline.

A candle, he thought. He wanted to see her, he had to see her. He stumbled over a chair leg and nearly cursed aloud. He got control of himself. He didn't believe he'd ever been so determined on a course in his adult life.

The candle lit, he walked slowly toward the bed.

13

There was a slight chill in the room. Knight quickly built up the fire. He wanted the room warm because he intended to have her naked.

He didn't move until orange flames were leaping upward. He approved his handiwork and rose, dusting his hands on his dressing gown. The front of the dressing gown parted slightly, and he was disgusted to see that he wasn't as indifferent to her as he told himself he was. Damnation, he hurt and he hadn't even seen her yet, hadn't even touched her. He pulled the belt tighter at his waist, but it didn't really help.

He stood over her, making no noise, simply staring down at her. The room was growing warmer by the minute, and he could see the shadows of the leaping flames on the wall opposite her bed. One arm suddenly came out from under the covers, and she pushed at the blankets in her sleep. They bunched up at her waist. Still he held himself back.

He wanted to look at her, to once and for all get his fill of her. Her hair was free and smoothed out over the pillow. Incredibly thick hair, so beautiful he swallowed, wanting desperately to run his fingers through it. Her lashes, darker than her hair, lay gently against her cheeks. In her sleep she looked very young, and very innocent. Innocent be damned. He nearly snorted his derision and self-contempt aloud.

His look became more derisive as he regarded her nightgown. It was virginal white, high-necked with small buttons marching from near her waist to her throat. He tried to imagine how she'd look in a confection like the one he'd bought for Daniella some months earlier. It was a peach silk affair that shadowed and framed and hinted at and defined. But as much as he tried, somehow he couldn't pin down the image.

He set the candle upon the small table by her bed. Enough was enough. He sat down beside her, still not touching her.

"A whore," he whispered to the empty room and the sleeping woman. "The most appealing woman I've ever known in my life, and she's a bloody whore." He laughed dryly.

Lily heard that laugh. It wasn't part of her dream, it was real. It was *here*, with her. Her eyes flew open. She turned her head slightly on her pillow and saw him.

"Knight?" How odd that he was here, sitting on her bed, smiling down at her. No, he was laughing. Surely that was strange. Had she said something amusing and not realized it? Was she still dreaming? "Are you truly here?" She raised her hand to his face, then dropped it. "Oh, dear, is something wrong? The children?"

"Hello, my dear Lily. Yes, I'm here, and no, nothing's wrong."

"Knight!" He was here in her bedchamber, in his dressing gown! "No! What are you doing here? Surely—" She broke off as she struggled to sit up.

Knight grabbed her shoulders and pressed her

back down. "Oh, no, Lily, I want you on your back."

She stared up at him, confusion written clearly in her eyes. "I don't understand you. What are you doing here? You promise nothing is wrong?"

He didn't laugh this time, but his lips twisted in a parody of a smile. He didn't release his hold on her shoulders. "Nothing at all, dear Lily. I'm here to test out a theory, no more."

"What theory?" she said blankly.

Ah, that incredible bewildered, innocent look. "You do that so well, Lily. Perhaps you could give acting lessons to the opera girls."

She didn't understand him; his words made no sense. "Are you foxed, Knight?"

"Nary a bit. It perhaps would have been better had I drunk myself into oblivion, but I didn't. No, I wanted to see, to understand, to know the results of my . . . experiment. Now, my dear, I want to look at you."

Something was very wrong. This man wasn't the Knight Winthrop she knew. But then again, that bitter, sarcastic man who'd insulted her endlessly and quite thoroughly earlier in the library wasn't either. She wasn't afraid, but she wished that he would say something sensible. His eyes were narrowed and the gold lights in them were pronounced in the candlelight. His fox's eyes, Mrs. Crumpe had called them. He was looking at her, looking beneath her lawn nightgown, and she understood then his intent. She sucked in her breath. "No," she said quite clearly. "Go away, Knight."

"Not this time, Lily. Now—" Suddenly without warning, he ripped the front of her gown from her throat to her waist. He yanked the material apart. She heaved and struggled frantically

against him, but it was no good. He simply held
her until she was too tired to fight him.

There was fear in her eyes now, but he refused
to be drawn in by it. That, too, was an act. There
wasn't a single thing real about her save her passion. At least that was what he believed, what he
intended to prove. He grabbed her wrists and
jerked them above her head. Then he stared down
at her breasts. ''Those gowns you wear, Lily, they
really don't do you justice. Your breasts are quite
nice, you know, full and so white, and your nipples, a very soft, dusky pink.'' He wanted to
touch her, to take her into his mouth. But no, he
had to retain control.

''Stop it, Knight. Why are you doing this? I'm
not a whore—please, you must let me explain!''

He said in a marvelously mocking voice, ''Ah,
very nice, Lily. You have something you wish to
explain to me? You had all the opportunity in the
world this afternoon in the library. But you didn't
say a single word, deny a single thing, did you?
Now, where was I? Oh, yes, your lovely breasts.
They're not that large, but your shape, Lily, and
the texture of your flesh—let me see about the texture—'' He held her wrists with one hand, and
with his other hand he touched his fingers to her
breast. His eyes didn't leave her face.

A deep, raw cry ripped from her throat. ''No!
You can't do this, Knight! You cannot force me!''

''Force you? You mean rape you? Of course I
shan't. It isn't my style. Not at all. I believe I already told you that. Oh, no, Lily, you like this,
don't you? Soon you will be babbling, you will
want me to touch you so much.'' His fingers were
teasing her nipple, and she saw in his eyes that
he wasn't going to stop. He was utterly determined on his course. She went berserk. She
bucked, pulling against his hold, kicking up

wildly with her legs. "Let me go, Knight! Damn
you, go away! I shall scream, I promise I shall—"

His hand left her breast and came down firmly over her mouth. He leaned close, his face
but a breath away from hers. "No, you won't,
Lily. I'm going to kiss you now and you'll want
me again, as you did that night in the carriage.
Hush now, Lily, and just see what I'll make you
feel."

She felt his warm breath on her cheek, saw the
male harshness in his eyes, and felt a spasm of
utter terror. Oh, God, no, she thought, and wildly
twisted her head away. But his hand clasped her
jaw, hard, and jerked her face back, holding her
still. "I'm not a whore, Knight," she said, but it
didn't matter. It was as if he were beyond her,
beyond understanding her. His mouth was covering hers now, warm and firm. She felt his
tongue lightly stroking over her lips. She moaned
her protest and he shuddered at the sound. She
had to stop this; she had to make him see reason.
His hold on her jaw loosened and she jerked
away, screaming, "No!"

"Damn you," he said, fury and cold purpose
filling his voice. He rolled over on top of her to
keep her still and found her mouth again. He held
her arms away from her body and she felt his full
weight. He wasn't gentle now, nor undemand-
ing. He deepened the pressure of his mouth, and
his sex strained hard against her belly. He pressed
downward, then forward, in a parody of the sex
act, and at the same time his tongue slipped into
her mouth, thrusting forward, then withdrawing.
Again and again he did it, and she thought: It's
Knight doing this, it's Knight making me feel
empty and hot and wanting, and it's so incredibly
erotic I can't bear it.

Knight knew the instant she responded to him.

He knew what was making her wild and he took immediate advantage. "Lily," he said into her mouth. He clasped her wrist and brought her arm down as he rolled off her. He pulled her hand on his belly. "Touch me, Lily. This is what you do to me." Her fingers brushed against him and his hips jerked despite his intentions. Suddenly her fingers tried to close about him through the thick velvet of the dressing gown. He felt intense frustration and groaned deep in his throat. He pulled back the dressing gown, then guided her hand to him again.

Lily couldn't believe what she was doing, what she wanted to do, what she was aching to do. Her fingers touched the alien male flesh, so hot and hard and smooth. She shuddered, her body quivering as her fingers explored him. She was frightened of his maleness, his strangeness, the size of him, and yet so excited she felt her own body trying to move toward him, to rub against him, to draw him inside her, into her.

He suddenly shoved her hand away. "Stop," he whispered, his voice jagged. "You're too skilled, damn you." He came down over her again, his mouth covering hers, his tongue instantly demanding entrance, and she gave it to him.

Skilled at what? she wondered, but then it didn't matter. She didn't care, not about anything except him and what he was doing to her, what he was making her feel.

He was touching her cheek, her nose, her throat. She wanted more, but she didn't know what it was she wanted. She felt a throbbing ache between her thighs and quivered. He reveled in the fact that it was he who was responsible. He settled himself between her legs.

"Wider, Lily. Open your legs wider."

She obeyed him without hesitation, without thought. Again he thrust toward her, and now there was only her ripped nightgown between them.

She was beyond herself now and he knew it. She was crying out, helpless cries into his mouth, and they filled him with triumph and a fierce joy that he denied. He leaned back, his manhood hard against her, and he pushed and heaved and she opened her eyes, stared up at him, and whimpered. Her hands were on his shoulders, jerking at his dressing gown.

"No, Lily!" He couldn't let her undress him. He would lose to her, he knew it. He couldn't let that happen. He wouldn't let her win. Quickly he rolled off her onto his side. She moaned his name, trying to turn toward him, find him, bring him back to her. Her hands were on his face, his shoulders, closing over his arms.

He kissed her again, deeply, and his hand went over her breasts and he felt the furious pounding of her heart, the soft ripplings of her flesh, her nearly consuming need. He splayed his fingers and rested his open hand on her belly. He felt the tension in her muscles, knowing that she was trapped now in her need. He had her. She was completely under his control. He'd won.

"Lily, look at me. Open your eyes! I want to see your face when I touch you. I want you to know I'm looking at you when I touch you."

Pleasure was pulsing through her body, pushing her, swamping her, and when she opened her eyes, she saw the intent look in his, the male triumph, not part of her but distant, controlling. "No . . . oh, please, no, Knight . . ." She couldn't allow this to happen, she couldn't. Why was he doing this to her? "Please, Knight . . ."

"Please what, Lily?" he said into her mouth.

He deliberately brought his hand back up and lightly laid it against her breast. He saw the disappointment in her eyes, felt her hips lifting, searching, and he smiled. "You're very passionate, Lily, and now you're mine. Don't you like this?" His tongue stroked hers and at the same time his fingers lightly touched her nipple. She cried out into his mouth. And felt his triumph, his immense male pleasure and satisfaction, and she hated herself and her body for its betrayal, but she'd never before imagined anything like this—when Tris had kissed her, she'd felt nothing, not a single stirring. But with Knight, she shivered even as the errant thoughts spun about in her head. Her lips parted wider, offering herself to him. His hand was firmer on her breast now, caressing her with skilled fingers, cupping her, lifting her, and suddenly his mouth left hers and closed over her nipple.

It was too much. Her back arched up and she moaned, deep in her throat. "That's it, Lily. Yes, that's it." Had he truly been in control, he would have stopped at this point.

As he suckled with his mouth, his hand found her other breast. He felt her heartbeat, galloping more wildly now, and for a brief instant he raised his face to look at her. Her eyes were closed, her head arched back against the pillow, her expression one of nearly painful pleasure. God, she was so beautiful, so touchingly . . . He quickly captured her nipple in his mouth. He wouldn't look at her again until he was certain he could handle it. It was a mistake. She was just another woman, another body, immensely desirable but nothing more. His hand went down to touch her waist, then flattened across her belly. She squirmed against him. He smiled, a cruel smile.

"Do you want me, Lily?"

She choked down a cry and he saw her hands in fists at her sides, wound around the bedcovers. "Touch me, Lily."

He willed her to open her eyes, and when she did, he commanded again, "Touch me, Lily."

Slowly she raised her hands and lightly touched them to his shoulders. Just that simple touch, not even on his naked body but on his bloody dressing gown, nearly did him in. He quickly encircled her wrists with his hands and pressed them back down to the bed.

"How do you feel, Lily?"

"I don't know." It was a wail, shrill, filled with frustration. She was breathing hard, her eyes wide and dilated, wild and frustrated.

His eyes still on her face, he moved his hand over her belly, then gently cupped his palm against her.

Her eyes narrowed as her body welcomed him. "Knight . . ."

"Don't close your eyes!"

She opened them.

"Now, tell me what you want. Tell me what you feel."

His fingers left her for just a moment. He ripped the nightgown a bit lower. He saw the dark blond fleece and smiled. "Tell me, Lily." His fingers found her and lightly pressed. Such triumph he felt. God, it was the most powerful feeling in the world.

"I—I . . . Knight—oh!"

He was astounded at the depth and quickness of her response. She nearly spun away from him in that moment, after he'd touched her for only a few seconds. Quickly he lifted his fingers, watching her face, watching her slowly open her eyes again and gaze at him in confusion and in something like desperation. He waited a bit longer; then his fingers stroked over her again.

"Knight . . ."

"Yes, Lily? That pleases you, doesn't it? You're so soft, Lily, and swelled and damp for me, just for me. Here, see? This is you, Lily." Lightly he touched his fingers to her cheek so she could feel her own dampness. She shuddered, and he felt his own body nearly explode in response.

He was very careful this time not to push her into her climax. He teased her, mocked her with his skilled fingers, stroked her, and knew that she was close, but he would be the one to decide what she received, and when.

Then, suddenly, her thighs parted and her hips pushed upward against his fingers, seeking, beyond pride, beyond anything, wanting only completion. He left her and just as quickly eased his middle finger into her. Oh, God! She was hot and tight and very small, and he groaned with the pleasure of it.

No, he couldn't. He had to get hold of himself again. He wouldn't let her affect him like this.

He brought his fingers down on her again and smiled painfully. Familiar territory, he thought, his movements rhythmic, light, then deep, teasing, then rough. He felt her climax building, reveled in the wild jerking of her hips, the stiffening of her legs, the uncontrollable cries tearing from her throat. At just the moment when she would have exploded in her climax, he left her.

He quickly rose to stand beside the bed. His chest heaved as he looked down at her. Her gown was split open to her thighs. He gazed at the expanse of smooth white flesh, her flat belly and the beautiful dark blond hair. God, she was exquisite and so responsive. *To any man fool enough to touch her.*

She was twisting her hips, arching upward, still beyond herself, and now she was crying, softly, helplessly. He tried to keep away from her. But he couldn't. He couldn't bear it.

"All right, damn you." He didn't stretch out beside her again, he couldn't. He sat there, one hand pressed down on her belly, holding her still, the other finding her again. Then he looked at her face. She stared at him and went unseeing as he brought her to climax. She screamed and he quickly covered her mouth. God, it was nearly too much. She was heaving against his fingers, trembling wildly. Still she stared at him even as she reached the height of her pleasure, and he felt her then, became a part of her for a brief instant.

It seemed to him as if an eternity passed. Slowly, very slowly, she began to quiet. He felt ripples go through her, gentle spasms and after-shocks of now fading pleasure.

He saw her eyes gradually clear. She was looking up at him now, really seeing him this time. She was herself again, apart from him, apart from his control.

He smiled down at her, a cruel smile, a very satisfied smile. "Next time, Lily, next time I'll have my mouth on you. Imagine my tongue stroking you instead of my fingers. You'll go crazy for it, Lily, and you'll beg me and beg me."

She shuddered at his words and he knew she was very nearly feeling his mouth covering her, caressing her. In the next moment, he saw that her mind had cleared and she was now understanding what he'd done to her.

She said nothing. She simply stared at him, mute, unmoving.

"You won't be a successful whore, my dear Lily."

Still she just stared at him, her expression unreadable to him.

"No, as I told you earlier, a whore is cold, very cold. She needs to be so that she can control the man, gain her ends, so to speak. But you, Lily, you are passionate, and a man would kill to claim your passion. But he wouldn't make you rich, oh, no. You see, he wouldn't have to. All he'd have to do is touch you and you'd go crazy wanting him to pleasure you. Everything would be free. Perhaps, Lily, if you are very kind to me, I will make you my mistress. Since I know who and what you are now, since there won't ever again be lies between us, we shouldn't have many difficulties. Would you like to be my mistress, Lily?"

Her lips moved, but there was no sound.

"Wouldn't you like to feel my sex inside you, Lily? I'd fill you, you know that, since you touched me and held me in your hand, and I'd drive you to such pleasure, stronger than what you just experienced. And my mouth, Lily. I'll give you more pleasure than Tris did. But then again, you've been several months without a man, haven't you? I know Ugly Arnold didn't count. You do have some standards, after all.

"You've become a mute? Haven't you tamped down on your passion yet? Do you want more? Well, I'm still hard for a woman. Any woman would do, naturally. But I'll give you more if you wish it, Lily. I'm a generous man."

Very slowly, she sat up. She clutched her nightgown together over her breasts. She closed her eyes against the harsh pain, the deadening humiliation. She heard him continue in that hateful, sarcastic voice. "Well, now you're beginning to bore me. I don't care for too much conversation in a woman, but a little wouldn't be remiss. Let me know in the morning, Lily. Perhaps I'll still be interested. Perhaps next time I'll even come inside you, though I would like to know how many men have preceded me before I do so.''

He turned to leave her bedchamber. In the next instant, a half-filled water carafe hit him hard between his shoulder blades. Knight stumbled, then whirled about.

He had no time to react, no time to think.

''You bastard!''

She was flying toward him, her shredded nightgown flowing like ghostly wrapping around her, her hair wild about her face. He saw her swing her arm, but everything was in a blur, a moment of disbelief, a fragment of a dream.

With all her strength, Lily brought up her fist and smashed it into his jaw. Pain exploded through his head. He was off-balance and went careening backward. She smashed her fist into his belly, all the while yelling at him over and over. ''Bastard! Unfeeling, damnable bastard!''

He slipped on the carpet in front of the fireplace and fell, striking his head on the corner of the mantelpiece.

He went down like a stone.

Lily stood over him, breathing hard, shaking her fist as the pain intensified in her now raw knuckles. ''I hate you, damn you, I hate you.'' She dropped to her knees and placed the flat of her hand over his heart.

It was strong and steady. ''Nothing would kill you, you miserable, obnoxious, half-witted—''

Lily drew in a deep breath. She rose and stared down at him. Then she smiled. She rolled and shoved until he was sprawled in the middle of a smaller carpet that lay in front of the wing chair. She tugged and pulled and heaved on the carpet. She dragged him from her bedchamber, stopping every few steps to regain her breath. By the time she'd gotten him outside his bedchamber, her arms were aching. She dropped the end of the carpet and stood straight.

The *master* suite, she thought, looking at the closed door. Some master. She left him lying there in the corridor, sprawled on his back, his dressing gown open to his hairy thighs, unconscious as the dead. She returned to her room, yanked two blankets from her bed, and went back to him. "You ought to die from nastiness, not from a stupid chill." She flung the blankets over him, wiped her hands in what was a grand gesture for her own private audience, then gathered her torn nightgown about herself, strode back to her bedchamber, and locked the door.

She was asleep in ten minutes.

14

"My lord!"

Knight awoke with a start at the sound of the high, shocked voice.

He cocked open an eye and saw Stromsoe bending over him. Odd that he was *over* him. He realized suddenly that he was very stiff and cold and that he was stretched out on his back on the hard wooden floor. He sat up abruptly. A pain thudded heavily in his jaw, another pain sliced through his head, and he tentatively rubbed his fingertips over the back of his skull. He came away with some blood on his fingertips. The place over his temple where Boy's bullet had grazed began to throb. He was a mess, a complete and utterly absurd mess.

"My lord! What are you doing here, in the corridor? I don't understand . . . I—"

"Be still, Stromsoe. I'm dying, or at least considering it." As he rubbed his aching jaw, then his aching head, every event of the previous evening trooped through his brain. The last troop he saw was the blur of Lily's fist, and he said, "My God, what a superb uppercut she has."

"What did you say, my lord? Superb *what*? Are your wits . . . well, my lord—"

220

"Stromsoe, shut your trap. Help my up. Lord, I'm stiff as a fat lady's corset."

"No wonder to that, my lord, if you slept all night on the floor. How did you get there? The blankets?"

"Interesting question, isn't it? Well, no answers for you, Stromsoe. Indeed," he added under his breath, "I don't have all the answers either." So Lily, in a spate of not wanting to see him frozen to death, threw blankets over him? He smiled, but it was painful. His jaw, his head, his back, all hurt like the very devil. If she'd wanted revenge—and only a long-suffering saint wouldn't have—she'd gotten it.

"A hot bath," he told Stromsoe as he walked slowly into his bedchamber, his valet flapping behind him. "A lot of very hot water to steam out all my evil humors." He plowed his fingers through his messed hair, accidentally brushed against the bump, and winced. As he lowered his hand, he caught her scent. He closed his eyes, suddenly remembering the look in her eyes as her pleasure took her over, hearing her cry out, feeling her move against his fingers . . . "Oh, God." He whirled about just as Stromsoe was leaving.

"Have you seen Mrs. Winthrop this morning?"

"No, my lord."

"Ask Duckett."

"Yes, my lord."

"Hurry, Stromsoe."

Stromsoe raised a brow at that tone but quickly nodded and took his leave. When he returned to his master's bedchamber not five minutes later, two footmen on his heels with the tub of hot water, he felt like the famed Greek messenger who'd delivered the bad news. That fellow had met a bad end, a very dead end.

"Well?"

"The hot water is right here, my lord, and very hot."

"Don't be such a damned nitwit, Stromsoe!"

"She's gone . . . left an hour ago."

Knight knew he paled. He shouldn't have, for it wasn't a surprise, not really. What had he expected? To see her smiling at him across the breakfast table and saying, *Why, good morning, Knight. I trust you slept well on the corridor floor after I smashed my fist into your jaw. Oh, yes, the pleasure you gave me, it was quite adequate, and yes, I've decided to become your mistress, but you must be careful, for I'm just liable to kill you because you're such a bastard.*

He laughed and his valet stared at him. Knight waved a distracted hand. "Don't mind me. Ah, there is steam rising off the water. Excellent. Get out now, Stromsoe. I want a little peace for my aching parts."

"Yes, my lord," Stromsoe said, heading for the door as fast as he could manage it.

"Send me Duckett."

"Yes, my lord."

"Damned rabbity fellow," Knight muttered.

He was naked and stepping into the tub of steaming hot water when Duckett slipped into his bedchamber not more than fifteen seconds later.

"My lord, you wished to speak to me?"

"You're slowing down in your old age. Close the damned door. It's bloody freezing and I'm bare-assed, as you can well see."

Duckett, made from a different bolt of cloth than Stromsoe, merely turned, no aplomb lost, and closed the door. Then he just stood there, his arms crossed, and waited. He knew what his lordship wanted, but he wasn't about to volunteer anything, not in his lordship's present mood. He wondered what had happened the previous

evening. The servants were buzzing with the tid-
bit of the viscount's doubtless drunken carousing.
Why else would he be lying on the floor? Why
else indeed? Duckett thought. He himself didn't
know the answer to that, but he did know that
the viscount hadn't been drunk. He knew the viscount drank only in moderation and never was
out of control.

Knight sank into the hot water and heaved a
deep sigh of pleasure. "This is better than a harp.
Do you think they give out hot baths in heaven,
Duckett?" He cupped a hand of water and poured
it over his head, winced as it hit the open cut,
then sighed again with pleasure.

"That is a theological question, my lord, fit
doubtless for the archbishop."

"All that, huh? No, don't answer that. Now,
Duckett, what time is it?"

"Nearly eight o'clock in the morning."

"Ah. When did Mrs. Winthrop leave?"

"At seven o'clock in the morning."

"How?"

"She was quite insistent upon riding back, my
lord." Duckett saw the viscount jerk up, his face
paling, and added in his most laconic voice, "I,
of course, insisted that Charlie ride back to Castle
Rosse with her."

At least she was returning to Castle Rosse. But
for how long? He wasn't worried about their two
jewel thieves. Monk would be laid up for a while
longer yet, and Knight doubted that Boy would
ever leave his side.

"I should have been quite against her leaving
had it not been for the weather, my lord. It is
unusual to be so warm this time of year."

"Why didn't a servant awaken me before
Stromsoe? What did they do, crawl over me?"

"No servant noticed you, my lord. Only Stromsoe goes to your bedchamber in the mornings."

Knight muttered something rather graphic and obscene, but Duckett, not at all moved, said nothing.

"When will you be traveling to Castle Rosse?" Duckett asked finally, seeing the viscount begin to carefully wash his hair. That Boy fellow had shot him over the temple. Could he possibly have yet another wound?

"Huh? Go to Castle Rosse? Why the devil should I?"

This was all very interesting. Duckett didn't flick an eyelid. "I really haven't the foggiest notion, my lord. Ah, here's Stromsoe. Will there be anything else, my lord?"

Knight opened his eyes and promptly got soap in them. "Go away. You're an impudent clod, Duckett."

"Yes, my lord."

"Keep Stromsoe away as well."

"Yes, my lord."

Two days later, Lily was alone, staring up at the near life-size painting of the fifteen-year-old Knight. She spoke to it quite seriously. "What you did to me was not a nice thing. That is, it was nice, more than nice, actually, but you didn't touch me because you wanted me or cared for me. No, Knight, you wanted to punish me and humiliate me and you did it quite well." She paused for a moment, realizing full well that it could be considered strange of her to be caught speaking to a portrait. However, she was alone, and it did allow her to vent her anger at him, and her embarrassment at her own unrestrained passion.

"You didn't win, my lord. I might not have

forced you to my will, but I did give you a great headache—at least I hope I did. I also hope you felt some humiliation at being found on the floor of the corridor by your servants. I wonder if you will count us even.'' She shook her head. ''No, you won't. I'm a fool to think for an instant that you will.

''If I remain, will you simply send me a message telling me to leave? No, that wouldn't be your style, would it? It would give you immense pleasure to come yourself and tell me to get out. Yes, you would enjoy that. You would do it with great panache and sarcasm in that cold voice of yours.''

A cough came from behind her and Lily whirled about, rattled. ''Oh, Mrs. Crumpe!''

''Mrs. Winthrop, I am sorry to bother you—and I myself occasionally speak to the portraits, they look so very lifelike, you know—in any case, Laura Beth has cut her finger and is carrying on as if she's dying at this very moment.''

''I'll come now,'' Lily said quickly.

Laura Beth was in the kitchen, sitting up on the stone-topped table, surrounded by Mimms, the cook; a scullery maid; Thrombin, the butler; and another servant Lily had never seen before. She was sobbing quite theatrically for her worried and quite adoring audience, and Lily was tempted to laugh.

''You naughty girl,'' she said, coming through the audience, which parted its ranks for her. ''How did you cut yourself? Hush with the crying, Laura Beth. I know it's a sham. Look, it's just a tiny little cut. You're acting like a baby.''

The sobs increased in volume.

''I suppose I will have to tell Sam. I can just hear him sneer about silly little girls.''

The sobs died an instant death. ''Mama? Oh,

Mama, I cut myself, I did, and it's bad and it hurts
dreadful!''

"Yes, I see that you did, snippet—"

"That's what Knight calls me.''

"Yes, I know.''

Mimms, the cook, broke into speech. "She
didn't mean to, Mrs. Winthrop, poor innocent little girl! It is all the fault of this stupid girl—'' A
powerful finger pointed at the hapless scullery
maid. "Agnes left the knife lying on the table
where anyone could pick it up and kill oneself
with it!''

Lily looked over at the pinch-faced Agnes and
smiled. "No harm done. I will see to it that four-
year-old little girls don't come wandering into the
kitchen and disrupt everyone's peace.''

This announcement brought a spate of dis-
claimers, but Lily only shook her head, her smile
never faltering. She thanked everyone again,
apologized again, lifted Laura Beth into her arms,
and bore her off.

"It hurts, Mama.''

"It probably stings, but just a little bit. I begin
to think you're becoming dreadfully spoiled,
Laura Beth.''

"Kiss it, Mama.''

"Oh, very well.'' Lily dutifully kissed the finger, then hugged Laura Beth close. What was going to happen? Would Knight force her to leave?
Leave the children? If she did, would Laura Beth
become a spoiled, demanding little twit? What
would become of Theo, her so serious Theo?
Would he become a recluse, a hermit surrounded
by books on steam engines? And Sam, would he
be shot stealing apples from a neighbor's or-
chard?

She was shaking her head even as the silent
questions drifted through her brain. And always,

ever since that night, thoughts of those intense, nearly painful feelings he'd made her experience flooded through her, leaving her once again excited, ashamed, and furious, both with him and with herself.

"What's the matter, Mama?"

"Nothing, darling. Nothing." It was remarkable, she thought, how well and how quickly one could lie to a child. She trusted the child in question was more interested at the moment in her cut finger than in any hidden motives from her mother. A mother who wasn't really a mother, and a mother who for the first time in her life had felt a woman's pleasure. Oh, stop it, she wanted to yell at herself.

She bandaged Laura Beth's finger, then patted her bottom. "I want you to play now with—" She broke off, staring fixedly at Czarina Catherine. She cleared her throat. "Laura Beth, I want you to find Theo and ask him to come and see me. All right? You can show him your bandage. It's rather grand, and Theo will be quite impressed."

That made the child leave her with more enthusiasm than otherwise.

Lily grabbed the doll and ran her fingers over the arms, chest, and legs. She could feel nothing. She hesitated to destroy Czarina Catherine, but the jewels—Billy's Baubles—had to be hidden in the doll. Tris had known that Laura Beth never let Czarina Catherine out of her sight. Never. The jewels had to be here. Very carefully, Lily pried loose the head from the body. The doll's huge painted eyes stared at her. "I'm not murdering you, for heaven's sake!" Lily said and continued with her prying. "I will fix what I unfix." The head came off at last. It rolled off her hand and landed on the bed, hollow neck up. The head was empty. Not a sight or a scent of any jewels. Lily carefully stuck her hand into the body stuffing. Nothing but horsehair and buckram wadding.

Lily felt a wave of hopelessness wash over her. The two villains were wrong. There weren't any jewels. No Billy's Baubles. If Tris had stolen them, if Tris had indeed hidden them, they were still in Brussels. Quickly she fitted Czarina Catherine's head back onto her body. It was loose, dammit.

She was plying her needle to the doll's neck when Laura Beth, followed by Theo, returned to the bedchamber.

"What is it, Mama?" Theo asked instantly. "John and I are working on his lordship's library."

Lily had forgotten to make up a lie, and lying to Theo was much more difficult than lying to Laura Beth. She looked him straight in the eye. "I forgot. Go back to John. If I remember I'll tell you at dinner. Oh, Theo, I'm sorry."

Theo cocked his head to one side, one of Tris's gestures, but at her continued silence, he took himself off.

Thankfully, Laura Beth noticed nothing amiss with Czarina Catherine. More than thankfully, she was ready for a nap, her dramatic performance for the kitchen staff having tired her out. Lily was at last free to be by herself for a while. Even Sam was occupied, helping Alfred, the head stable lad, with the horses.

Lily considered going riding, then felt pity for poor Violet. She'd ridden her hard from London two days before. Let her rest another day. No, a walk was what she needed.

To think and to walk.

The jewels had to be somewhere, they simply had to be. Without them, she was trapped. Knight would come, she knew it. She had to find those jewels, sell them, and escape with the children, leave England. She thought suddenly of Theo's books. He'd brought seven or eight of his favorites. Perhaps the jewels were sewn somehow into the binding. She couldn't imagine how that would work, but she would shake and bend and feel every one of them very carefully.

Where else?

Lily sighed and walked toward the ornamental lake that was at the edge of the sloping east lawn. Huge, sprawling oak and willow trees skirted the perimeter of the lake. Now naked-branched, the trees looked as miserable and dull and empty as she felt. The water was a flat gray, the few ducks that lived there evidently bored with their surroundings, for they were nowhere to be seen. Lily walked, thinking, discarding ideas as fast as she came up with them. While she walked, she pulled the pins out of her hair, tossing them to the ground, throwing them at trees, all in all paying no attention whatsoever to anything outside herself and those bloody jewels.

Billy's Baubles. She shuddered, thinking of those two wretched characters, Monk and Boy. Even if she found the jewels, even if she managed to sell them and escape England with the children, they wouldn't give up. They would keep looking until they found her.

Lily slumped against an oak tree, defeat washing over her.

That was how Knight first saw her. She looked beaten, her shoulders slumped forward, her glorious hair loose down her back and over her shoulders. Her gown was old, a muddy brown wool, and her heavy shawl looked fit for the trash. He felt something stir deep inside him.

It was contempt.

He felt it for himself until he drew a deep breath, took another look—realistic this time—and saw a young woman deep in thought, very probably trying to figure out how to best him.

The jade.

Lily *was* thinking about him. Again. She didn't want to; she wanted him to disappear, to fall into some faraway oblivion. But he wouldn't. She could still feel the touch of his mouth, his hands, his hot male flesh quivering as she touched him . . .

"Lily."

She groaned; now she was hearing his voice. It was too much. She straightened her shoulders and walked away.

Knight, nonplussed, shouted, "Lily! Wait!"

Oh, no, it couldn't be! Lily looked over her shoulder, saw him striding toward her, and broke into the fastest run she could manage.

"Stop, dammit!" It didn't take Knight long to bring her down. His legs were longer, stronger, and he wasn't hampered by silly petticoats and skirts.

He grabbed her arm and spun her around.

Lily swung her free arm at him, but this time he caught her wrist in the air, three inches from his jaw.

She made no sound, said nothing, merely stared up at him, eyes narrowed, her breath coming heavy and fast.

"You won't strike me again, Lily. I won't allow it."

He didn't release her wrist. And now he grabbed the other one, holding her hands together in front of her with one of his. She was breathing hard, and it was difficult for Knight to keep his eyes off her breasts.

"Why did you run from me?"

Stupid question! Damn him for a fool, a thousand times a bloody fool. He couldn't, wouldn't, let her see any weakness in him. She'd take advantage of it in a flash. He wouldn't let a woman like her bring him low.

She stared at him straightly, showing no emotion, no expression, and said calmly, "You humiliated me. I dislike you. I don't want to see you. I certainly don't want you to touch me."

"Well, that's a pity," he remarked, clasping her wrists more firmly. "I'm here and you're looking at me, and I am touching you, Lily, not where I would like—indeed not where you would like—but I am touching you."

She sucked in her breath and tugged, but his grasp did not give. Then she stood very still, simply waiting, staring down at her hands and his, holding them.

"Of course you knew I would come. This is my home." He paused for a moment, looking out over the ornamental lake. "Dervin Winthrop widened this from a stinking little pond into a lake some eighty years ago. It really is quite impressive, don't you agree? Saying nothing, then? Well, it is impressive and very beautiful in the spring and summer." He waited for her to respond—to say anything—but she didn't. "I wondered, actually, if you would still be here. I expected you to find the jewels and be gone by the time I arrived."

"I haven't found them." No harm in telling him the truth about that.

"Where have you looked?"

"In Czarina Catherine." No harm in telling him the truth about the doll either.

Knight looked much struck. "An excellent hiding place. Laura Beth doesn't let the doll out of her sight. No luck, then?"

"No."

"Listen to me, Lily. If we find the jewels—yes,

it's *we* now—they will be returned. They're this Billy's property, whoever the devil he may be, but I will discover his identity. I have no intention of becoming a criminal."

She looked up at him now. Her voice and face were equally cold. "I don't mind. Being a criminal would be better than being a poor relation."

"Relation?" A dark eyebrow shot up a good inch. "You're no relation at all, Lily," he said slowly, looking into her eyes. "You're no relation to the children, no relation to me." At least not yet she wasn't. His eyes widened at that vagrant thought and he cursed.

She made a low sound deep in her throat and tugged again. He held fast.

"No, I really don't wish to chase you to ground any more today. Just hold still."

She became quiet again, too quiet.

He wanted to get a rise out of her. It was perverse, he knew it, but he couldn't help himself. God, the tumult she'd put him through since she'd just strolled into his life such a short time before. "I see you didn't bother to deny it this time. You aren't Laura Beth's mother, are you?"

He could see it in her eyes, the question of whether or not to lie to him. "Tell me the truth, damn you!"

"No," she said. "I am not the woman who gave birth to her, but I *am* her mother."

He should have been warned, but he wasn't. He was immersed in thought, and in erotic images too vivid to abide, when suddenly she kicked him, hard, in the shin. He released her and she jumped back even as he sucked in his breath and hopped on one foot.

She turned quick as a hawk in flight and sped away, back toward the huge manor house.

He didn't go after her this time. If he had, when

he caught her he'd have thrashed her. Soundly. That or kissed her until they were both insensate.

No, he'd bide his time.

He returned to the manor house. He hadn't even been inside yet since his arrival. One of the stable lads had seen Lily walking toward the lake and had told Knight, who immediately followed her.

Thrombin didn't seem at all surprised to see him now, just bowed as low as his age and arthritis would allow and gave him a beaming smile. Knight saw that there were even fewer teeth in Thrombin's mouth than the last time he had been here, and felt a stab of concern. Lord, Thrombin had known him since his birth. They chatted for a moment, then Knight heard his name shrieked out.

He looked over to see Laura Beth bounding down the stairs as fast as her short legs would allow.

"Be careful and slow down!" But she didn't, of course. He strode toward the staircase, and when Laura Beth landed on the third-to-last step, she launched herself at him.

He heard Thrombin moan in consternation. Knight just smiled and caught her, drawing her up against his chest and kissing the smiling little mouth. "Well, snippet?" He tossed her into the air, and her screams brought every Castle Rosse servant.

Mrs. Crumpe came to a panting halt in the entrance hall. She stared. "I don't believe it," she said aloud.

She watched her urbane, sophisticated master toss the little girl again, then catch her and hug her until the child squeaked with delight. She watched as Laura Beth nearly choked the viscount, giving him wet smacking kisses on his cheek.

"Sir!" Theo, older and trying to be as sedate as an indifferent adult at a surprise visit from a favorite uncle, made his way down the stairs slowly, but he was speaking at a great speed. "Oh, Cousin Knight, wait until you see what John and I have done in the library! Do you know that I'm already to the L's? Do you know how many volumes are there, some that haven't even had their pages cut?"

"No, Theo, I don't know. To the L's, huh? Remarkable, my boy, quite remarkable." Theo held back just another very short instant; then, as Knight shifted Laura Beth to hold her in one arm, Theo, with a big smile, flung himself against Knight's side.

"I'm glad you're here, Cousin Knight," Theo said. "Mama's been so unhappy and we were so afraid you were really hurt bad, even though she told us you were all right."

"It's Cousin Knight!"

"I've only got two arms," Knight shouted as Sam pelted through the front doors.

If there had been four children, perhaps it would have been a problem. However, Knight simply gathered both boys against him, and for a moment he closed his eyes. God, dear God, they were his and he'd missed them so much. He just hadn't realized. . . .

"Hello, my lord," John said. "We're delighted to see you restored to good health. We were all quite concerned when Mrs. Winthrop told us of the attack in London."

"Mama was crying," Sam said, looking up at Knight, "but she made us promise we'd be good because she was riding to London immediately to take care of you."

Knight didn't like to hear that. He hugged each child again and released them. "Ah, hello, Mrs.

Crumpe. Mrs. Allgood sends her love. It's good to see you again. All of you,'' he added, encompassing all the servants he saw. He must have put on quite an unexpected show for them. ''What do you think of these monkeys? Are you ready to run screaming from Castle Rosse?''

''Oh, Cousin Knight, we've been good as—''

''Good as what? Dross?''

''What's dross?'' asked Laura Beth.

''Nothing important, snippet. How would all of you like to have some of Mimms's lemonade and some cakes? Of course you would, and I also. There's greed shining from all our eyes. If you please, Mrs. Crumpe? We'll be in the drawing room—no, make that the library. I have to examine all the tomes to the L's.''

Theo beamed with pride.

''I've got so much to tell you about the horses,'' Sam confided, sticking his hand into Knight's. ''It's all right, I washed them after I mucked out Violet's stall. You know, we need to have some work done on the southern paddock,'' Sam continued, all seriousness and plans.

Knight swallowed and listened, to all three of them. At once.

15

Knight bided his time until an hour before dinner. Lily hadn't shown her face or any other part of her. But he'd learned a lot from the children that afternoon.

And he saw, really saw, how much they adored her. She was their mother, no way around it. While he'd been in his royal snit, when the children hadn't been there in London, he'd forgotten.

"I thought Mama was going to fall over, she was so upset," Sam had confided to Knight over lemonade and cakes. "But you know what she's like—she never cries, her lips just get all stiff. She left with Charlie really soon after he arrived."

"Sam's right," Theo said. "And Mama was real quiet when she came back. We were worried, Cousin Knight, but she promised us you were all right."

Knight could just imagine how quiet she must have been.

"I prayed real hard for you," Laura Beth said, beaming up at him, her mouth full of scone and strawberry jam.

As he began dressing himself for dinner, he gave unscrupulous thought to how he was going to get Lily to the dinner table. He smiled to himself when he hit upon just the correct approach. As he shrugged himself into his evening coat, he found he missed Stromsoe for the first time. He grinned to himself, remembering how Stromsoe had nearly burst into tears at the thought of his master touching his high-gloss Hessians with less than immaculate fingers.

Knight was whistling when Thrombin arrived for his message to Lily. "Ah, yes, Thrombin, please tell Mrs. Winthrop that I've come to a decision. Tell her that I expect her downstairs to dinner, that it is essential to her future and to the children's future that she come."

He grinned into his mirror as he studied his cravat. Even without Stromsoe directing his every article of clothing, he was pleased with his appearance. He looked formal and elegant, yes indeed.

He was pacing the drawing room, waiting for Lily. She was two minutes late. His breath caught in his chest at the sight of her. She was wearing the same brown wool gown, a relic with long, tight sleeves and a nun's neckline. She hadn't gotten to within ten feet of a hairbrush, had the stoniest expression he'd ever seen on a face, and still she looked lovely.

"Good everning, Lily," he said and gave her a smile. It wasn't much of a smile, but it did pass muster.

She gave him a mockery of a curtsy. "How lovely of you to ask me to dinner," she said in a faraway voice. "Is this to be my last?"

He shrugged. "Who knows? Ah, here's Thrombin. I trust Mimms outdid herself?"

"Yes, my lord, I believe you will be pleased."

"A fatted calf, undoubtedly," Lily said, and she was quite serious.

"For the prodigal viscount?"

Knight allowed Thrombin and Thomas, a footman, to serve the first course; then he dismissed them with a kindly "We'll see to ourselves now, thank you."

He turned to Lily. "Would you care for bacon-cheek garnished with greens? They're one of Mimms's specialties."

Lily helped herself, saying nothing.

Knight served himself a good portion of rump steak and kidney pudding, ate two bites, felt it thud in his stomach, and sat back in his chair, his eyes on Lily. He picked up his full wineglass and twirled the delicate stem between his long fingers.

"You expect me to kick you out?"'

"Your message was that you'd come to a decision. I'm waiting." She hadn't looked up as he'd spoken. It seemed to him as if she were finding her vegetable marrows of great interest. "As you pointed out, I'm not even a poor relation. I'm not anything at all, as a matter of fact."

"I wouldn't say that's true. You're a very beautiful woman, Lily. And a very passionate woman as well."

She stiffened up like a poker at that observation but still didn't look at him.

He simmered, perversity singing through his veins. Damn her for her aloofness. "What a man loves to hear is woman's breathy little cries, to feel her fingers digging into his arms, to know that she wants him to—"

"Stop it, damn you!"

He eased at that and smiled. He'd won; at least he'd gotten her eyes off her vegetable marrows and onto him. "All right. All I wanted was your attention. Answer me a question, Lily, and no, don't look back down at your plate."

"Very well."

"Tell me why Tris didn't marry you."

She looked as if she'd like to slam her fist into his jaw again. Then she looked incredibly weary, shrugged, and said, "Why not tell you, even though you won't believe me. Tris did ask me to marry him. I refused him, particularly before my father's death. After his death, I had no money, no home, and Tris asked me again. I continued to turn him down. I was very fond of him, but I didn't love him, you see, not the way I think a woman is supposed to love the man she will marry. But there were the children. Finally I agreed. We would have been married by now if he hadn't been killed."

"I see. How long did you live with him?"

"Six months. And I didn't live *with* him, I simply lived in his house."

"Naturally. How very crass of me to state things so crudely. You were, of course, the children's nanny?"

"That's right."

"In Tris's house?"

"Yes, that's correct."

He took her completely off guard when, after pausing for a long moment, he cocked his head to one side and said, "You've quite a right uppercut. Did you knock me out?"

She would never understand a man's mind, she thought, staring at him. They were the most curious of creatures, their thought processes defying logic. "No, after I hit you, you stumbled, lost your balance, and struck the back of your head against the edge of the mantelpiece. That knocked you out. I did, however, add another blow to your stomach."

He dropped his hand unconsciously to his belly. "Thank you. I couldn't remember anything beyond your right to my jaw."

Lily said nothing. She took a drink of her wine,

set down her glass carefully, then folded her napkin. "Would you care to tell me what decision you've reached?"

He waved her question away. "I was pleased to see the children." He frowned the moment the words were out of his mouth. "I hadn't realized that I'd missed them."

"They were pleased to see you. Of course, they don't really know what you're like, but—"

"Nor do you."

"If it makes you feel all the more powerful to hear it, you were all they could talk about. They doubtless went to sleep talking about you. They'll doubtless have wonderful dreams about you."

"That sounds quite nauseating, doesn't it?"

"Yes, quite. What is your decision?"

"You're not much for light dinner conversation."

She pushed back her chair and made to rise.

"Sit down! I'm not through with you, Lily, not by a long shot. Sit down!"

She wasn't about to obey him. Her chin went up in the air. "Why should I? You have no hold over me. You're just enjoying playing with me as a cat would with a mouse."

"Sit down and I'll tell you my decision."

She looked mutinous, but finally gave in and eased back into her chair.

"Good. Now, I've decided not to boot you out, so to speak, if you and I can come to some sort of mutually satisfying agreement. It would be worth your while to listen, Lily."

"I won't be your mistress, Knight."

"I wouldn't consider you for that position. I doubt you have the requisite skills."

She raised her eyebrows, trying to freeze him with a glance. Finally she just shrugged. "It's bound to be an insult in any case," she remarked, more to the cold vegetable marrows on her plate than to him.

"I hope not," he said coolly.

"Very well, say what you will, Knight. I'm listening."

"I want you to marry me."

If he'd told her that he was Lazarus and he'd just been away on a trip for three days, she couldn't have looked more taken aback. She turned as still as Lot's wife, her pallor nearly as white as that pillar of salt.

He said again, "I want you to be my wife. At last you can be a Winthrop."

Still she stared at him. Then, "I will be gone by tomorrow morning. I will not stay here and be toyed with any further."

"I'm not toying with you, nor, I trust, am I insulting you. I'm asking you to marry me."

"Why?"

"Why not?"

"You despise me! You think me a trollop, a whore, a—"

"No, I don't," he said, but she knew he was lying. And he knew that she knew. "All right, I do have serious questions about your character, but I don't care. It's that simple. I don't give a good damn. I want you and I want the children. I can't have one without the other. I'm not such a monster to separate you from them either. So you're part of the package. Marry me."

"I could simply be their nanny! This is absurd for you to—"

"No, you can't be their nanny. Remember the reason you left London? All that damned gossip? Well, it simply won't go away. You're too damned beautiful. And too damned young. Another thing, my dear. I can't simply tell myself not to touch you. If you don't marry me, you will end up in my bed. I want you very much and I know, as we've already proved, that you want me as well. Marriage is the only solution.''

"But you're not forty!"

He blinked at that, then threw back his head and laughed deeply. "However did you hear of that?''

"From Mrs. Crumpe, when we were looking at your portrait. 'Tis a major tenet of your philosophy of life.''

"I see. I don't suppose she stopped with that? No. All right, she also filled your ears with a lot more.''

"Yes, quite a lot more.''

He could just imagine, particularly the part about him disliking children and planning to ignore his own, just as his father had ignored him. Had he really believed such nonsense? "No, I'm not forty, I'm a mere twenty-seven, and marrying you will give me three children, a ready-made family. My father would howl about that if he were here to see it. But I've made up my mind. Now, will you marry me?''

She looked at him steadily. It was a solution, a perfect solution, if one could be cold-blooded about such things. He wanted her body. That was all. And the respectability of marriage. To protect his name and the children. But he didn't love her. At least Tris had loved her, in his way. She shook her head. "No,'' she said. "No, I can't do it.''

"How many men were there before Tris? That was why he wouldn't marry you, wasn't it? You'd already had a protector. Or perhaps he did ask you. Did you use the children as a lever to get him to come around?''

She laughed at that. He was getting back to normal. "Good night, Knight. How odd that sounds! In any case, perhaps I will see you in the morning. On the other hand, perhaps I might experience a bit of luck and not see even your shadow.'' She got to her feet.

"What of the children, Lily?''

"What do you mean?''

"If you don't marry me, you will have to leave them. Doesn't that bother you? Don't you care? Is your love for them only an outward show? A sham?''

She went right over the edge with that final shove. "You're a bastard, a fool, an idiot! I will leave, my lord, but I will find the jewels first. Then the children and I will go together. I'm certain you'll be delighted when we're out of your selfish, boorish bachelor's life!''

He was out of his chair now, and at her side in a moment. He clasped her wrist none too gently between his fingers. "You listen to me, you stupid woman, you're not going anywhere, and if you do, it will be quite alone and quite without a single damned sou to your name! Do you understand me, Lily?''

She looked up at him in that moment, and it was his undoing. He clasped her face between his hands and kissed her, hard. His tongue was probing against her tightly closed lips. His hands left her face and stroked down her back, then held her tightly against his chest. His hands were in her hair, pulling out the pins, shifting through the thick tresses.

"Oh, God, Lily.'' He moaned into her mouth.

"No,'' she said. "No!'' But she didn't mean it, he knew she didn't mean it, and in any case, it didn't matter. Her lips parted and his tongue met hers and she froze, then melted faster than a Gunthers ice on a day in July.

He felt it and reveled in it. He had her now. He wouldn't let her forget how she responded to him. Never. How she doubtless had responded to all the men before him.

He raised his head and looked at her. Her eyes were vague and dazed. He could see the pulse pounding wildly in her throat. If he wanted to, he could take her right here, in the dining room, on the floor, on the table, standing against the wall. He could lift her and bring her down onto him, deep and deeper still, until . . .

He forced himself to calm down, to count his breaths.

"You see," he said at last, "you aren't a virgin mother goddess. No need to pretend you are, not with me, Lily."

"Virgin mother goddess," she repeated slowly, trying to collect her wits. He'd done her in yet again. She was weak and a fool. She had to get hold of herself. "What a splendid sound that has to it. But all right, I'll stop trying to make you believe it. Good night, sir. Perhaps you'll leave in the morning? The weather is quite fine for travel, isn't it?"

Knight didn't say anything for a long time. He just looked at her, at the perfect bone structure, the naturally arched brows, the narrow nose, the soft mouth. He wanted her. He wanted her more than any woman he'd ever known, ever seen, ever dreamed about. More than any lady, more than any courtesan.

"We will discuss our wedding tomorrow. Sleep well, Lily, but not too well. Dream of me. And when you do, dream of yourself naked, lying under me, and me stroking you with my hands, with my tongue—"

She drew in a shattered breath, jerked away from him, and fled the dining room.

She was a jade, but he didn't care. He wouldn't allow himself to care. One thing was certain,

though. He'd never have to worry if she was
playing him false. He'd never let her out of his
bed.

The next morning the weather continued fine.
Knight took himself to the nursery after breakfast.
Lily, he was told, had just left.

Laura Beth was so excited to see him that he
stayed with her a good thirty minutes. He saw
the fine stitching around Czarina Catherine's
neck. Where were those bloody jewels? He and
Lily needed to discuss that.

He joined John and Theo for a few minutes, but
Theo was in the midst of a geometry lesson and
it was more than Knight could stomach. As for
Sam, he was at the stables, mucking out a stall.
It was Sam, bless him, who told him that Mama
had gone riding on Violet. ''To the west, sir. She
likes that oak forest. Now, Cousin Knight, you
must look at the paddock.''

And he did. He had no choice, not really. He
wasn't about to disappoint Sam, whose enthusiasm over the horses and everything to do with
them gave Knight serious food for thought.

He rode out thirty minutes later toward the ancient oak forest. It was a beautiful spot, even in
late fall. He smiled, a very cynical, very determined smile. He would do whatever was necessary.

And he would do it this morning.

Lily needed to have things explained to her,
that was all.

As for Lily, she'd allowed Violet her head and
was enjoying the crisp breeze pulling at her riding
hat.

It felt good to be away from the house, away
from the children for a while—oh, tell the truth,
you wretched fool! You had to get away from
Knight, and his wretched marriage proposal.

What to do? She wouldn't marry him; she couldn't. She knew what he thought of her and she would be utterly stupid to marry a man who believed her a woman of loose moral character. She could tell him the truth about that, but he wouldn't believe her.

What to do? She felt herself trapped, just the way she had with Tris. She couldn't leave the children, yet not leaving them gave her no choice but to take the man who was their legal guardian. No, it wasn't the same as it had been with Tris. She had to be honest with herself. It was the fact that Knight didn't love her that made her shake her head. And she, fool that she was, she wanted him, desperately. She didn't know why she did, but she did and there it was.

If she continued in her refusal, would he boot her out? The answer was a rather obvious yes, at least to her. Her face froze in a mask of dismay. I won't think about him, she said in a whisper. I won't.

She tried to force her mind onto the scenery, dutifully regarding the denuded rolling hills to her left, the small village of Cranbourne ahead to her right.

She rode toward the oak forest, said to have been inhabited by Druids centuries before. She'd discovered it the second day at Castle Rosse, and now, whenever she went out for a ride, she returned here again and again. It was private, a place to be at peace. And if there were ghosts, they were as calm and peaceful as the sweet air itself.

If she saw a ghost she'd ask him or her where the wretched jewels were. She'd examined every one of Theo's books. No luck.

There was simply no place else to look.

What was she to do?

Just as he'd seen her the day before by the ornamental lake, he saw her again, her back against a thick oak, staring down at her riding boots. Her hair wasn't loose and flowing today; it was in a severe knot at the nape of her neck.

"Good morning, Lily," he said, all affability, as he strode toward her.

She threw her hand out in front of her, to ward him off, he supposed, but Knight only smiled and kept on coming toward her. He saw the indecision on her face and said quickly, "No, don't run from me today, Lily. I'm frankly not in the mood for another chase. Just stay put."

"Why don't you leave?" she wailed. "Go back to London! To your damned mistress! Just leave! There'd be no talk if you weren't here."

"I can't leave," he said and stopped only six inches from her.

"The weather is fine. Of course you can."

"No. Neither of us will leave until we're married. Then we'll take a wedding trip. Where would you like to go?"

"Knight, stop it! I pray you to leave be."

"I'm delighted it's such a warm day. Just fancy, it's early November and I'm actually sweating." He smiled down at her with such warmth that she felt herself heating to a near sweat herself.

"Would you like to know what I intend to do, Lily?"

"You will tell me. I usually have no choice where you're concerned."

"First I'm going to ask you again. Will you do me the honor of becoming my wife?"

"No."

"All right," he said, still all sweetness and affability. He shrugged out of his coat, loosened his cravat, and tossed it to the ground.

"What are you doing?"

"I'm undressing myself. Then I'm going to undress you. Then I'm going to make love to you,
right here, under this beautiful old oak tree."

16

Lily stared at Knight. He was musing about the history of the oak forest even as he began to unbutton his shirt. He couldn't be serious. No, it was impossible. It was the middle of the day.

On the other hand, he had entered her bedchamber, he had ripped open her nightgown, he had touched her and kissed her and made her scream with pleasure. A pleasure she'd never even known existed. A wonderful pleasure. A pleasure devoutly to be sought. Oh, dear, she had to do something.

"No, damn you!" Lily picked up her riding skirts and bounded away from him.

"Not again," Knight said, frowning after her. "Lily, I really don't want to marry a mountain goat!" He would have caught her quickly enough if they hadn't been in that damnable oak forest. She whipped behind a tree. He went one way and she went the other.

He stopped immediately and waited. Her head peeked around one side. He didn't move. Neither did she.

They stared at each other.

"You wouldn't consider coming here, would you?"

"No."

He sighed. Of course, she'd played this game with the children. She probably knew the moves better than he did.

"Lily, when was your last monthly flow?"

She actually squeaked.

"I didn't mean to embarrass you, well, perhaps I really don't care, but you see, if I get you pregnant—and out here in the forest you can't do anything to prevent it—well, then, that will solve our problems. Now, do you have an answer for me or just another mouse sound?"

All he heard was her harsh breathing.

"Lily, you can be certain that I'll stay inside you for as long as I can. To give us the best chance—of getting a child in you, that is. Now—"

"Go away, Knight! You miserable man, you don't love me!"

"The last I heard, love had nothing at all to do with marriage, Lily. I beg you not to be a twit, a romantic twit, a weak-headed romantic twit."

"Knight, please, just go away. I'll have nothing to do with you, nothing."

"Lily, enough. Come along now."

She was pale, a bit openmouthed. "You expect me to come out, to say, 'Why, certainly, my lord, please rape me'?"

"Don't be a fool," he said, feeling irritated now, his mood more disagreeable than otherwise. "I'm not about to force you, just give you a bit of, well, encouragement, that's all."

"Liar! Listen to me, Knight. You don't even like me, you despise me, you believe me a whore, the lowest kind of female. You can't want to marry me. You can't!"

"Well, I do, so there's an end to it. I will simply forget all about the others. As a matter of fact, I will keep you so occupied in my bed you won't have the time or the energy to pursue any other gentlemen.'' As he finished speaking, he lunged, but Lily, no slouch, was faster. She dashed to the cover of another oak tree, this one so gnarled and twisted Knight was certain it must have been the site of many a religious sacrifice in the misty past.

He grabbed for her but was left with a handful of air.

He cursed, then set himself to masculine, and thus superior, stratagems.

Lily watched him, distrusting that concentrated look on his face. His fox's eyes gleamed yellow. Then he looked straight at her and she knew, knew deep down, that she'd lose. She also knew that she just might want to lose. Perhaps it wasn't really losing at all. . . .

He feinted left, then in a flash dipped right and was on her in the next moment. She yelled, turned, but he had her arm in a firm grip.

''I've got you,'' he said with great relish and jerked her against him. ''I have got you, Lily,'' he repeated, then kissed her. ''Today is the beginning of our lives together, and dammit, you will admit that's true.''

She wasn't about to admit to anything, but she did want that kiss, and another one after that and another. Why not admit that she would quite willingly do anything he asked if he would keep kissing her like this? She gave up her struggles.

Her arms went around his back and she felt the smoothness and musculature of him. It was heady stuff, this man's body and to feel his flesh beneath her fingers. . . . Lily moved closer. Knight deepened his kiss. His tongue was lightly exploring her mouth, not ravishing her by any means. Her tongue tentatively touched his and she froze for a moment at his moan. She could do that to him?

"Knight," she said, worried now because her hips were pressing against him and she could feel him hard against her, and it was embarrassing to feel like this, to see in his eyes that he knew she was feeling this heat deep in her belly.

His hands stroked down her back and cupped her buttocks, lifting her against him, pressing her hard against him. The heat exploded and she forgot her embarrassment, forgot that she didn't want him to know what she was feeling. She simply didn't care. She just wanted more and more. . . .

He was so hard and she was squirming against him, her hands around his neck now, her fingers tangling in his hair, her mouth ravishing his. Oh, goodness, she wanted more and more and he gave and gave and oddly, at least to Lily, everything he did, every touch of his fingers, his lips, the pressure of his body, made her wilder than the moment before. How could he know? How could he possibly realize what he was doing to her?

She was in a frenzy for him now as his hands caressed her buttocks, molding and working her against him. He quickly turned, pressing her back against an oak tree. He drew away for a moment, knelt, and yanked up her riding skirt.

She groaned and he rose to quickly cover her mouth again. She felt his fingers moving toward her knees. Her knees, for goodness' sakes! She was trembling wildly, waiting, seeing his fingers on her stockings, moving upward, ever upward, where her woman's flesh was heated, damp and aching. And she didn't care. She parted her legs for him and heard him suck in his breath.

His fingers moved slowly, ever so slowly, and now they touched her garter, then the top of her stockings. She was dizzy with expectation, with anticipation, with uncertainty.

"Lily," he said, his breath jagged and warm in her mouth. "Do you like this?" His fingers skimmed lightly over the bare flesh of her thigh. "What are you feeling, Lily? Tell me."

He lifted his face and looked down at her. Her eyes were closed, her lips parted. Her breathing was ragged. "Open your eyes."

She did and the embarrassment was gone, or perhaps it had never been a real part of her. "What do you feel, Lily?" he asked again, his eyes never leaving hers.

His fingers stroked over her inner thigh, then moved higher. When they found her, she cried out, tensing, her back arching, her hands tightening about his arms.

"You are so beautiful and so warm and so very soft. What do you feel, Lily?"

She moistened her lips. "I . . . oh, God, Knight, please, oh!"

He slipped his middle finger inside her, easing upward as he pressed her back against the tree, and her eyes glazed with pleasure.

"Please what, Lily?"

He withdrew his finger, then inserted it again, just a small way, then repeated the movement, many times. She was narrow, very tight, actually, and he was going mad. She was breathing hard, but she still looked at him, and he could see everything she felt in her eyes.

Then his fingers probed further and she cried out, her hands fists now, pounding against his shoulders, and he wanted to yell himself at the pleasure of it. He would bring her to her climax now, bring her so much pleasure she'd be beyond thought, beyond any more of her stupid arguments. He wouldn't take her this time, no, he simply wanted her agreement to marry him. And he would have it. She was his now and she had to know it. She had to admit it. To him, aloud.

He felt an ungodly painful protest in his groin at his damnable decision. But he wasn't a randy boy, he could control his lust, and he certainly would. He wouldn't take her until she'd said yes to marriage to him.

His fingers wove passion through her and she grabbed him suddenly, bringing his mouth back down to hers. And he kissed her hard.

He could feel her tensing. He eased the pressure, smiling to himself, knowing he would just make it build and build until she was crazy for him, crazy for the pleasure he would give her. She'd say yes to anything.

"Lily, will you marry me?"

For a brief instant, she was apart from the passion and she looked lost and frightened. He hated it. He wouldn't stand for it. He caressed her again, making her eyes dazed with pleasure, making her hips push against his fingers.

He heard the shouts before she did.

"Mrs. Winthrop! Lord Castlerosse!"

No, he thought, no, it wasn't fair, it couldn't be.

The shouts were coming nearer.

She was close, so very close, moving against his fingers, her breasts heaving madly, her breath hot and wild against his mouth.

"Lily," he said very softly against her parted lips. "Sweetheart, I'm sorry."

His fingers left her and still she writhed against him, her body searching, wanting. . . .

"Lily."

"Mrs. Winthrop! Lord Castlerosse!"

Her eyes slowly regained their focus, the vagueness slowly receding. She became aware that her body was still moving against his, begging for his fingers to . . .

She cried out in mortification.

He understood. He rubbed her arms, up and down. "Lily, I'm sorry. Sweetheart, are you all right? Damn, I'm so very sorry, you were so close."

Close to those awesome feelings he'd brought her to that other time. She finally made her body become perfectly still. She felt a near pain between her thighs. Her head dropped forward onto his shoulder. He pulled her away from the tree and stroked his hands up and down her back, saying over and over, "I'm sorry, God, I'm so sorry to leave you like that."

He'd called her sweetheart. It sounded wonderful.

"Mrs. Winthrop!"

She raised her head, her eyes intelligent with awareness now. "Who is calling us? Oh, it's John. Something's happened . . . oh, no, what's happened? The children, oh, God . . ."

"Shush, Lily. Hold still a minute." He quickly straightened her clothes, then his. There was nothing he could do about the jacket he'd tossed to the ground. He scanned her face but decided that only he could see the remnants of passion there, hidden now but simmering, waiting for him, just for him.

He drew a deep breath and smiled at her, tenderly. He lightly touched his fingertips to her lips, his smile widening at her reaction, and called out, "We're here, John."

John wasn't a particularly worldly young man. On the other hand, neither was he stupid. He felt like a clod and he was embarrassed to the tips of his boots. But he couldn't leave.

"Ma'am," he said, his Adam's apple bobbing.

"It's Sam, he was mucking out a stall and got kicked. His leg is sprained, I think, but not broken."

Knight quickly took hold of Lily's hand. "Has Thrombin sent for the doctor?"

"Yes, my lord. Please don't be frightened, Mrs. Winthrop. I examined him and it's really not all that serious. He's quite all right, but he wants you and his lordship."

"Yes, yes, I'm coming. Oh, where is Violet?"

"We'll be right along, John," Knight said, and there was dismissal in his voice. John nodded and rode away with alacrity.

"It's all right, Lily. Just a simple sprain. He's a boy, you know, and boys are always doing stupid things."

Knight could see that she was frantic with worry, and that worry for Sam was mixed with the knowledge that she'd been standing against an oak tree, a man's fingers driving her to distraction, while Sam was being kicked. He saw shame wash her face clean of any color.

"Stop it!" He shook her. "You have nothing to feel guilty about. You couldn't have stopped the horse from kicking Sam. Come along. The boy needs us."

Lily drew a deep breath. She looked at him straightly. "You're right. Thank you."

He dropped his hands and smiled. She strode away from him, twisting her hair up into a chignon as she walked.

Then she realized she had no pins. Angrily, quite aware of her stupidity, she stuffed her hair down into her collar. And kept walking until she saw her riding hat on the ground. She leaned down and picked it up, not looking at it.

She slammed it on her head.

I've got you now, Lily, he thought. Be as furious as you please. It won't do you a bit of good. You're mine.

Bear Alley
Whitehall, London

Monk gave a loud bark of laughter, then moaned just as loud.

"Oh, aye, Monk, 'old still now, ye're not yet 'ealed."

"Ye got that right, Boy." Monk allowed Boy to settle him against the dirty pillows again. He sighed. "But what ye said, I liked that. Aye, 'ire one of them bloody solicitors to get them sparklers back. Aye, I like that. Send the fellow to 'is bloody lordship with a proposition."

"A rare scrawny little cove," Boy said, envisioning this solicitor. "With a big black 'at and a funny way of talking."

"We'll get the sparklers, Boy, aye, we will. Another few days, then I'll be fit again. Then I'll get that bloody damned lordship!"

"'Is sticker went pretty deep, Monk. At least three more days, that bloody doctor said."

"'E set us up, ye know," Monk said, ignoring his cohort's words. "'E set us up and we walked right into 'is trap."

"Who? What?"

"The viscount," Monk said, more patient than usual since he was dependent upon Boy's goodwill to keep him fed and watered and his bandage changed.

Monk's eyes narrowed, but it wasn't just the thought of revenge that narrowed them. It was his own body stench. The room was small, the single window nailed shut. "If ye 'adn't popped 'im one, 'e and 'is friend would have nabbed us but good.''

Boy was pleased with that faint praise. ''I've never been much good with stickers,'' he said modestly.

''No, ye're a bloody ass with a sticker. Ye can't wound a man properly. Lookee what ye did to ole Tris. But I'll get 'is lordship, and with my special sticker. 'And me my stiletto, Boy. Aye, a fine piece of work, ain't it?''

''We'll kill 'is lordship, don't ye worry about it, Monk.''

''Aye, we will,'' Monk agreed, his eyes on the sharp, narrow silver blade of the stiletto. ''But you know, I quite liked 'im. A brave cove, 'e is, and full of pluck and guts. Aye, I'll tear 'is gullet out.''

Boy tried a smile, decided it wasn't appropriate, and downed a glass of stale ale instead.

Castle Rosse

''You're such a brave boy, and no, I won't leave you, Sam.'' Lily felt his small hand tighten its grip about hers. ''Just a few more minutes, love, and Dr. Mumfries will give you a piece of hard candy, your favorite.''

''Licorice, Mama?''

''Licorice,'' Lily repeated firmly.

Sam caught a groan and bit down on his lower lip.

''It's all right, love, go ahead and scream your head off. I would.''

''But you're a girl, Mama,'' Sam pointed out with unerring accuracy. ''Boys can't make mewling sounds.''

Knight grinned at that, wondering if the sounds

he made when stroking Lily's body could be
called mewling.

"You can groan," Knight told him. "That's
manly, I swear it. Why, just last week I was
groaning to beat anything."

"When those footpads attacked you?"

Ah, Lily thought, Knight had managed to di-
vert his attention. Lily moved slightly so Knight
could sit down beside Sam. She saw him take the
boy's hand, heard his mesmerizing voice, and
watched Sam respond to him.

". . . then, unfortunately for me, the other fellow, Boy is his name, shot me. I ducked, but not
quite in time. Then Julien St. Clair came along
and the two of them scurried away. That's right,
Sam, a nice tearing moan. Good, I quite liked the
sound of that. And Dr. Mumfries is finished with
you."

"But what about Monk? The one you sliced
up?"

"I don't know. I will tell you when I find out,
though, I promise you, my boy."

Dr. Mumfries, a man new to the county, was
impressed with the viscount but didn't understand how he came to have three children living
with him and why, more importantly, this beautiful young woman was called Mama by the children. He supposed it was none of his affair. He
smiled at Sam and said, "You're game, my boy.
A pleasure to take care of you. Now, you'll be off
that leg for one week, no sooner, mind, else it be
the worse for you! Here's some laudanum in your
lemonade. Drink it."

Sam, too tired to argue, opened his mouth.

Five minutes later he was fast asleep.

Lily smiled at Dr. Mumfries and thanked him
for the dozenth time. "He'll sleep like the de—
well, soundly," Dr. Mumfries quickly amended.

"Is he all right, truly, sir?"

Knight saw a white-faced Theo standing against the corridor wall. He looked worried enough to be sick and Knight said quickly, "Of course he's all right, Theo. What did you expect? Sam's much too much a pain in the . . . well, he's a real goer, an absolute terror, you know that, Theo."

"I'll sit with him, sir. Mama, I'll take care of him, I promise. I'll read to him and—"

Knight put his hand on Theo's thin shoulder. "Theo, you are his brother. You aren't his mother or his doctor or the horse that kicked him. I'm counting on you to finish up my library. If you spend all your time with Sam, you won't finish my library and very likely you'll end up by strangling your brother. Then poor John would be out of a job."

"But how, sir?"

"Why, my dear Theo, you would go to Newgate, then to the hangman's noose, for murdering your brother. Sam would go to either heaven or hell; I'm not sure which place would have him. John would be stuck with Laura Beth. On second thought, the poor fellow would probably leave Castle Rosse, his eyes crossed."

Theo laughed, a weak sound, but still a laugh.

"Come along, let's have some lemonade. Have you tasted Mimms's lemonade? Certainly you have. It'll make your mouth pucker for at least an hour."

Knight nodded to Dr. Mumfries, then strolled down the corridor, his hand still on Theo's shoulder.

Dr. Mumfries shook his head and smiled. "The viscount is excellent with children. I'm surprised he doesn't have a dozen of his own. Of course, he's still young. Not so very surprising after all."

"That's right. He isn't forty."

"Good heavens, no! Now, Mrs. Winthrop, I prescribe a small bit of brandy for you. You've suffered quite a shock."

More shocks than you know of, Doctor, she thought, but her smile didn't slip.

There were only the faint shadows cast by the banked fire in the grate. Lily moved quietly, straightening Sam's covers and his pillows. He was sleeping soundly, a good thing, she knew, for healing. Poor little mite. He would hurt and he would doubtless become an incredible handful as the sprain mended. Enforced bed for a week. It made even Lily shudder.

She looked up at the faint noise. It was Knight, garbed in his dressing gown and slippers. The temperature had dropped sharply as the evening had advanced, and it was now as it should be for eary November.

Knight said nothing, merely nodded toward her and turned his attention to the fireplace. He built up the fire, then rose, dusting off his hands.

Lily had watched his every move, particularly his hands—strong, well shaped, narrow, the nails short and buffed. Why was he in his dressing gown? Surely he didn't intend to continue where he'd left off this afternoon?

That thought made her heart thud, loudly and quickly.

"What do you want?" she whispered, her mouth incredibly dry. "It's very late."

Knight smiled at her and strolled over, bringing a chair with him.

"I'm here to see my little patient, of course," he said easily and sat down. He saw her eyes go the length of his legs and added quietly, "Don't worry, Lily, I shan't make you howl with plea-

sure here. We don't want to disturb Sam's rest.
When you howl, we'll be quite alone."

"Stop it!"

"All right. He's still sleeping soundly?"

She nodded. "No fever, thank God. Dr. Mumfries believes Sam's too sturdy to get a fever."

"Too mean, too mischievous, too . . . well, I
can't think of any more alliterations. He's a good
boy, Lily. You've done well with him. With all
the children."

She could but stare at him. A compliment? For
her, a trollop, a fancy piece, a—

"Don't look so surprised. Of course you're a
good mother. And despite all my leanings in the
other direction, I fancy that I will be an adequate
enough father to the little devils."

He sat back in his chair and stared toward the
opposite side of the bedchamber. "I never believed I would even be in the same room with a
child. Now look at me. How odd life is. I also
never thought I would wed at such a tender, un-
ripe age, yet look at me. You've changed my life,
Lily."

"If you would but help me find the jewels, the
children and I can unchange it."

"Too late, my dear. Much too late. I should,
however, like to find Billy's Baubles. Otherwise I
fear that our two villains will cross our path again
and again until I kill them or they manage by hook
or by crook to do me in."

He heard her suck in her breath. "My being
killed bothers you, Lily?"

"A groundhog's death would bother me if it
was unnecessary."

"Ah, I see. So, my dear, next week is all right
with you? Just as soon as Sam is up on crutches?
Or sooner? Tomorrow?"

Lily slipped out of her chair only to feel his

hand close over her wrist. He tugged her off-balance and pulled her down onto his lap.

"Kiss me, Lily, and then pick a date."

"No," she said, then leaned forward to be kissed.

He laughed softly and kissed her.

Time stopped for Lily. She was drowning and loving it. She snuggled closer, her fingers tightly holding the lapels of his dressing gown. She felt him hard against her buttocks and it was unbearably exciting.

"Mama, why is Knight cuddling you?"

Knight cursed very softly and very explicitly.

17

Lily stared stupidly at Sam. "Oh, dear," she managed and tried to pull away from Knight. He didn't let her go.

"How do you feel, Sam?" Knight asked, his voice calm.

"Real funny, like the room's spinning all around. You and Mama are spinning, too."

"Nothing for you to worry about. That's the laudanum. No pain in your leg?"

"Maybe a little. What's my mama doing on your lap, Cousin Knight? And you've got your arms around her."

Knight didn't miss a beat. He'd had a minute to develop a believable lie. "She's very worried about you, my boy. Very worried, and she was crying. I'm just trying to comfort her, that's all. Doesn't she cuddle you when you're worried or crying?"

"I don't cry."

"Worried, then?"

"Yes," Sam allowed, but his voice was slurred and his eyes were drooping.

"Go back to sleep, Sam."

"Good night, Mama, Cousin Knight."

Lily sat on Knight's thighs, her head bowed, her hands clasped in her lap. She felt his large

264

hand stroke over her back and she stiffened
straight as a birch rod.

"Lily, don't be silly," he said, his hand settling
for a moment on her hip. "When we're married—
tomorrow or Friday or Saturday—the children will
see us cuddling all the time."

"No."

"You are the most stubborn woman," he marveled aloud.

"Just because I don't want to be tied to a man
who doesn't love me?"

Knight said nothing to that. He was swinging
a meditative foot. Lily could feel the movement
beneath her bottom. She squirmed just a bit and
the bounder smiled.

"I wish you would leave now, Knight."

"Why? Do you have a lot of heavy brooding to
do?"

"No, my mind is quite made up."

"Lily, if I have to, I will take you to my bedchamber right now and make love to you. I might
not let you out until Sam is ten years old. I will
make love to you until I get you with child. And
that's the end to it."

And he would, too. She knew him to be easy-
going, charming, for the most part, and kind, for
a goodly amount of the time. Until he'd made up
his mind about something, until he'd set his
course. Then he was as immovable as the Regent's Cumberland corset.

To argue would gain her naught. Nor would
she allow him to seduce her, a task as remarkably
easy for him as trouble was for Sam. So she
smiled and nodded. "All right, Knight. I will
marry you if you promise to keep your distance
until after the ceremony."

He grinned, wagging a finger at her. "That was

awfully quick, that quick change of yours. You don't think me much of a mental giant, do you?''

"You may set the date," she said, her teeth clenched.

He was quiet for a moment, weighing both her words and her expression. He simply didn't know if she was lying or not. Well, it didn't matter. He had her, here, at Castle Rosse. Sam was in bed. She couldn't, wouldn't, leave. He gave her a sunny smile. "Very well, then. Friday. I'll get a special license from Bishop Morley. He and my father were great friends. Should you like to be married by a bishop?''

"A bishop," she repeated, trying for brightness, for some enthusiasm.

At that instant, he knew she was lying. She couldn't hide anything from his discerning eye, at least not for long. He decided to let it go. What, after all, could she do? "Incidentally, Bishop Morley didn't agree with my father's precepts. Indeed, he's a romantic from the old school.''

"What old school?''

"I'll ask him when I go to see him tomorrow.''

She turned her head and he looked at her clean, utterly beautiful profile. Slowly, he brought his hand up and cupped her breast.

She gasped, twisting about on his thighs to see his face. "Knight—''

"You feel better than nice, Lily," he said and moved his fingers over her breast, circling her nipple. He saw that she was holding her breath. He saw her cheeks flush and her eyes glaze. He gave her a smile of pure triumph. Then he dropped his hand.

"It will take me a very long time to slow you down, I think," he said. He stood then, quickly, and dumped her off his lap and onto the floor. "Good night, Lily. If you have any trouble with

Sam, call me. You do know where my bedchamber is.''

His last sight was of her staring at him, completely nonplussed, her gown settled around her on the floor.

He was hard and throbbing. His hand was tingling. Friday, he thought. Friday, and she would be his legally.

But she was a jade.

On the other hand, she was genuinely fond of the children and they of her. Surely children would know if they were being treated honestly; they would feel it somehow. No, she loved the children.

Where were those damned jewels?

He resolved to spend his time until the wedding searching through every one of their belongings.

He had no time for searches the following morning. He left Castle Rosse to ride to Blimpton, to the home of Bishop Morley. He didn't return until three o'clock that afternoon. He found his household in an uproar.

Sam, the battered victim, wasn't involved. He was, evidently, sleeping the peaceful sleep of the angels.

Nor was Theo anywhere to be seen.

Laura Beth, in the very pink of health that morning, was rolling about on the entrance hall floor, clutching her stomach and screaming at the top of her lungs.

Lily looked ready to drop. She was trying to soothe Laura Beth, trying to hold her, but the child was carrying on to bring down the roof.

Knight observed the hand-wringing servants, Lily's helpless ministrations, and Laura Beth's god-awful loud performance. And it was a performance. He shook his head. Children were amazing, truly amazing.

He strode to the child, stood with legs spread and hands on his hips. "Be quiet!"

Laura Beth cocked an eye at him, then shut down like a clam.

Lily looked up, blistering words on her tongue, but Knight just shook his head at her.

"Now," he said. "Now we have quiet. No, Laura Beth, keep your bellowing behind your teeth, my girl, or it will go badly for you. Lily, what is wrong?"

"It's her stomach. She's complaining of severe cramps."

Mimms, the Castle Rosse cook, heaved through the door that led to the nether regions. "She ate two of my oatmeal cookies, my lord, that's all. Oatmeal! How could she get sick from my food, I ask you?"

"A very good question," Knight said. "Lily, leave her and come here, if you please."

"Knight, really, she—"

"Come here, Lily. I won't ask you again."

Lily was so tired she didn't have the energy to argue with him. She'd been up half the night with Sam, and now Laura Beth was acting as if she were dying. Acting! She shot Knight a suspicious look, then stood, weaving a bit before she walked over to him.

Once he had her next to him, Knight said in his sternest voice, "Laura Beth, you will now get up, straighten your clothes, apologize to Mimms and to your mother, and take yourself to your room."

Laura Beth let out a howling shriek.

"If you don't immediately do as I tell you, my girl, you'll feel my hand on your bottom."

Laura Beth gave him the most pathetic look he could ever have imagined on a child's face. He held a tight rein on the incredible urge to enfold her in his arms and promise her the moon.

"Go," he said, pointing a finger toward the stairs. "Now, Laura Beth. I am most displeased with your behavior, particularly the way you have upset your mother."

Lily wasn't overly surprised when Laura Beth scrambled to her feet, gave her dress a few tugs here and there, and whispered, "I'm sorry, Mama, Mimms." She gave a tiny sob, but Knight grabbed Lily's arm to hold her still.

"Go," he said again.

The child turned as slowly as dripping water and, small shoulders slumped pathetically, began her long hike up the stairs.

"Don't go after her, Lily," Knight said. "Leave her be until after dinner."

"It was an act," Lily said blankly, staring after the small bundle of impressive talent.

Knight grinned down at her, then dismissed Mimms and the other servants. "Now, my dear, come into the drawing room. You are in need of a strong cup of tea."

He saw her pallor, her fatigue, but said nothing. Obviously Sam had kept her up, but she hadn't called on him for help, damn her beautiful hide.

He watched her ease into an old, comfortable wing chair. She closed her eyes, leaning her head back.

"Didn't you get any rest?"

"Yes," she said, not opening her eyes. "Toward morning Sam finally quieted."

"May I ask why you didn't call on me during the night?"

"You aren't Sam's father, and I—" Her voice stopped dead the instant she realized what she'd said.

"That is a truth I can't deny," Knight agreed. "Ah, here's Thrombin with some tea."

He said nothing more until the butler had bowed out of the drawing room and Lily had sipped several times on the hot, strong brew.

"You know, Lily, you would have seen through Laura Beth's remarkable act had you not been so bloody tired."

"She wanted attention, my attention."

"True, but she must learn that she isn't the only inhabitant in the world."

"She's just a little girl, Knight."

"Now, hopefully, she's a somewhat chastened little girl, at least for the next thirty minutes or so."

"Perhaps fifteen minutes," Lily said and gave him her crooked grin that made him instantly and overpoweringly as randy as the head herd goat.

"I don't like this overmothering of yours," he said. "It smacks of being a martyr and I find that nauseating."

She remained quiet and Knight developed his theme. "I had hoped, Lily, that you would have more sense. I don't want my bride-to-be white-faced and skinny, her eyes red from lack of sleep."

He was very talented at goading her into giving herself away, she thought, even as she and her temper slid over the edge. She was shouting as she rose. "Why won't you believe me? I don't want to be your damned bride!"

"I do hesitate at calling you a liar, Lily, but if you don't want to be my bride, then it must be the position of mistress you're aspiring to. Whichever, you want my poor body very badly. Why, last night all I had to do was touch your breast, caress you ever so lightly, and—"

She threw her teacup at his head. He ducked,

but not before hot tea splattered over the front of his coat.

Knight picked up a napkin and patted the tea stains on the pale blue superfine material. "Should you like me to thrash you for that, Lily?"

She drew a deep breath and tried to draw on a near-exhausted supply of patience, but she was so tired. "I'm sorry I threw my teacup at you, but you deserved it, Knight."

"It wasn't my intention to revolt your finest feelings, Lily, just to point out the truth to you. You're a very responsive woman, and after Friday I'll see to it that every need, every twinge you feel, is satisfied."

Every line of her body bespoke her weariness. Knight went over to her and drew her into his arms. He kissed her hair and his hands lightly stroked up and down her back. After a few moments, she leaned into him and rested her head on his shoulder.

"I will take care of the children until their bedtime. Rather, I will see to Sam and direct John to earn his generous wages and look after Theo. Our little actress will stay in her bedchamber until— well, how about dinner? I don't want her to go hungry. But don't give in to her and let her out until then. And you, my dear Lily, you will go to your bed, unfortunately alone."

She stiffened just a bit and he chuckled in her ear. "That was a very small attempt at humor, no more."

"You give orders so smoothly."

"Naturally. I'm a man."

Her fist curled hard into his belly and he obligingly grunted for her. He kissed her hair again, hugged her hard, then set her away from him.

"There's another thing I'm going to do. You're not interested? Well, I'm going to search everything you and the children own and I'm going to find those damned jewels. Are you with me? Tomorrow morning?''

Lily sighed and rubbed her fingers over her temples. She could count on her left hand the number of headaches she'd suffered in her lifetime. One was coming and it wasn't going to be pleasant. She spoke before she thought. ''I've already looked. I can't find them. In fact, I looked last night after—''

''Do continue.''

''Very well. After you humiliated me again last night, I went on another search. I tell you, there aren't any jewels.''

''Hmm,'' Knight said and stroked his jaw. That paled quickly and he brought Lily back against him. It was on the tip of his tongue to apologize to her, even to deny what he'd done, but the fact of the matter was that he had tried to dominate her, to make her realize that she wanted him and he was the one in control and he always would be and there was nothing she could do about it.

Thinking about it in such stark terms made him feel quite petty and small. He was aware that he was hard and throbbing and that if he pulled her any closer she would feel how much he wanted her. It was a matter of control. He didn't want to relinquish it. It was frightening as hell.

''What's the matter?''

''Just a headache.''

''Do you have many headaches?''

She shook her head. ''Hardly ever.''

''I suppose these circumstances warrant one. Come, let me walk with you to your bedchamber. Shall I lock you in? It would keep you in and all the children out.'' He paused, flicked his fingertip over her soft cheek. ''And me as well.''

''Give me the key.''

He grinned. "No."

He left her at her door, looked down at her beautiful face, and smiled. "Don't worry, Lily. Everything will be fine. You might consider trusting me, just a bit."

She said nothing. Her head was pounding and she felt nausea roiling about in her belly.

"You might even consider that marriage to me won't turn out to be the awesome degradation you're envisioning. We'll deal well together, you know."

He gently pushed her into her room and closed the door. He wished he could lock her in but knew even he couldn't get away with something that gothic.

Knight was thoughtful as he walked down the long corridor to his bedchamber. She would try something, he knew her that well. He would simply have to spike her guns, the sooner the better. He paused outside Sam's door and smiled.

He allowed another hour for Laura Beth's punishment, then had the child fetched to Sam's room. She gave him a bright smile which made him instantly wary until he realized she was four years old and didn't harbor the least bit of ill-will toward him.

When Theo arrived he gave Knight a very uncertain look, the kind that Knight had hoped to have disappear by now. He smiled at the boy and motioned him to sit on Sam's bed.

"Now that we're all here," Knight said, looking at each of the children in turn, "I have something to tell you. I'm going to marry your mother. On Friday."

Utter silence.

"That is the day after tomorrow."

Sam looked at him with very narrowed eyes.

"You were cuddling her last night. Is that why you're marrying her, Cousin Knight?"

"Cuddling is part of it. Your mother and I are fond of each other. We wish to do what is best for us and for you."

"It's awfully soon," Theo said, his thin face pale and suddenly tense.

It *was* awfully soon, Knight thought. "Come here, Laura Beth." He gathered her up and placed her on his knee. "Theo, please attend me. Sam, are you comfortable enough?" At Sam's nod, Knight continued. "You are my legal wards. Your mother agreed to that so Ugly Arnold couldn't ever again threaten her about your welfare. Fortunately, even though your aunt Gertrude is more closely related to you than I am, I have the resources to ensure that they can't hurt you or take you away from me. Unfortunately, Lily isn't your real mama, so she can't protect you by herself."

"She is!"

"She's my mama!"

Knight held up a quieting hand. "You love her, I know that, but the fact remains that—"

"She's my mama!" Laura Beth cried again, bouncing up and down on his knee.

"No, snippet, she isn't your real mama, but that isn't important. She's your mama in every way that counts. But, you see, the English courts wouldn't take that into account."

"We had to do that, sir," Theo said.

"Do what, Theo?"

Sam shrugged. "Tell him the truth, Theo. He already knows most of it."

Theo gave Knight a long, searching look, seemed satisfied, and began. "When we went to the Damsons in Yorkshire, Lily told them the truth, that she had been our father's fiancée. Aunt Gertrude didn't behave like a lady toward her and

Ugly Arnold tried to hurt her, but I stopped him. We all escaped the next morning. The only thing we could come up with was to make Lily Laura Beth's mother and my father's widow.''

"She is my mama," Laura Beth said again, turning on Knight's knee. For the first time he noticed a resemblance to her father. That stubborn chin of hers.

"Once she is wed to me, no one will ever challenge it. Theo, what's the matter? You're worried about something?"

"Mama is very beautiful. Men are always staring at her. Usually she doesn't even notice. But sometimes they are very obvious and it makes her unhappy. Sam and I have tried to protect her. We truly like you, Cousin Knight, but Mama comes first. Do you promise that you're not forcing her to marry you?"

My God, Knight thought, poleaxed, from the mouth of a nine-year-old. He couldn't answer that question. He wouldn't. He said instead, "Is it that you mind having me for a father?"

"You're too young to be our father," Laura Beth said, twisting around to look up at him. Her thumb promptly went back into her mouth. Why? he wondered. Because she was afraid of both her statement and his reply?

"Not really. I'm twenty-seven. Surely that's a great enough age to have sired the lot of you."

He saw the flash of pain in Theo's eyes and added quickly, "You had a father, a wonderful father. Tris was my cousin and I cared about him. Unfortunately, he had to leave you. I will be your stepfather and I hope you will allow me to take care of you. Even though you're all devils, absolute heathens, I do find that I'm quite fond of you. Most of the time."

"You like to order us about," Sam said.

"That's right. Particularly your actress sister here."

Laura Beth took her thumb out of her mouth and gave Knight the most beatific smile he'd ever had shone upon him.

"Will we have to go to Eton?" Sam asked in his most belligerent voice, but he couldn't quite meet Knight's eyes.

"Certainly. I went there, as did my father before me. It's a tradition among Winthrop men, you know."

"Did Papa go to Eton?"

"Yes, Sam, he did. He was a terror there. A scourge, and he had many friends, I understand."

"When will we go, sir?" Theo asked.

"Perhaps in January. We'll see."

"Will you hurt Mama?"

"Oh, Sam, of course not. I will take very good care of her and you. If, that is, you promise to stay away from an angry mare's hind legs."

Sam grinned.

Theo rose and extended his hand. Knight, nonplussed, shook it. "What's that for, Theo?"

"We'll let you marry Mama," Sam said.

"Thank you," Knight said in his most serious voice. "Thank you very much for trusting me."

Laura Beth took her thumb out of her mouth and beamed at Knight. "You're Papa now."

If Knight didn't look utterly taken aback, he certainly felt it. He stared at the child, thinking: I, a father? Ridiculous, absurd! Oh, God, they are mine now and I am responsible for them.

"Now, Laura Beth," Theo began, and Knight saw that he was rubbing his hands together, a nervous habit. "Cousin Knight isn't used to children. Surely he doesn't want—"

"Stow it, Laura Beth," Sam said more force-fully. "Cousin Knight is our guardian, not our papa."

Knight rose slowly, setting Laura Beth on her feet. He looked from Sam to Theo to Laura Beth. "Actually, I think if you can bring yourself to call me Papa, I should like it very much."

"Papa," said Laura Beth.

Sam's lower lip suddenly jutted out. He shook his head. "No," he said in a very aggressive voice. "No, my papa's dead. I shan't forget him. I shan't!"

"I should hope not," said Knight. He felt at a loss for a moment and wondered if it had been such a good idea to speak to the children without Lily being present. He drew a deep breath. "Think about it, Sam. I'm truly not trying to take your papa's place." But he was and he realized it at that moment. He wanted the children, wanted them to love him and look to him when they were in trouble, which, he thought with a small smile, just might make him gray-haired in a very short time.

"Sir," Theo said, clearing his throat, "we will think about it."

"Oh, close down your scarmy trap, Theo!"

"Sir, Sam's not feeling too well right now and—"

Before Sam could take further exception to his brother's diplomatic excursions, Knight said, "I understand. Now, Theo, Laura Beth, let's leave Sam to garner his strength. He needs it to be on crutches next week." Knight paused and smote his forehead with his palm. "Oh, Lord, what will you do on crutches, Sam? Should I warn the neighbors and the magistrate?"

* * *

"You *what?*"

"I spoke to the children and they gave me their permission to marry you."

"But Laura Beth didn't say a word to me, not a single word! And Sam was asleep and I couldn't find Theo—"

"I told them to keep mum. I'm impressed with Laura Beth. She really kept quiet?"

Lily was clearly distracted. A nice job of spiking her guns, Knight thought, and cut a hefty bite of his fillet of grouse.

"Yes, she did. You bribed her. You let her out well before dinner, Knight. That's not fair."

He grinned at her shamelessly. "Anything, Lily. Anything at all until you're my wife, all right and proper. Then I'll revert immediately to my former obnoxious, overbearing, cloth-headed self."

"No," she said, her voice laced with sad acceptance, "no, you won't, because you aren't any of those things. What you will revert to is being nice again."

He arched a dark brow. "Nice, huh? You're sure about that? You're finally convinced that I do have a fine and wonderful character?"

"You shouldn't have gone behind my back with the children."

"Why not? I thought it excellent strategy. You're in my net now, so to speak, and you're well and truly caught. Give it up, Lily. If you like, we can tell the children about the jewels. If they're anywhere amongst their things, they will turn up. Can you just imagine Sam with an assignment like this?"

"No, I don't want them to know about the jewels. They wouldn't let it rest there; they would want to know everything. I don't want them to know that those awful men killed Tris."

Lily had racked her brains, headache and all, to try to figure a way out of Castle Rosse and away from Knight Winthrop. Now he'd done her in. Aloud, she said, "I don't know what to do."

"If you'll tell me the problem I will try to help, truly."

She looked up, clearly startled.

"You spoke out loud, Lily."

"I didn't mean to. Oh, Knight, can't you simply settle some money on the children? I'll take them away with me and you won't have to be bothered ever again. Please, I'll—"

His partially empty wineglass sailed by her head.

She froze, staring at him.

"Why are you looking so appalled? You have shot missiles at me more times than I can count."

"Just twice!"

"With deadly intent."

"You deserved it!"

"Well, unlike you, I wouldn't have hit you. I did intend the red wine to spill on your bosom, though. Very interesting result. Would you like me to mop you off, Lily?"

Lily looked down. This one gown wasn't cut high as were her others, but it wasn't low either. She suddenly felt the wine snaking down between her breasts. "You've ruined my gown," she said, not looking at him. "I only have three, you know."

"It doesn't matter. I'll buy you a hundred."

She felt a dull thud of pain at his words. "I don't want a hundred gowns. I don't want you to buy me anything."

Knight sat back in his high-backed chair. He regarded her closely, saying nothing. Finally, in his Adult-to-Sam voice, he said, "I don't really give a good damn what you want at the moment.

Your wardrobe is lacking, to say the very least. I will see you suitably gowned. Now, have you anything else to say to me? Take care, Lily, the bottle of wine is at my elbow.''

"You're marrying me for all the wrong reasons, Knight. Can't you see that?''

"You speak in such a persuasive tone, my dear. Now, here is your betrothal ring.'' He pulled a ring from his pocket and held it out to her. Lily stared at it. It was an immense emerald surrounded by diamonds set in a delicate gold band. It was the most beautiful piece of jewelry she'd ever seen in her life.

"Billy's Baubles?''

"Amusing, aren't you? The ring belonged to my mother and my grandmother before her.''

"It must be ancient then, given the fact that the Winthrop men never wed until they are forty!''

"No, that nonsense began and ended with my father. I am twenty-seven and nearly the husband of a very beautiful woman and stepfather to three children. It's amazing, I freely admit it, but it is very nearly done, Lily. Day after tomorrow, my dear, and you will be a viscountess. I'm rich as well as titled. Doesn't that stir any greedy embers in your soul?''

"Yes,'' Lily said, smiling at him. "Yes, it does. I am marrying you for your money and what you can give me. You were right about why I came to London when I'd heard you were hurt. I hoped you would marry me on your deathbed, then I would have had everything.''

"Excellent,'' he said, sitting back in his chair and giving her a charming smile. "This way is better, don't you think? You will have all the money you wish, and in addition, you will also have my randy man's body as often as you can handle it.''

Lily could think of no words.

It wasn't until she was lying wide awake in her bed some three hours later that it occurred to her that she hadn't even asked Knight how the children had responded to his news.

They'd probably shouted hallelujahs.

Even as she thought it, she shook her head. No, it was much too soon for them to accept Knight in Tris's place. She would speak with them in the morning.

She'd accepted things, she realized. What choice had she but to marry Knight?

She couldn't say that she found him repellent.

Nor could she say that he was wicked and mean like Ugly Arnold.

But she could say that he didn't love her. And that hurt, awfully. Damn his title and his money. Damn his ruthlessness. Damn him for being the most wonderful man she'd ever known in her life.

Lily stopped her damning in an instant at the sound of a loud crash. Sam! She ripped back the covers and pulled on her dressing gown even as she was running out of her bedchamber.

18

Lily's yell died in her throat. She skidded to an abrupt halt just inside Sam's bedchamber. She stared.

Sam and Knight were tangled together on the floor, two blankets wound about them.

The night table beside the bed lay on its side, the pitcher cracked and empty on the wooden floor, water snaking toward Knight's elbow.

Sam's splinted leg was nearly vertical to his body. He was laughing.

Knight was trying to keep Sam's leg straight. He was cursing.

"May I ask what's going on?" Lily heard herself ask in the calmest voice imaginable.

"Mama," Sam said, then went off again into a fit of giggles.

"You're not hurt, I gather."

Knight clamped down on his curses. "No, that is, Sam certainly isn't hurt, not with me holding his leg in the air for him. As for myself, this damned splint of his weighs at least five stone. Don't you dare laugh, Lily! Help me get Sam up. He's under the influence of a goodly amount of laudanum. He, the dear little chap, doesn't feel a blessed thing."

Lily let a giggle escape her own throat until she

realized that Knight was in his dressing gown and the dressing gown was open to his waist and he wasn't wearing anything underneath. She gulped and stared at him. He knew that she was staring, and even if he'd been embarrassed to the roots of his hair he couldn't have prevented his body's announcement of his feelings. Thank God the room was cold. That helped, that and the fact that Lily now kept her eyes on Sam's face.

"Oh, dear," she managed, then doubled over with laughter. Knight eyed her as she hugged her stomach.

Sam giggled.

Knight gave him a stern look. "You've enjoyed enough laughter at my expense, you foul brat. Go back to sleep now and dream about all the wedding delicacies you'll doubtless consume." He patted the boy's face, straightened his blankets, then stepped back. He looked over at Lily, who had finally managed to contain her hilarity.

Indeed, he saw that she was looking up at him, and that look did him in immediately, irrevocably. It could have been fifty degrees colder in the room and it wouldn't have mattered. Oh, God. He was hard, and there was nothing, absolutely nothing, to leave to her imagination. He wanted to grab her, he wanted her to take him in her hand and caress him, he wanted to feel her beautiful breasts while her mouth . . .

"Oh, Cousin Knight, could you stay a minute? Er, Mama, would you leave, please?"

"Leave? Whyever for?"

"Mama, I have to relieve myself."

"Oh, that," Lily said and gave an exasperated sigh. "Don't be silly, Sam."

"You shouldn't be here, Mama. Cousin Knight will help me. Won't you, sir?"

Knight patted Lily's shoulder. "You're barefoot, my dear. Go back to your bed. I'll take care of the brat here. Go."

She went, but not before she heard another giggle from Sam.

She wasn't surprised, not really, when she heard her door open quietly a few minutes later.

"Is Sam all right?"

"Certainly. He much enjoyed oversetting me, I think. Bringing me to my knees, so to speak. I believe he's just like his mother in that regard."

"But I wouldn't bring you to your knees, I—"

"Lily," he said. He was closer now, standing beside her bed, looking down at her. "Lily, after we are married, you *will* have me on my knees. First I intend to strip you naked, very slowly, and I'll keep you standing, close to the fire, of course. I wouldn't want you to catch a chill. Then I'll kiss every inch of you—I'll lift the hair off your neck and nibble my way around your throat to your soft mouth. Ah, and then your breasts, Lily. Can you imagine how you will feel when I caress your breasts in my hands and caress your nipples with my mouth? Then you'll feel my tongue on your belly, then lower, until my tongue is sliding inside your beautiful body and then—" He broke off at her gasp and frowned. "Surely you are quite knowledgeable in all matters carnal?"

"No, I'm not."

"Lily, don't." He sat beside her, able to make out her features now in the dim light. "Don't ever lie to me. I don't care about the past, you must believe me. All I care about is you and me and the children and our future together."

"Of course you care about the past. You become incredibly nasty whenever you think about me with other men. I told you, Knight, I didn't live with Tris, I lived in his house. There is an immense difference, if you would but admit to it.''

But those men knew of you, he wanted to shout at her. They called you Tris's fancy piece, Tris's whore. . . .

''I want you now, Lily.'' Before she could say anything, he was stretched out beside her. ''Kiss me.''

I can't let this happen, she thought. She twisted her face away, so that his kiss landed on her left ear. If he kissed her mouth she would succumb immediately.

His right hand held her wrists, his left stroked over her throat, downward, until his fingertips touched her breast. She sucked in her breath, reared up, and pulled away from him. She rolled to the far side of the bed. ''Go away, Knight. You won't do this to me.''

He lay there, feeling equal parts foolish, bereft, and furious with her. Then he laughed. ''You're right. It's just that I want you so much I forget I'm a gentleman, a civilized man.'' He rose, straightened his dressing gown, and said in a calm voice, ''Good night, sweetheart. Tomorrow we'll find Billy's Baubles. Dream about me, Lily.''

''Good night, Knight.''

He laughed and was gone.

She didn't dream about him. She dreamed about Monk and Boy and knew fear. They had to find the jewels.

They didn't find the jewels. Knight made a game of it with the children. He told them only that if they found anything of interest in their belongings, they would be rewarded. Every item of clothing the children owned was closely examined, every toy squeezed, taken apart, and otherwise probed and prodded. Nothing.

"You were right," Knight said to Lily at luncheon. "Not a blessed thing." Saint John, as Lily now called the young tutor, was speaking to Theo, neither of them paying any attention to Knight or Lily. Laura Beth was happily forking down Mimms's plum pudding. Lily merely nodded, saying nothing. Knight fell silent, and Lily knew he was trying to decide what to do about Monk and Boy.

She was on the point of excusing herself when Knight said suddenly, "Lily, please come into the drawing room in, say, ten minutes. I have something for you."

"What? What?" Laura Beth demanded.

"None of your affair, snippet," Knight said. "Sit still and finish your plum pudding."

"What?"

"Laura Beth, Cousin Knight wants you to be quiet or else he'll send you to the nursery."

"That's an excellent threat, Theo," Knight said. "It's cold up there, Laura Beth, and you would probably freeze Czarina Catherine's toes off."

The child laughed.

"Mama, I'll go spend some time with Sam."

"Thank you, Theo. John, you deserve some rest."

"Theo and I are going riding later, Mrs. Winthrop. That will be my outing."

"Another martyr," Knight remarked to no one in particular.

Exactly ten minutes later, Lily closed the drawing room door. "You wanted to see me?"

Knight brought out a huge box from behind his back. She stared at it. "What is it?"

"Why don't you open it and see?"

She walked slowly toward him. "If you like what you find, perhaps you'll give me a kiss," he said.

"Perhaps," she said and took the box. He watched her carry it to the spindle-legged marquetry table. She lifted the lid and pulled away the silver tissue paper and gasped.

"Knight!"

He said nothing, merely watched her lift the exquisite white silk gown from the box. The rounded neck was edged with Valenciennes lace, as were the long, fitted sleeves and the hem. The moment he'd seen it, he knew that it had to belong to Lily.

"It's your wedding gown," he said after a long moment of silence.

She looked stunned. "It's incredible, but—"

"No buts, if you please. When I visited Bishop Morley, I also went to the modiste and talked her out of it. It should fit you. Her assistant was about your size and I judged it on her." He paused, realizing he was carrying on at a fine clip and Lily was as silent as a drugged mouse.

Her head was lowered.

"Lily?"

She shook her head and turned her back to him.

Knight frowned. "It doesn't please you?"

"Of course it pleases me, you idiot!"

He grinned. "I was beginning to think you'd turned into a female watering pot on me. I know the groom isn't supposed to see his bride in all her finery before the wedding, but—"

"No, you shan't." She turned around to face him, and to his surprise, she looked as composed as a saint. "Thank you, Knight. You're very kind."

He regarded her intently. "Perhaps you'll contrive to believe it, Lily. As of this time tomorrow, you'll be my wife and all of us will be a family. It isn't such a repellent thought, is it?"

She shook her head. "We couldn't find the jewels," she said, and he wanted to throttle her.

"I see," he said at his most sardonic. "If you had, you would have escaped from here—this scabrous prison—in the dawn of the morning, just as you did from Damson Farm."

"Yes," she said, and he took a step toward her, throttling a very real alternative to him now.

Lily clutched the gown to her breasts and took a quick step back. "I should like a marriage of convenience!"

He stopped cold in his tracks. "You *what?*"

"A marriage of convenience. For three days perhaps?"

"A very short marriage of convenience. After three days you will decide you want me in your bed?"

"Please, Knight, just three days. That isn't too long, and I would very much appreciate it."

"I begin to see. You still hope to find the non-existent jewels, then? Three more days to search without the fear that I'll get you with child?"

She was silent.

He was enraged. He grabbed the gown, wadded it into a ball, and threw it across the room. "Madam, you may have three years, thirty years! I don't care! I will give you fifty thousand pounds. You can leave. You can't, however, take my children. Do you understand me?" He grabbed her arms, shook her, and shouted, "You won't take my children! I won't let you!"

Lily didn't struggle with him. She was listening to him, really listening. "You've known the children less than a month. Surely you can't care that much for them."

He snarled at her, beyond himself now. "You make one move to remove them from my protection and I'll personally—"

"Personally what?" she asked, very softly.

He stared at her, knowing himself vanquished without a whimper. He hated her in that moment. He hadn't felt like a normal human being since she'd come into his well-ordered life and turned it arse over heels. He hated not being in control. Of himself or all those about him.

"God, I wish I could cut you out of my heart!"

She smiled up at him and wrapped her arms around his waist. He stiffened but he didn't pull away. She hugged him tightly.

"Knight?"

"What, you damnable irritant?"

"Am I really in your heart?"

"No, I didn't mean that at all. It was a momentary lapse, an abberation. What I really meant was that you're only in my groin. My manly parts have no sense whatsoever."

"Oh."

His hands were on her arms, rubbing lightly, up and down. "Lily, that sounded like real disappointment to me, as if you really care about me."

"I suppose I don't find you completely repellent, Knight."

"Will you marry me?"

"Yes."

"No more three days of convenience?"

"Not even an hour. Not now."

He felt as buoyant as a butterfly. He clasped her about her waist and lifted her above his head. "It's about time, you silly woman. Kiss me. Like you mean it, like you will tomorrow night when we're in bed."

He lowered her slowly as she kissed him, and she felt the hardness of him, his strength, his gentleness. She kissed him with great enthusiasm and, if he'd but realized it, great innocence.

The marriage ceremony of Knight Carden Paget Winthrop, eighth Viscount Castlerosse, to Miss Lily Ophelia Tremaine was quite a satisfactory affair, though there were only the children and the Castle Rosse servants in attendance.

Bishop Morley's cousin, the eminent solicitor Mr. Drake St. John, gave the bride away, thinking as he gently placed her hand into Lord Castlerosse's that her groom was the luckiest man to grace the face of the earth.

Knight, had he been applied to at that moment for his opinion, would have agreed, devoutly. As did the children.

"Mama's an angel," Laura Beth informed Mimms.

"Shush," Theo whispered nervously.

Sam gave his brother an impatient look and said loud enough for Knight to hear, "Mama is prettier than the Castle Rosse peacocks."

There was only one peacock currently in residence at Castle Rosse, and he was a mangy sight. Lily choked.

"Mama's prettier than Violet," Laura Beth added, not to be outdone.

Sam looked over at the bishop. "Violet is Mama's mare," he explained.

Laura Beth, in a spate of confidence sharing, tugged on the bishop's black coattails. "Look at Mama's ring! It's an airloom and very old because all of Cousin Knight's papas were old when they got married."

"Laura Beth!"

"But Cousin Knight loves Mama so much he's marrying her real young."

Theo said in a strangled voice, "No, please, Laura Beth . . ."

"It's all right, Theo," Knight said, swallowing a laugh. "Laura Beth just got her story mixed up, well, a part of it anyway. I will ask her after the ceremony where she got this bit of news."

"Why, from—"

Lily reached over and firmly clamped her hand over Laura Beth's mouth. "Suck your thumb! All right?"

"But you don't like me to, Mama."

Lily rolled her eyes heavenward and Knight said peremptorily, "Be still, Laura Beth, or you won't get a single piece of Mimms's cake."

That did the trick.

Knight nodded to Bishop Morley, a gentleman blessedly endowed with an active sense of humor.

Lily heard Knight's words, strong and deep, and felt him squeeze her hand. Her own responses were equally firm.

". . . I pronounce you man and wife. My lord, you may kiss your lovely bride."

"They're going to cuddle," Sam said and promptly shuddered.

"More than that," Theo said wisely. "Just watch."

"Do you mind?" Knight whispered against Lily's closed lips.

"Mind our vocal audience? Yes, but I'll get them. I'm just not yet certain how—"

His mouth came over hers and it was all Lily could do to stay still and not fling herself against him and hurtle him to the floor.

When he released her, he looked into her eyes, was pleased with what he saw, and gave her a very male smile. "Think about tonight, Lily. Or this afternoon. Perhaps even an hour from now if I can manage it."

Lily was humming, from the inside out. She accepted congratulations, not really understanding the words, but with a smile that never faltered.

Theo and Laura Beth crowded about them. Sam called from his royally placed chair, "Mama, will we have to watch that all the time?"

"Watch what, Sam?"

"Cousin Knight touching you and putting his mouth all over your face."

"Yes, my boy, you will. Now, John is going to carry you into the dining room. You've been a trooper, and it's time for your reward."

"I want Mimms!" shouted Laura Beth and tried to take John's hand.

"I'll see to them, Mama," Theo said and dashed after his beleaguered tutor.

"They are wonderful children, my lady," the bishop said, taking her hand.

My lady! Oh, goodness, Lily hadn't even thought about that consequence. "It is kind of you to say so. They were so excited this morning. Mr. St. John, thank you so much for being here."

Mr. St. John would have liked very much to resurrect that marvelous privilege, the droit de seigneur, if, that is, he could have demoted the viscount to a peasant. He sighed. Some things weren't meant to be.

Mimms had outdone herself. The wedding cake was three tiers with the sweetest frosting Lily had ever tasted. It settled in her stomach, mixing with the champagne and the knowledge that she was now married for the first time in her life, to a man who obviously wanted her female body more than he wanted anything else about her, which, she'd already decided, was quite enough for the present. Perhaps more importantly, he wanted the children. And that was a shock. To him as much as to her, Lily suspected, and smiled as she wiped a dab of frosting from Laura Beth's mouth.

"Are you thinking about all the very wicked things I'm going to do to you just as soon as I can clear out the house?"

"No."

Knight managed a very creditable wounded expression. "I expected you to be more malleable now that you're married, Lily. I am disappointed."

"Very well. Yes."

"Yes what?"

"I was thinking that—" She stopped, leaned toward his ear, and whispered, "Actually, my lord, I was thinking about all the wicked things I was going to do to you."

He jerked back, so surprised he sneezed into his glass of champagne. In that instant, he pictured her on top of him, her mouth on his belly, her hands moving downward, caressing him as her soft lips followed, and he nearly groaned aloud.

"Don't."

She cocked her head at him. "It seems only fair to me," she said. "Can't I be outrageous on rare occasion?"

Knight didn't say another word. He quickly sat down, crossing his legs. He sipped on his champagne, looking not at his wife but at Sam's rapt expression as he ate his second slice of wedding cake.

His wife. That had a quite acceptable ring to it. Even though he was only twenty-seven years old.

Even though his eldest child was nine years old. Even though . . .

"That's a rather vacuous grin on your face, my boy," said Bishop Morley as he seated himself beside the viscount. At Knight's continued grin, the bishop perjured himself without hesitation. "Your father would have been proud. Your wife is a beautiful woman, and is kind and good-natured as well. You are a lucky man, no doubt about that."

"My father," Knight said, staring the bishop straight in his rheumy eyes, "would have shipped me off to Africa, hoping I'd either gain some much-needed sense or rot if I didn't. You know he had no patience for anything related to the fair sex and a man's whimsical emotions."

"Your father was quite wrong," the bishop said. "But he was so very amusing, his wit so outlandish, one scarcely ever saw through to the lacks in him. I doubt he rarely noticed them. Odd how you have his wit, my boy, and he didn't spend more than two weeks a year with you."

"Well, he's laughing at me now, or howling, or whatever it is a heavenly sire does when his earthbound son disregards all his advice. He was quite like Lord Chesterfield, you know, forever writing me letters crammed with his philosophies."

"No matter now. I repeat, my boy, your wife is a fine lady. Now, I must take dear St. John— you've doubtless noticed that he's been gazing at your wife as he would at a holy relic or a plum tart. Still, he's a good-hearted fellow, you know."

Knight sighed. "I know. Most men do stare at her with succulent devotion. It can't be helped. Lily, bless her heart, rarely notices."

"Ah, you aren't a possessive husband, then?"

"I don't really know yet," Knight said thoughtfully, watching Mr. St. John—a portly gentleman old enough to be Lily's father—pat her hand, then her wrist, then her elbow. He stopped there.

The man obviously valued his hide.

Laura Beth tugged on Knight's trouser leg. "Papa," she said, giving him a sunny smile.

"Where's Czarina Catherine?" Knight asked around the sudden lump in his throat.

"She didn't have a nice enough dress to wear to Mama's wedding. I made her stay in bed."

"I should have thought of that. Come up, snippet, and say wise and intelligent things to Bishop Morley."

"I don't like black," said Laura Beth and poked her thumb in her mouth.

A wedding night should be remembered until one stuck one's spoon in the wall, Knight was thinking as he watched Lily speak to each of the servants in turn. A night that Lily would remember—in great detail—and what she remembered would make her smile, even in fifty years.

Knight looked out through the bow windows in the huge domineering formal dining room. It looked cold, the sky overcast with fat rain clouds. He turned, and saw Lily watching him. She smiled shyly.

He smiled back, thinking that she would go to bed with him every night and wake up with him every morning.

At six o'clock that evening, Knight stopped off to say good night to the children, then wended his way downstairs to the small breakfast room where he and Lily would dine alone. Dear John, bless the fellow, was entertaining the

boys until bedtime, and that saintly Mrs.
Crumpe was Laura Beth's closest friend for the
evening.

Now, Lily, he thought, it's your turn. And
mine.

19

"How can you be more beautiful than you were only an hour ago? It is obviously a metaphysical question that has no answer." Knight raised his champagne glass. "To you, Viscountess Castlerosse, my lady, my wife, my helpmeet, my—"

"You're fast going downhill!"

Lily quickly tapped the fine crystal glass to her husband's. "To us," she said, grinning. "It is odd," she continued, watching Knight serve her plate, "but I never thought to be a viscountess or any kind of 'my lady.' There was no money, you see, after Father and I left England, and I was always told that gentlemen only wed ladies with ample dowries."

"You had something better than money, Lily, a commodity of which I am already plentifully endowed."

"Oh? What, pray tell?"

He smiled at her and said simply, "You brought not only yourself but also a family. Both very strong inducements."

Lily wasn't certain if he was serious. He seeemed to be, but she still didn't know him well enough to be sure. "Well, the children are wonderful."

"And you're not?"

"I'm just me, Knight, a woman who is really quite ordinary."

"You won't speak of my wife as being ordinary, if you please, Lily. God, I'm glad it's over with. Can you admit to feelings of relief at being my wife?"

"I don't know," she said slowly, fiddling with her wineglass. "It's all been so fast and . . . well, I don't know what to think."

"I'm relieved enough for both of us," he admitted. "You're mine now, and I swear to take good care of you."

She was watching his mouth as he spoke; then she looked down at his strong hands, at the moment underemployed with serving her carrots, and imagined how it would feel to have his hands on her body, on her—

Knight stilled. "Stop looking at me like that else I'll fling you between the plate of roast hare and the bowl of scalloped oysters and have my way with you."

"That's an odd way of saying it," Lily said, trying to wipe the look—whatever it was—from her face.

"You're right. It's probably more accurate to say that you, my dear, will have your way with my poor body." That hungry look was back for a moment, and Knight groaned. "Here," he said and set her plate before her.

"Mimms has done marvelously."

When Knight settled into his chair, he smiled at her and said, "Do you think you can eat something? Just twelve bites, Lily. You'll need your strength."

Her fork trembled, just a bit, but Knight saw it, and his smile grew very pleased. A wife—an honest-to-God wife—who was a lady born and bred and who wanted to have sex with her husband. It was a heady thought, and he refused to allow any other into his mind. If she'd had just Tris or she'd slept with several men, it didn't matter to him. He'd meant what he'd said to her. The past wasn't important.

They ate in silence. Knight's eyes glittered as brightly as the branch of candles on the table.

"Lily."

She looked up and grew very still at his expression.

"This is our wedding night."

"Yes, I know."

"You aren't nervous, are you?"

"Certainly. Are not you?"

"No."

"A foolish question. You are, after all, a man."

"I can't argue with that assessment. But it is our wedding night and I want you to trust me. All right?"

"This is so different from what I am used to. Being married means I'm no longer responsible just for myself and the children. I must now include you."

"Why not just make me responsible for all of you? You can take a rest and get used to being my wife."

"Don't you have to get used to being my husband?"

"All I'm saying is that you don't have to be so alone anymore, Lily, you don't have to be so independent. I'm here now."

"Yes, you are. I'm really not hungry, Knight."

"Eat. Ten more bites, that's all. Now, do you remember that afternoon we were in the oak forest? The unforgettable afternoon Sam sprained his leg?"

She didn't want to say yes, give him more fodder for his masculine display of superiority, but she couldn't help herself. Those few moments were crystal clear in her mind. She swallowed, remembering the wild feelings that had coursed through her. She nodded.

"Do you remember what we were doing?"

"Please, Knight. Eat your mashed potatoes."

"You were standing against an oak tree, remember? The one with the very thick, old bark? I was kissing you and you were crazy for more. I leaned down then and put my hand beneath your riding skirt."

He paused for a moment, watching her place her fork first in her right hand, then in her left. Then she put it down. She didn't know what to do with her hands. She picked up a napkin.

"I have long arms, thank the good Lord," he continued, his voice lower now, softer. "Remember how I caressed the back of your knee, then very slowly moved upward, along your beautiful thigh? You were trembling, Lily, making those little female noises in your throat, and I kissed you again even as my fingers splayed upward, nearly touching you."

"Knight—"

"When my fingers found you, you were hot and all swollen for me, and you wanted me, Lily. Do you remember how I stroked you, caressed you until you were crying into my mouth, wanting me so much you couldn't help yourself?" Knight's voice was becoming ragged; he was losing control just recounting that afternoon of the week before. Lily was sitting very still.

"What are you thinking, Lily?"

She ran her tongue over her bottom lip. Then she closed her eyes for a moment. "Your fingers," she whispered. "The feelings low in my stomach when you touched me. And your mouth and the feel of your body pressed against me.''

He nearly leapt out of his chair. Oh, God, he'd thought to control things and look at him. He was hurting more than she was, he knew it. He was a man, after all, and men hurt more than women when it came to sex. He just hadn't expected her to be so very . . . honest.

''Do you know what I'm going to do to you tonight?''

She shook her head, cogent thought and even simple words hovering beyond her reach. He'd seduced her now as surely as he had that afternoon in the forest.

''We haven't an oak tree in the house. It's too cold to take you back to the forest. But, Lily . . . no, I shan't tell you. I'll show you. You won't be nervous, Lily, or afraid.''

Knight scraped back his chair, his intent clear on his face. Then, to Lily's bemused surprise, he seemed to shake himself mentally. He turned away from her and said over his shoulder, ''Would you like to play the pianoforte for me?''

She stared at his back blankly. ''Certainly,'' she said. ''That is what I should like to do more than anything in the world.'' What she really wanted, she thought somewhat forlornly, was for her husband to tell her that he cared for her. But it was just her body he wanted. He kept making that clear enough. Lily wasn't a hypocrite. Even as she thought those things she admitted that she wanted him as well, immensely. But she cared for him, dammit. Cared for him more than any man she'd ever known.

They left the dining room with nearly as much food present as before they'd come to dinner.

Lily, something of a realist, knew that any music except for the simplest piece would be quite beyond her fingers tonight. What was he up to? Tonight, she thought, she would become a woman, and it was so wonderfully exciting that she wanted to throw herself in his arms right now, right in the middle of the drawing room.

Instead, she played an Irish ballad that was, thankfully, very slow and blessed with only four different chords.

Knight watched her, watched the candlelight shimmer around her head, making her thick blond hair glow with golden highlights. The wedding gown was beyond what even he'd envisioned. The soft lace around the neckline framed her white shoulders and hinted at the soft breasts beneath the silk. He shook his head. If he continued thinking along those lines, he would be well and truly lost. He'd asked her to play the pianoforte so he could distance himself a bit, but it wasn't working.

He had to maintain control. These odd and utterly disconcerting feelings he had for Lily had to be contained. He would not be ruled by his groin. But was that all it was?

"That's enough, Lily."

He got to his feet and picked up the branch of candles. Lily's fingers fell on a minor chord and she looked at him, startled and, had he but known it, vastly relieved. He was playing some sort of game with her and she wanted it to end. She wanted him to make love to her. Once she knew what it was all about, she thought she'd have a prayer of regaining a bit of equilibrium. Not much, but a small portion at least.

She rose slowly, smiling shyly at him. He held out his hand and she placed hers into his.

"I had all your things moved into my bedchamber," he said as they walked side by side up the stairs.

"That was kind of you."

"Kind? I simply want you with me. Next week we'll begin to replenish your wardrobe."

"It doesn't matter," she said. "My wedding gown is beautiful, Knight. And so is my ring. I didn't mean to sound ungrateful."

"Gratitude has nothing to do with anything, Lily. I don't want it, in any case. I want you, nothing more."

"You have me."

"Not yet," he said, and he sounded as if he were in pain.

When they reached his large master suite at the end of the corridor, Knight opened the door, smiled down at his bride, and said, "Here, take the candles."

She did and walked into the bedchamber. He turned and pulled the heavy oak door closed. Then he faced her again, leaning against the door. "Please stand still for just a moment. I want to look at you."

Lily felt foolish and exposed, which she wasn't, not at all. The candles shook in her hand and Knight retrieved them.

He set them on the mantelpiece. "It's quite warm in here," he remarked, leaning down to add yet another log to the fire. "I told Thrombin I wanted it that way."

"There's no screen in here, Knight, and I—"

He held up his hand. "I'll be your lady's maid, Lily, but not yet. No, not yet." He walked toward her, very slowly, his eyes on her face. "You are so beautiful," he said, stopping in front of her. She closed her eyes as his fingers lightly stroked over her cheek, her jaw, her ears.

"And you, my lord. Has no woman ever told you how beautiful you are?"

"Not more than a dozen. I didn't believe them."

"Will you believe me?"

He looked at her for a long time. "We'll see. In the morning. Now, my dear bride, I want to kiss you until my ears ring."

She lowered her head, embarrassment filling her, but his long fingers closed under her chin and he raised her head. "Lily," he said, and she felt his warm breath on her mouth. She placed her hands on his shoulders and moved against him. He looked at her mouth for a very long time, then kissed her lightly, small nipping kisses that made her smile and open her eyes.

His fingertip stroked her mouth. "Part your lips."

She did and he deepened his kisses. She tasted him, the sweet taste of the champagne, the tart taste of the lemon pudding, the warm taste of him, Knight, a wonderful man, her husband. It was exquisite and no longer forbidden to her. She felt free for the first time in her life, free to be herself, free to show him what she felt for him. His tongue touched hers and Lily jumped in surprise. Then she accepted him.

She was his now, completely in his power, and he could do as he wished with her. He ignored the painful throbbing in his groin, cupped her buttocks in his hands, and lifted her. He carried her across the room, near the fireplace. He pressed her back against the wall and came against her. He felt her soft breasts against his chest, felt her breasts heaving as he rubbed his straining sex, now hard and demanding, against her belly. She gasped with the feel of it.

"You like that, don't you?"

She couldn't think of any words, and her response was to deepen her kiss and dig her fingernails into his upper arms.

Lily felt the wall against her back, felt him pushing himself against her, and she was straining toward him, unable to help herself. Then she remembered his words about the oak tree and what he'd done to her that day. She was embarrassed, excited, nearly incoherent with anticipation.

Then he was gone from her and her eyes flew open in consternation. "Knight?"

"A moment, Lily."

He was on his knees in front of her, lifting her wedding gown. "It's more delicate than your riding habit, you know, and thus requires more care. I don't wish to rip it."

She felt the cool air on her legs. Then he was standing in front of her again, his head coming down so he could kiss her, and she felt his hand on her thigh. She gasped, her arms wrapping around his back, straining toward him.

His hand moved upward, very slowly, and he kissed her again. Then he said softly into her mouth, "Do you like that, Lily? Nearly there, my dear, I'm nearly touching you. Oh, God, do you have any idea what you feel like to me?"

His fingertip lightly brushed through the curls to find her. She cried out and shuddered helplessly against him.

"No interruptions this time. Not a one."

His kiss was deep now, his tongue stroking hers just as his fingers were rhythmically caressing her soft woman's flesh, making her wild, making her moan and cry out beyond herself, making her press against his fingers to know more. . . .

He slipped his middle finger inside her and Lily

fell forward, her head on his shoulder. "Knight, I can't—"

Deeper into her. "Can't what? You're so warm, Lily, so tight, and—"

His sex was pumping, running quite rampant now, out of his control, and he withdrew from her. He wanted to bring her to a climax before he took her.

His fingers slid upward until they found her again. He smiled and nudged at her face until she raised her head for his kisses. "You like that, don't you, Lily? I know you do. You're wet and soft and I—" His tongue eased into her mouth.

She couldn't have spoken if the house had been on fire.

She moaned, flinging her head back, offering him her throat and her breasts. His fingers delved and teased. He felt the tension building in her, felt her legs stiffen, and knew that in just another moment she would reach her climax, and when she did he would be watching her face. He wanted to hold back, build the tension in her even higher, but he knew he couldn't wait.

He pushed her then, his fingers burning deep, driving her to a frenzy. Her back arched, her hips thrust forward, and she closed her eyes, crying out.

"Open your eyes!"

She did and he saw the wonder in them as her body exploded, then the vague surprise and the hopeless wash of feelings that swamped her, feelings that she could never hide from him.

He continued caressing her, his motions now soothing, more gentle, as she slowly quieted. Then, without warning, he released himself from his trousers, lifted her, and said sharply, "Put your legs around my waist!"

Lily did as he said, not understanding, not caring in any case. His hands were shoving away her wedding gown, baring her legs and hips. "Knight," she whispered, then froze as his fingers parted her. She sucked in her breath at the feel of him. His sex was against her, pushing hard, and he was hot and throbbing and she was trying to draw back, unable to help herself. He was large and insistent, and suddenly, without warning, his hands were lifting her and he was thrusting upward inside her body. She stiffened, then screamed with the pain.

Knight drove deeper, making her take more of him. He was aware of her smallness, how tight she was, but she'd wanted him and she was slick and hot and he was inside her and he wanted to howl with the feelings that were making him wild. He heard her cry out.

No, it was a scream, and she was fighting him. He didn't understand. He shoved her more closely against the wall to hold her still.

His hands were firm about her waist now and he lifted her, then drew her down on him, hard. God, she was so tight, and there was something wrong, something . . . He tore through her maidenhead and seated himself to his hilt. He could feel her womb.

She was hitting him with her fists, crying, her body shuddering with pain, her long legs tightening about his flanks.

She was a virgin and he'd just taken her roughly. Knight couldn't comprehend the consequences. He was inside her, deep inside her, and he could feel her pain, feel her muscles clenching about him, and for an instant he got hold of himself. "Lily, I'm sorry. Hold still, no, don't move! God!"

But she was trying to get free of him, and her struggles sent him over the edge. He was beyond himself, beyond her, as he worked her with his hands, thrusting faster and deeper until he yelled and stiffened and fell forward against her, spewing his seed deep inside her.

He was insensate for many moments, his breath coming harsh and ragged as he pressed his face beside hers against the wall. It was the sound of her hoarse sobs that brought him back to his senses.

She had been a virgin.

He felt her legs sliding from his flanks. Gently, he eased himself out of her and winced at her moan of pain. He lifted her in his arms and carried her to his bed. Her beautiful wedding gown was a tangled mass of silk. He smoothed it about her after he laid her on her back. Her eyes were closed and he could see the trails of tears down her cheeks. She looked like a damned virgin sacrifice.

"Lily," he said, sitting beside her. "Come, open your eyes."

"No," she said, very clearly. "I don't want to."

"I don't blame you. I—" He'd started to say he didn't know, hadn't believed she was a virgin, but he wasn't stupid. "I'm sorry, it's just that you made me wild and I wanted you so very much, Lily."

She opened her eyes and looked at him. "That hurt horribly. I thought it would be nice."

"I'm sorry," he said again. "But it won't ever hurt again, I swear it to you. Next time we'll be so close, Lily, and you'll want me inside you."

She wasn't so certain about that, even though

he appeared to be. "Is that what you would have done to me in the forest that day if John hadn't come?"

"No. I wanted to, but I decided I wanted only to give you a woman's pleasure. Your pleasure is beautiful to behold, Lily."

She studied his face, silently. "Could you please leave me now, Knight?"

"No. Let me help you, Lily. Don't argue with me—you know you can't get all those tiny little buttons by yourself."

He helped her up and began unfastening the length of buttons down her back. He was efficient and quick. He paused only when she was standing in her chemise. Lily looked down and saw the blood spots on the soft white lawn and gasped. She looked up at him, horrified. He gave her a pained smile.

"No, no, it's all right. Come and lie down and I'll bathe you."

"But, Knight, I'm bleeding!"

"Just a bit. It's from my tearing through your maidenhead. Now hold still."

She said nothing. In truth, she couldn't think of a thing to say, even when he pulled her chemise up to her waist and bathed her with the soft wet cloth. She knew he was looking at her, but still she didn't move. He pressed the cloth against her and the soreness receded a bit.

Knight stared down at her as his hands gently kneaded her inner thighs, pushing them wider apart. He'd bathed off the blood and his seed. And now he just wanted to look at her, touch her, and the wet cloth gave him an excuse. God, she was beautiful, those long white legs of hers sleekly muscled and so wonderfully soft, and he saw her again, her long white legs wrapped around his flanks, and he wanted her. Again. Lightly he touched her and she flinched. "Do you still hurt?"

He looked up, and for a moment she just looked at him.

He laid his warm palm over her. "The next time, Lily, you will be smiling at me, and ordering me not to leave you."

"It's hard to believe that."

His smile never wavered. He couldn't blame her. He'd been an ass, no doubt about that. A complete clod. "Here, let's get that chemise off you."

"No," she said, and to his surprise, she folded her arms protectively over her breasts. Her thighs were spread wide and she was covering her breasts. He grinned. "You're wonderful, my lady," he said, grasping the bottom of the chemise and ripping it off her. "Move your arms."

When she was naked, sprawled on her back, he still held himself back. He lightly laid his palm on her flat belly. Then he leaned down and took her nipple into his mouth.

Rampant, wild pleasure. She arched her back without conscious decision.

"Would you like more, Lily? I won't come inside you again, you're too sore, but I can pleasure you."

She moaned, her hands roving over his shoulders.

"I believe that's a yes."

She wanted to tell him that he was still clothed and she wanted to see him, touch him, but she felt his warm breath on her flesh as he moved down her body.

He was kissing her belly, his fingers finding her, then pushing her legs apart. He came between her legs, lifted her, and his mouth was on her, hot and deep, and she was crying with the wonder of it, the strength and power of it, and she screamed as her body shuddered and tensed.

She was gone from him, yet oddly a part of him, something deep inside her swirling about him, binding her to him, and she forgot then everything but the magic of his mouth and her body's response to him, and it went on and on.

She slid away from him as she quieted, falling asleep even as he lifted his head to smile at her. In triumph.

She was truly asleep, he saw. He supposed he should be quite satisfied with himself. He'd exhausted her with pleasure. He gently eased off the bed and rose. He looked down at her. Her hair was tangled in glorious disarray about her head, her white body was sprawled for his pleasure, and his pleasure in looking at her was great. Even her narrow feet were beautiful. He was a lucky man, a very lucky man. She was passionate and loving.

He couldn't imagine now ever entertaining the belief that the wise man should wait until he was forty to enjoy a woman who was his wife.

Knight stripped off his clothes, tossing them to the floor. He was normally ordered and neat, but he wanted more than anything to hold her against him, to feel her warm breath against his shoulder, her smooth palm on his chest. He eased in beside her and pulled the blankets over them.

She murmured something he couldn't understand.

He kissed her temple and stretched out on his back, tightening his hold on his wife. Life was just fine. There was nothing he would change, not a single thing.

Knight woke slowly, aware that something wasn't quite right. But even before he opened his eyes he thought of Lily and smiled like a vacuous sod. No, it wasn't . . .

He opened his eyes to see not Lily but Laura Beth. She was curled up between them and her elbow was in his throat.

He started, then held himself still. His wits were scattered to the four winds. At that moment, Lily opened her eyes. She stared at Laura Beth, then at her husband.

She grinned and whispered, "Oh, dear. Where did this little baggage come from?"

"I should have locked our door," Knight said.

"At least she's between us. Sometimes she sleeps right on top of me and I wake up barely breathing."

"Hello, Papa. Hello, Mama."

A small elbow barely missed jabbing into his Adam's apple. Knight felt a very wet kiss on his cheek.

"Laura Beth," Lily began, then started to laugh. She turned onto her back and laughed harder.

"Mama, you don't have any clothes on. What happened to your nightgown?"

"Oh, dear," Lily said again, straightening up at once.

"Papa doesn't have a nightgown either, I don't think."

Knight brought his arms up to pillow his head. He gave Lily a lazy look. "I want to see how you handle this four-year-old problem."

Lily had only a minute to look at her husband's bare chest. He was perfectly lovely, as lovely as she'd remembered from that afternoon when he'd stripped to his trousers to bathe Laura Beth. He wanted her to get up and parade about without her clothes on. She fretted with her lower lip, then said, "Laura Beth, I want you to hand me that towel. See, over there, near the screen."

"It's cold," Laura Beth wailed and snuggled down against Knight's chest.

Knight chuckled and brought an arm down to tousle her hair. "Listen, snippet—"

Laura Beth raised her head. "Why are you in here with Mama? This isn't her room. I was scared because I couldn't find her."

"Your mama married me yesterday, Laura Beth. That means that she will always be with me, everywhere, all the time, without exception, particularly when she's sleeping."

"Oh." Laura Beth's thumb settled into her mouth.

Lily tried again. "Get me that towel."

Knight decided to take pity on her. He leaned over and pulled on the bell cord beside the bed.

"Now, just be still and someone will come soon enough. It isn't that early."

It wasn't just someone who came, it was Stromsoe, and he turned red as a sailor's sunset. He'd arrived only two days before and had kept his distance from everyone except Knight.

"We need your assistance, Stromsoe," Knight said easily, enjoying his valet's discomfort. The prig. "Hand me my dressing gown, then take yourself off to the kitchen and tell Mimms we want our breakfast served up here in, say, thirty minutes. A very noble breakfast, if you please."

"Yes, my lord."

Stromsoe carefully averted his eyes when he

came to the bed, Knight's dressing gown in his hands. He understood his lordship's problem, naturally, a little girl in his bed, of all things! This would never have happened before she . . . He shot the new viscountess a look from the corner of his eye. He saw her then, not as an intruder, but as a woman, and he nearly swallowed his tongue. God, she was bloody fine, she was. He quickly stepped away and fled the bedchamber.

"I do believe old Stromsoe was a bit embarrassed."

"So am I. I will forgive him all his lapses of the past. You're a dreadful tease."

Knight eased into his dressing gown. Laura Beth wanted to help him and he finally sighed. "Lily, please take this little brat and hold her down. Thank you."

He heard Laura Beth giggle as he rose from the bed, quickly pulling his dressing gown into very proper lines.

"Please, Knight. A nightgown for me and my dressing gown?"

He grinned at Lily but gave in.

Over breakfast some thirty minutes later, he said to her as he buttered a slice of warm bread, "We're leaving in two hours for Brighton."

"What?"

"I don't think a wedding morning should include a four-year-old girl who not only pokes her elbow into her new papa's throat but giggles and wonders why we're sleeping together."

"But Brighton? It's winter, Knight."

"I know. There shouldn't be a soul about. Just you and me. When we're not in bed, we can talk about it or sing about it, or perhaps even chant about it."

She laughed, became warmly flushed, and felt that wonderful surge of pleasure spread over every inch of her body.

"You're mad," she said. "Two hours?"

20

The day was cold and clear, the sky a steel blue. Knight couldn't keep the grin off his face. He leaned out the window of the carriage and waved one last time to the children, who were lined up on the front steps, Theo holding Laura Beth, Sam held upright by two footmen.

"Mind John," he shouted. "And Thrombin. And any other adult who tells you to do something!"

"Laura Beth," Lily called out, squeezing in beside Knight, "keep your thumb out of your mouth and your fingers out of Mimms's cookies!"

"I'll make sure they obey," Theo called.

Knight shook his head. "That boy will either become a vicar or turn into a fanatic revolutionary. No middle road for him."

Lily smiled at him, that crooked smile that never failed to arouse him. He pulled her onto his lap as the carriage rolled forward down the long, curving drive of Castle Rosse.

"Are you warm enough?"

"Oh, yes, my cloak is wonderfully warm."

Knight stroked the soft ermine lining. "Your father must have been in a very wealthy period to buy you this."

"Yes, it's from Russia. A Count Something-or-other had bought it for his wife, and my father won it from him in a game of piquet."

She snuggled into his arms and laid her face against his. "Are you warm enough?"

"God, if you only knew, Lily. Keep moving your lovely bottom like that, and it will be the worse for you."

She giggled. It was such an unexpected sound, so sweet and clear. Knight felt something deep within him shift. He wanted her, that was all. She was a beautiful woman and she was his wife, and the combination was quite enough to make him feel more things than he'd felt in many a benighted year.

"Hold still. I mean it, Lily."

"All right," she said agreeably. "Shall I move to the other seat?"

"No, we need to share our warmth."

Lily settled herself close against him. He pulled the carriage blanket over her legs and his.

"Now, I want to talk to you."

"That sounds serious. You're not going to change, are you, Knight?"

"Why the devil should I change? You want me to become a thoroughly nasty master?"

She shook her head against his shoulder. "There were no gentlemen before you, Knight."

"I know. I was stupid. I was ignorant and obnoxious and blind. I was the greatest fool alive and—"

"You'd best stop. You've given me enough ammunition for a good decade."

"You will forgive me?"

She kissed his jaw. "Yes. Now, husband, tell me what you wished to talk about."

He tightened his arms around her and dropped a kiss on her temple. "I was just thinking perhaps we could visit Burke and Arielle Drummond—

they're the Earl and Countess of Ravensworth—perhaps on our way back from Brighton. Burke and I were boys together, attended Oxford together, joined the army together, and served together in the Peninsula. I was in Paris at the time of the Battle of Toulouse this past April. Burke was wounded, and both of us came home. Of course, with Napoleon's abdication, we sold out. It was time for us to become civilians again. For Burke in particular, I suppose."

"I didn't know you'd been a soldier."

"Don't tell the children. I'll be pounded and pummeled for all my adventures, and believe me, most of them are sordid in the extreme. Now, about Burke and Arielle. You and Arielle are the same age, I think. She and Burke haven't been married long at all. They are both thoroughly nice people."

"Will they be surprised? Or do they know about us?"

"No, they don't know a bloody thing. I can just imagine the look on Burke's face, though."

"Ah, Knight Winthrop's infamous philosophy—marriage-at-forty and children are to be protected from their sire's vagaries."

"Exactly. However, once Burke sets eyes on you, my dear, he'll know I had no choice at all in the matter."

"That's nonsense," Lily said, and Knight couldn't deny the absolute sincerity in her voice, even though it was muffled against his coat. "You obviously married me for the children."

He laughed at that, then said in a serious voice, "Lily, I don't think you will ever cease to surprise me."

He kissed her again. "I think we'll stop at The Waddling Goose late this afternoon. It's a quaint old place in Godalming. Then tomorrow, my dear, we'll travel on to Brighton. It should be cold and overcast, the elements quite inhospitable, in fact, and as private as we could wish.''

That sounded just fine to Lily. ''No four-year-old little girls to snuggle between us?''

''No, a twenty-seven-year old husband will be doing all the snuggling.''

Their arrival at The Waddling Goose in Godalming brought out the ostler, a Mr. Turnsil, himself. Unfortunately, both Knight and Lily were in no mood for the overly friendly Mr. Turnsil. They'd been kissing and fondling each other for the past hour. Knight was grateful that it was winter and his greatcoat covered his intense and painful arousal. He looked at her hungrily as he helped her from the carriage, but Lily kept her head down. She *knew* that anyone who glanced at her would see the mad desire in her eyes, see her reddened mouth, and know exactly what they had been doing in that carriage.

She climbed the narrow inn stairs in front of Knight, her hand on the old wood railing. Suddenly she felt his hand caress her bottom and she jumped.

''Knight!''

''You'd best pick up your skirts and run, Lily. It's going to be an awfully close thing.''

She did, lifting her cloak and her long skirts and dashing to the top of the stairs.

''To the right,'' he called to her.

Once inside the bedchamber, a large, airy room with several wide windows that gave onto the village green, Knight drew a deep, steadying breath. Never in his adult life had he felt this way. He studied his fingers as they worked the key in the lock.

"We'll have dinner later," he said, slowly turning to face Lily. She'd taken off her cloak and was unfastening the long row of buttons over the bodice of her gown.

"Lily."

She paused, then smiled, a pained smile, and in the next instant she hurled herself into his arms. "How can you make me feel like this?" she was wailing into his ear. Then she clasped his face between her hands and began kissing his chin, his nose, his eyebrows. "Oh, truly, Knight, I can't—"

His hands beneath her buttocks, he lifted her against him, and she arched her back, pressing her belly against him. "It's too much, truly, too much—"

"I know," he managed between kisses. "Dear heaven, I know, love."

Knight carried her to the bed and eased her down onto her back. "Damned clothes," he said and stepped back, his fingers working his shirt buttons.

Lily tried to calm herself. This was insanity, she thought, this incredible array of sensations that boiled up to swamp her whenever he touched her. An hour of him fondling her in that carriage, whispering all those things he wanted to do to her, and she wanted . . .

"Knight?"

He didn't look up from his task. "Hmm?"

"Do you know something? I've never seen you completely without your clothes before."

That made him smile and pause. "That's true enough. And powerfully odd. Last night, well, that was rather strange, I guess you could say. I'm just a man, Lily. You won't be afraid of me, will you?"

"Can I assist you, my lord?"

His hand shook on the buttons of his trousers.

"Why, yes, I believe you can."

Lily, her bodice gaping open, focused all her attention on her husband, whose shirt was on the floor and whose hands were on the waistband of his trousers.

"Touch me, Lily."

She saw the thick bulge and her fingers glided downward, closing around him. He jerked forward and she sucked in her breath. "I don't know if this is such a good idea," he said, and she thought he sounded as if he were in intense pain.

"I'll help you," she said and dropped to her knees in front of him. Quickly she unfastened the buttons. Slowly, she pulled down his clothes. When he was standing, perfectly naked, Lily sat back on her heels. He looked down just as she looked up.

"You're incredible," she said, and he watched her fingers move upward, lightly skimming his thighs to touch him. He moaned even before she touched him. It was too much.

"Lily, I can't wait. I'm in very dire straits."

"Yes," she said, wanting him so much that her body was nearly humming with desire. "Oh, yes. But just a moment, Knight. Just one single moment." And then she touched him, her fingers warm and delicate on his flesh, and he wanted to howl and let himself go. He wanted her mouth on him, but when she leaned forward on her knees, he quickly stepped back. "No, Lily, I can't. No more, at least not now."

She slanted him a look, but he didn't explain. She frowned just a bit, then rose and began pulling and tugging at her clothes. Knight laughed and helped her. When she was naked, he lifted her and carried her across the room, tossing her onto the bed. In the next instant he came down on top of her. Lily closed her eyes at the feel of his body against hers.

"There can be nothing better than this in the whole world."

"Oh, yes, there can. Just you wait."

He moved over her, pressing his hips inward, watching her face. His touted control was a thing of the past. He came into her then, a single powerful thrust that drove him deep. Lily cried out and he froze. "God, did I hurt you?" He was holding himself still over her, his body trembling with the pressure.

"No. Oh, no."

It was enough. Her arms came around his back and she lifted her hips. "Move, Lily. Move your hips with me."

She didn't really understand what he wanted her to do, but her hips moved anyway. He groaned, throwing his head back, and she wanted to caress the cord in his powerful neck.

She was small and slick and so hot he knew he couldn't hold back much longer. And she was Lily and she wanted him, perhaps she even loved him a little, and more than anything he wanted her pleasure first. His voice was a hoarse, raw sound. "Lily, I . . ."

His fingers were between their bodies, finding her, and she bucked against him. He fell onto his side, bringing her with him, then turned once again until he was on his back and she was astride him, looking down at him blankly, not understanding until he closed his hands around her waist and lifted her, positioning her above him, and he felt himself at her womb, so deep was he.

Her hair was loose and wild about her face and she stared down at him, feeling his hands moving upward to cup her breasts. She arched her back and he went even deeper into her.

"Lily, move on me. Do as you wish. Anything you want."

She lifted herself, feeling him come slowly out of her body; then, without warning, she came down on him quick and hard and he groaned. He was caressing her breasts, kneading them, rubbing her nipples, and she wondered if he knew that in a second, in less than a second, her body would explode.

But his knowing hands left her breasts then and she was held on the edge, her body pulsing, wanting more. He slid both hands downward until his skilled fingers were caressing her, and she arched her back wildly, sending her hair flying about her head, and he watched her beautiful face as she bucked and twisted over him, taking her pleasure and taking him with her.

Lily fell forward, her head nestled against his throat. "I won't survive this."

Knight said nothing. He simply couldn't believe what had happened. He'd given himself completely to another person, released all control, indeed hadn't even thought about it. It should have been frightening to him, a man who'd always regarded himself as a woman's master, as her natural ruler, as the one who controlled, who knew when and how he would give a woman her pleasure whilst he observed and applauded his own skill, his own talents, his own power.

His own generosity.

His hands were slowly, automatically, stroking

her back. Nothing that had just passed between them had a thing to do with power or generosity or control. His hands stilled. She was kissing his shoulder and he was hardening inside her, filling her again. She felt him and pressed down, taking more of him.

"Lily, you're sore, and here we've—" He moaned, his hands moving down to fill themselves with her soft buttocks. He didn't give her the chance to come up on him again, but rolled her onto her back, balancing himself above her.

Her legs came up to clutch his flanks and he rode her hard, harder still, until she was crying and clutching at his hips and kissing him. And this time he'd thought it would be slow and gentle and easy. It was anything but. It was fierce as a raging storm and fast.

"Lily."

She couldn't move, didn't want to move. She was enjoying the feel of him, slick with sweat, his body hot and hard and so wonderful she wanted to burrow inside him, become part of him. She sighed. She would touch him, and keep touching him forever. She just hadn't known, hadn't realized. . . .

"Knight? I know that you've, well, experienced other ladies before and—"

He grinned at that but said only, "And?"

His mouthy Lily was fumbling for words. This was interesting. "Yes?" he prodded.

"Well, did they enjoy you as much as I do?"

"I don't know. Tell me how much you enjoy me, and I'll try to give you an answer."

"You're slippery, Knight."

"With sweat, from all my exertions and yours, and—"

Her fingers squeezed his buttocks, and he

dipped his head down to kiss her pursed lips.
"You're the only lady I want until I cock up my
toes and pass to the hereafter. The others are well
past. They don't matter."

"I please you, then?"

"If you pleased me more I should be dead."

He sounded positively serious and she giggled.

"Don't laugh. It doesn't help."

"Did they become wild like I do?"

Ah, so that was the crux of it. Could the perfect
lady also be perfectly wanton? She was afraid.
"No," he said. "Well, yes, but not in the same
way. You are giving and open and loving. Few
ladies are so wonderful as you, Lily, as natural as
you."

"Then it doesn't shame you that I am so very
. . . well, I guess you could say that—"

"Shame me? You silly wigeon!" He rolled her
onto her side and they lay nose to nose. "You're
mine, Lily," he said and began kissing her. "Mine
forever."

Lily slept, those final words of his floating
through her mind, pleasing her more than she
could have ever imagined. When she awoke it was
to more kisses. She smiled and his tongue eased
into her mouth. "Knight," she whispered and
held out her arms for him.

"No, Lily. I have ordered our dinner. We need
sustenance. Here is your dressing gown."

Mr. Turnsil had provided roast hare, lark pudding, oyster patties, and two vegetables. It was a
feast, and Lily took one look at the munificence
and fell upon it like a starving woman. Knight
watched his wife. His *wife*. "A trencherwoman of
note," he remarked as he poured her some excellent bordeaux.

She swallowed her bite of hare and gave him a

wide grin. ''A trencherwoman must keep up her strength.''

''Do you have any idea how utterly beautiful you look right this minute?''

Lily cocked her head to one side and gave him that crooked smile of hers. ''You like ratty hair, do you?''

''Yes. And I particularly like the way your dressing gown is slipping open over your breasts.''

That got her attention, and to his immense surprise and amusement, she flushed. ''Remarkable, absolutely remarkable. A toast, Lily, if you can resist your hare for a moment.''

Their glasses clicked together.

''To tonight.''

She raised a brow.

''To breaking a record.''

She blinked.

''To reducing myself to an exhausted heap by morning.''

''Here, here!''

''Greedy woman,'' he remarked fondly to a lone oyster patty on her plate. ''Another toast. May I be plagued my entire life by this one single greedy woman.''

''Here, here!''

But Knight wasn't to break his record that night. He was holding her, calming her breathing, lightly caressing her heaving breasts, when suddenly, without warning, the bow window opened and a familiar voice whispered, ''I know ye're awake, me fine cove.''

Knight froze.

''Oh, no, don't move, me lord. Lookee, Boy, 'e's still atop the little piece, 'e is. At least we

gave ye time to wring out yer rod. Ye've plowed
the little piece more than yer share, though.''

"Knight? What—''

Knight turned quickly and placed his finger
over Lily's mouth. "Hush and don't move.''

"What's wrong?''

"We've company.'' She turned stiff as a stone
but didn't move. Knight pulled the covers over
them and waited.

"Close the window, Boy. It's bloody cold. We
need to 'ave a little chat with our friends 'ere.
Aye, that's it. Light the bloody candle. Now, my
fine lord, ye're through with yer little tart. Ye
don't 'ave to cover 'er up, ye know. Boy and I,
well, we done seen all she's got, wot with ye
plowing 'er yet again.''

Lily sucked in her breath. It was the men she'd
seen, the ones who'd killed Tris. Fool! She'd forgotten all about the damnable jewels.

Knight didn't respond to the taunt. He couldn't
afford to. He and Lily were naked, in bed, and
his pistol was in his greatcoat pocket, on the far
side of the bedchamber.

"Gawd, but she's a beauty, Monk, purtier than
I remember. Just lookee at all that 'air she's got.''

"I know,'' Monk said, "but we got better things
to do now, Boy.''

"I'd hoped I'd sent you to the devil,'' Knight
said to Monk.

The big fellow merely grinned as he seated
himself quite at his ease at the small table where
Knight and Lily had enjoyed their dinner not
many hours before. "Ye gave it yer best, milord.
Now, ye gives us the baubles and we'll be on our
way again. Boy will leave the little tart alone, all
aboveboard. I like ye, ye see. Poor Tris! 'Is own
blood cousin in 'is tart's belly, and 'im not un-

derground for more than three months. No loyalty in this world, no indeed.''

"She is my wife," Knight said.

"Yer what? Well, ye 'ear that, Boy? 'Is fancy lordship 'ere married Tris's little fancy piece. Well, now, 'tain't none of our affair. Where's the baubles?''

"I'll tell you if you let my wife go.''

"Sorry, but we'll keep yer missus right 'ere. She'll keep ye in line.''

"Let her go. She has nothing to do with any of this. Nothing.''

"No, Knight, I won't leave you.''

"Lily, be quiet.''

She shook her head, straightened a bit so she could see Monk. "Listen to me, both of you. We don't know where the jewels are! We've looked and looked. I'm telling you the truth. Tris never said a word to me, not a single word. I don't know about the jewels and neither does his lordship.''

"She's smooth as old Tris," Boy said. "Only she's lots purtier, she is. Look at them titties, Monk. Gawd.''

Her breasts were covered. She didn't move. She felt Knight's hand tighten on her arm. "Please keep quiet. It won't do any good to plead with them. Please, just do as I tell you.''

Lily looked at him numbly. She felt curdled with fear. Oh, God, what if they hurt Knight? It would be all her fault. She'd brought these men into his life.

"She's not lying to you. We don't have them," Knight said. "We can only believe they're still in Tris's house in Brussels. We've looked everywhere.''

Boy scratched his ear and said to Monk,

"Maybe they're telling us the truth, Monk. Do ye think that—"

"Ye don't know nothing about this world, Boy; ye're too innocent and trusting. Men is men, and they're greedy coves when all's said and done. One look at the sparklers and our fine lordship 'ere would likely sell 'is little tart, er, wife. Out of yer bed, both of ye, and dress yerselves."

"No," Knight said quite calmly. "You will take me into the corridor as a hostage while my wife dresses. You will not watch her, gentlemen."

Perhaps it was the command of the soldier of many years, but it worked. Monk scratched his belly. Boy was already moving to the door. "Awright," Monk said, standing. "Give 'im a dressing gown, Boy, and bring 'im along. As for ye," Monk said, looking long at Lily, "ye 'ave two minutes, no more, mind ye, else we're in again to look our fill."

Lily nodded, beyond words. She watched Knight, beautifully naked, ease out of the bed, stand straight, and hold out his hand for his dressing gown. She watched until the bedchamber door had closed behind the three of them, then dashed from the bed. She was clothed in a trice.

She was looking frantically about for a weapon, anything, when the door opened and Monk peered around it, an abstracted look on his face.

"Pity," was all he said. "Now, yer turn, yer lordship."

"Sit down, Lily," Knight said, motioning to the chair at the table. He wasn't about to allow them to take her into the corridor. Where the devil was Turnsil? Where were any other guests? Were they the only ones in the inn? Perhaps Monk had paid old Turnsil to keep his mouth shut and his door closed. What Monk had said was, for the most part, quite true. Greed ruled many men.

He needed his pistol, and he would have it once he donned his greatcoat. Then he'd look for the right opportunity. He gave Lily a reassuring smile, stripped off the dressing gown, and dressed himself. In a total of ten minutes, the odd quartet was quietly going down the stairs and out of the inn.

Old Kenny, his driver, would give the alert, Knight thought, when he found them gone in the morning. But what a mess. What would he say? What could he possibly tell anyone?

It was black as pitch outside. No moon, the stars obscured by low dark clouds. It was colder than it should be, the air heavy with the threat of snow.

Within five minutes the carriage, now driven by Monk, was bowling along the road. Not toward Brighton, Knight realized, but north and east.

Boy was seated on the seat opposite them, muffed to his ears in a scruffy wool scarf. He kept a pistol aimed at Lily's chest. "Just a little trip," he said after a while. "Me and Monk got this little cottage. 'Ired it, we did, just the way real folks do. Ye'll come about once we're there."

Neither Lily nor Knight said anything to that bit of news.

Several hours later, the carriage turned off onto a rutted side road and continued for some ten minutes more before taking another left turn. Knight had no idea where they were. Finally Monk pulled the horses to a halt in front of a small, dilapidated cottage, its one story completely covered with ivy.

"Nice place, ain't it?" Boy asked. "Monk saw to us getting it. 'E 'as refined taste, 'as Monk."

Knight could only marvel at the man. He was something of a half-wit, something of a cunning animal, and a murderer. Both men were murderers. He couldn't forget that.

Monk pulled open the carriage door. "Ye all right, Boy?"

"Aye, Monk. Nary a bit of trouble from our fancy cove 'ere."

The cottage was dark. Knight and Lily waited on the narrow, sagging porch, Boy standing guard over them while Monk went inside to light the candles.

"Bring 'em in!" Monk shouted.

The interior of the cottage was as depressing as the exterior. Lily looked at the low-beamed single room, a smoking fire at one end, a curtained-off partition at the other end, hiding, she assumed, a bed and perhaps a table. The kitchen looked rusted and unused.

"Ye get over there and build us up a fire," Monk said, waving his stiletto toward Knight. "And ye, me fine little lady, ye can make us all some dinner."

Lily didn't say a word. She walked into the kitchen area and flinched at the grime. "There's no water," she said.

"I'll fetch ye some. There's vittles—ye'll find 'em on that counter. 'Urry up now, we want tea."

Lily took off her beautiful cloak and carefully laid it over the back of a chair. From the corner of her eye she saw Knight remove his greatcoat, discreetly removing the pistol with it and hiding it in the folds of material. He would do the right thing at the right time. She had to believe that.

Lily was frying two thick slabs of beef when she felt a man's hot breath against the back of her neck. She continued with her task, not moving.

"Oh, aye, old Tris wanted ye, wanted ye more than anything. We did ye a favor, 'uh? Got rid of 'im and gave ye a rich man. Ye still got the brats? That little one, 'e got me good, right in the shin. That little nipper deserves a pounding."

Lily closed her eyes for a moment. Words were nothing. Words didn't hurt or kill. Suddenly his arms came around her and Monk jerked her back against him.

"Let her go," she heard Knight say calmly. "Now, Monk, or I swear I'll kill you, very slowly and with more pain than you've ever imagined."

Monk laughed in her ear. He brought up his hand, brushed it across her breasts, then released her and stepped back. "Later, 'uh? Me and Boy knows ye love it—we watched ye sweating with yer 'usband enough. Gawd, it made us both 'ard as tree trunks!"

Lily served the fried beef and some softly cooked potatoes. She was aware of Monk's assessing eye on her, but she forced herself to remain calm.

"I've made up me mind," Monk announced, not waiting to swallow the mouthful of beef before he spoke. "Nothing will move ye, either of ye, at least not logic and persuasive words. So, me fine lordship, me and Boy 'ere will take yer little wife, right in front of ye, iffen ye don't tell us where ye 'id the sparklers. Ye got that, me fine cove? We'll spread 'er legs and plow 'er little belly, and ye'll watch."

"Me first, Monk?"

"Ye ain't got enough even to tease 'er, Boy. Nay, I'll plow 'er good, open 'er up, so to speak, then ye can 'ave yer fun. Now, me two pigeons, wot do ye think of that plan?"

21

Fear ripped through Lily, but she held herself still. Completely still. She wouldn't show them her fear.

Stay strong, Knight was urging her silently; don't break. God, he wished he were close enough to touch her, to take her hand, but he wasn't. He blustered a few minutes, threatening them, swearing mightily, all in all giving them a marvelous show. Was Lily feeling disgust at his weakness? Did she understand? He simply didn't know.

Finally he said, defeated fury lacing his words, "All right, you damnable bounders! I'll tell you where the jewels are. Just keep your hands off my wife. The stones are back at Castle Rosse. Lily and I found them in one of the children's toys just before we were married. I hid the jewels in the stables. I can't tell you specifically where, I must show you."

"Ah," Monk said and sat back. "Ye see, Boy," he continued, giving his friend the benefit of his wisdom, "our fine lordship 'ere jest needed a bit of proper encouragement. 'Uman nature, Boy, ye 'ave to know 'ow to appeal to 'uman nature. Now, in the morning, we'll go back to Castle

Rosse and 'e'll fetch us Billy's Baubles all right
and no more 'emming about.''

''But what about 'er?'' Boy sounded petulant,
like a child who would be deprived of a promised
candy.

'' 'old yerself, Boy,'' Monk said mildly. ''Jest
'old yerself.''

''I don't want to 'jest 'old myself,' I want to
'old her. Ye saw her titties, Monk. Gawd, they're
lovely and round, and them white legs of 'ers, all
open wide, and 'im going into 'er like—''

''Ye're too sick to enjoy 'er, Boy,'' Monk interrupted and stood to his intimidating height.
''Ye've got a chill, and I knows that ye can't de-
plete yer stock when ye've got a chill.'' Boy subsided, but he continued to voice his complaints.
They only dropped an octave.

Knight's belly was cramping. He drew several
calming, deep breaths.

''We'll leave at first light,'' Monk said to
Knight. ''Ye and yer little piece rest now, iffen ye
don't want to take 'er again. No? Well, then,
we've got to tie ye up, no sense in ye taking
chances with Boy and his pistol. I don't want Boy
to shoot ye.''

''Like he knifed Tris?''

''That's right. That were a mistake, but Boy
learned 'is lesson. I coshed 'is 'ead fer that one, I
did.''

In short order Knight's hands were bound behind his back with rough hemp. He moved closer
to the fireplace and leaned against the sharp-hewn
stone.

Monk rose and dusted his hands. ''Now, mi-
lady, 'tis yer turn. Sit down beside 'is lordship
'ere.''

He tied Lily's hands in front of her, not tightly,

but with a maze of complicated knots that would have brought compliments from a sailor.

"Now, Boy, ye watch 'em close for four hours, then wake me up. Stay up, ye 'ear? No snoring. 'Is lordship ain't a proper clod to be left unattended."

The only warmth in the cottage was from the sluggish fire in the fireplace. Knight nodded to Lily and she moved closer to his side. "No fondling 'is lordship now," Boy said to Lily, a vacuous remark considering the rope around her hands.

Lily leaned against Knight's shoulder. "I know," she whispered softly. "I know." She relaxed trustingly against him.

Knight said nothing, but he wished he had the confidence in himself that Lily appeared to have. He waited until he heard Monk's noxious snores. Just Boy now, he thought.

"Be ready," he said quietly in Lily's ear as he kissed her temple.

There were two pistols: the one in Boy's hand and the one tucked loosely in the folds of Knight's greatcoat. Unfortunately, his greatcoat was slung over the back of a chair on the far side of the room. Soon, though, Boy would fall sleep, he was sure of it. Then he would make his move. Slowly, very slowly, he rubbed the ropes about his wrists against a protruding jagged stone on the fireplace.

"Ye know, Monk didn't say nothing about me jest touching 'er, now did 'e?"

Lily stiffened.

"If you do," Knight said easily, "I won't show you where I hid the jewels. Lily doesn't know, so I'm your only source, and without me, Boy, you won't get the sparklers. Monk just might cancel out your friendship, eh? He might do more this time than cosh you in the head. He might slide that stiletto of his into your heart.''

Boy's eyes narrowed. Knight saw his indecision and prayed. His prayer was answered in a way he couldn't have anticipated.

''Awright, then ye take 'er. She'll open yer britches, then she ken climb on top of ye. Ye'll stick it in 'er, and I ken watch.''

''No,'' Knight said. ''You forget, Boy, a man has to be aroused to do anything at all with his rod. My hands are tied behind my back, I'm bloody uncomfortable, my shoulders feel like they're being pulled out of their sockets, I'm a bit cold, and my rod's deader than an Egyptian scarab.''

''What's a scare-ab?''

''A scarab is a long-dead black dung beetle.''

''Well, I 'opes it's long dead!''

Boy subsided. He wrapped himself up tightly, winding his filthy woolen scarf about his throat. But he never fell asleep. Not that it mattered much to Knight. The ropes seemed impervious to the jagged stone. His hands cramped. His fingers went numb. He wanted to yell with frustration.

When Boy roused Monk, Knight pretended sleep. He watched the big man settle himself across from him and Lily, Boy's pistol on his lap.

He'd have to be more careful now.

Knight fell asleep finally, and into a vicious nightmare. He was completely and utterly alone, his arms and legs chained to a bare stone wall. He could hear Lily screaming, but he couldn't see her, couldn't help her. It went on and on. It was the horror of the nightmare that finally jerked him awake. He heard Monk chuckle as he shook his head to clear it of the lingering images. The nightmare had been a blessing. It had brought him awake again. He went back to work with renewed energy and strength on the damned ropes.

Lily slept fitfully beside him. Monk said nothing, merely watched both of them. It was near dawn when the rope unfrayed and Knight could pull his hands free. He kept very still. He had to get feeling back into his hands before he had a prayer of overcoming Monk and Boy.

Monk untied Lily and ordered her to make coffee.

"I'll need water to make the coffee. There isn't any here."

It was Monk who went outside the cottage to fetch water, from where Knight didn't know. He hoped it was a good distance away.

Knight moved then, moved more quickly than he had in his entire life. He was on his feet and on Boy in an instant. His fist landed hard in Boy's stomach, next on his nose, and he drew back to give a smart kick in Boy's groin.

Boy screamed with pain and fell to his knees.

"Gawd damn ye! Oh, I'll kill ye for that . . . ah!"

Knight brought the pistol butt down on Boy's head and he crumpled unconscious to the dirty floor.

Knight raced to the window and peered out. No sign of Monk. Thank God.

"Quickly, Lily."

Within a minute Knight and Lily had eased out of the cottage and around the side to the stable.

Knight's fingers felt clumsy and numb, his knuckles bloody. Lily helped him saddle the big raw-boned stallion that had pulled the carriage. "He'll carry both of us. We'll let the other horses out. Hold still now, Lily. Don't move."

Knight peered around the stable door. He saw Monk drop a pan of water at a yell from Boy.

"Go! Quickly!"

Knight grabbed the stallion's reins and pulled him outside. Lily prodded and waved her cloak to get the other horses out of the stable and away.

Then she looked up and froze.

"Knight! Oh, God! He's got a pistol!"

Knight whirled about, dropping the horse's reins, pulling his own pistol up. He and Boy fired very nearly at the same instant. In that brief moment, Lily flung herself in front of him, screaming, "No!" and he felt her body take the bullet, felt its impact as it hurled her back against him.

"Oh, God, no!" His arm went around her waist to hold her up. "Oh, God, Lily!"

Time seemed to stop. Knight heard an agonized scream, but it seemed far away, far removed from him, until his eyes focused and he saw Boy go down, clutching his chest. Monk yowled with fury as he came running toward his friend. Knight's pistol was empty. He quickly lifted Lily into his arms, grabbed the loose reins of Monk's horse, and swung himself into the saddle.

A bullet whistled past his ear. He ducked his head and dug his heels into the horse's sides, sheltering Lily with his body.

"Ye damned bastid!" Monk yelled after him. "I'll kill ye for this! Ye soddin' bastid! Oh, Gawd, Boy!"

Another bullet tore through Knight's greatcoat, missing his arm by a hair's width. Yet another bullet? Did Monk have another pistol? Knight kept his head down, Lily tucked tightly against his chest.

At last all was silent. No more bullets, no more Monk screaming curses after them. A snowflake hit his nose, then another. Knight looked up at the dawn-streaked sky. Freezing cold and now

snow. The clouds were nearly black, bloated with
snow.

He looked down at Lily's quiet face. She was
so damnably pale. He had to stop soon, had to
stanch the bleeding. He slipped his hand into her
cloak and pressed it over her heart. The beat was
slow and steady.

He heard no sounds of a horse following them
and knew that for the moment, at least, Monk
wasn't behind them. He brought the horse to a
halt beside a brace of naked-branched maple trees.
As gently as he could manage it, he dismounted,
holding Lily high against him with his one free
arm.

He eased her to the ground and opened her
cloak. Her chest was covered with blood. He saw
the hole the bullet had made high on her left
shoulder, through her cloak and through her
gown. He gently lifted her and allowed a small
moment of relief. The bullet had torn through and
exited her back. But the bleeding was still copi-
ous. He ripped open her gown and pulled her
chemise aside. Carefully, he cupped snow in his
hand, then flattened his palm against the wound.
That should slow the bleeding and cleanse the
wound as well. He repeated the procedure on her
back. Once, then again, longer this time, until his
hand was numb with cold, his fingers blue. The
bleeding stopped. Then he lifted the hem of her
gown and ripped off the flounce of her petticoat.
He wrapped it around and around her shoulder
and back, and tied it tightly. Oh, please, God, he
prayed, please let her survive this.

She was unconscious. He made the decision not
to try to rouse her. Her pain would be unbearable
when she awoke. He looked around, trying to get
his bearings. Where the devil were they? It was
impossible to tell. There was no sun rising in the

east. The snow was coming down faster now, thicker, obscuring any signs that would give him a clue to their whereabouts.

He had to get them to a warm place. Lily must have a doctor. And he, her wonderful protector, had no idea which direction to take. He mounted once more, settled Lily against him, and gave the horse his lead. They were on a country road, to be sure, but at least it was well traveled, which was heartening. Sooner or later there had to be road signs. There had to be farms and cottages and people who were not villains.

Knight felt the cold seeping through his great-coat. The snow was coming down thick and fast, nearly blinding him. Suddenly Lily stirred, struggled against him, her arms flailing, and screamed, "Knight, no! No! He can't kill you, I won't let him! Oh, God, Knight!"

"It's all right, truly, Lily, I'm all right. Hush now, don't move. I can't hold you still and keep our horse on the road." She quieted again and he continued speaking to her, nonsense really, but oddly enough, she seemed to find it reassuring.

He didn't know how much time had passed before he saw the barn, a rickety old structure that had seen better days a good twenty years before. But it was shelter, and it was off the road. In the thickly flying snow, he couldn't see if there was a farmhouse near. Well, it was a beginning.

The barn was a mass of drafts. Boards had fallen off the sides, leaving huge gaps for the wind and the snow. Then he saw what looked to be a pile of dry hay in one dim corner of the barn. Good enough, he thought. They could keep warm until it stopped snowing. Then he'd find the farmhouse that had to be nearby.

He was terrified for Lily. Her clothing was damp and there was nothing he could do about it. He carried her to the protected corner and gently laid her down. He took off his greatcoat and wrapped it over her, then piled her with the dry hay. The horse was blowing, his sides quivering. He had to take care of their only means of transportation. Knight ran his hands over the horse's neck, telling him what a brave, stout fellow he was, rubbing him down with handfuls of hay until his sides were still and he butted Knight with his nose.

"All right, old fellow, you come over here and eat your fill. And rest; you'll need it."

Once he'd taken care of the horse, Knight returned to Lily. He wasn't particularly cold because of all his exertions. He eased down beside her, holding her close to give her all his warmth. The piles of hay over them held in their heat, and he could feel her body slowly relaxing against him. He slept a while, then woke with a start, his heart pounding, sweat beading on his forehead.

Monk! The noise came again. God, he'd found them. Knight became as taut as a bowstring, tensed and ready to move quickly. Nothing.

They were alone. The horse had nickered, that was all.

A bird had taken flight. Nothing more.

There wasn't another human about.

Knight sat up slowly, careful not to disturb Lily. Through a substantial hole in the far side of the barn wall, he could see that it still snowed heavily. Damn and blast. He hadn't any idea how much time had passed. There was nothing he could do. Nothing.

He eased back down and looked at his wife. So dreadfully pale she was. "Lily," he said softly, and glided one fingertip down her cheek.

To his surprise, her eyelashes flickered and her

eyes opened. She looked at him, and remarkably, she smiled. "Hello."

"You're awake," he said.

"Yes. Are you all right? Where are we?"

"Hush, I'll tell you everything. I'm wonderfully well and I haven't the foggiest notion where we are. It's snowing too hard, you see, and I couldn't make out any road signs. We're in a very drafty barn, in the only corner that doesn't have boards ripped off the side. Are you warm enough?"

"Oh, yes." Suddenly her body communicated with her mind that all was not well. "Knight!" She pressed her head back against his arm, feeling the searing hot pain in her shoulder. It was like nothing she could have ever imagined. Deep, burning deep, and tearing pain. She wanted to scream, to try to pull away from it, but Knight was holding her still and she refused to scream, refused to let the pain win.

"Take slow, deep breaths," she heard him say, his breath warm on her cheek. "It will help the pain. Slow, Lily, very slow breaths. Try it. Come on."

She did. It took incredible will, but she did it. Slow and deep. Slow and deep.

"That's right. You're controlling it. I knew you could do it. We'll be all right, Lily, I swear to you. As soon as the snow stops, I'll be able to take us to safety and you to a doctor. That's right—slow and deep."

He continued to speak to her, coaching her, encouraging her until once again she fell into a stupor.

He didn't know whether to be relieved or scared out of his wits. At least she was free of the pain for a while. He looked up to see a swirl of snow cascade through a wide hole in the barn's wall.

It was several hours before Lily opened her eyes again. Knight was staring at her, praying that she wouldn't be fevered. If she were, he knew it would mean defeat. He'd seen too many men wounded in battle succumb, not to their wounds, but to the raging fevers that sucked the life out of them. She was cool to the touch.

"Knight?"

"Lily. Breathe slow and deep. That's right."

"It's warm, you're warm."

"It's the hay, it's keeping our body heat in. It's still snowing hard. But not much longer, Lily. Even now it looks to be clearing. At least Monk can't be following us in this weather."

"Did you kill Boy?"

"I don't know. I saw him clutch his chest and fall. I pray I didn't; then Monk will stay with him."

"Otherwise, Monk will be after us."

"He won't find us, Lily."

"I can control the pain, Knight. It's there, you know, and like a caged animal tearing at the bars to be free, but I won't let it, I won't."

"You're wonderful, Lily, and don't you ever forget it." He kissed her lightly on her forehead. "You also saved my hide. I thank you for it, but, Lily, the price is high. Promise me you'll be all right."

Now he was begging her, not reassuring her. She forced a smile. She thought he was marvelous. "I promise, Knight. I don't want to leave you now. Not ever."

"You won't. Now, you try to relax. No, don't fight the pain. That's right, deep and slow. I want to tell you what we're going to do when this is all over. When you're well again, you and I are going to Italy. I want to take you to Venice. We'll stay in the Palazzo di Contini. It's near St. Mark's Square, on the Grand Canal. The patriarch Contini himself will welcome us, and you, my dear, will be feted and indulged and thoroughly spoiled until you become a completely insufferable person. Then we'll come back to England because we'll both be picturing the children as bereft little angels, pining for our return, wasting away on Mimms's cooking. Of course, the little devils will look at us and demand to know what presents we brought them.

"And, naturally, we will have brought Theo some outlandish treatise on a machine that flies to the moon. Let's see, for Sam it will have to be a fleet of gondolas—those are the means of travel in the canals in Venice—and for my littlest devil we'll bring back a special Medici doll, one that still has some poison in her ring on her left hand." Did Lily chuckle? He wasn't certain. Her eyes were closed, her expression still. He continued. "Then we'll settle into Castle Rosse until late spring. By that time you'll have my child in your womb. You won't be ill in the mornings—I won't allow it. Our child, Lily. Shall we have a boy or a girl?"

"A boy, to look just like you," she said, not opening her eyes. "He'll have fox's eyes, all gold and brown, yellow when he's angry. Yes, I like that, Knight, all of it. When did you say we could leave for Italy?"

He hugged her close. "Soon, Lily. Very soon." He kissed her forehead, then lay back. He was feeling something he'd never experienced before, something warm and immensely satisfying that was expanding and filling him. He felt tears sting his eyes. He was afraid, terribly afraid, and he felt so damnably helpless. He cursed, long and fluently.

The horse whinnied.

Lily slept again. Or was unconscious. He didn't know which. He continued to pray.

It stopped snowing late that afternoon. Knight eased away from Lily and walked to the barn door. There would be enough light for perhaps another hour. He had to discover where they were. He had to find help.

Within ten minutes Knight and Lily were on the horse, back on the country road. It was bitterly cold, the wind howling through the trees, the snow swirling about the horse's hooves. It was like a loud whistle, and a heavy coat simply didn't stop it from penetrating. Knight felt the cold penetrate his greatcoat, felt the numbness spread. He held Lily as close as he could, giving her all his warmth.

Knight saw smoke rising just beyond a thicket of maple trees. A farm. Warmth and help. He started to flick the horse's reins when suddenly there was a fork in the road and a signpost. Crawley to the right, and ten miles away. Crawley. My God, Knight thought, excitement flowing through him. Burke Drummond lived within five miles of Crawley. He wasn't all that far from Burke's home, Ravensworth. He felt a shock of relief so strong he nearly yelled aloud.

Ravensworth was to the south and to the east. So Monk and Boy had been taking them back toward London by a roundabout route.

"Lily," he whispered, "we're almost safe. God helps fools and half-witted viscounts."

It turned dark. Snow-bloated clouds hid the stars. Knight kept to the widening road. He almost missed the sign. So close now, so very close.

Knight had no idea what time it was. It had

begun to snow again and the wind had died down
a bit. But it was bitter cold now that night had
fallen.

Then he saw the great iron gates of Ravensworth, the gateman's cottage, and sent a prayer
of thanksgiving heavenward.

He'd never before thought that the Ravensworth drive was long. It seemed endless this
night. Bloody endless. Then the huge three-story
house came into view, and there were lights burning from several windows. The earl and the
countess were in residence, thank the heavens.

Knight yelled at the top of his lungs as he drew
his tired mount to a stop in front of the wide stone
steps.

The front doors creaked open.

The Ravensworth butler, Montague, stuck his
head out the door.

"Hurry, man," Knight called out as he dismounted. "Have a stable lad fetched to see to my
horse!"

The next minute Knight was striding across the
entrance hall, Lily in his arms.

Burke Drummond, the Earl of Ravensworth,
hearing the commotion, came through the library
door at that moment. He saw Knight standing in
the entrance hall, and of all the unexpected
things, he was carrying an unconscious female in
his arms.

"Well, good evening, Knight. What the hell is
going on?"

Knight barely paused. "Please, Burke, have a
man sent to fetch the doctor. Please hurry. She's
been shot and it's bad."

Burke Drummond didn't bat an eyelid. Instructions given, he led Knight to the library.

The Countess of Ravensworth, Arielle Drummond, was standing beside a chair, looking toward the door.

"Knight! Good heavens, what is happening? Who is that?"

"Arielle, quickly. She's been shot and she's very wet. Can you bring some dry clothes?"

"For you as well, Knight," the earl said.

"Certainly," Arielle said, and without another word, without another question, she left the library.

Knight laid Lily on a long, narrow settee, then moved it closer to the blazing fire. He pulled off his coat, then gently eased her out of her cloak. Her beautiful cloak, he thought vaguely as he tossed it onto a chair. There was a black hole through it now, and blood was streaked over the ermine.

Her gown was damp, as was the bandage. He began unfastening the long row of buttons. "I will tell you everything, Burke, once I see to her."

"Here, drink this."

"In a moment."

Burke Drummond regarded his friend as he gently pulled the bodice of the ripped gown down to the lady's waist. He saw the makeshift bandage and winced at the soaked-through blood. She'd been shot, all right, and it didn't look very good to Burke. He heard Knight saying softly over and over, "It's all right now, Lily. I swear it's all right. The doctor will be here soon. Yes, soon."

Knight untied the bandage and eased it away. He sucked in his breath. The wound was sluggishly seeping blood.

He felt Burke's hand on his shoulder.

"Dr. Brody will be here soon, Knight. She'll be all right. Now, drink the brandy. Lord knows, you need it."

Knight quickly downed the liquor. "Thank you,

Burke. God, she's hurt and it's all my fault. She saved my life, dashed in front of me when Boy fired. I—''

Burke said reasonably, ''Here's Arielle with some dry clothes. She can change the lady if you wish.''

''No, no. She's mine, you know.''

Burke didn't know. He stared for a moment, silent as a clam.

He turned away, nodding to his wife. Who the devil was the young woman? God knew, even disheveled as she was, she was still a beauty. Knight's latest mistress? But what had happened?

Arielle and Knight stripped off Lily's damp clothing and wrapped her in one of the earl's dressing gowns. Arielle handed Knight a folded clean handkerchief and silently watched him press it against the lady's shoulder.

''I asked Mrs. Pepperall to bring some blankets. Ah, yes, there they are. Thank you, Burke. She's also having a bedchamber prepared.''

Once Lily was wrapped to her chin in the thick blankets, Knight stood up. ''I've been so frightened,'' he said to no one in particular as he rubbed his hands together in front of the fire. ''Then I saw the Crawley signpost. You can't imagine the relief I felt.''

''Who is she, Knight?'' the earl asked.

Knight turned slowly and smiled. ''Why, she's my wife.''

''Your *what*?''

''My wife,'' Knight repeated with great relish. ''There's so much to tell you, so much you don't yet know . . .''

Arielle laid her hand on his arm. ''Soon, Knight. First you must change into something warm. She'll need you to be well, not sneezing your head off.''

"I'll wait for the doctor. I'm only a bit damp around the edges."

Arielle took another look at the unconscious lady—Knight's wife!—and said, "I'll fetch some hot tea and sandwiches."

Dr. Michael Brody arrived some fifteen minutes later. "My lord," he greeted the earl; then he turned to Knight. "It's Lord Castlerosse, isn't it?"

"Yes. Quickly, it's my wife. She's been shot."

If the doctor thought this a rather unusual occurrence, particularly in the great house of a local nobleman, he didn't let on. He sat beside the woman and pulled back the blanket. He opened the dressing gown and lifted off the handkerchief.

He leaned close to Lily's breast, listened to her heartbeat, then closely examined the bullet hole. "The bullet is still in her?"

"No, it went out her back."

"That was lucky for her. When did it happen?"

"Early this morning. It started to snow hard and I couldn't see where we were going. Luckily we came upon a barn, and I took her in there until it stopped snowing. She's been unconscious most of the day."

"No fever as yet. An excellent sign. The bleeding has nearly stopped."

Dr. Brody motioned to Knight, and together they lifted her so the doctor could examine her back. The exit wound wasn't as neat as the entry. It would need stitching.

"I'll bathe the wound and rub in some bacilicum powder, my lord, and set a few stitches in her back. Then we'll see."

"Thank you," Knight said. "I'll carry her upstairs now."

"All right." Dr. Brody paused for a moment, then asked, "How did it happen? Footpads?"

"I suppose you could call the villains that. She

saved my life. She took the bullet that was meant for me."

"Knight?"

Knight quickly went down on his knees beside the settee. He stroked his fingertips over Lily's brows, her nose, her lips. "It will be all right now, Lily. You're safe. I must take you upstairs."

"You're all right? You swear it?"

"I swear it." When he lifted her, she moaned.

"Slow breaths, Lily, and deep. You remember. Do it."

Burke Drummond and Dr. Brody exchanged glances.

As Knight carried her up the wide Ravensworth staircase, he was aware of his friend, Burke, regarding him intently. He planned to tell his host everything, but not yet, not until Lily was safe and out of danger.

"In the Diamond Room," Burke said, moving ahead to open the door. A fire had already been lit, and Mrs. Pepperall stood beside the bed, drawing back the counterpane.

Lily didn't want Knight to leave her. When he laid her on her back, she clung to him, sobbing, "No, Knight, please don't go. You promised we'd go to Venice. Forever, you said. Don't go!"

"I won't," he said, his voice as soothing and soft as warm butter. "I won't leave you. But I want you to go back to sleep, Lily. Do you think you can?"

"Don't go!"

Knight leaned over her and kissed her mouth. "It's all right now, love. Don't you believe your husband? I wouldn't lie to you, you know. Everything is all right."

"No, you wouldn't lie to me," Lily said and stiffened at a particularly sharp jab of pain. She

arched her back and a cry broke from her throat.
Then, just as suddenly, she moaned very softly
and fell back against the pillows.

Dr. Brody shoved Knight out of the way.

22

Dr. Brody slowly straightened. "It's all right, my lord. She's unconscious from the pain. I was going to give her laudanum, but her body simply removed her from the pain for a while. Sleep is the great healer, you know, and that's what she needs."

Knight looked as if the weight of Atlas's world had been lifted from his shoulders. "Thank God," he said and sank down on the bed.

"You should take off your wet clothes, Knight." Burke handed him the dressing gown. "Arielle, love, take yourself off for a while, all right?"

"Certainly," the countess said. She patted Knight's arm and left the bedchamber.

However, Knight didn't move until Dr. Brody had set the stitches in Lily's back and rebandaged her shoulder. When he'd finished, Knight methodically began stripping off his damp clothes.

"You know, my lord," Dr. Brody said thoughtfully, looking down at Lily, "there is something here I don't understand. If she dashed in front of you and took the bullet that was meant for you, then where is it?"

Knight's head came up and he stared at the doctor.

"I mean, was she truly in front of you, or was the shot actually wide?"

Suddenly, without warning, Knight felt a sharp jabbing pain in his ribs.

"It tore through her," Dr. Brody continued. "But where did it go? I thought you said she was in front of you."

"She was in front of me." Knight stripped off his shirt and looked blankly down at his bloody chest. "Well, I'll be damned," he said, slowly raising his head to stare in bewilderment at Burke and the doctor. "Your mystery is solved, Dr. Brody. It looks like I got shot after all. Funny, though—I never felt a thing."

With those words Knight gave Burke and the doctor a crooked smile, then crumpled to the floor.

When he woke up, Arielle's concerned face was above him. "Hello, Knight."

"Lily?"

Arielle didn't believe for a moment that he was delirious and confusing people. "She's asleep, not unconscious but really sleeping this time. She woke up and Dr. Brody gave her some laudanum. You're in the chamber next to hers. Now, I'm delighted you're with us again. And truly, Lily is just fine. As for you, my lord, Dr. Brody removed the bullet. It was nestled right up against a rib. It didn't break or shatter anything or do any real damage. So it was very shallow, thank the heavens, and you'll be quite all right soon." Arielle paused, then lifted Knight's left hand in hers. Bandages were wrapped about his wrists. "Your wrists were raw and bloody, so that's why they're bandaged. Ah, here's Burke, ready, I wager, to drive you mad with questions."

The earl gave his countess a wounded look. "Not at all—well, perhaps just a few. My curiosity is eating me alive, Knight. You were bound. And you were shot. And you're married, for God's sake.'' He added thoughtfully, ''That is without a doubt the biggest shock of all.''

''I'm so hungry I could eat your curiosity, Burke. Any chance for a half side of beef or something?''

''All right, I'll see to it, but only if you swear to tell me everything. After you eat.''

The earl was good to his word. He didn't ask another question, merely spoke of the weather until Knight had finished eating. ''Here's another bit of brandy for you.''

Knight sighed deeply, replete, and closed his eyes for a moment. ''I am married, and no, Lily isn't pregnant, and no, she wasn't my mistress, and you won't believe this, but I'm also a father. I have three children, and they're little devils and I love them as dearly as I do their mother.''

''My God.''

''Lily was engaged to my cousin Tris Winthrop. They're actually his children. I hadn't seen Tris in well over five years. In any case, my cousin was evidently a master thief until he pulled a rather incredible blunder. He double-crossed two villain partners of his, and they killed him. Ah, there's so much more. Let's see, Lily took the children and left Brussels with scarcely fifty pounds in her pocket. Did I tell you about Brussels?''

It required many questions from the earl, but eventually he was in possession of the facts and had arranged them in their proper sequence.

''Not a single idea where those bloody jewels are, then?'' Burke asked.

''No. Believe me, Lily and I examined every one of the children's toys, all their things, really. Billy's Baubles have got to be in Brussels. There's simply no other place."

"Billy's Baubles," Burke remarked. "That's interesting. Is there a story behind that?"

And Knight, so tired now he could barely make sense, told Burke about Billy and his betrothed, Charlotte, and how she'd told Billy she no longer wanted to marry him and he'd taken back the jewels. And on their way back to Brussels, Tris and his men had stolen them.

"Billy and Charlotte," Burke repeated. "That would be William and Charlotte. Hmm. Brussels."

Knight would have agreed if he'd had the energy, but he didn't. He fell asleep, deeply.

"Very interesting," the earl said quietly and rose. He stared down at his lifelong friend. "Very interesting indeed."

Lily awoke slowly. She was so thirsty her tongue felt swollen. She managed to croak, "Water. Please, water."

In an instant she felt the glass against her mouth and an arm lift her head. Cool water dribbled into her mouth and down her chin. "Thank you."

Arielle smiled at one of the most beautiful women she'd ever seen. Lily's thick, dark blond hair was tangled and spread over the pillow, her face was dreadfully pale, but still she was lovely, every feature complementing the other so perfectly it was impossible to find a flaw. "You're most welcome. Now, I would imagine you're hungry?"

Lily thought about that for a while and discovered that she could probably have eaten the water glass. "Oh, yes, please."

"Any pain?"

The pain was there, but at a distance. "I can control it, at least for a while."

"Good. The laudanum is still at work."

Arielle fed her guest some porridge sweetened with honey and rich, thick cocoa to drink. "You'll be dancing again soon, Lily."

"Who are you? You know my name. Where's Knight?"

"Oh, dear, there's so much to tell you. First of all, your husband is just fine. Like you, he's in bed, recovering. You see, my dear, when you took that bullet for him, it went through you, then into his chest, settling against a rib. He never even felt it. But he is fine. Michael—that's Dr. Brody—said it was very shallow. Nothing to worry about. He is also of the opinion that Knight didn't feel a thing because he was too frightened for you. Now, my name is Arielle Drummond. You're at Ravensworth Abbey, in a very pretentious bedchamber called the Diamond Room. And I can see that that's enough for now. You can barely keep your eyes open. Go back to sleep, Lily."

And Lily did as she was bidden. "You have beautiful hair," she heard herself say as she slipped away. "The color is remarkable, not red, but not really gold either, sort of like the color I've seen in some old Italian paintings, but I'm not sure. . . ."

Arielle smiled at her and patted her hand. "And you, my dear, have accomplished a miracle. Married to Knight Winthrop and well before he can shout to the world that he's middle-aged. I shall try to check my curiosity until you can tell me how you managed this feat."

"Talking to yourself, hmm?"

"Oh, Burke! I was just talking to Lily. Of course, she can't hear me, but still—"

Her husband hugged her, then kissed her

lightly on her mouth. "Our invalids are both quite fine, I gather."

"This one is. She ate all the porridge and drank the cocoa. There was lots of sugar in the cocoa, just as Michael ordered. You know something, Burke?" Arielle continued without pause. "She's the most beautiful woman I've ever seen."

Burke looked down at the sleeping Lily. "She is," he said in a pontifical voice, "quite passable, I suppose. You think she snared our Knight with her beauty?" The moment the words were out, Burke was shaking his head. "No, Knight appreciates beauty, and God knows, he's enjoyed his share of beautiful women, but to marry a woman because of it, no, never."

"And children? Did you tell me there are three of them?" At her husband's nod, Arielle just shook her head. "I can't seem to take it all in. Knight Winthrop with a wife and three children. Do you remember him at Lannie and Percy's wedding? He was sweating like a pig, nearly babbling with paranoia what with all the matchmaking mamas eyeing him like a succulent feast at the reception, and vowing over and over not to wed until he was well past his fortieth birthday."

"Ah, yes, and his disgust with Percy and Lannie, calling Percy a fool and a dimwit." Burke began to chuckle; then he broke into a full laugh.

Together, the earl and the countess left the bedchamber, the earl still laughing.

The earl wasn't laughing a few minutes later. He was shouting at his valet, Joshua. "He's what? That's utterly absurd! Good God, he can't!"

Burke dashed into Knight's bedchamber and skidded to a stop. Knight was dressing, slowly, to be sure, but he was managing. There was a wide bandage about his waist and small bandages about his wrists. He needed to shave, his clothes were wrinkled and dirty, and he looked quite determined.

"That's enough, Knight."

Knight looked up, shaking his head. "No, Burke. I probably killed Boy. If I did, then Monk will either be scouring the countryside for me and Lily or heading back to Castle Rosse and the children. I told him the jewels were in the stable. He doesn't know where to look, but look he will. And if he can, he'll nab one of the children. I can't take the chance. I've got to make sure they're safe."

"You've quite made up your mind about this? You won't allow me to fetch the children?"

"No; they're not your responsibility. If you will keep Lily safe for me, I'll get them. I should be back with them sometime tomorrow evening."

"I can't allow this, Knight. You're not in any shape to go anywhere."

Knight told his friend very concisely and without excessive heat what he could do with his opinion.

Burke stared at him for a moment; then, when Knight's britches were about his knees, Burke stepped forward and slammed his fist into his friend's jaw. Knight went down without a sound.

"Sorry, old man," the earl said as he rubbed his knuckles, "but you've been quite noble enough. Any more of your nobility and nausea will overcome me."

"Oh, Gawd!"

Burke turned to smile at his valet, Joshua. "His lordship will be just fine. He'll doubtless wake up cursing me to hell and back, be the proud possessor of a sore jaw, but he'll recover. Now, Joshua, here's what I want you to do."

"Remarkable, absolutely remarkable." Dr. Brody stood up and smiled down at Lily. "No fever, color in your cheeks, and the wounds are healing quite nicely. If I could say the same for your husband's temper, then—"

Lily paled. "Where is Knight? What's happened to him?"

Arielle sent Michael Brody a disapproving look, and he murmured, "Sorry," and quickly stepped back from the bed.

Arielle said in her most soothing voice, "Now, Lily, my dear, your husband is just . . . well, he's just—"

"Cursedly furious, for starters, Arielle."

"Knight!"

"Hello, Lily." Arielle saw Knight's expression alter radically. He was suddenly all tenderness and gentleness. "You look wonderful, wife. I can't imagine why they put me into another bed-chamber. My place is beside you, naturally." He kissed her forehead, clasped her hand in his, then looked over at Arielle. His expression went back to being ferocious. "As for your husband, Arielle, when I get my hands on that damned bounder, I fully intend to smash my fist—"

"You just be quiet, Knight Winthrop!" Out of sheer surprise, Knight shut his mouth. Arielle Drummond, that slight, slender person, was standing, arms akimbo, looking ready to kick him in a very vulnerable spot. "No, you, too, Lily! Just hush, both of you. You will listen to me. Knight, in his condition, was going to return to Castle Rosse to fetch the children, Lily. Burke merely rendered him temporarily unable so that—"

"He waited until I'd pulled my britches to my knees, then planted me one in the jaw!"

"That's what I said," Arielle replied with great patience. "So Burke is going to bring the children here. More than that, he's sent for a Bow Street

Runner who's worked for us before, Ollie Trunk. You, Knight, and Lily and the children will remain safely at Ravensworth until they've caught this fellow Monk. Now, do either of you have any questions?''

"I do," came a diffident voice.

"Well, what is it?" Arielle snapped as she turned on the hapless Dr. Brody.

"Do you mind if I examine Viscount Castlerosse's rib?"

Lily laughed, laughed until she hurt. "Ah, Knight, you've been disposed of quite nicely. I've learned a doubtless very valuable lesson here."

Knight said nothing, nodded to Dr. Brody, then climbed into bed beside Lily. "All right. Examine away."

"You're an awful man!"

"I'm your husband. You can't order me out. I intend to stay here and let Arielle mother both of us. Once the children arrive, it will be chaos and bedlam and you'll regret your kindness, Arielle. The little devils will bring Ravensworth down around your toes. They'll reduce all of you to wearing mufflers over your ears just to stay reasonably sane. Then, just when you'll be ready to muzzle them, they'll smile at you or give you a look that would melt a stone, and you're a goner and they've got you and it all begins again. The servants will no longer be loyal to you but to them. You'll see."

Arielle could only marvel silently. Knight Winthrop was saying these things? About *children*?

"I intend to tell them about all the presents we'll be bringing them from Venice, Knight," Lily said.

"I think that—ow! God, that hurts, dammit!"

"Do hold still, my lord," Dr. Brody said and proceeded to probe the flesh covering Knight's rib. To Knight's consternation, Lily picked up his hand and patted it.

"Done in," he said under his breath. "Done in and hung out to flap in the wind."

"At least I have both of you in the same place now. If you give me any trouble, I can simply lock the door." Arielle beamed down at them and Knight cursed.

"When you're done, Michael, why don't we leave them alone to rest? The viscountess is very reasonable. They *will* rest, I doubt not."

Dr. Brody mumbled something under his breath and Knight said, all surprise, "Why, I believe he's embarrassed! You're a bloody doctor, Michael! I— ow!"

"There, my lord, all done now. Rest, as her ladyship instructed. I'll see you both on the morrow."

When Knight and Lily were finally alone, Knight came up on his elbow and looked down at her. "We made it."

"That we did. I still have difficulty understanding why you never felt that bullet hit you."

"I guess the doctor is right. I was so scared for you, my body kindly decided not to further strain my poor brain." He leaned down and kissed her mouth, her chin, her nose. "Look outside, Lily. It's snowing again. Damn, how can Burke travel in this wretched weather? How can the children?"

"Burke is an inventive man and not a fool. That's what you told me. No, don't go into a snit again. Lie down and hold my hand and tell me exciting things."

"I met Ollie Trunk this past summer," Knight remarked, his eyes on the naked cherubs that smiled vacuously down upon them from the ceiling molding. "I guess Arielle forgot. In any case, he's a good fellow and tenacious as a bull terrier. He'll help. Perhaps he can even find out about this Billy and Charlotte.''

"I love you so much, Knight," Lily said clearly, and in the next moment was deeply asleep, her breathing even and soft.

Knight tensed from his ears to his ankles.

His heart began to pound. Loudly.

This incredible woman loved him? Dear God, he'd neatly forced her to marry him; taken her body as his natural right as her husband without regard to what she wanted; put her in mortal danger—and she loved him. Well, damn and blast, he was as happy as a man could be in six decades. He grinned. He wanted to howl and dance. He winked at the cherubs overhead.

Then he shook his head at himself. He supposed he wasn't really surprised that he loved his wife as well. He'd told Burke he loved her, but he hadn't really *felt* it while he had said it. It had come as stealthily as a thief in the night, this love business. It hadn't happened to his father. So it had skipped a generation. He'd make certain it didn't skip any more generations in his family. "That makes two of us," he told the sleeping Lily. "But I'll wager I love you more. I'm older by seven years, after all. I have more experience, more skills involving things that are, well, er, related. Yes, I'll wager you that you haven't come close to what I feel for you, Lily Winthrop. But I'll let you work at it. We can examine this in another ten years or so and see. But I'll still be ahead. Oh, yes, I will." Grinning like a besotted village idiot, Knight kissed his wife's left ear, then turned onto his back, still grinning like a fool, and was snoring sonoriously within minutes.

When Lily awoke the following morning, Knight wasn't in bed beside her. She called his name. He wasn't in the Diamond Room either. She didn't want to disturb her hostess, but finally worry made her pull the bell cord.

Arielle appeared some ten minutes later. She looked none too pleased. Indeed, she looked ready to kill. "Your husband," she said slowly, as if keeping a wild fury under control, "left two hours ago, nearly at the crack of dawn. He left this note for you." She handed the scrap of paper to Lily.

Lily,
I'm off to Castle Rosse. Will return with the children soon. Don't worry and don't do anything stupid.

Knight

"That . . . that . . ."

"Noble blind bounder? Foolish, foolish man?" Arielle supplied.

Lily's hands were fisted on her lap. She wadded up the note and tossed it across the room, then promptly groaned from the pain in her shoulder. "I'll kill him. Damn him, Arielle. He's hurt!"

"I know," Arielle said, then regretted that she'd shown so much anger to Lily. This patient was rapidly becoming quite upset. "Now, Lily, he'll be all right. Burke has told me that Knight is a man who can take care of himself. He said he was a survivor, that he'd trekked through the hills of Portugal one summer when it was so hot the rocks were nearly melting, and he made it to the sea with two French spies in tow. The wound wasn't grave, Lily. He'll be just fine."

"When he gets back here, he'll have to survive me. Right now I'm feeling a lot meaner and a lot tougher than two Frenchmen."

"They weren't men. They were Frenchwomen."

"Arrgh!"

At least it had stopped snowing. Thank the
powers for something. Now he could keep his
horse at a steady gallop. Knight knew a shortcut
northwest to Castle Rosse. Burke didn't. He
wouldn't be surprised if he caught up with the
earl before reaching home.

His rib hurt, but not excessively, and the extreme cold kept him pretty well numbed. He'd
lain there beside his beautiful wife, wondering,
worrying, then finally realizing that he simply
couldn't allow Burke to ride into possible danger.
Burke didn't know how vicious Monk was.

Knight changed horses at three different posting houses. At Netherfield, the ostler at the Wild
Goose Inn had nothing to rent him but a slope-
shouldered gelding that had more heart and grit
than a racer. The journey to Castle Rosse ended
up taking him a mere six hours.

There was no sign of Monk.

There was a good deal of pandemonium when
Knight walked through the great oak doors into
the Italian-marble tiled entry hall of Castle Rosse.

He hadn't beat Burke, but then again, Burke
had been one hell of a soldier and tracker.

"Papa!" Laura Beth lost her footing on the
staircase and tumbled down three steps to land
on the floor at Knight's feet. He scooped her up,
tossed her high in the air, and then held her so
tightly against his chest that she squeaked.

Burke Drummond came out of the drawing
room to witness this reunion. He stared.

Theo said from just behind him, "Cousin
Knight is here! I thought you said he was at Ra-

vensworth, sir. Oh, goodness! He doesn't look well. Laura Beth will strangle him!"

Theo raced around Burke and right into Knight's quickly freed right arm. "Theo, Theo, I've missed you like the very devil."

"You're hurt. Uncle Burke said you were hurt by that awful man. Was it the one who tried to kidnap Sam in London? The one who attacked you in London?"

"Yes, that was the one. I'm not badly hurt, Theo. Stop shaking. So it's Uncle Burke, is it? Laura Beth, stop kissing my ear! It's getting all wet inside. Ah, here's Sam. Come here, lad, and tell me what a saint you've been."

"Mama. Where's Mama?"

"Didn't Burke—Uncle Burke—tell you?" He carefully hugged Sam, who was being held in Charlie, the footman's, arms. Knight cupped the boy's face in his palm. "Your mama's all right. She's in bed, being utterly lazy and ordering Uncle Burke's servants about, throwing her water glass at anyone who dares to disagree with her. All in all, she's fine."

Sam giggled and Theo expelled a relieved sigh.

Knight looked up and straight at Burke.

"I couldn't let you have all the fun, Burke."

"I see that. However, you do look like bloody hell."

"Yes, my lord, bloody hell indeed," Thrombin said.

"Aye, indeed!" Charlie said, adding his oar to the water.

Knight looked around at his servants, previously silent. Mrs. Crumpe had her arms folded across her ample breasts. Even Mimms was standing in the doorway, a plate of goodies in the crook of her dimpled arm. But Thrombin was the awesome one. He looked utterly disapproving. His lips were so thin as to be nonexistent.

"His lordship," Thrombin continued, "has told us that he's here to remove the children back to Ravensworth. He also assured us that you were all right, but wounded, my lord, and, I might add, quite safe in your bed."

"All right, now listen to me, Thrombin. All of you. Laura Beth, stop chewing on my ear. Sam, hold still or Charlie will drop you and you'll deserve it. Theo, stop wringing your hands like the mourners in a Greek chorus. Mrs. Crumpe, we'll be in the drawing room. I'm starving. Please bring food and whatever else you deem proper. Come along, Burke. We have a lot to discuss."

"Papa," Laura Beth said and squeezed his throat. "Did you bring Czarina Catherine a present?"

"Yes, me."

Laura Beth didn't find this answer to her liking, but she was distracted. "Your face is all scratchy."

"Yes, and I'm filthy as a winter goat. No, Betty," he continued to Laura Beth's new nurse, "I'll keep the urchin with me for a while. But only if you behave yourself, snippet."

"All right, Papa," Laura Beth assured him and he groaned, knowing that sweet, utterly guileless smile.

Charlie carried Sam into the drawing room and placed him on a couch. Theo fussed over his brother until Sam, disgusted, told him to stick his head in a ditch. Laura Beth was quite content curled up against Knight's shoulder. That made his rib hurt, but it didn't matter. Everything seemed so blessedly normal again. It helped erase the nightmare of the past two days.

It was another half hour before Burke and Knight were alone, the children carping and complaining but nonetheless off to their beds. There was a blazing fire in the fireplace, and Burke brought out the brandy bottle.

"Your children are delightful."

Knight smiled sleepily. "Yes, the little devils are quite unique. Czarina Catherine is Laura Beth's doll."

"Thank you. It was a question that was weighing on my poor brain."

"No sign of our Monk?"

"No, not a one. I only beat you here by three hours, though. I did, however, alert all the servants, particularly the stable lads. They're ready, Knight."

Knight nodded. "Now what we need is a trap for our villain."

"You've got an idea?"

Knight sat forward and rubbed his hands toward the leaping flames. "Yes," he said, his eyes narrowing, "yes, and it should bring Monk here in short order. The damned bastard."

23

Arielle brought George Curlew, the earl's steward, and Dr. Brody with her to visit Lily in her bedchamber the following morning for a cup of tea.

"I thought you would like to see a face that wasn't mine for a change," Arielle told her.

Lily nodded and sipped at the tea. "This is so good."

"Would you like a bit of laudanum?" Dr. Brody asked.

Lily shook her head. The pain was deep and it was steady, but she didn't want to see her guests through a haze. "Not just yet, thank you."

Arielle chatted with profound determination, all the while keeping one eye on Lily, who was quiet, too quiet. Even though she was still confined to her bed, Arielle had brushed her hair and arranged a lovely pale blue silk peignoir around her shoulders. She saw that George Curlew and Michael Brody were looking at Lily with new eyes, and very masculine eyes at that, and paying her endless compliments. Arielle grinned to herself. If they'd looked at *her* like that during the past summer, or told her even once that her gown was lovely, she would have been terrified and probably fled the vicinity.

But Lily was beautiful, Arielle remarked without a spark of envy. It was something beyond just the excellent complementing of her features; it was something more, something glowing and soft and brilliant. Arielle had more than a sneaking suspicion that Knight Winthrop was responsible. She looked over to see how Lily was taking this abundance of male appreciation.

Lily didn't even notice. Arielle was concerned that Lily's shoulder was hurting her more than she was letting on, but Michael hadn't said anything, so she held her peace. Once Lily had crumbled her second scone, Arielle said with just a hint of a smile, "Lily, I must now assume you're thinking about Knight, and worrying. Well, you know very well that Burke and Knight were soldiers and officers. They're both quite resourceful, intelligent—"

"They're idiots!"

"Yes, well, they're men, so that is also true."

"I will kill Knight!"

"He'll doubtless be gratified that you've worried about him. Now stop your dithering. It can't be good for your recovery."

"Did you say *two* Frenchwomen?"

"They were spies, Lily, French spies. Not really women, but enemies."

"Hah! How long was he alone with them in those hot, arid hills of Portugal?"

"Not long at all. Not more than a fortnight, or perhaps it was three weeks. I don't remember. It's not important. It was an assignment, a very difficult one, but just another assignment."

"I believe," George Curlew said, anxious to provide information to this exquisite confection of womanhood, "that Lord Castlerosse was alone with the spies only for a sennight. Then, my lady," he added, turning to Arielle, "I think the earl joined him and the two of them brought the French spies to the English command near Oporto, I believe it was."

Arielle turned on the hapless steward. "You're telling me that *Burke* was also escorting those wretched women?"

"Now, Arielle," Lily said, "they were spies, enemies. It was just another assignment, difficult no doubt, but just another assignment."

"I'll kill him!" Arielle's hair looked fiery red at that moment, not at all a soft titian. "More tea, Michael?" she added between her teeth.

Lily laughed at Dr. Brody's alarmed expression, then moaned from the jab of pain in her shoulder.

The doctor rose immediately and came to her. "I must leave soon, my lady. A local woman is in labor and I need to lend a hand. May I examine you now?"

How odd that title still sounded. Lily nodded. Arielle and Mr. Curlew left the bedchamber. Dr. Brody was all efficiency as he bared the wound. "It hurts dreadfully?"

"Yes, but for the most part I can control it. It is just times when, for example, I laugh that I pay a high price."

"I will tell Arielle to be morose."

Dr. Brody helped her onto her side and eased her gown down to look at her back.

He straightened, finally done, and smiled at her. "You are the most remarkable patient I've ever had. You've no sign of fever or poisoning of the blood, and the wound is pink and healthy. Still, my lady, you must rest and do nothing at all strenuous until further notice from me. By strenuous I mean doing more than lifting your own teacup. If you continue at this phenomenal rate, I'll remove the stitches from your back next

Tuesday or Wednesday. Then—'' He shrugged, smiling.

"I'll be dancing at a ball," Lily said. "And then to Venice. After, that is," she added, her eyes darkening, "I've murdered my husband.'' But she was soon thinking about Monk, wondering if Theo and Sam and Laura Beth were in any danger, and trying to convince herself that Burke and Knight could well handle any attempt on Monk's part to hurt the children, or them for that matter.

They should all be arriving tonight.

She missed the little heathens. She wondered how they'd greeted their steppapa.

The pain worsened late in the morning, and Lily took some laudanum willingly. She slept throughout the remainder of the day. Arielle ate her dinner with Lily in the bedchamber, both ladies keeping an ear trained for the sounds of a carriage arriving at Ravensworth. Nary a sound of anything.

Nor did they arrive the following day.

"Stop fidgeting, Arielle," Lily finally said to her new friend as she watched her pace back and forth across the bedchamber, stopping every few minutes to twitch the heavy draperies aside to look outside.

"I just don't like it. That miserable philanderer could be in trouble."

"They were spies, Arielle, enemies." Lily giggled.

"It's snowing again," Arielle said. "How can they travel in this weather? Didn't you say Sam's leg was hurt? However will they manage?"

Lily didn't know. To think about it made her head hurt nearly as much as her shoulder.

Late that afternoon Lily fell into a light sleep. Her dreams weren't pleasant. Monk was chasing her and Knight through narrow canals filled with brackish water. They were riding in long, narrow boats that Knight called gondolas. Suddenly the gondola tipped from a vicious shove from Monk's oar. Lily felt the black water close over her head, heard Knight yelling frantically for her. She moaned and jerked awake.

She wasn't alone. She was staring up into Monk's very real and very mean face. One huge hand was clamped tightly over her mouth. Before she could react, he stuffed a dirty handkerchief into her mouth and quickly tied another over it and knotted it tightly behind her head.

He wasn't supposed to be here, she thought blankly. He was supposed to be at Castle Rosse.

He looked very pleased with himself. ''Ye're alive and now I've got ye. Why are ye in bed?''

Lily could only stare at him.

Monk shook his head, grabbed her hand, and pulled her upright. Lily swallowed a cry of pain. Monk frowned and jerked open the bodice of her nightgown, paying no attention to the scattering buttons. He saw the bandage.

''So Boy did make that bullet fly 'ome, jest the wrong one. I weren't sure about that. 'Ow bad is it?''

She could only shake her head. This time Monk pulled the gag from her mouth. ''My shoulder,'' Lily whispered. ''Please, it hurts dreadfully.''

Monk cursed loud and long. ''I don't want to kill ye yet,'' he said. ''Damnation, 'is lordship won't give me the sparklers if ye're dead. Oh, damn and blast! If I carts ye out of 'ere, ye'll bleed to death on me, won't ye? Jest to spite me, I'll wager.''

Lily thought that would probably be the outcome, but she didn't say that spite would have nothing to do with her probable demise. Her shoulder throbbed, making her close her eyes against the pain. She heard Monk curse again.

"Well, I ain't got no choice."

He lifted her over his shoulder, not bothering to tie her hands and ankles, for he knew she didn't have the strength to fight him. "Ye jest 'old still and ye won't bleed, leastways I 'opes not." He cursed again. "It's cold out there, wot with the snow and all. I'll 'ave to wrap ye up." Monk grabbed two blankets off the bed and threw them over Lily, then continued to the wide bow windows that faced the eastern lawn.

He was on the point of climbing out when suddenly he came face-to-face with a man he'd never seen before, a man whose face was remarkably like a monkey's and who looked at once completely taken aback and chagrined.

The man shouted right in Monk's face: " 'Old there, you blighter! I've got you now! Drop the lady and throw out your popper!"

Monk jumped back from the window. "Who the 'ell are ye?" he roared.

"Ollie Trunk's me name and I'm the law. I'm taking you to London to 'ang for murder! Careful now, you put the lady down real careful."

"I'll see you in 'ell," Monk shouted and smashed his fist into the man's face. Lily heard the scream, knew her would-be savior had lost his grip and fallen to the frozen ground. She heard running footsteps, shouts, and the lower rumble of frantic speech.

Monk stood undecided for a moment by the window. He looked outside, saw a half-dozen men milling about, saw the little monkey-faced man rise and dust himself off. "I don't understand," he said, more to himself than to Lily. He seemed to realize that he was still holding her over his shoulder. He carried her back to the bed and laid her back down, automatically covering her up. Pain pulsed through her.

"Everyone was supposed to be at Castle Rosse—the earl wot owns this pile, yer 'usband, the nippers, Lord knows, everyone! That's why I came 'ere. I ask ye, 'ow'd that Runner get 'ere so fast anyways? It don't make no sense, no, it don't."

Lily didn't care about any sense. She wanted, quite simply, to die.

" 'Ere, now, wot's wrong? Yer shoulder?" He leaned over and shook her. Lily moaned. "Don't ye dare stick yer spoon in it! I need ye! Ye're me 'ostage! Oh, 'ellfire!"

But Lily did stick her spoon in it. She didn't know how long she was unconscious, but it seemed a very short time. She heard pounding. It seemed to come from a great distance away. More pounding, and then Knight's wonderfully familiar voice.

"Open the door, Monk! Now! You hurt my wife and I'll carve you into small pieces!"

"Wot's 'e doing 'ere?" Monk raised his voice, bellowing, "I've got yer wife! Ye keep up yer blathering and I'll make 'er mighty uncomfortable!"

There came the low hum of conversation, then Burke Drummond's voice. "Listen, Monk. I'm the Earl of Ravensworth. You let the lady go and I'll give you the jewels."

"Billy's Baubles? Ye've got 'em?"

"Not those particular jewels, but heirlooms in my family for hundreds of years. That or money. Whatever you wish. And you'll leave here a free man."

"No, my lord! Ye can't do that. That bloke's a criminal, and I've gots to take 'im to Lunnon!" It was the monkey-faced man's voice; Lily recognized it.

In the corridor outside the bedchamber, Knight grabbed Ollie Trunk by his shirt collar and lifted him off the floor. "Shut your mouth, you damned fool! The man's a murderer all right. And he just might kill my wife!"

Ollie shut up. "I ain't ever been in no situation like this afore," he said, straightening his collar. "I don't want the lady dead, but ye can't jest let that Monk fellow fly off hide-free."

"We've no intention of that, Ollie," Burke said, and motioned the man to silence.

Knight pressed against the bedchamber door. "Lily," he called out.

Monk looked toward the door and drew out his pistol. To Lily he said, "Ye don't try nothin' and we'll get along jest fine. Answer the man, it won't matter none."

"Knight? I'm fine, truly." But her voice broke. Oh, please, God, she prayed, don't let him do anything foolish.

"I wants the sparklers," Monk shouted. "I want wot's mine and Boy's."

Knight drew a deep breath. The truth, he thought. Why not the truth, at least for now? "Listen, Monk. I told you the truth. We couldn't find the jewels. It stands to reason that they were never brought to England. It's true. I wouldn't lie to you, not with you holding my wife."

Oh, God. He'd kill her now. Lily felt lightheaded. Her shoulder was ripping with pain and she wanted to writhe away from it, but she couldn't do anything save lie there and let the pain consume her.

Suddenly Monk was leaning over her. "Ye're awful white about the gills, but no matter. Jest don't die on me quite yet. Is 'e telling the truth?

Ye didn't find the jewels? Ye tell me, or I'll find a way to kill 'is lordship, kill 'im real dead.''

"Please, please, we couldn't find them. It's the truth.''

"They wasn't in the stables at Castle Rosse?''

Lily shook her head, mute.

"I guessed as much. That's why I came 'ere and didn't follow yer 'usband back to Castle Rosse. Oh, no, I found out 'e'd been 'ere, at Ravensworth Abbey, and 'e was not with ye, so ye still 'ad to be 'ere. Ye was the key, I knew. Yer 'usband would do anything to 'ave ye back safe. But those damned sparklers! Damn that Tris! Damn 'im for a wily cove! If only Boy 'adn't stuck 'is sticker in 'is back! If only that watch 'adn't come along when 'e did!'' Monk cursed, railed, and looked about the large bedchamber. For what, Lily couldn't begin to guess. So Monk had followed them here, had watched Burke, then Knight, leave.

Everything was silent now. Very silent. She closed her eyes, wishing she had just a modicum of strength so she could overpower Monk. Do something to end the nightmare once and for all. But she couldn't even lift her hand. She felt warm stickiness and knew the shoulder wound was seeping blood. She wondered if she was going to die. She didn't want to die, not now, not now that she was happy.

Where were the children? Oh, God, what had Knight done with the children? They had to be safe. They simply had to be.

At least if she died, they had Knight. Lily felt tears sting her eyes. She didn't want to die. She didn't want to leave Knight or the children. She tasted a salty tear in her mouth.

"Monk.''

It was Knight's voice.

"Let me come in now. I must see that my wife is all right. You can keep me for your hostage, but let her go."

"No!"

Lily didn't know where she found the strength to scream that single word. She lay back, panting, waiting, praying that Monk wouldn't let Knight into the room. "No!" This time it was just a whisper.

"Awright," Monk called. "But no tricks, or yer little piece will meet 'er maker this minute!"

"No," Lily said again, so quietly this time she herself barely heard it. She saw Monk unlock the door, saw the door slowly open, saw Knight stride in. God, he looked wonderful, vigorous, strong. Monk aimed his pistol at him and told him to raise his arms. Knight did as he was bidden. Monk ran his hands over his body, then straightened, nodding. "Ye're clean," he said.

Knight looked at the man who'd been his nemesis for the past month. God, he wanted to kill the blighter. He immediately went to the bed. "Love," he said softly and sat down beside her. "It will be all right, Lily. Just hang on, love. Just hang on, please." He kissed her cheek. "Trust me, Lily," he said more softly.

"Yes," she whispered. "You're wonderful, Knight." He gave her a slow smile and she saw something else, something in his golden fox's eyes—determination, that was it. "Please take care." He nodded, then straightened, coming slowly to his feet.

Monk was standing like a towering giant in the middle of the room, his legs spread, the pistol in his right hand. "You've made our lives a misery for far too long, Monk," Knight said. "I'll give you the money the jewels would have brought you. I want you to leave. Now."

"I'll take 'er with me."

"No, you won't. She's far too weak. She'd only slow you down. If you did take her, I'd follow you. For as long as it took, I'd track you down and I'd kill you. Surely you'd rather live and spend all your groats."

"Ye killed Boy. I'll kill 'er. It's fair."

"Go away, Monk. Leave us be. You'll have all the money you could spend in two lifetimes."

Suddenly, without warning, there was a loud crashing noise from the window. Monk whirled about. Burke Drummond, a rope about his waist, bounded through the window into the room, rolled, then came up on his feet, a pistol at the ready. Lily heard a man shout from outside, "He's safe! I let him down and he made it!"

Burke ignored the voice, jerked up his pistol, and would have fired that moment, but Monk had his own pistol aimed, not at him or Knight, but at Lily. "Jest ye try it," Monk yelled. "Jest go ahead and do it, and I'll bury the little piece right 'ere, right now!"

Burke spat on the floor and snarled, his voice filled with scorn and contempt, "Your mother was a gin-soaked whore who should have smothered you at birth!"

With a ferocious bellow of rage, Monk jerked, his gun leveled now on Burke's chest.

Knight smoothly pulled the knife from his sleeve, poised it to its mark, then sent it straight and fast toward Monk just the instant before Monk fired.

The blade sank into one side of Monk's neck, the red-tipped point protruding obscenely out the other side, under Monk's right ear. Burke hit the floor as the bullet went high and wide. Monk stared at Burke, then, turning slowly, stared at Knight. "A stiletto, ye kilt me with a stiletto, jest

like me mother gave me." He tried to say something more, but it was garbled sounds, liquid with
his own blood.

Lily saw the knife sticking through Monk's
throat. She saw him drop the pistol, saw him
slowly crumble, his huge body seeming to fold in
on itself. It was odd, but his body made scarce a
sound when it hit the wooden floor. She saw
Burke come to his feet, stand there, unmoving;
saw her husband, his arm still outstretched.
Slowly, she opened her mouth. Only a sob
emerged.

Knight rushed to the bed. "Lily, it's over now,
all over."

She stared up at him, unable to raise her hand
to touch his face. "I couldn't help you. I couldn't
do anything except lie here like some wilting,
weak female and watch Monk hurt you."

"He didn't hurt me. He's dead now, Lily, dead
and gone. Please, love, it's all right. *I'm* all right."

Slowly, the room turned dark, then darker still.
Lily tried to fight it off but she couldn't.
"Knight," she whispered, then softly slid into
unconsciousness.

Three days later, midmorning in the Diamond
Room, Lily was surrounded by three children, a
husband, an earl and a countess.

Sam was proudly demonstrating his ability with
his crutches. Theo was trailing after him, a close
shadow, ready to catch him if he fell. Laura Beth
was cuddled next to Lily on the bed, Czarina
Catherine in her arms.

"Not a bit of room for me," Knight said.
"Won't you go away, Laura Beth? Perhaps play
with your uncle Burke? He looks terribly lonely,
doesn't he?"

The child took her thumb out of her mouth and

grinned at Knight. "Papa," she said. She nodded, apparently pleased with the sound, and
stuck her thumb back into her mouth.

"I suppose that's an answer of sorts. Sorry,
Uncle Burke, maybe later. Careful, Sam, you'll fall
out the window! Theo, sit down. May I have a
cup of tea, please, Arielle? All this fathering is
wearing me to a bone."

Lily smiled and touched her husband's coat
sleeve. "You're a wonderful father."

"But not yet all that wonderful a husband,"
Knight said, hoping that only she heard him.

"I have an excellent memory, my lord."

"So do I. I hurt, Lily. Would you please speed
up your recovery? It was, after all, only a bullet
wound through your shoulder. Barely a scratch.
Have you so little stamina?"

"Knight, would you please take a seat and leave
Lily to Laura Beth and her doll?" Arielle said.
"Here's your tea. Now behave. You're quite as
active as the children."

Knight meekly did as he was asked.

"You as well, Arielle," Burke told his wife.
"Lily was just asking me about Knight's plan."

"The one that didn't work," Arielle added.

"Well, it was a try," Knight said. "And really
quite simple. I just sent out a good half-dozen
men to canvass all innkeepers and shop owners
and let drop that we'd turned up these fabulous
jewels at Castle Rosse and, being lawful folk, we
were dispatching them to London. Mentioned the
date and the time, of course. It was a fairly decent
plan, even if it didn't work, since Monk was here
rather than there."

"Did you truly have someone traveling to London with something?" Lily asked.

"Yes, Burke's valet, Joshua. He had two other
men trailing him in case Monk made a move.

Joshua was peeved that he missed all the excitement here.''

Burke said, ''Joshua was my batman in the army. This was his first excitement in some months and he was ready to bash some heads. He's been doing nothing but complaining since he came back.''

At that moment, the Ravensworths' butler, Montague, came into the room and spoke quietly to Burke. Burke frowned for a moment, then nodded. Montague withdrew.

''How bizarre,'' Burke said. ''Ollie has just arrived from London. He asks to speak to you, Knight.''

''I did pay him, did I not?''

''Yes,'' Burke said. ''Perhaps he's back for a bonus.''

''No, sir,'' Ollie said as he came into the room, sounding much affronted. ''We Bow Street Runners are an 'onorable sort, we are, not bleeding milkers.''

''I was just jesting, Ollie. Do come in. What have you to tell his lordship?''

Ollie looked at each of them in turn, then eyed the children with something akin to terror. He cleared his throat. ''Billy's Baubles,'' he announced.

Everyone stared at him.

''Billy's Baubles,'' he said again. ''The bloody jewels. Don't you understand?''

''No,'' Knight said.

''Billy, as in William,'' Ollie explained in a tone of exaggerated patience. He still got no response. ''You're all a bunch of loobies! William—bloody Prince William of Orange! That's who Billy is. 'E was betrothed to Charlotte—Princess Charlotte of England! She done told the prince to stuff it this past summer, said she didn't want to marry 'im.

'E took the jewels back and sent 'em 'ome to Brussels, but they was stolen. All I 'ad to do was ask about it quiet-like. Lord Kittaker knew all about it. Since it didn't 'appen 'ere in England, no one knew much about it.''

"Oh, my goodness,'' Lily said. "Imagine that. No wonder they were so valuable.''

"My God,'' Knight said. "And I was thinking this Billy was a rich Cit or something of the sort.''

"The Princess of England,'' Lily said. "Jewels for a royal princess.''

Arielle was shaking her head. "Well, it doesn't matter who owns them. We still don't have any idea where the devil they are.''

There was no answer to that.

Ollie earned a bonus of one hundred pounds for his information.

The following afternoon, Mrs. Pepperall, the Ravensworth housekeeper, walked into the draw-ing room looking unduly perturbed. Knight had carried Lily downstairs and had tucked her care-fully onto a sofa near the fireplace.

The children were outside with John, who had recently arrived, playing in the newly fallen snow.

Mrs. Pepperall cleared her throat. "My lady, the strangest thing has happened.'' In her hands she held Lily's once beautiful ermine-lined cloak.

"Yes, Mrs. Pepperall? Oh, the cloak.''

"Yes, ma'am. We tried to clean it, but the blood . . . Well, one of our girls was trying to snip out the blood-covered fur from the rest of the er-mine so's you could wear it again, and the strang-est thing happened. Look what she found wrapped up real tight in linen in the lining.''

Mrs. Pepperall held up a glittering necklace, earrings, and bracelet. Diamonds, emeralds, and rubies spilled over her hand, shining wildly in the afternoon sunlight.

"My cloak! They were in my cloak all the time, and it never occurred to me—"

"To either of us," Knight said. "Merciful heavens, would you look at the size of those diamonds!"

"They're real?" Mrs. Pepperall said, her voice a high squeak, and she promptly dropped the jewels into Knight's hands.

"Quite real," Knight said, sifting the brilliant jewels through his fingers. "Thank you, Mrs. Pepperall. You've solved the mystery."

"Not at all, my lord," said Mrs. Pepperall, beaming at the compliment. "It wasn't much at all, really."

"Irony," Knight said. "I've had quite enough of irony."

✹✹✹ EPILOGUE ✹✹✹

Venice, Italy
April 1815

On a bright afternoon in early April, Lord and Lady Castlerosse stood on the open balcony off their bedchamber in the Palazzo di Contini, looking over the Grand Canal.

"Thank God it's only early spring and not the middle of summer," Knight said, leaning on the polished wood railing. "It was my misfortune to visit Venice in August some six years ago. The stench was nearly overpowering. But now . . ." Knight paused and breathed in the cool spring morning air.

"I have been wondering what's under that dark water," Lily said, peering down from their third-story view. "It's menacing and murky, a lover of the gothic would say."

"I shudder to know what's under it."

"Ancient Greek coins, perhaps? Roman urns and centurions' shields? I know, Attila the Hun left his sword here, and it sank."

"Someone's dead cousin, more's to the point. The Venetians aren't known for their forgiving natures."

Lily shuddered and turned, to lean her back

385

against the balcony railing. ''You're not a romantic, Knight.''

He grinned at her, that quite lascivious grin that made her want to leap into his arms and wrestle him to the floor. ''And have my way with you,'' she finished aloud.

''What?'' He immediately put his fingertip to her lips. ''No, don't repeat what you said. It's possible I misunderstood. I prefer to believe that you want to fling me down and rip off my clothes and caress me with your hands and mouth and—''

''You're terrible! But yes, that's it exactly. You've been distant today, Knight. Admit it.''

His grin faded a bit. He pulled her into his arms, settling her there exactly where she belonged, her head on his shoulder, her hands around his waist. ''It's like you've been with me all my life,'' he said, kissing the top of her head. ''You're feeling quite perfect again? You promise?''

''I promise.''

''We've been here for three weeks now. We've attended nine balls, three in our honor, gambled away five hundred pounds—''

''I lost only fifty pounds! It was *rouge et noir*, and you said I was cheated.''

''Well, I knew it was some vast amount. In any case, we've ridden in the gondolas until you were nearly seasick, we've fed every damned pigeon in St. Mark's Square, we've trudged over the Rialto Bridge a good three hundred times, and you almost locked me in the dungeons in the Doges' Palace—''

That brought out a giggle. ''I didn't really lock you in.''

''You made me think so. I found a gray hair the very next morning. Now, where was I? Oh, yes,

I've had Tintoretto for breakfast, Carpaccio for lunch, Parodi for afternoon tea, and Bellini for dinner. The only activity that hasn't paled in the least, in fact the one that just keeps bounding heavenward, is making love with you.''

He felt the small shudder go through her at his words and smiled.

"I suspect that won't pale for a very long time."

"Fifty years, Lily?"

"At the very least. Now, what is really on your mind?"

Knight sighed. She knew him well, his wife. "I miss the children," he admitted. "We've been gone from them nearly two months now. And even though it's been wonderful—"

Lily laughed and kissed him. "What are you *really* trying to say?"

"Haven't you wondered if Castle Rosse is still a fine old manor house and not a squalid remnant from the past? If our servants are still sentient people and not blathering idiots? If the upstairs maids haven't gone shrieking to Bedlam after putting their hands in Sam's bread dough?"

Lily was laughing so hard she couldn't speak. "Oh, stop," she managed. "You're so funny, Knight. How did I live so long without the wittiest, the handsomest, the most wonderful, the—"

"The best lover?"

"Yes, the best lover and nearly the youngest husband in the entire world?"

Knight moaned. "All my fine philosophies— shredded and tossed to the winds. I, a young man, captured in his prime, hurtled into captivity, forced to service a woman who has endless appetites for my young, virile body. How can it be borne?"

"What is it to be, then, my lord?"

"It's my turn."

"To hurtle me to the ground? I, a young lady, to be captured in her prime?"

He laughed and squeezed her tightly against him. "Enough talk for a while. It's time we both did some servicing—to each other."

They did, and it was sweet and fierce and slow and very, very fine. The sun was sinking into twilight before Knight was able to string more than two words together. "If I had met you when I was forty, you would have killed me within a week. I'm damned lucky I'm young; it's the only way I could survive being married to you."

"True," Lily said and kissed his shoulder.

Knight kissed the tip of her nose. "When did you plan to tell me?"

Lily was caught in mid-yawn. "Tell you what?"

"That you're pregnant."

She gave him a radiant smile. "Next month, I thought. No, don't frown at me. I wanted to be certain. How did you know? You're a man."

"Even a man notices if his wife doesn't have her monthly flow. That, love, and your breasts. They're fuller, more sensitive, more tender. Haven't you noticed how careful I've been when I've caressed you?"

"No," she said quite honestly. "When you touch me, all I notice is that I'm wild and hot and aching for you."

"Ah," Knight said, his hand going to her belly, his fingers splaying over her. "That is very nicely said. When can I expect my fourth child to enter this world?"

"The end of November, I think."

"You're feeling well?"

"Oh, yes, extremely fit. I haven't been at all ill in the mornings."

"Doubtless it's due to your remarkable husband and his excellent care of you." Knight glanced at the puckered scar on her shoulder. He felt a shock of memory, then resolutely shook it off. That was over, long over. "What was I saying? Oh, yes. Now, I've decided I'll give you the reward and not keep it for myself, even though I am certain I earned it."

Lily blinked up at him. "Whatever are you talking about?"

"The reward. For the return of Billy's Baubles."

"What reward? From the Prince of Orange?"

"Certainly from the prince. I got a letter this morning from Burke. Billy, my dear, wants us to accept a token of his esteem and profound thanks for the return of his sparklers, in the form of a small seventeenth-century manor house he owns in Cornwall, near Lostwithiel, I understand."

"A house for the return of some paltry jewels?"

"Not quite so paltry. Evidently they were worth something in the neighborhood of sixty thousand pounds."

"Goodness," Lily said. "And they were sewn in the ermine lining of my cloak! What if I'd lost the cloak? Sold it? Oh, dear—"

Knight's fingers were on her lips; then he leaned down and kissed her. "When will I stop wanting you all the time? The manor house is called Swanson Grange. I was thinking we could change the name to something more noble. Perhaps—"

Lily lightly caressed him and he forgot everything except her soft hand and her soft mouth on him.

"Perhaps what?" she asked, her breath warm in his mouth.

"Attila's Hall? Napoleon's Grange? The Turk's Abbey? I don't know, I don't care."

Lily didn't either at that moment.

"I know," he said some thirty minutes later.

"Know what?"

"We'll christen it Medici Manor. We could build old, dank prisons. We could sell poisons, import the Italian concept of vendetta."

Lily giggled. "You're making me laugh too much."

"My mission in life. Get used to it."

"All right," Lily said and kissed him.

"And that's your mission, wife."

"All right," she said again, enthusiasm and laughter filling her voice.